Debra Webb is the award-winning *USA TODAY* bestselling author of more than one hundred novels, including those in reader-favourite series *Faces of Evil*, the *Colby Agency* and *Shades of Death*. With more than four million books sold in numerous languages and countries, Debra has a love of storytelling that goes back to her childhood on a farm in Alabama. Visit Debra at www.debrawebb.com

Elle James, a *New York Times* bestselling author, started writing when her sister challenged her to write a romance novel. She has managed a full-time job and raised three wonderful children, and she and her husband even tried ranching exotic birds (ostriches, emus and rheas). Ask her, and she'll tell you what it's like to go toe-to-toe with an angry 350-pound bird! Elle loves to hear from fans at ellejames@earthlink.net or ellejames.com

WITNESS PROTECTION WIDOW

DEBRA WEBB

DISRUPTIVE FORCE

ELLE JAMES

MILLS & BOON

First Published in Great Britain 2020
by Mills & Boon, an imprint of HarperCollins*Publishers*
1 London Bridge Street, London, SE1 9GF

Witness Protection Widow © 2020 Debra Webb
Disruptive Force © 2020 Mary Jernigan

ISBN: 978-0-263-28017-3

0220

MIX
Paper from
responsible sources
FSC™ C007454

This book is produced from independently certified FSC™
paper to ensure responsible forest management.

For more information visit: www.harpercollins.co.uk/green

Printed and bound in Spain
by CPI, Barcelona

WITNESS PROTECTION WIDOW

DEBRA WEBB

Those employed by the US Marshals Service and the Federal Bureau of Investigation are some of the finest law enforcement folk in our nation. I am in awe of all these dedicated men and women do. As I wrote this story, I took artistic license with certain protocols and operations. After all, romance fiction is about the love story between two people. Everything else is secondary. Enjoy!

Chapter One

Four days until trial

Sunday, February 2
Winchester, Tennessee

It was colder now.

The meteorologist had warned that it might snow on Monday. The temperature was already dropping. She didn't mind. She had no appointments, no deadlines and no place to be—except *here*.

Four days.

Four more days until *the* day.

If she lived that long.

She stopped and surveyed the thick woods around her, making a full three-sixty turn. Nothing but trees and this one trail for as far as the eye could see. The fading sun trickled through the bare limbs. This place had taken her through the last weeks of summer and then fall, and now the end of winter was only weeks away. In all that time, she had only seen one other living human. It was best, they said. For her protection, they insisted.

It was true. But she had never felt more alone in her life. Not since her father died, anyway. That first year after his death, she had to come to terms with being only twenty-four and an orphan. No siblings. No known distant relatives. Just alone.

Bob nudged her. She pushed aside the troubling thoughts and looked down at her black Labrador. "I know, boy. I should get moving. It's cold out here."

She was always keenly aware of the temperature and the time. When it was this cold, the idea of an accidental fall leading to a serious injury haunted her. Other times, when she couldn't bear the walls around her a minute longer, no matter that it was late in the day, she was careful not to stay gone too long. Allowing herself to get caught out in the woods in the dark—no matter that she knew the way back to the cabin by heart—was a bad idea. She started forward once more. Her hiking shoes crunched the rocks and the few frozen leaves scattered across the trail. Bob trotted beside her, his tail wagging happily. She'd never had a dog before coming to this place. When she was growing up, her mother's allergies wouldn't allow pets. Later, when she was out on her own, the apartment building didn't permit pets.

Even after she married and moved into one of Atlanta's megamansions, she couldn't have a dog. Her husband had hated dogs, cats, any sort of pet. How had she not recognized the evil in him then? Anyone who hated animals so much couldn't be good inside. Whatever good he possessed was only skin-deep and primarily for show.

She hugged herself, rubbed her arms. Thinking of him, even in such simple terms, unsettled her. Soon, she hoped, she would be able to put that part of her life behind her and never look back again.

Never, ever.

"Not soon enough," she muttered.

Most widows grieved the loss of their spouses. She did not. No matter the circumstances, she had never wished him dead, though she had wished many, many times that she had never met him.

But she had met him, and there was no taking back the five years they were married. At first, she had believed the illusion he presented to her. Harrison had been older, very handsome and extremely charming. She had grown up in small-town Georgia on a farm to parents who taught her that fairy tales and dreams weren't real. There was only reality and the lessons that came from hard work and forging forward even when the worst happened. Suddenly, at twenty-six, she was convinced her parents had been wrong. Harrison had swooped into her life like Prince Charming poised to rescue a damsel in distress.

Except she hadn't been in distress, really. But she had been so very hopeful that the future would be bright. Desperately hopeful that good things would one day come her way. Perhaps that was why she didn't see through him for so long. He filled her life with trips to places she'd only dreamed of visiting, like Paris and London. He'd lavished her with gifts: exquisite clothing, endless jewels. Even when she tried to tell him it was too much, more came.

He gave her anything she wanted...except children. He had been married once before and had two college-aged children. Though he was estranged from those adult children, he had no desire to go down that path again. No wish for a chance to have a different outcome. She had been devastated at first. But she had been in love, so she learned to live within that disappointing restriction. Soon after this revelation, she discovered a way to satisfy her mothering needs. She volunteered at Atlanta's rescue mission for at-risk kids. Several months after she began helping out part-time, she was faced with the first unpleasantness about her husband. To her dismay, there were those who believed he and his family were exceptionally bad people.

The shock and horror on the other woman's face when she'd asked, "You're married to Harrison Armone?"

Alice—of course, that wasn't her name then—had smiled, a bit confused, and said, "I am."

The woman had never spoken to her again. In fact, she had done all within her power to avoid her. At least twice she had seen the shocked woman whisper something to another volunteer, who subsequently avoided her, as well. Arriving at the center on her scheduled volunteer days had become something she dreaded rather than looked forward to. From that moment she understood there was something wrong with who she was—the wife of Harrison Armone.

If only she had realized then the level of evil the Armone family represented. Perhaps she would have escaped before the real nightmare that came later. Too bad she hadn't been smart enough to escape before it was too late.

She stared up at the sky, visible only by virtue of the fact that the trees remained bare for the winter. She closed her eyes and tried to force away the images that always followed on the heels of memories even remotely related to him. Those first couple of years had been so blissful. So perfect. For the most part, she had been kept away from the rest of the family. Their estate had been well away from his father's. Her husband went to work each day at a beautiful, upscale building on the most distinguished street in the city. Her life was protected from all things bad and painful.

Until her covolunteer had asked her that damning question.

The worry had grown and swelled inside her like a tidal wave rushing to shore to destroy all in its path. But the trouble didn't begin until a few weeks later. Until she could no longer bear the building pressure inside her.

Her first real mistake was when she asked him—

point-blank—if there was anything he'd failed to disclose before they married.

The question had obviously startled him. He wanted to know where she had gotten such a ridiculous idea. His voice had been calm and kind, as always, tinged with only the tiniest bit of concern. But something about the look in his eyes when he asked the question terrified her. She hadn't wanted to answer his question. He had been far too strangely calm and yet wild-eyed. An unreasonable fear that he would track down her fellow volunteers and give them a hard time had horrified her. After much prodding and far too much pretending at how devastated he was, he had let it go. But she understood that deep down something fundamental had changed.

Whether it was the idea that the bond of trust had been fractured, or that she finally just woke up, she could not look at him the same way again.

The worst part was that he noticed immediately. He realized that thin veil of make-believe had been torn. Every word she uttered, every move she made was suddenly under intense scrutiny. He became suspicious to the point of paranoia. Every day was another in-depth examination of what she had done that day, to whom she had spoken. Then he allowed his true character to show. One by one those ugly family secrets were revealed by his actions. Late-night business meetings that were once handled at his father's house were suddenly held in their home.

One night after a particularly long meeting with

lots of drinking involved, he confessed that he had wanted to keep the fantasy of their "normal" life, and she had taken it from him.

From that moment forward, she became his prisoner. He punished her in unspeakable ways for taking away his fairy tale.

Now, even with him dead, he still haunted her.

She shook off the memories and focused on the moment. The crisp, clean air. The nature all around her. She'd had her reservations at first, but this place was cleansing for her soul. She had seen so much cruelty and ugliness. This was the perfect sanctuary for healing.

And, of course, hiding.

Only a few more days until the trial. She was the star witness—the first and only witness who had survived to testify against what was left of the Armone family, Harrison Armone Sr. The man had built an empire in the southeast, and Atlanta was his headquarters. The Armone family had run organized crime for three generations—four if you counted her husband, since he would have eventually taken over the business.

But he no longer counted, because he was dead.

Murdered by his own father.

She had witnessed Mr. Armone putting the gun to the back of Harrison's head and pulling the trigger. Then he'd turned to her and announced that she now belonged to him, as did all else his son had hoarded to himself. He would give her adequate grieving time, and then he would expect *things* from her.

Within twenty-four hours, the family's private physician had provided a death certificate, and another family friend with a funeral home had taken care of the rest. No cops were involved, no investigation and certainly no autopsy. Cause of death was listed as a heart attack. The obituary was pompous and filled half a page in the *Atlanta Journal-Constitution*.

It wasn't until three days after the funeral that she had her first opportunity to attempt an escape.

She had prepared well. For months before Harrison's death she had been readying for an opportunity to flee. She had hidden away a considerable amount of cash and numerous prepaid cards that could not be traced back to her. She'd even purchased a phone— one for which minutes could be bought at the supermarket. When the day came, she left the house with nothing more than the clothes on her back. The money and cards were tucked into her jacket. The entire jacket was basically padded with cash and plastic beneath the layer of fabric that served as the lining. She'd worn her favorite running shoes and workout clothes.

This was another way she had prepared. Shortly after her husband had started to show his true colors, she had become obsessed with fitness and building her physical strength.

The week before her own personal D-day, she

had gone to the gym and stashed jeans, a sweat-shirt, a ball cap, big sunglasses and a clasp for pin-ning her long blond hair out of sight beneath the cap in a locker.

When D-day arrived, she had left the gym through a rear exit and jogged the nearly three miles to the Four Seasons, where she'd taken a taxi to the bus sta-tion. She'd loaded onto the bus headed to Birming-ham, Alabama. In Birmingham, she had boarded another bus to Nashville, Tennessee, and finally from Nashville to Louisville, Kentucky. Each time she changed something about her appearance. She picked up another jacket or traded with another trav-eler. Changed the hat and the way she wore her hair. Eventually she reached her destination. Scared to death but with no other recourse, she walked into the FBI office and told whoever would listen her story.

Now she was here.

The small clearing where her temporary home— a rustic cabin—stood came into view. The setting sun spilled the last of its glow across the mountain.

In the middle of nowhere, on a mountain, she awaited the moment when she would tell the world what kind of monster Harrison Armone Sr. was. His son had been equally evil, but no one deserved to be murdered, particularly by his own father.

Those last three years of their marriage, when he'd recognized that she knew what he was, his decision to permit her to see and hear things had somehow been calculated. She supposed he had hoped to keep her scared into submission. She had been scared, all right. Scared to death. But she had planned her escape when no one was looking.

The FBI had been thrilled with what she had to offer. But they had also recognized that keeping her alive until and through the trial wouldn't be easy. Welcome to witness protection. She had been moved once already. The security of the first location where she'd been hidden away had been breached after only three months. She'd had no idea anything was going on when two marshals had shown up to take her away.

So far things had gone smoothly in Winchester. She kept to herself. Ordered her food online and the marshal assigned to her picked up the goods and delivered the load to her. Though she had a small SUV for emergencies, she did not leave the property and put herself in a position where someone might see and remember her.

Anything she needed, the marshal took care of.

The SUV parked next to the house was equipped with all-wheel drive since she lived out in the woods on a curvy mountain road. US Marshal Branch Holloway checked on her regularly. She had a special phone for emergencies and for contacting him. He'd made her feel at ease from the beginning. He was patient and kind. Far more understanding than the first marshal assigned to her had been.

For this she was immensely grateful.

Yes. She had married an evil man. Yes. She had

been a fool. But she hadn't set out to do so. She had been taught to believe the best in everyone until she had reason to see otherwise.

Two years. Yes, it had taken a long time to see past the seemingly perfect facade he had built for her, but she was only human. She had loved him. She had waited a very long time to feel that way again after her first heartbreak at the age of twenty-one.

"Get over it," she muttered to herself. Beating herself up for being naive wasn't going to change history.

This—she surveyed the bare trees and little cabin—was her life now. At least until the trial.

In the movies witness protection was made to look like a glamourous adventure, but that could not be farther from the truth. It was terrifying. Justice depended on her survival to testify in court, and her survival depended upon the marshal assigned to her case and on her own actions. The FBI had shown her how much bigger this case was than just the murder of her husband and the small amount of knowledge she had absorbed. The Armones had murdered countless people. Drugs, guns and all sorts of other criminal activities were a part of their network. She alone held the power to end the Armone reign.

No matter that the family was so obviously evil, she still couldn't understand how a father could murder his son—his only child. Of course, it was Harrison's own fault. He had been secretly working to overthrow his father. The old man was nearing seventy and had no plans to retire. Harrison had wanted to be king.

Instead, he'd gotten dead.

She shuddered at the idea that his father—after murdering him—had intended to take his widow as his own plaything.

Sick. The man was absolutely disgusting. Like his son, he was a charming and quite handsome man for his age. But beneath the surface lived a monster.

Once the trial was over, she hoped she never had to think of him again, much less see him.

Staying alert to her surroundings, she unlocked the back door and sent Bob inside ahead of her. He was trained to spot trouble. She wasn't overly concerned at this point. If anything had been amiss, he would have warned her as they approached the cabin.

The dogs were a new addition to the witness protection family. She hadn't had a dog at the first location. It wasn't until she'd arrived here and had Bob living with her that she'd realized how very lonely she had been for a very long time. Since well before her husband was murdered.

She locked the door behind her, taking care to check all the locks. Then she followed Bob through the three rooms. There was a small living-dining-kitchen combination, a bedroom with an attached bath and the mudroom–laundry room at the back. Furnishings were sparse, but she had what she needed.

Since cell service was sketchy at best, she had a

state-of-the-art signal booster. She had a generator in case the power went out and a bug-out bag if it became necessary to cut and run.

She shivered. The fire had gone out. She kept on her jacket while she added logs to the fireplace and kindling to get it started. Within a couple of minutes, the fire was going. She'd had a fireplace as a kid, so relearning her way around this one hadn't been so bad. She went back to the kitchen and turned on the kettle for tea.

Bob growled low in his throat and stared toward the front door.

She froze. Her phone was in her hip pocket. Her gun was still in her waistband at the small of her back. This was something else Marshal Holloway had insisted upon. He'd taught her how to use a handgun. They'd held many target practices right behind this cabin.

A creak beyond the front door warned that someone was on the porch. She eased across the room and went to the special peephole that had been installed. There was one on each side of the cabin, allowing for views all the way around. A man stood on the porch. He was the typical local cowboy. Jeans and boots. Hat in his hands. Big truck in the drive. Just like Marshal Holloway.

But she did not know this man.

"Alice Stewart, if you're in there, it's okay for you to open the door. I'm Sheriff Colt Tanner. Branch sent me."

Her heart thudding, she held perfectly still. Branch would never send someone to her without letting her know first. If for some reason he couldn't tell her in advance, they had a protocol for these situations.

She reached back, fingers curled about the butt of her weapon. Bob moved stealthily toward the door.

"I know you're concerned about opening the door to a stranger, but you need to trust me. Branch has been in an accident, and he's in the hospital undergoing surgery right now. No matter that his injuries were serious, he refused to go into surgery until he spoke to me and I assured him I would look after you, ma'am."

Worry joined the mixture of fear and dread churning inside her. She hoped Branch wasn't hurt too badly. He had a wife and a daughter.

She opened her mouth to ask about his condition, but then she snapped it shut. The man at her door had not said the code word.

"Wait," he said. "I know what the problem is. I forgot to say 'superhero.' He told me that's your code word."

Relief rushed through her. She moved to the door and unlocked the four dead bolts, then opened it. When she faced the man—Sheriff Tanner—she asked, "Is he going to be okay?"

The sheriff ducked his head. "I sure hope so. Branch is a good friend of mine. May I come in?"

"Quiet, Bob," she ordered the dog at her side as she backed up and allowed the sheriff to come inside before closing the door. She resisted the impulse to lock it and leaned against it instead. Holloway wouldn't have trusted this man if he wasn't one of the good guys.

Still, standing here with a stranger after all these months, she couldn't help feeling a little uneasy. Bob sat at her feet, his gaze tracking every move the stranger made.

"Is there anything you need, ma'am? Anything at all. I'll be happy to bring you any supplies or just…" He shrugged. "Whatever you need."

The kettle screamed out, making her jump. She'd completely forgotten about it. "I'll be right back."

She hurried to the kitchen and turned off the flame beneath the whistling kettle. She took a breath, pushed her hair behind her ears and walked back into the living room.

"Thank you for coming, Sheriff, but I have everything I need."

"All right." He pulled a card from his shirt pocket and offered it to her. "Call me if you need anything. I'll check on you again later today and give you an update on Branch's condition."

She studied the card. "Thank you." She looked up at him then. "I appreciate your concern. Please let the marshal know I'm hoping for his speedy recovery."

"Will do." He gave her another of those quick nods. "I'll be on my way then."

Before she opened the door for him to go, she had to ask. "Are his injuries life-threatening?"

"He was real lucky, ma'am. Things could have been far worse. Thankfully, he's stable, and we have every reason to believe he'll be fine."

"What about his wife?"

"She wasn't with him, so she's fine. She's at the hospital waiting for him to come out of surgery. If you're certain you don't need me for anything, I'm going back there now."

"Really, I'm fine. Thank you."

When the sheriff had said his goodbyes and headed out to his truck, she locked the door—all four dead bolts. She watched as the truck turned around and rolled away. She told herself that Marshal Holloway's accident most likely didn't have anything to do with her or the trial. Still, she couldn't help but worry just a little.

What if they had found her? What if hurting the marshal was just the first step in getting to her? Old man Armone was pure evil. He would want her to know in advance that he was coming just to be sure she felt as much fear as possible. Instilling fear gave him great pleasure.

Harrison Armone Sr. had a small army at his beck and call. All were trained mercenaries. Ruthless, like him. Proficient in killing. Relentless in attaining their target. They would be hunting her. If being careful would get her through this, she had nothing to worry about. But that alone would never be enough. She needed help and luck on her side.

With this unexpected development, she would need to be extra vigilant.

"Bob."

He looked up at her expectantly.

"We have to be especially alert, my friend."

The devil might be coming.

And he wouldn't be alone.

Chapter Two

Winchester Hospital

Jaxson Stevens left Nashville as soon as he heard the news of the accident. He and Branch Holloway had been assigned together briefly before Holloway transferred back to his hometown of Winchester. Holloway was a good guy and a damned fine marshal. Jax was more than happy to back him up until he was on his feet again.

He parked his SUV in the lot and headed for the hospital entrance. He hadn't been in the Winchester area in ages. He hailed from the Pacific Northwest, and he'd taken an assignment in Seattle when he completed training with the marshal service. He had ended up spending the better part of the first decade of his career on that side of the country. Then he'd needed a change. He'd landed in Nashville last year.

Truth is, he'd hadn't exactly wanted to spend time in the southeast, but it was a necessary step in his career ladder. There was a woman he'd met when he was in training at Glynco. The two of them had a very intense few months together, and he'd wondered about her for years after moving to Seattle. They'd both been so young when they first met. He'd kept an eye on her for years while she finished college, certain they would end up together again at some point. He'd anonymously helped out when her father passed away.

Then his notions of a romantic reunion had come to a grinding halt after she moved to Atlanta.

She had gotten married. He shook his head. All those years, she had haunted his dreams. He'd thought he had known her, thought they had something that deserved a second go when the time was right. He'd definitely never felt that connection with anyone else.

But he had been wrong. Dead wrong.

A woman who would marry a man like she had was not someone he knew at all. He imagined she fully comprehended what the world thought of her choice about now.

Irrelevant, he reminded himself. The past was the past. Nothing he could do about the years he wasted wondering about her. He was happy in Nashville for now. He had just turned thirty-two, and he had big career plans. There was plenty of time to get serious about a personal relationship. God knew his parents and his sister constantly nagged him about his single status.

Maybe after this case was buttoned up. The witness had to be at trial on Thursday. After that, he was taking a vacation and making some personal decisions. Maybe it was time he took inventory of his life rather than just pouring everything into the job.

The hospital had that disinfectant smell that lingered in every single hospital he'd ever stepped into. The odor triggered unpleasant memories he'd just as soon not revisit in this lifetime. Losing his younger brother was hard as a ten-year-old. He couldn't imagine what his parents had suffered.

His mom warned him often that he shouldn't allow that loss to get in the way of having a family. He had never really considered that he chose not to get too serious about a relationship because of what happened when he was a kid, but maybe he had. His parents had spent better than twenty years telling him that what happened wasn't his fault. Didn't matter. He would always believe it was. He should have been watching more closely. He should never have allowed his little brother so close to the water's edge.

He should have been better prepared to help him if something went wrong.

Why the hell had he gone down that road?

Jax shook his head and strode across the lobby, kicking the past back to where it belonged—behind him. A quick check with the information desk and he was on his way to the third floor. He followed the signs to Holloway's room.

His gaze came to rest on his old friend, and he grimaced. The left side of the man's face was bruised and swollen as if he'd slugged it out and lost big-time. What he could see of Holloway's left shoulder was bruised, as well. "You look like hell, buddy."

Branch Holloway opened his eyes. "Pretty much feel like it, too. Glad you could make it, Stevens."

Jax moved to the side of his bed. "What happened? You tick off the wrong cowboy?"

Tennessee was full of cowboys. Jax had tried a pair of boots. Not for him. And the hat—well, that just wasn't his style. He was more a city kind of guy. Jeans, pullovers and a good pair of hiking shoes and he was good to go. He was, however, rather fond of leather. He'd had the leather jacket he wore for over a decade.

"I wish I could tell you a heroic story of chasing bad guys and surviving a shootout, but it was nothing like that. A deer decided my truck was in his way. I didn't hit him, but I did hit the ditch and then a couple of trees. One tree in particular tried real hard to do me in."

Jax made a face. "Sounds like you're damned lucky."

"That's what they say, but I gotta tell you right now I'm not feeling too lucky. My wife says I will when I see my truck. It's totaled."

"Can I get you anything?" Jax glanced at the water pitcher on the bedside table.

"No, thanks. My wife was here until just a few minutes ago. She's hovered over me since the paramedics brought me in. Between her and the nurses, I'm good, trust me."

Jax nodded. "You didn't want to discuss the case by phone. I take it this is a dark one." Some cases were listed as dark. These were generally the ones where the person or persons who wanted to hurt the witness had an abundance of resources, making the witness far more vulnerable. Sometimes a case was dark simply because of the priority tag associated with the investigation. The least number of people possible were involved with dark cases.

There were bad guys in this world, and then there were *really* bad guys.

"Need-to-know basis only," Holloway said. "We're only days out from trial. Keeping this witness safe is essential. At this point, we pretty much need to keep her under surveillance twenty-four hours a day until trial. This couldn't have happened at a worse time."

"Understandable," Jax agreed.

"I'm sure you're familiar with the Armone case. It's been all over the news."

Jax's eyebrows went up with a jolt of surprise. "That's not a name I expected to hear. I knew the patriarch of the family was awaiting trial, but I haven't kept up with the details. Besides, that's a ways out of our district."

"The powers that be felt moving her out of Georgia until trial would help keep her safe. They've kept the details quiet on this one to the greatest extent possible. Even with all those precautions and a media blackout, her first location was jeopardized."

Her? A bad, bad feeling began a slow creep through Jax.

"Hell of a time for you to be out of commission," he said instead of demanding who the hell the witness was. *This* could not happen. Maybe it was someone else. A secretary or other associate of the old man. Or maybe of the son, since he was dead. His death may have prompted someone—an illicit lover, perhaps—to come forward.

"Tell me about it," Holloway grumbled.

"Why don't you bring me up to speed," Jax suggested. "We'll go from there."

"The file's under my pillow."

Jax chuckled as he reached beneath the thin hospital pillow. "I have to say, this is going the distance for the job."

"We do what we have to, right?"

"Right." Jax opened the file, his gaze landing on the attached photo. He blinked. Looked again. She looked exactly as she had ten years ago.

"You okay there?" Holloway asked. "You look like you just saw a ghost."

"Full disclosure, Holloway." Jax frowned. "I know this woman." No. That was wrong. He didn't just know this woman—he knew her intimately. Had been disappointed in and angry with her for years now.

"Well, hell. If this is a problem, we should call

someone else in as quickly as possible. I've got the local sheriff, a friend of mine, taking care of things now. But I can't keep him tied up this way. No one wants this bastard to get away this time. We've got him. As long as she lives to testify, he's not walking."

Holloway was right. The Armone family had escaped justice far too long. "I've got this." Jax cleared his head. If Holloway thought he was not up to par, he would insist on calling in someone else. Jax was startled, no denying it. But he wanted to do this. He had to do this. For reasons that went beyond the job. Purely selfish reasons. "You can count on me. I just wanted to be up front. We knew each other a long time ago."

"If you're sure," Holloway countered. "I'm confident I can count on you. I just don't want to put you in an unnecessarily awkward situation. Sometimes the past can adversely affect the present."

Jax felt his gut tighten. Maybe he wasn't as ready for this as he'd thought.

No choice.

If he didn't do this, he would never fully extract her from his head.

The what-ifs would haunt him forever.

"I can handle it. Like I said, we haven't seen each other in years," he assured the other man. "No one wants this family to go down more than me."

That part was more true than he cared to admit.

"If we're lucky, that family will be history when this trial is done," Holloway said. "The son is dead.

Now all we need is for the father to be put away for the rest of his sorry life." Holloway searched his face as if looking for any uncertainty. "I can ask Sheriff Tanner to show you the way to her location if you're sure we're good to go."

"That works."

"Thanks, Stevens. I'll owe you one."

THE CABIN WAS well out of town. Sheriff Colt Tanner had met Jax at the courthouse and led the way. Tanner had last checked on the witness an hour ago. At this stage, Jax wasn't going to simply check on her—he was to stick with her until she walked into that courtroom to testify. Protect, transport…whatever necessary.

On the drive to her location, he had decided he really didn't have a problem with doing the job. He couldn't deny that he had spent a great deal of time trying to find Allison James, aka Alice Stewart, the widow of Harrison Armone Jr., illegal drugs and weapons kingpin of the southeast. In fact, he wanted to do this. He wanted to learn what had happened to the sweet young woman he had known during his training. How had the shy, soft-spoken girl become the wife of one of the most wanted bastards on the minds of FBI, ATF and DEA agents alike? Maybe it was sheer curiosity, but he needed to understand how the hell that happened.

The actual problem, in his opinion, was how she would feel about him being the one charged with her safety. She no doubt would understand that he was well aware of who she had gotten involved with and would be disgusted by it. Members of law enforcement from Atlanta to DC had wished for a way to eradicate this problem.

He guessed he would find out soon enough.

Jax parked his SUV next to hers and got out. She was likely watching out the window. Tanner had updated her on Holloway's condition and told her that a new marshal would be arriving shortly. Jax had no idea whether the sheriff had given her his name. If he had, she might be waiting behind that door with her weapon drawn. Not that she had any reason to be holding a grudge. He'd asked her to go with him to Seattle, but she had turned him down. No matter that he shouldn't—didn't want to—he wondered if she had attempted to track him down at any time during those early years after he left and before she made the mistake of her life.

Had she even thought of him?

He hadn't asked her to marry him, but they had talked about marriage. They had talked about the future and what they each wanted. She'd had expectations. He had recognized this. But that hadn't stopped him from leaving when an opportunity he couldn't turn down came his way. She wouldn't go. Her father was still alive and alone. She didn't want to move so far away from him. What was he supposed to do? Ignore the offer he had hoped for from the day he decided to join the marshal service?

That little voice that warned when he had crossed the line shouted at him now. He had been selfish. No question. But he'd had family, too, and they had been on the West Coast. An unwinnable situation.

He walked up to the porch. Climbed the steps and crossed to the door. Aware she was certainly watching, he raised his fist and knocked.

She didn't say a word or make a sound, but he felt her on the other side of the door. Only inches from him. He closed his eyes and recalled her scent. Soft, subtle. She always smelled like citrus. Never wore makeup. She had the most beautiful blue eyes he had ever seen.

The door opened and she stood there, looking exactly the way she had ten years ago—no makeup, no fussy hairdo, just Ali. The big black Lab the sheriff had told him about stood next to her.

For one long moment, she stared at him and he stared at her.

He inhaled a deep breath, acknowledged the scent of her—the scent he would have recognized anywhere.

"Say it."

For a moment he felt confused at her statement.

"Say it," she repeated. "I'm not letting you inside until you do."

He understood then. "Superhero."

She stepped back, and he walked in. The door closed behind him, locks tumbling into place. The dog sniffed him, eying him suspiciously.

She scratched the Lab's head, and the dog settled down. "No one told me you were the one coming."

She stood close to the wall on his left, beyond arm's reach. Now that he had a chance to really look, she was thinner than before. Fear glittered in her eyes. Beyond the fear was something else. A weariness. Sadness, too, he concluded.

"I didn't know it was you until I arrived in Winchester." He held her gaze, refused to let her off the hook. He didn't want this to be easy. Appreciating her discomfort was low. He knew this, and still he couldn't help it. "I'm glad I'm the one Holloway called. I want to help. If that's okay with you."

"I'm certain Marshal Holloway wouldn't have called you if you weren't up to the task." She shrugged. "As for the past, it was a long time ago. It's hardly relevant now."

She was right. It had been a long time. Still, the idea that she played it off so nonchalantly didn't sit so well. No need for her to know the resentment or whatever the hell it was he harbored related to her decisions or the whirlwind of emotions she had set reeling inside him now. This was work. Business. The job. It wasn't personal.

He hitched a thumb toward the door. "I picked up a pizza. It's a little early for lunch, but I was on the road damned early this morning."

"Make yourself at home. You don't need my permission to eat."

No, he did not. "I'll grab my bag and the pizza."

He walked out to his SUV. He took a breath. Struggled to slow his heart rate. He had an assignment to complete, and it was essential he pulled his head out of the past and focused on the present. What happened ten years ago or five years ago was irrelevant. What mattered was now. Keeping her safe. Getting her in that courtroom to put a scumbag away.

He grabbed his bag and the pizza and headed back to the cabin. She opened the door for him and then locked the four dead bolts. He placed the pizza on the table and dropped his bag by the sofa. He imagined that would be his bed for the foreseeable future. The place didn't look large enough to have two bedrooms.

"This is Bob, by the way," she said of the dog who stayed at her side.

He nodded. "Nice to meet you, Bob."

Bob stared at him with a healthy dose of either skepticism or continued suspicion.

"Would you like water or a cola?"

Since beer was out of the question, he went for a cola. She walked to the fridge and grabbed two. On the way to the table, she snagged the roll of paper towels from the counter and brought that along, as well. She sat down directly across the table. Apparently she had decided to join him. He passed her a slice, grabbed one of his own and then dug in. Eating would prevent the need for conversation. If he chewed slowly enough, he could drag this out for a while.

She sipped her drink. "You finally get married?"

He was surprised she asked. Left her open for his questions. And he really wanted a number of answers from her. At the moment dealing with all the emotions and sensations related to just being in the same room with her was all he could handle.

"No. Never engaged. Never married."

Silence dragged on for another minute or so while they ate. Keeping his attention away from her lips as she ate proved more difficult than he'd expected. Frankly, he was grateful when she polished off the last bit.

"Technically," she pointed out as she reached for a second slice, "*we* were engaged—informally."

He went still, startled that his heart didn't do the same. He hadn't expected her to bring that up under the circumstances. *"Technically,"* he repeated, "I suppose you're right."

"How long were you in Seattle?"

"Until last year." He wiped his hands on a napkin. "I'm sorry about your father."

"It was a tough time."

"Yeah, I'm sure it was." He had come so close to attending the funeral, but he had wondered if he would be welcome, so he hadn't.

He bit into his pizza to prevent asking if that was why she'd ran into the arms of a criminal. Had she wanted someone to take care of her? A sugar daddy or whatever? Fury lit inside him. He forced the thoughts away. It didn't matter that they had spent months intensely focused on each other, practically inseparable. That had been a long time ago. Whatever they had then was long gone by the time she married Armone. All this emotion was unnecessary. Pointless. Frustrating as hell, actually.

"What about your parents?" She dabbed at her lips with a napkin. "Your sister?"

"The parents are doing great. Talking about buying a winter home in Florida. Is that cliché or what?" He managed a smile, hoped to lighten the situation.

She looked completely at ease. Calm. Maybe he was the only one having trouble.

Her lips lifted into a small smile. "A little."

"My sister is married with three kids." He shook his head. "I don't know how she does it."

"She's lucky."

"You have kids?" He knew the answer, but he didn't know the reason.

"No. *He* didn't want children. He had two with his first wife." She stared at the pizza box for a moment. "Looking back, I was very fortunate he didn't."

For now, he guided the conversation away from the bastard she'd married. He asked another question to which he already knew the answer. "You were determined to finish school. Did you manage?"

"I did. With taking care of my father it took forever, but I finally got it done."

"That's great."

More of that suffocating silence. He stared at the pizza, suddenly having no appetite.

"Your career is going well?" she asked.

"It is. The work is challenging and fulfilling."

She stood. "Thank you for the pizza."

He watched as she carried her napkin and cola can to the trash. She stood at the sink and stared out the window.

The urge to demand how she could have married a man like Harrison Armone burned on his tongue, but he swallowed it back.

"I think maybe they should send someone else."

Her words surprised him. Flustered him. He stood, the legs of his chair scraping across the wood floor. "Why? I see no reason we can't put the past behind us."

She turned to face him but stayed right where she was, her fingers gripping the edge of the countertop as if she feared gravity would fail her. "If *he* finds me, he will kill me. If you're in the way, he'll kill you, too."

Chapter Three

The man she had fallen head over heels in love with when she was barely twenty-one stared at her as if she'd confessed to the world's most heinous crime. How could he be the one they sent to protect her?

It shouldn't be him.

She didn't want it to be him.

Too dangerous.

"I'm a highly trained US marshal with a decade of experience under my belt. You don't need to worry about me, Ali."

Ali. Her throat tightened as she attempted to swallow. His voice, the one that had haunted her dreams for a decade. Even when she'd told herself she loved her husband—before she learned his true identity—this man had stolen into her dreams far too often. No matter that the monster she had married had showered her with gifts, no matter that she had bought into the whole fairy-tale life…all of it, every single moment, had been an attempt to erase this man from her heart.

Hadn't worked.

Now, here he was, prepared to put his life on the line to protect hers. Or maybe he wanted to see the person she had become. The widow of one of the most sought-after criminals in the country.

A lie.

Her entire existence these past five years had been a lie.

She had no one to blame but herself. She had allowed herself to buy completely into the fantasy.

Now she would be lucky if she survived.

"Why?" she demanded.

His gaze narrowed—those brown eyes that made her shiver with just a look. "Why what?"

"Why you? There's what, a couple thousand marshals? Why you?" she repeated.

"Holloway and I worked together in Nashville for a while before he relocated to Winchester. When he had his accident, he reached out to me. There wasn't time to go through the usual red tape. He needed someone with you ASAP. So here I am."

She shook her head. "This doesn't work for me."

She surely had some choice in the matter. After all, she was the witness—the *star* witness, according to the prosecutor. Without her, their case would fall apart at the hands of the dozen or so powerful attorneys Armone kept on retainer.

Jax shrugged. "I can pass along your objection to the powers that be. It's possible someone else could take over for me, but that would take time, and time is short. The trial is in four days. We don't want to do anything that might draw attention to where you are."

No. This would not work. She couldn't be this close to him. Night and day in such a cramped space. Impossible. More important, she did not want him to get hurt. "Call them. See what they can do."

He took a step toward her. Then another. She told herself to breathe, but her lungs refused the order.

"Is there some reason you don't trust me? Maybe you believe I'm not capable of handling the job?"

"I have no idea what your credentials are," she improvised. "I'm just not comfortable like this... with you."

He nodded once. "I see. You don't like being alone with me?" Another step disappeared between them.

Her heart refused to stop its pounding. She stared at him and told the truth. The truth was all she had left. "In light of the circumstances, I would like to be reasonable, but I'm having some difficulty. Yes."

For a moment he hesitated, then he said, "I'll stay out of your personal space. You have my word."

He backed away, turned and crossed to the other side of the room, and sat down on the sofa.

When she could breathe again, she dragged in a lungful of much-needed air. "I usually take a walk at this time every afternoon."

It wasn't necessary for him to know she'd already taken a walk this morning. Sometimes she took a couple of walks in a day in addition to a nice long run. Right now, she needed out of this too-tight space. She needed to breathe. To think.

"All right." He stood. "I'll go with you."

Well, that didn't work out the way she'd planned. "I usually go alone. With Bob, of course."

"Starting today, you don't go anywhere alone."

No point arguing the decree. He likely had been briefed on things she was not privy to as of yet. She understood there were aspects of the case she shouldn't or couldn't know. At first she hadn't been happy about that part. Eventually she had come to terms with focusing on her role and allowing the marshal and the prosecutor to do what they needed to do.

Frankly, it wasn't that different from her life with Harrison. He had told her what to do and when to do it. The funny thing was, she hadn't realized how controlling he was at first. In the beginning, their life together had felt as if he were pampering her and taking exquisite care of her. Her entire adult life had been about taking care of others. First her mother and then her father. Not that she had minded. She had done what any daughter would do. College had been more of the same. Go to class, do the work. Since she'd had to squeeze college in around the health issues of her parents, she had been twenty-five when she finally attained her undergraduate degree. Then she'd moved to Atlanta and met Harrison, and everything had changed.

Suddenly someone was taking care of her. Mak-

ing the decisions. Showing her the world and showering her with luxurious gifts.

It was hard to believe now that she hadn't recognized her fairy-tale life was too good to be true.

The trouble was, she had needed it to be true.
Sometimes a need was so powerful that it overrode
good sense.

She had thrown good sense and logic out the window.

Beating herself up about it more wasn't going to
change the facts. She'd done what she'd done, and
now she was in the middle of this situation.

"Let's go, Bob." She patted her thigh, and he
jumped up to follow her.

She locked up and handed Jax the key she typically kept in her pocket. If he was in charge, she
might as well turn that over to him, as well.

The sun hovered near the treetops as they walked
away from the cabin. She surveyed the blue sky.
It was supposed to snow late tonight or tomorrow.
Snow would be nice. A dusting or two had happened since she arrived in this location. A whole
two inches had fallen on Christmas Eve night. She
had needed that beautiful display of nature. She'd
felt so intensely alone.

Christmas afternoon Marshal Holloway had
shown up with a veritable buffet of goodies. His wife
and mother had made a lovely Christmas lunch, and
they had wanted to share with her. He'd also brought
a little decorated tree. The sort you picked up at the

grocery store. Those simple gestures had touched her so deeply. That was the moment when she realized she might actually be okay eventually.

If she survived beyond the trial, she could make a new life. There were still plenty of good people in this world. She would be fine.

If she survived.

"What's your plan for when this is over?"

The sound of his voice, the deep rumble that had whispered in her dreams for so long, made her pulse flutter.

"I really haven't thought that far ahead. Mostly I'm focused on surviving."

"I'm sure you've met with the AUSA in your case and done the necessary prepping."

Assistant US Attorney Samuel Keller was the federal prosecutor in the case against the Armone family. Ali had met with him twice. An attorney had been assigned to represent her interests, and she'd met with him the same. The situation was fairly cut-and-dried. She had never been involved with the family business. She had only in the past two years started to learn and document information she intended to one day take to the FBI.

"Yes. His name is Keller. Samuel Keller."

Jax nodded. "I'm familiar with Keller. He has a high conviction rate, and he's ambitious. Two important assets for the case."

Ali hadn't liked him very much. He'd made her feel cheap during their first meeting. When they'd met the second time, he had been far kinder. Perhaps someone above him had warned that he shouldn't frustrate or anger their star witness.

"I don't think he's a very nice man," she admitted. Not that she could trust her instincts as well as she'd once believed. They had steered her wrong with Harrison. Dead wrong.

"Being nice isn't necessarily a good thing when it comes to prosecutors. Ruthlessness and fearlessness are far more attractive in their line of work."

The notion made some sort of sense, she supposed. "I guess so."

Bob galloped ahead, spotting a bird or a squirrel. A gust of chilly wind whipped through the trees. She shivered, despite the sweatshirt she wore.

"When did you move to Atlanta?"

She studied his profile a moment, noting the little differences. A laugh line or two around the eyes. Slightly more angular jaw. He was leaner. "I finished my last semester of college, and I just couldn't see going back home to that empty house. Mom and Dad were both gone. I needed a fresh start. Something new. A challenge." She shrugged. "I was offered a position with an up-and-coming company. It felt right, so I threw caution to the wind."

More so than she intended.

"Did you sell the farm?"

He had been to her parents' farm once. It wasn't anything to brag about. A rambling old house on a hundred acres. She had loved the barn and the big old oak trees best of all. She'd lived there her whole life except for when she was away at college and then had moved to Atlanta afterward.

"I did. It was a difficult decision, but I couldn't stay. There were no career opportunities in the area, and I was reasonably certain that farming wasn't my strong suit. I was pleased that a guy who attended high school with me had just gotten married and wanted to buy the place. He and his wife have two kids now. They've fixed up the house and are really making a go of the farming gig. My dad would be happy."

Silence settled for a long while. The sun was dropping, leaving the sky streaked with faded grays and blues. The temperature was dropping, too. She should have grabbed her jacket. But she had been thinking of only one thing—getting out of that tiny cabin.

"Does your father still build boats?"

Ali had met his parents twice. Once when they came to Georgia to visit him and once for Thanksgiving when she and Jax flew out to visit them. They lived near the water, and boating was his father's love—second only to his family. He was one of the few people who still built fishing boats by hand. The craftsmanship was utterly amazing. Despite the gray hair, it had been easy to see that Jax had inherited his good looks from his father. His mother was a schoolteacher and a very lovely woman. She and Ali had quickly connected. Ali's mother had died the year before, and she had desperately needed that bond.

"He is. I can't see him ever stopping. He loves it too much."

Ali appreciated that level of passion. "What about your mother? Is she still teaching?"

"She is, but not in the classroom. She's the middle school principal now." He chuckled. "I'm just glad that didn't happen when I was in school. It was bad enough knowing she was in the same wing teaching biology during eighth grade."

Ali smiled. "She insisted you were a really good student."

"She only told you that because she liked you and didn't want to scare you off." He glanced at her. "I was a bit of a class clown."

Ali looked away. She watched as Bob sniffed at the undergrowth farther up the path. She wondered if she would be able to keep Bob when this was over. She couldn't imagine life without him. They'd been together for six months. The same amount of time she and Jax had spent together a decade ago.

Ali picked up her pace. It was getting colder, and the sun would set soon. They should probably turn back at the top of the next rise. As they reached it, she called Bob to come and waited for him to reach her side. Then they started down together, Jax trailing after.

The idea that he would be sleeping on the sofa no more than thirty feet away needled at the back of her mind. She didn't want to be that close to him in the darkness.

Too late to do anything about that now.

BY THE TIME the clearing came into view, it was dark and the occasional snowflake floated down in front of them.

Bob abruptly froze. A growl sounded low in his throat.

"What's the matter, boy?" Ali surveyed the area as she spoke.

Jax suddenly pulled her into the tree line. "Someone's at the house."

The whispered words no sooner brushed against her ear than she spotted the man peering into the house via the back door. He looked for a moment and then moved to a window. He tried the sash to see if it would move. It didn't. She kept the windows locked. Then he moved around the corner of the house.

"Take Bob and disappear deeper into these trees," Jax whispered with a nod to his left.

She nodded and did as he'd told her, ushering Bob along when he wanted to stop and stare and growl. Thank God he didn't bark. She crouched down between two trees and watched the clearing. Bob sat next to her, his warm body reassuring.

The quiet was deafening. She stretched her neck in an attempt to see Jax. It was too dark to see well. She could see the cabin because she'd left the lights on. The moonlight lit up the area around it the slightest little bit. She tried not to blink for fear she'd miss Jax or the other man.

Shouted voices echoed in the night. She strained to see.

Wherever they were, it wasn't on the back side of the cabin.

More angry voices. Then only one.

Jax.

She pushed out of her crouch and started forward. Bob stayed right on her heels. She moved closer to the clearing, careful to stay in the tree line. Jax had the man pushed against the cabin, his weapon boring into his skull.

Was this someone Armone had sent?

She eased closer still.

Jax repeated his demand to know the man's name. Finally he sputtered, "Teddy Scott. I work for the utility company. There was a call about the service out here. I came to check it out."

"On Sunday?" Jax asked, his skepticism clear.

"Hey, man, I just do what I'm told. I work nights, days, weekends. Whenever the call comes."

Except no one had called. Not from this address.

She dared to slip from the tree line. The guy's gaze strayed to her. Jax jerked his errant attention back to him.

"Everything okay?" she called out to Jax.

"Maybe," he said. "Maybe not. Go out to my car and grab the handcuffs from the console, would you?"

Ali hurried around to the front of the cabin. She

went to his SUV and opened the passenger side door. She leaned over the seat and opened the console. She reached in and grabbed the metal cuffs.

She rushed back to where he held the man and handed him the cuffs.

"Turn around," he ordered the interloper.

The man turned around. "Seriously, if you'll just call the utility company, you'll learn I'm telling the truth. The call came in, and I came out."

"I'm not saying I don't believe you, Mr. Scott." Jax snapped one cuff onto the man's right wrist and one onto the metal pole attached to the cabin. "The problem is, I have to be sure."

Needing someplace to look besides at the man who may have been sent to find her, Ali traced the path of the pole. It went up to the roof. *Antennae.* As many times as she'd walked that path beyond the cabin, she hadn't paid the slightest attention to the antennae. It was just a part of the house.

And now it was the part that would keep Mr. Scott right here until Jax figured out exactly who he was or what to do about him. He withdrew the man's wallet and checked his ID, she presumed. He carried no weapon, which seemed odd for one of Armone's thugs.

Jax started toward her. She braced herself for his touch as he reached for her. His fingers wrapped around her upper arm. "Get your purse, if you carry one, and let's go for a ride. I'll call Sheriff Tanner and let him get to the bottom of this."

Ali hurried inside and grabbed her cross-body bag. She tucked the emergency cell phone inside. "Come," she said to Bob.

Her faithful friend followed her to the front, where Jax waited. He was on his cell phone, presumably with Tanner. He provided the man's description and the name he listed on his ID, which was the same one he'd given. Jax listened for a bit and then ended the call.

"Is Tanner coming?" Her stomach churned with uncertainty. Six months and this was the first time another living soul besides Holloway and Tanner, then Jax had set foot up here.

Couldn't be good.

"Tanner and one of his deputies are coming up to talk to the man. If he was sent by Armone, hopefully we'll know soon."

"Where are we going?" She told herself not to be nervous. If she had to move again, she would move again. Whatever she had to do to get through this.

Four more days.

"Away from here." He ushered her and Bob toward his SUV. "We're not waiting around to see how this turns out."

Chapter Four

Jax drove faster than he should on the narrow dirt-and-gravel road that would lead to the main highway at the bottom of the mountain. This was not the place to run into trouble. The road was only wide enough for one vehicle. If someone else appeared on the road…

He wasn't going there just yet.

From the corner of his eye, he saw Ali struggling with the panic no doubt clawing at her. She was worried. She had a right to be. *He* was damned worried.

He didn't take a deep breath until they hit the Y in the road. Left went up another mountain road, while the right went to the highway. He gunned the accelerator and barreled to the right. Ali grasped the armrest on her door.

Car lights on the road ahead had him holding his breath again.

The vehicle passed. No brake lights lit up in the rearview mirror. Good. The driver kept going.

"What do we do now? Are we going someplace specific?"

He glanced in her direction. "I don't know. I'm not familiar with this area. You?"

She shook her head. "No. I've been here six months, but I've only left that mountain a couple of times."

They drove on through the darkness, the silence thickening.

Tanner would call and they would make a plan. Until then, Jax would drive.

"Could I go to the hospital and see Marshal Holloway?"

Her question gave him pause. Sometimes witnesses grew very attached to the people assigned with the responsibility of their protection. He'd heard stories of bizarre obsessions, but he didn't believe this was one of those times. She'd asked about his condition after she learned of the accident, but she hadn't appeared unduly concerned. Maybe a stop at the hospital would get her mind off whatever was going down back at the cabin.

"I don't see why not." He reached beyond the console into the back seat and grabbed the ball cap he'd tossed back there and passed it to her. "You might want to tuck your hair up."

"Okay."

As her fingers threaded into all that blond hair, a jolt of tension roared through him. His mind instantly conjured dozens of images of him running his fingers through the silky length. Feeling the whisper of it against his skin.

He blinked away the images and focused on regaining his bearings. He'd driven from the hospital to the sheriff's office and then here. But that had been in the daytime. There weren't that many identifying road signs.

A few more miles had him reasonably certain he was lost. Then he spotted the sign he needed. Left to Winchester. It wasn't long after that left when he began to see familiar landmarks. The drive to the hospital only took a few more minutes from the city limits.

Jax decided to park at the ER entrance and go in from there. Ali gave Bob a rub behind the ears. "We'll be back soon, boy."

Jax's thinking was that anyone watching for Ali would more likely be waiting in the main lobby. He wound through the corridors until he found a staff elevator. Ali glanced around nervously as they waited for the doors to open. Once they were inside and moving upward, she seemed to relax.

When the elevator stopped he said, "Almost there."

He didn't know why he felt compelled to make her feel more comfortable. He'd told himself he wouldn't feel anything like that toward her, but he did all the same. The doors opened, and a scrub-clad woman stared at them as they exited. Jax gave her a nod and kept walking. Ali stayed close behind him.

At the room where he'd visited Holloway earlier that day, he hesitated and knocked.

The door opened, and a man Jax didn't recognize looked directly at him and asked, "Can I help you?"

Jax glanced at the bed about the same time Holloway said, "It's Stevens. Let him in."

They walked into the room, and the stranger closed the door behind them. Holloway frowned. "What's going on, Stevens?" He gave Ali a tip of his head. "Ma'am, you okay?"

She nodded. "I wanted to see if you were okay and to speak to you. Privately."

"I should probably go," the stranger said. He thrust his hand toward Jax. "I'm Chief of Police Billy Brannigan."

Jax shook his hand. "Jaxson Stevens."

"The marshal who's filling in for me," Holloway explained to the chief. "Keeping a low profile," he added as he shifted his attention to Jax.

"We had a guy claiming to be from the utility company show up. Tanner is checking him out. I didn't want to hang around in case more trouble was headed our way."

"Maybe I ought to check with Colt and see if he needs any help," Brannigan offered.

"Thanks, Brannigan. I would appreciate it."

"In that case, I'm gone."

When the door closed behind Brannigan, Holloway looked from Jax to Ali. "Is something wrong besides your unexpected visitor?"

"I'd like to speak to you privately," she repeated.

Jax got it now. "I'll be outside."

If the woman didn't want him on the case, he wasn't going to argue with her. She could do as she pleased.

He left the room, pulling the door closed behind him. Rather than pace the corridor, which was his first thought, he leaned against the wall and waited.

Frustration twisted inside him. He supposed he should have handled the situation better. He'd thought they had reached an agreement of sorts. He would do his job and stay out of her personal space. Four days. It was barely more than half a week. He could get through four days. Why couldn't she?

Damn it all to hell. He shouldn't have allowed the past to color his attitude. This was an important case. She needed the best protecting her.

Maybe she didn't think he was up to the job.

He resisted the impulse to storm into the room and tell her she was wrong. There wasn't anyone better.

Damn it.

"Have a seat, Ali," Marshal Holloway said, worry lining his bruised face.

Ali suddenly regretted having come here this way. It was selfish of her to impose upon this injured man. She sighed. Closed her eyes for a moment. "I'm sorry."

"First off, you don't need to be sorry."

She opened her eyes. "Are you sure you're okay? I really should have thought this through better. This is not a good time for you and—"

"Second," he interrupted, "every single thing related to this case is about you. Whatever you need, all you have to do is tell me. Marshal Stevens or I will make it happen. You can count on that."

"Marshal Stevens is the problem." Her throat ached from having held the words back so long. But they were out there now. Marshal Holloway looked even more puzzled now.

"Is there a problem with Stevens? He mentioned that the two of you knew each other, but he assured me there wouldn't be a problem."

Now she was the one confused. "He knew I was the witness in this case before he came to Winchester?"

"No, ma'am, we've kept your identity and location as deeply covered as possible. He learned who you are when he arrived and I showed him your file."

So he'd seen her file. A cold hard knot formed in her chest. "Everything?" She moistened her lips and tried to swallow to do the same to her suddenly dry throat. "He knows everything?"

His blue eyes lit with understanding. "No. No. None of that is in the file I showed him. Ali, those parts of what happened aren't necessary for Marshal

Stevens to carry out his duty. Information about you and this case is on a need-to-know basis."

Thank God.

She nodded. Grateful for that small measure of relief. "Still, I would prefer someone else. I don't want to cause any trouble for Marshal Stevens, but I'm not comfortable with him."

Holloway released a big breath. "I can make the call and try to get someone here, but be aware that every exchange of information creates a possible opportunity for that information to end up in the wrong hands. It's a shame that we can't fully trust all the players in a case, but they're only human. Every human has his or her breaking point. Some have a price. It doesn't usually start out that way, but life happens. People change."

He was right. She understood this. She wasn't completely naive to these sorts of things. Harrison and his father had had only a few they trusted with everything. The rest were only allowed a tiny piece of knowledge—only what was required to carry out their mission.

But she had to be firm. This was what she wanted. "I apologize for making this difficult for you, Marshal Holloway—especially under the circumstances—but I'm willing to take the risk. I would like you to send Marshal Stevens back to Nashville."

He studied her a moment. "If you'll tell me the real reason you want him to go, I promise I'll make it happen if that is truly what you want."

The real reason. She glanced back at the door. She had promised herself that she would never allow lies into her life again. If that rule didn't start with her, what was the point?

"We both know there is a strong chance Armone's people will find me no matter what we do or how careful we are." When he would have interrupted, she held up a hand to stop him. "It may be as I walk up the steps at the courthouse or as I enter the court-room." She shrugged. "In the car on the way to the airport. At the airport. There are just a million op-portunities for it to happen."

The weariness and probably pain he struggled with filled his expression, but Holloway nodded his understanding. "You're right. It's possible one of those scenarios could happen. Are you having sec-ond thoughts?"

Startled by his question, she pressed her hand to her chest. "No. Not at all. Whatever happens, I'm going to testify as long as I'm still breathing. It's not me I'm worried about. It's him."

Realization dawned on his face. "You're con-cerned that if they come after you, anyone in the way will be hurt or worse."

"Yes. I don't want to cause *him* harm." How did she explain this without sounding like a fool? "I know his family. His mother is a wonderful woman. He has a sister with three kids. I don't want to risk being the cause of his family losing him."

Holloway seemed to consider her explanation for

a moment. "Ali, that's incredibly noble of you." He spoke as if he were choosing his words carefully. "But you must be aware that Marshal Stevens risks his life every day on the job. If he leaves this assignment, he'll only go to another that could be even more dangerous."

She couldn't deny the former, but she had her doubts about the latter. Armone, the bastard, was completely ruthless, and he had endless resources. There had to be something she could say that would change his mind. What he'd said to her at the onset bobbed into her frantic thoughts.

"You said whatever I wanted," she reminded him. "All I had to do was ask."

He gave a nod. "You've got me there." He stared at her for a long moment. "Jaxson Stevens is one of the very best. We're very lucky he was available. Anytime there's a touchy situation, he's the one they go to. They would likely have put him on this case instead of me, except he wasn't available then."

He was going to say no. Her hopes fell.

"All that said," he went on, "if you're set on having someone else, I'll make it happen. But I think it would be a mistake. Has he done or said anything to you that has you feeling upset or uncomfortable?"

"No, not really." Truth, she reminded herself. "I was deeply in love with him once." She shrugged. Felt like a fool.

Holloway held up his hand to prevent her from saying more.

"I need to say this," she warned. "The truth is maybe I still am even after all this time. All I know is that I can't allow him to risk his life for me."

"You don't get to make that decision."

Her heart dropped to the floor at the sound of his voice.

Holloway sighed. "I tried to stop you when the door opened."

He had, and she wouldn't listen. Her back was to the door, and she'd had no idea. Oh God, he'd heard her declaration. She told herself it wasn't entirely true…only partly so.

Jax joined her at the marshal's bedside. Ali couldn't look at him. Not after what she'd said. How she wished the floor would crack open and swallow her up. Good grief, could she have stuck her foot any deeper into her throat?

"Ten years," Jax said, his voice oddly neutral. "It's been ten years. We've both moved on. Whatever you think you feel is more likely resentment because I left."

Heat scalded her cheeks even hotter. Lovely. Now Holloway knew the rest of the sad story of their shared history. She and Jax had had an intense relationship ten years ago, until he got an offer he couldn't refuse and then he was gone.

She was a fool. Then and now.

Ali turned to him. "Or maybe you're just feeling guilty for walking away and now you have something to prove."

He moved his head slowly from side to side. "Trust me, I have nothing to prove. You're a witness in a high-profile, very important case. I'm here to make sure you stay alive until you've testified. Nothing more."

Anger fired inside her. She shifted her attention back to Holloway. "Fine. Let him stay. If he gets himself killed, it won't be on me."

Holloway struggled to sit up straighter. Ali winced at the pain on his face.

"I don't like this one damned bit," he said then grimaced, "but we are too close to risk a screwup." He stared at Jax. "Can you handle this?"

"What the hell, Holloway? You know better than to ask."

"Tell me you won't get distracted."

He shook his head. "I will not get distracted. Like I told you, whatever we had was over a long damned time ago."

His words were like a slap to her face. Ali pinched her lips together. Anything else she said at this point would only make her look more foolish.

Holloway slumped against his pillow. "If I could get out of this bed, we would not be having this discussion."

"I've got this, Branch," Jax said, using the marshal's first name.

Apparently the two knew each other better than she had realized.

Jax reached into his jacket pocket and pulled out his cell. "It's Tanner."

He answered the call, explained their situation and set the phone to speaker. "Go ahead, Tanner."

"The man posing as a utilities worker is Rafe Sanford."

Holloway looked from Jax to Ali and back. "Sanford is a local thug. In and out of trouble all the time."

"Always has been," Tanner reiterated. "Mostly petty crimes, but there have been rumors of bigger jobs but no evidence to ever tie him to any of it. I've got him in lockup now. He says a man sought him out and hired him to see if a certain blonde lady was holed up anywhere around town. He suggested Rafe keep an eye on Marshal Holloway and me, as well as Chief Brannigan as a way of finding what he was looking for."

Ali's mortification from what Jax had overheard vanished as her fears were realized. Armone had found her again.

"He says he was caught before he could report back to the guy. He has a cell number to call. He says the guy was wearing a suit like he was some big hotshot. Waited for him at the pool hall. Looked about as out of place as a bald guy at a barbershop."

"Have you confirmed his story?" Jax asked.

"I did. Kenneth Prince, owner of the pool hall, described the same guy hanging out twice this week."

"Is Sanford supposed to meet with him again?"

"Only if he finds her location. He gets one thousand dollars in cash."

Ali felt sick to her stomach. That was the Armone way.

Holloway was trying to sit up again. Jax shook his head and ushered him back down.

"You think we can set up a sting operation?" Holloway asked.

"We?" Jax laughed. "You're not leaving this hospital. I'm taking this witness—" he glanced at Ali "—someplace safe."

"I've already notified the FBI," Tanner said. "They want this guy."

"Damn." Holloway blew out a breath. "The more activity in this area, the more attention we draw."

"Deputy James Carter is headed to your location now. Stevens, he'll take you to a place to stay tonight."

"We need security at Holloway's home and on his room here at the hospital," Jax said.

Ali hated this. She didn't want anyone else hurt because of that bastard.

Holloway protested. "I don't need—"

"Don't argue," Jax ordered.

"Making that happen now," Tanner said. "We can't be sure what this man knows. If Sanford doesn't come through for him, he may move onto bigger fish."

Holloway muttered a curse.

While Tanner and Jax continued to talk, Holloway looked at Ali. "You okay?"

She managed a nod. "You guys have the tough job. All I have to do is stay alive."

Falls Mills Bed & Breakfast

SHERIFF TANNER WAS friends with the owner of the historic bed-and-breakfast. Since there were no guests tonight, he had turned the place over to Tanner.

The bed-and-breakfast was a small two-story cabin built in the late 1800s, according to the brochure on the table by the door. The location was sort of off-the-grid. Not as much as the cabin where she'd stayed for the past six months, but definitely on a road less traveled.

She glanced at the clock—almost nine. Not so late, but she was exhausted. The owner had closed and locked the gate to the main property. Of course that wouldn't stop a man like Armone.

"Here we go."

Jax was on one knee in front of the fireplace; Bob watched him intently, his tail wagging. Jax had started a fire. He had a bit of trouble in the beginning. Ali had thought about telling him that she could do it, but she'd decided to avoid conversation as much as possible. She did not want him to ask her about what she'd said to Holloway. She'd come up with an excuse to explain it away, but she'd rather not talk about it.

Ever.

He stood. "You hungry? Tanner said the place was stocked. We can have a look, see what's available."

"I think I'll just go to bed." She needed some time alone to regroup and pull herself together.

She could not linger here any longer and have him stare at her the way he was right this second.

"We eat and then we sack out."

"Okay." She started toward the kitchen, moving past him as quickly as possible. Bob trailed behind her.

Jax followed. She didn't have to look back—she could feel his nearness. How could she be so keenly aware of him after all these years?

To distract herself from him and to get this whole eating thing over, she perused the cabinets and the fridge in the small kitchen. Nothing she saw made her the slightest bit hungry. But he was right. She had to eat or she wouldn't be able to function at her best. She grabbed a can of soup and crackers along with a bottle of water. While he prowled, she heated her soup in the microwave. There was no dog food, so she opened a can of little sausages for Bob. Then she went to sit on the floor by the fire.

She couldn't get warm.

She needed a shower. A toothbrush and clothes.

It felt as if this nightmare was never going to be over. She forced herself to eat the soup and munch on a cracker. It would be nice to say she couldn't wait to go home, but she had no home. She had nothing. Not even a vehicle. The one at the cabin didn't belong to her.

Nothing belonged to her. Not even the few items of clothing in the bureau in that cabin she would never see again.

Tears burned her eyes, but she refused to cry. Crying was pointless. Besides, she was utterly exhausted. She lacked the energy to cry.

Every family photo she possessed was at the house she had shared with Harrison. The necklace her father had given her for her sixteenth birthday, the watch her mother had worn every day of her life and dozens of other mementos.

Armone had probably had them destroyed.

He would love hurting her that way. Bastard.

"About the thing at the hospital."

She dropped the spoon into her empty bowl. Somehow, she had finished the soup. "What thing?"

"What you were saying to Holloway."

He was staring at her. Waiting for her to look at him. She refused. Kept her gaze locked on the bottle of water in her hand. "I said what I thought I had to say to get him to take you off the case."

It was a good excuse and kept her from looking totally pathetic.

"I see." He scooped up another spoonful of cereal.

"Good night." She got to her feet and started toward the kitchen with her bowl.

"For the record," he said.

She stopped but didn't look back.

"It doesn't matter. This is what I do. Nothing more."

She took another step and then another until she reached the kitchen. Careful not to drop the bowl, she placed it in the sink, her hand shaking. The crackers went back into the cabinet. He came into the kitchen and placed his bowl in the sink next to hers. She braced herself for walking past him once more.

"Good night," he said as she passed.

She kept walking, Bob on her heels.

Chapter Five

Three days until trial

Monday, February 3

A sound woke her.

The room was pitch-dark. Ali lay still and listened. The distant sound of the falls, the occasional splat of something wet against the metal roof. More snow?

She had no idea what time it was.

Throwing the handmade quilt aside, she sat up. Her bare feet settled on the cold wood floor. Her eyes slowly adjusted to the darkness. Across the room the other bed was empty. The white linens beneath the other handmade quilt confirmed her conclusion.

Where was Jax?

Maybe he'd awakened early and gone down for coffee. Ali drew in a deep breath. Since the loft was open on one side to the first level, the scent of brewed coffee would surely have wafted up to her.

No hint of coffee lingered in the air. Just the cold air flavored with the slightest scent of lavender. There were bunches of the dried herb neatly placed throughout the room. Pushing up to her feet, she righted her clothes. The sweatshirt had twisted around her waist, and the jeans had crawled up above her ankles. Somewhere around the bed were her socks and shoes. She should find them before going downstairs. She moved slowly around the bed, swiping one soundless foot across the wood until she bumped the pile of abandoned footwear.

Where was Bob?

Settling on the floor, she gathered the socks first and tugged them on. Then the shoes that were her favorites. This was the only footwear she'd brought with her when she walked away from that gym. When this was over, she would certainly need to refresh her wardrobe.

Assuming she needed something more than a burial dress.

She shivered. The cold, she told herself. She wasn't afraid. Not really. Especially now. She was far more afraid of Jax being hurt than she was of her own mortality. She had bought in to this tragic nightmare. He had not. He was only attempting to do his job. She cringed at the memory of him hearing what she'd said to Marshal Holloway. It wasn't true, of course. The assurance rang hollowly in her head. Yes, she had feelings for him. He had been her first love. But she wasn't still *in* love with him.

Not possible.

She got up and moved quietly to the stairs. They were narrow, not made for more than one person at a time. Downstairs was just as dark as upstairs. She opened her mouth to call his name, but some deeply entrenched instinct stopped her.

It was too quiet.

If he was up, why wasn't a light on? Why didn't she smell coffee?

Another step downward and then another. Maybe he'd gone outside to look around. Check the perimeter or whatever bodyguards did.

She took the final step down to the lower level and turned toward the kitchen area. Moonlight filtered in through the window. No Jax.

A firm hand closed over her mouth. Her scream lodged in her throat.

A strong arm locked around her and flattened her against a hard body. "Quiet," he whispered.

Jax.

Thank God.

Holding her tight against him, he shuffled soundlessly away from the stairs and the meager light trickling into the kitchen.

When they were in the darkest corner of the room, his mouth brushed her ear again. She shivered, and it had nothing to do with the cold.

"There's someone outside."

Her pulse accelerated. She pinched her lips together to prevent any sound from escaping. Holloway had been right. The closer the trial date got, the more desperate Armone would become. All these months had been so quiet, so uneventful. She closed her eyes and focused on steadying her breathing.

Where was Bob? She opened her mouth to ask, but the dog's warm body brushed against her leg, alleviating the need. Her fingers trailed the length of his back.

Jax guided her to the area beneath the narrow stairs. Bob scooted in next to her. Jax touched her lips with one finger in the universal sign for quiet.

As he moved away, she lost sight of him in the darkness. The other windows in the cabin, including the one in the door, were covered with curtains. Jax had carefully closed them all when they first arrived. Only the kitchen window was uncovered. If trouble was here, they needed backup. He shouldn't do this alone.

She reached into the hip pocket of her jeans, thankful her phone was still tucked there. Squatting deeper beneath the stairs, she turned it on and waited for the home screen to appear. Her fingers shaking, she quickly typed a text message to Holloway.

SOS

The promising dots that he was responding appeared, and she held her breath.

Relief swam through her veins. A thumbs-up meant he had received the message and would send help. Since there were two thumbs-up images, she assumed Jax had already called for assistance.

Everything would be okay. *If* they arrived in time. As far as she could tell driving in the dark last night, they were sort of in the middle of nowhere.

A scratching sound whispered through the darkness.

The air trapped in her lungs.

The urge to rush out there and help in some way hurtled through her.

Be still!

This entire case depended on her survival to testify. If something happened to her, the old bastard would get away with everything the same way he had for decades.

She could not allow that to happen.

Glass shattered at the front of the cabin. Next to her, Bob's body tensed. The door opened.

Ali twisted just enough to see beyond the stair treads. The staircase was open with no risers or anything that would block her view.

With the door open, moonlight arrowed across the floor. The instinct to draw away nudged her, but she didn't dare move. A shadow blocked the light.

Her heart bolted against her sternum. Bob pressed closer against her, his fur standing up. She gave him the hand signal to stay. He was trained not to move or to make a sound when given that signal.

The slightest brush of a shoe sole against the hardwood. Then another and another. He—whoever he was—moved about in the darkness. Ali held her breath. Tried to make herself as small as possible.

The sigh of his weight settling onto the first tread sent fear roaring through her.

Another brush of rubber against wood as he braced a shoe on the next step.

A grunt echoed in the darkness.

The tread squeaked with movement.

For a moment there were only grunting sounds and fabric rustling. She tried to make out what was happening, but she could only see movement in the darkness. It was impossible to discern what she was looking at other than she understood the two men were struggling.

"Do not move."

Jax.

His order was directed at the other man. Bob issued a low growl.

Again, the urge to get out there and help somehow prodded at her.

Blue lights suddenly throbbed in the darkness.

Backup had arrived.

"On your feet," Jax instructed.

With the headlights of the official vehicles shining on the cabin, she could see the man scramble to his feet.

"Hands behind your head."

He obeyed Jax's command.

Tanner and two uniformed deputies filed in through the door. Chief Brannigan followed. Someone flipped on the overhead light. Ali squinted until her eyes adjusted to the brightness.

"Everything okay?" Tanner asked.

Jax nodded. "Just caught this scumbag trying to slip in and mess up my vacation."

The last was an effort to throw the man off. No one wanted him reporting back to whoever hired him that he had indeed found the witness.

Tanner cuffed the man's hands behind his back.

"I have a few questions for him before you take him away," Jax said.

"Let's step outside and have a chat," Tanner suggested.

Flashlights bobbed in the night. Ali supposed there were other deputies out there searching the area. There was always the possibility that this guy hadn't come alone.

Before walking out, Jax said something to Brannigan for his ears only.

When the door closed, Brannigan came around to the back of the staircase and couched down. "You all right, ma'am?"

Bob's tail thumped on the wood floor as if he recognized one of the good guys.

"Yes." The word was rusty. She managed her first deep breath since waking up.

"I think it's safe for you to come out now." He offered his hand.

Ali put her hand in his and scrambled from her hiding place, Bob right behind her.

"Thank you."

"Anytime."

Brannigan was like Tanner and Holloway. He wore the cowboy boots and the hat. He had the same polite manners, as well. All this time she'd believed cowboys were overrated. Maybe not. Her mind was whirling with silly thoughts and ideas. She was too tired and too stressed and coming down off an adrenaline rush fueled by fear. On cue, her knees attempted to buckle.

"Steady there." Brannigan took her by the arm and ushered her to the nearest chair.

She sat, managed another thanks. When she'd composed herself a bit, she asked, "Do we know if he's one of Armone's men?"

"I figure we'll know that any minute now."

He was probably right.

The phone still clutched in her hand vibrated.

She looked at the screen.

?

Holloway wanted to know if she was okay. She sent him a thumbs-up, and he shot back a smiley face.

She suddenly felt tremendously lucky to have been stashed in Winchester. Everyone had been so nice to her. It wasn't at all like her first location, where she'd felt like a prisoner, an outsider…a criminal.

Before she could stop the reaction, tears spilled

down her cheeks. She felt like a complete idiot. Bob set his head on her knees and stared at her with sad eyes.

Brannigan crouched down beside her chair. "Hey, now. We've got the situation under control. No need for tears."

He stood and crossed the room, came back with a box of tissues.

She pulled out a couple and swabbed at her cheeks. "Sorry. I guess I was due for a little breakdown."

"I'm certain of it," he assured her. "We all need a way to blow off steam from time to time. There's no rule that says you can't do it this way."

She sucked in a big breath and attempted to compose herself.

"You need a place to stay until we figure out what happens next," he said. "I thought you and the marshal could stay in town at the funeral home."

"Funeral home?" A frown pulled at her weary face.

"Several generations of DuPonts grew up there," he said with a smile. "I live there with Rowan DuPont. But there's plenty of room in the living quarters above the funeral home. You'll be safe there."

She'd expected to possibly end up in a funeral home before this was over. She just hadn't expected to be alive.

JAX MADE SURE Ali and Bob were tucked in for the night before going into the living room. Chief Bran-

nigan waited for him. He'd introduced Rowan Du-
Pont, the owner of the funeral home, to them when
they first arrived an hour ago. She had gone to bed
soon after, up on the third floor. Brannigan had explained that Rowan's family had built the funeral
home more than a century and a half ago. DuPonts
had lived on the second and third floors since. Rowan
was the only one left now.

Jax had heard about her. Before her father's death,
Rowan had worked with Nashville Metro. A serial
killer had become infatuated with her and murdered
her father. In fact, the bastard was still out there,
haunting her from afar.

Sometimes it felt like the bad guys won too often.

Kept guys like him fighting an uphill battle.

"Tanner brought me up to speed on the case,"
Brannigan said. "He and Holloway will have a new
safe house for the two of you by daylight."

Jax nodded. "Good. I'll need to inspect my vehicle
more closely in the light of day first. The guy pretending to be from the utility company, Teddy Scott,
stuck a tracker on my SUV. If I hadn't been in such
a hurry to get out of there I would have thought of
that and checked first."

He wasn't sure he could forgive himself for that
mistake. Ali could have been killed. The bastard
he'd taken down wouldn't talk other than to demand
a call to his lawyer. A quick cell phone pic sent to a
deputy at the jail, and Scott had confirmed the man
was the same one who had hired him to look for Ali.

Armone hadn't sent him. He was a damned investigative reporter from Atlanta. Jax had known something was off when the man broke the glass in the door. What kind of hired killer announced his presence by busting his way inside?

There was always the chance he had a team with him, in which case it wouldn't have mattered, but one man alone would have wanted to keep his presence unknown for as long as possible.

Outrage rushed through him again just thinking about the kind of person who would put a photo op before a person's life—including his own.

"I have people who can help with going over your vehicle," Brannigan assured him.

"I appreciate your support, Chief." Jax couldn't remember the last time he'd felt so tired. Lots of cases were tough, but this one was taking it out of him fast.

Doesn't have anything to do with the identity of the witness.

The lie echoed in his brain.

Brannigan shook his head. "The dead husband was one sick puppy."

Jax knew a great deal about the man professionally, but he knew very little about his personal life. One of the reasons the bastards had escaped justice so long was because of their ability to keep their personal lives as tight as a vault.

"Most of them are." He'd never met a criminal at Armone's level who was anything but pure evil.

"Frankly, I don't see how she survived. It took

real courage not to just take the easy way out and end the pain."

What the hell was he talking about? "I don't know what you mean."

Ali had married Harrison Armone of her own volition. Had stayed married to him for five years.

"You didn't read the file?"

"I read the file Holloway showed me at the hospital, but there wasn't any information about the relationship between her and him other than the fact that she was his widow."

Surprise flashed across Brannigan's face, but he quickly schooled his expression. "I see."

Jax went inordinately still. "You read a different file."

It wasn't a question. What he had been shown was the bare minimum. After all, he was a US marshal, the same as Holloway. He knew who and what the Armone family was. He hadn't needed all the dirty details.

"I was made aware of additional information." Brannigan stood. "I think I'll try to get a couple more hours of shut-eye. You should do the same."

Jax stood. "I'd like to know what you saw that I didn't."

Brannigan held his gaze for a moment. "You should talk to Holloway about that, or maybe the lady in question. Good night, Stevens."

He headed for the stairs that would take him to the third floor.

Jax walked down the hall to the room where Ali slept. Rowan had explained that it had been her parents' room. The night-light in the hall cast a dim glow into the room and across the bed. Ali slept soundly.

What had she been through that she didn't want him to know? Not just her. Obviously, Holloway had made the decision that passing along those personal details wasn't necessary for Jax to do his job. And it wasn't.

But he wanted to know.

His gut tied up in knots when he considered the possibilities. There were some sick individuals in this world.

He couldn't help wondering if he'd stayed in Georgia with her if he could have…

He pushed away the thought. He couldn't undo the past. He wasn't even sure he would want to if he could.

Before he started kicking himself for that long-ago decision, he needed to know the truth. He had regretted his decision on some level, sure. He'd been crazy about her ten years ago. He'd wanted to spend forever with her. Whatever forever meant to a twenty-two-year-old guy with a burning desire to save the world.

She had only wanted to get through college. She'd had to delay starting for more than a year after high school to help her father take care of her mother. After her mother passed, she'd resumed her plan.

That was how they'd met. She was in college and he'd been at Glynco, and they'd ended up at the same pizza place.

She was the prettiest girl he'd ever seen and so shy. The shyness had really intrigued him. He'd had to dig for every nugget of information. She was the only woman he'd ever taken home to meet his family.

His mother and sister had adored Ali. His father, too. He'd told Jax that she was the one. At twenty-two, who listens to their old man?

The whole family had been upset with him when he moved to Seattle alone. On some level he had known it was a mistake, as well. But he hadn't taken steps to make it right until it was too late and she'd married a monster. He hadn't allowed her to creep into his thoughts again…until yesterday.

No point beating a dead horse. It was done. It was over. She was the one who'd married someone else.

He checked the door locks and the security system key pad then slipped quietly into the room where she slept. Bob was stretched out on the floor next to the bed. He lifted his head, eyed Jax for a moment, then relaxed on the floor once more. Jax went into the en suite bath and closed the door before turning on the light.

Rowan had supplied fresh towels and toiletries. He placed his weapon and cell phone on the floor next to the shower, turned on the water and shed his clothes and shoes. He stepped under the hot spray and just stood there for a while, allowing the water to slide over his body.

Every muscle tightened when he thought of the way Ali's body had felt against his when he'd pulled her to him to whisper in her ear. Even under the circumstances, he had felt that old familiar need to keep holding her, to turn her around and to kiss her the way he used to.

He didn't want to feel that way. Not after she'd lived with a man like Armone.

Scrubbing the soap over his body, he tried his level best to banish thoughts of her, but she wasn't going anywhere.

He thought of the comment Brannigan had made. Had he been wrong all these years?

No. He let the hot water wash away the soap then he reached for the shampoo. She'd married the bastard because she wanted to. No one forced her. He'd seen them together.

The idea that he had watched her for days five years ago after he had discovered she was married was another of those memories he would like to evict from his head. No matter that he had been the one to walk away, he had somehow always expected to end up with Ali. When she finished school, if he still felt as strongly about her, he would hunt her down and sweep her off her feet. Dazzle her and change her mind about moving to the northwest. He'd wanted that time and distance to give her a chance to decide what she really wanted. He had been certain his shy, small-town love wasn't going anywhere. She would be waiting for him. Only he'd been wrong.

He had been an arrogant fool.

She had found someone new.

He had made the mistake of his life.

She was just as pretty as he remembered, but she was with *him*.

He'd told himself that she couldn't possibly understand what kind of man Armone was, but his pride had overrode any doubt or sympathy,

He turned off the water and climbed out of the shower. That was the part that didn't add up. Why would she even go out with a man like Armone? Didn't she recognize evil when she saw it?

She couldn't possibly have married him without at least some idea of who he was.

This was the part he couldn't overlook. That really got to him. That he couldn't forgive.

She hadn't looked back, either. Hadn't tried to call him. Hadn't called his mom or his sister. She had just gone on with her life and married someone else. That part was on him. No denying it.

He toweled off and pulled his clothes back on. Whatever Brannigan knew that he didn't wouldn't make any difference.

Maybe that made him heartless, but if you didn't want to be bitten, you didn't climb into a den of snakes.

Chapter Six

A dusting of snow had fallen during the wee hours before daylight.

Ali stared out the window over the yard behind the funeral home. Funny, it looked like any other backyard. Freud, Rowan's German shepherd, pranced around the yard as if he wanted to make as many footprints in the snow as possible.

But this was no typical residence. Downstairs people were prepared for their final journey in this life. Funerals and wakes were carried out. She shivered. How fitting that she would be in this place. Her life the past five years had been nothing more than a facade for a dead marriage to a killer.

With a shudder, she pushed the thought away. She'd stirred at some point just before daylight. Jax had been sleeping in a chair on the other side of the bedroom. A lamp on the table next to the chair had cast a soft glow over his face.

Taking care not to make a sound, she had sat up in bed and watched him for a long while. The few lines around his eyes had relaxed in sleep. A day's beard growth shadowed his jaw. She didn't want to smile, but her lips formed the expression, anyway. He had hardly changed. Still good-looking. A little leaner in places, more heavily muscled in others. The boy right out of college and psyched about attending marshal training had been full of energy and excitement. This Jax was all man. All grown-up and slightly jaded after a decade in his chosen career.

He was quieter...more still. She suspected all that energy and excitement had calmed a bit and that the newer, deeper emotions were kept close, behind the tin star he carried. But in sleep, he looked so much like the very young man she had fallen so hard for. She had been so naive, which was kind of sad, since she hadn't started college until she was twenty. Certainly she hadn't been the starry-eyed eighteen-year-old fresh out of high school. Ali had spent two years taking care of her mother before she passed away. She'd barely gotten three years of college under her belt when her father had fallen ill. Another year at home with him, and then she'd found herself completely alone. Those final two semesters of college had been so lonely. Moving to the big city had seemed like the perfect change.

Instead, it had been the biggest mistake of her life.

Somehow she'd drifted off to sleep again, and now she dreaded leaving this quiet room. She'd heard people stirring. Heard the low rumble of Jax's voice as well as the softer voice of a woman. Rowan Du-

Pont, she imagined. Ali had met her only briefly last night. Like Ali, she had long blond hair. She, too, had that look in her eyes—the one that said she had experienced deep pain.

Ali righted her sweatshirt and smoothed a hand over her jeans-clad hips. Bob waited by the door watching her. He was probably starving. Rowan had a dog, too. Thankfully Freud hadn't seemed to mind the company—not even Bob. The two dogs had eyed each other speculatively but neither bothered to growl.

Ali needed fresh clothes. Hopefully, Sheriff Tanner could bring her clothes from the cabin. She slipped on her shoes and ran a brush through her hair again. Then she headed out to learn what would happen next.

The living room was empty. Listening for the voices, she followed the sound into the kitchen. Both Jax and Rowan turned her way as she entered the room.

"Good morning." Rowan smiled. "The coffee is strong and hot, and Billy made breakfast before he had to head to the office."

A chief of police who cooked. Judging by Rowan's smile, she was very happy that he did. "Thank you."

Jax poured a mug full of the steaming brew and passed it to her. She thanked him.

"There's cream and sugar," Rowan said, "if you don't like it black."

"Black is fine." Ali noticed that Jax remembered.

She kept her gaze away from his for fear he would recognize that she had noticed.

Rowan crossed the room and picked up a plastic bowl filled with kibbles and placed it on the floor. "Bob," she said to the dog, "this is for you."

Bob trotted over to the bowl and dug in.

"Thank you," Ali said to her, immensely grateful for the extra mile.

Rowan smiled. "Well, I have a client coming at nine. I should probably start preparations."

"Thank you so much for your hospitality," Ali offered. She was immensely grateful to all the people who had gone to such lengths to help her do this.

"Good luck, Ali," Rowan said. "You're doing the right thing."

Ali nodded and watched her go. She wondered at the things the woman had been forced to do in her life. There was a sadness about her, but it didn't overwhelm her. Ali hoped the past few years would not define her for the rest of her life.

She stared at the lovely breakfast spread across the counter. Eggs, biscuits, bacon. Her stomach knotted at the thought of eating.

"You have to eat."

She turned to the man, who could clearly still read her like an open book. "I'm really not hungry."

"You're going to need all the strength and courage you can muster. To do that, you need to eat."

"What about you?"

"I've already eaten."

She gathered a plate and fork and went through the motions, forcing herself to consume a few bites of egg and a biscuit. Once she started, her appetite roused and kept the ordeal from being entirely awful.

The coffee gave her a shot of energy, chasing away the lingering shadows from last night's drama.

"How long will we be staying here?" It wasn't the idea of the funeral home below that bothered her. The trouble was that her presence put Rowan and anyone else here in danger. Ali didn't want anyone to suffer because of her.

"Tanner and Holloway should have a new safe house for us in a few hours. The last time we spoke, he was going to check out a location."

She downed the last gulp of her coffee. "What about my clothes from the cabin? Is there any chance he can bring those?"

"One of his deputies brought your things to the sheriff's office. They'll be at the new location when we arrive."

"Great." She needed a shower. She needed clean clothes and some time away from the rest of the world.

This time three days from now, she would be sitting in a courtroom preparing to testify against old man Armone. It seemed strange that the idea of testifying didn't scare her. She looked forward to the opportunity. Worry about who would get hurt ensuring she had that opportunity gnawed at her relentlessly. She thought of Marshal Holloway and his wife and daughter. Sheriff Tanner and his family. She thought of Chief Brannigan and Rowan. And she thought of Jax.

So many people who could be hurt.

Rather than dwell on the worrisome thoughts, she busied herself cleaning up. She tucked the dirty dishes into the dishwasher. Someone had already cleaned the stove and washed the cooking utensils. There was really nothing else she could do in here. Rather than try making amiable conversation with Jax, she went back to the bedroom and made up the bed.

When she was finished, she lingered. The desk in the room was covered with dozens of notebooks. She walked closer and decided the notebooks were journals. This had been Rowan's parents' room. They were both gone now. She wondered if the journals were her mother's.

She touched an open page, traced the handwriting. Her own mother hadn't kept a journal. But she had meticulously documented each photo in the family photo albums. Time and place and a note about whatever was happening. Her father had been far more pragmatic. He was eternally focused on work and what needed to be done next. A farmer's life was challenging. Hard work, lots of worry and rarely a decent payoff for the two.

Certain she had sequestered herself in this room for as long as possible without risking Jax showing up to check on her, she walked back into the living

room. He was in the kitchen, his low voice and the
cell phone tucked against his ear telling her he'd
heard from someone. Perhaps there was news about
what happened next.

Then again, it could be a personal call. He'd said
he'd never married and had never been engaged—
which was not entirely true—but that didn't mean he
was without a girlfriend. He could have someone up
in Nashville waiting for him to come home. The idea
hadn't even entered her mind. She had expected him
to be married and have a kid or two. That he was not
had thrown her for a bit of a loop. Maybe he enjoyed
the bachelor lifestyle too much.

He was only thirty-two. He could certainly enjoy
a decade more of the single life before bothering
to settle down. Made life far less complicated. As
a marshal, he could be gone for days or weeks at a
time. Without a wife or children to worry about, he
was free as a bird.

He hadn't been pathetically needy and lonesome
the way she had been.

Bob most likely needed to go outside and do his
business. It was possible Jax had taken him out earlier, but she couldn't be sure. She didn't see any reason why she couldn't take him out.

"Come," she said to the animal as she patted her
leg.

Bob trotted over, and the two of them exited the
living quarters, heading for the staircase. Since there
was a fenced backyard, she wouldn't have to worry

about the leash. At the top of the stairs, she looked down at the lobby. The place was certainly grand enough. Behind her a towering stained-glass window depicted angels ascending toward heaven. As she descended the staircase, she surveyed the numerous elegant sitting areas—conversation groupings of furniture. The double entrance doors were equally grand.

It really was a beautiful place.

"Hey, Ali."

She turned to Rowan, who was walking toward her down a corridor. On the wall, arrows pointed to that corridor showing that the lounge and restrooms as well as the office were in that direction.

"Hi. I thought I should take Bob out, if it's okay."

"Of course. Follow me."

Rowan led the way through a set of doors labeled Staff Only. Another corridor seemed to lead to the back of the house. Doors lined the corridor, but none were labeled. Toward the end was an elevator. Next to the back door was another set of double doors and a second staircase, this one rather narrow.

Her guide opened the back door and waited for Bob to trot out across the porch.

She watched him for a moment then smiled at Ali. "He'll be fine outside. Did you need anything else?"

Ali shook her head. "No, thank you. I'll just wait here to let him in."

"All right."

Rowan walked away, and Ali's gaze returned to the backyard.

Bob and Freud were prancing around in the snow.

She would love to go out there and join them, but it wouldn't be safe.

For nine months now, everything had revolved around keeping her safe. She'd lived like a recluse. Barely setting foot outside where anyone might see her. Bob had been her only constant companion.

If she survived this, she wanted to do more with her life. Have a real career. Make a difference.

Have a family.

The idea that Jax's face came immediately to mind when she thought of family warned that she was in more danger than anyone knew.

THE HOUSE WAS rustic like a cabin but with all the amenities of a contemporary home. It sat deep in the woods, high on a hillside. To reach the house, Jax had to drive across a stream and up a steep, curvy road that was just barely wide enough to accommodate his SUV. The narrow road had been carved out of the mountainside. Looking over the edge might have been a little unsettling if not for the dense, soaring trees on both sides. Many were bare for the winter, but many more were evergreens and blocked the view of the dirt track from the paved road below.

Not that Jax was particularly worried about anyone finding them too quickly. The right he'd taken off Highway 64 as they neared Huntland had wound deep into the countryside. The only sign of civilization was the worn-out asphalt that was just shy of two actual lanes and the occasional farmhouse. They drove for miles without seeing a thing except trees and that faded asphalt snaking out ahead of them before a small white house surrounded by barns two or three times its size and sweeping pastures appeared. More trees followed.

This, Jax decided, was the sticks. He made a left just past the curve Tanner had described. If possible, this road was even less populated. Trees, trees and more trees. He spotted the wide stream, ice crusting its outer edge. The temperature hadn't risen high enough to melt off the snow. It clung to the branches of trees and the landscape like a coating of powdered sugar on the chocolate cake his mom made every year at Christmas. The memory had his stomach rumbling. Breakfast had been hours ago.

After a meeting with Holloway and Tanner, they sat in on a conference call with the AUSA from Nashville, Adam Knowles. He and his counterpart in Atlanta had decided that a conference call was necessary to ensure Ali was ready for trial. Tomorrow morning at eleven they were to be in Nashville at the AUSA's office.

Jax didn't like it. He didn't like it one damned bit. Holloway was mad as hell. He'd refused at first, but eventually the AUSA had won him over. Now it was up to Jax to take all sorts of back roads and unexpected routes to get Ali to the man's office. She hadn't objected. She'd basically agreed to whatever he suggested. Even her damned attorney, who was also on the call, hadn't objected.

Who the hell was the guy working for?

Still furious, Jax unloaded the last of their supplies from his SUV. This house and its forty mountainous acres belonged to a close friend of Tanner's. It was unoccupied just now, but the power remained on for insurance purposes. The house remained furnished, since the family used it from time to time when they visited their hometown. Just beyond the house, a large water tank sat on a towering stand and gathered water from the underground streams coming from the mountainside. The house also had a generator and a basement.

All the comforts of home—and fully self-sustainable.

Tanner had provided Jax with additional ammo and an extra handgun. Jax had turned on the lights downstairs and checked the two bedrooms upstairs. There was a bathroom upstairs and down. A big kitchen and nice-size family room. The fireplace was huge. Firewood was stacked on the back porch.

It was almost like a vacation rental, except it wasn't.

Ali stood by the fire he'd started as if she couldn't get warm after walking around the property to get familiar with the territory.

"You hungry?" She hadn't eaten much at breakfast.

"I'm good with a peanut butter sandwich." She turned and walked toward the kitchen.

Bob looked at him before following her.

He did the same. "Peanut butter it is, then."

Food wasn't usually such a dominating subject on his mind, but it was a topic he could broach with her without worrying where it might lead.

After she had prepared her sandwich, he did the same. While he placed two slices of bread on a napkin, she went to a fridge for a bottle of water. She passed one to him.

"Thanks." He placed it on the counter and continued spreading peanut butter on one slice of bread.

Without a word, she took her lunch to the family room.

"I guess I'm in for the silent treatment," he said to Bob, who had hesitated before following her.

He slapped the two slices of bread together and grabbed his water, then took the same path she had taken. She stood at the front window peeking through the blinds. Her sandwich and water had been abandoned on the coffee table.

"It's snowing again."

She said this as if she were speaking to herself rather than to anyone in particular. He joined her at the window and leaned his head to the right far enough to see through the two slats she had parted. She drew away the slightest bit.

"Looks like the meteorologist got it right for

once." Snow had been in the forecast, but in this part of the country there was rarely a follow-through.

She released the slats and walked back to the sofa. It was a large L-shaped one. He settled on the opposite end from her. He didn't need a crystal ball to tell him she wasn't interested in having him too close.

"You worried about tomorrow?" He tore off a bite of the sandwich and chewed as he waited for her response.

"Not really." She nibbled her sandwich, eating like a bird.

"I've already mapped out a route." He'd been thinking about it since the command performance was issued. There was little likelihood of them being discovered en route with the precautions he had outlined. There was always the risk that their travel plans could be leaked. It had happened before. To ensure that didn't happen again, he had not provided the route he intended to take to anyone. Better to be safe than sorry.

"I'm not worried," she said in case he hadn't gotten it the first time.

She chewed and swallowed, chewed and swallowed. Clearly she wasn't enjoying the food. He figured if he hadn't mentioned that they should eat, she wouldn't have bothered. It was his job to keep her safe and to ensure she was ready to testify at trial on Thursday. To that end, his duties included seeing that she ate, slept and behaved responsibly.

"If you have any questions about how things will

go on Thursday, I can probably answer them." She hadn't asked a single question during the conference call.

"I don't have any questions." She drank more of her water and wadded the napkin she'd used for a plate.

"Good." He finished his sandwich and chugged the rest of his water.

The silence was deafening. He considered going back to the kitchen and making coffee, but the enthusiasm just wasn't there. There were things he wanted to ask…to say, but none of it would come out the way he wanted. He was too angry about what she had done. *Angry* might not be the right word. He wasn't exactly angry. He was disappointed. The crazy part was he had no right to feel either way.

As she had so accurately pointed out, he'd been the one to leave.

No point going down that path again.

He stood and returned to the kitchen. Tossed his trash and made a pot of coffee. The silence was a lot easier to tolerate if he found some way to occupy himself.

The scent of fresh-brewed coffee filled the air, and he relaxed marginally. Today and tonight were going to pass painstakingly slowly. They had both said plenty, maybe too much on some subjects. There was nothing else to discuss.

Words weren't going to change deeds.

What was done was done.

"I do have one question."

Surprised that she had walked into the room without him detecting her presence, he turned to face her. "What might that be?"

"The day we go to trial, will you be wearing a bulletproof vest?"

So they were back to his safety, were they? "I've already told you there's no reason for you to worry about me. I know how to do this."

She stared at him, unblinking, determined. "You asked me if I had any questions. That's my question."

"Yes. And so will you."

Apparently satisfied with his answer, she turned and walked away.

Was it possible that she was actually that worried about him?

He shook his head. Made no sense.

Chapter Seven

The snow had stopped, leaving enough to cover the grass and adorn the trees and rooftop. Ali had always liked snow, but growing up in Georgia she had rarely seen it outside Christmas movie marathons. On the rare occasion it did snow, it was a given that it wouldn't last long. Vivid memories of both her parents romping in the snow with her when she was a child assaulted her, took her breath.

Bob nudged her with his nose, and she smiled down at him. "Sorry, boy, I was lost in thought."

Somewhere close by, Jax would be trailing her. There wasn't really any place to go unless she wanted to attempt climbing higher up the mountain. The edge of the tree line provided a sweeping view of the valley below. Even the faded asphalt far below that zigzagged through the valley was covered in snow. Not a single vehicle had driven along that road since their arrival. She hoped they would be safe here until the day after tomorrow, when they headed to Atlanta for the trial.

According to the conference call this morning, they were booked under aliases on a commercial flight from Huntsville, Alabama, to Atlanta. The airport in Huntsville was less than an hour away. Jax had said they would leave early Wednesday morning and, per the usual protocol, take back roads until they had no other choice.

When this began, her attorney had mentioned to her the possibility that dedicated followers of old man Armone might haunt her for many years after his incarceration. Assuming she survived to testify and all went as expected during the trial. There was always the chance, she supposed, that a jury could be intimidated or bought off.

But no one was going to let a man who shot his own son get away with it. Right?

Ali hugged her jacket tighter around her and turned back toward the house. Jax lingered a few yards behind. His gaze caught hers briefly as she walked past him. She had been thinking that it might be best to try and make amends of some sort. If she didn't live through this, the idea of him spending the rest of his life harboring this resentment he felt toward her was more than she wanted to take to her grave.

He was the one who'd left, and in her mind he owed her the apology, explanation, whatever. Not vice versa. But he didn't see it that way. All he saw were the facts. She had married a ruthless criminal.

Had stayed married to him for five years until he was murdered. Admittedly, that didn't look so great.

But there were so many things he didn't know. Things she could not bear to tell anyone beyond the official statement she had given over the course of a week when this thing began.

Rather shortsightedly, she had walked into that FBI office in Kentucky and identified herself. No further explanation had been needed. Immediately, the powers that be were gathered into conference rooms across the southeast and decisions were made. She was interviewed over and over for weeks. Finally when a course of action was decided upon, she was whisked away into hiding to await trial.

There had been no fanfare, no sense of adventure or excitement. Just more loneliness. The deep, sad loneliness she had felt for years by that point. At least the physical pain had stopped.

Oddly, the physical pain was the only aspect of those last three years of her marriage that reminded her she was still alive. She had felt dead most of the time. A body floating through time. The numbness that had overtaken her life had been profound—except for the physical pain he wielded. Sometimes she even looked forward to the moments when the pain reminded her that her heart was still beating.

She wasn't sure what a psychiatrist would say about that. Most likely she didn't want to know.

Stamping the snow from her shoes at the back door, she smiled as Bob shook himself, as well.

"Come on, boy."

They went inside, and Jax followed. She peeled off her jacket and hung it in the mudroom before continuing on into the kitchen. Rubbing her hands together, she went in search of a treat for Bob. She found a small bag of jerky that was still in date.

Bob shifted from paw to paw with excitement as she opened the bag. She gave him a piece, and he sauntered off to pile up in front of the fireplace. Bob liked being near the heat and maybe the crackle of the logs. Then again, it didn't take a lot to make him happy. The occasional scratch behind the ears, walks and food.

In her opinion, he had the right idea. She longed for simple again.

Finally, she turned to face the man watching her. "We need to talk."

He lifted one shoulder and let it drop. "Talk."

"Can we go in the other room and sit while we talk?" No matter that the sun was dropping, light poured into the kitchen's western-facing windows. She didn't want to have this discussion in such unforgiving light.

He gestured to the other room. "After you."

She sat in a chair near where Bob lay. The fire had died down a little while they were out walking. Jax added a couple more logs to fuel the flames. He settled on the sofa, which allowed him to stare directly at her.

"Just so you know," he said before she could

begin, "you don't owe me an explanation. You're right. I left. You had every right to move on with your life as you saw fit."

His face told her he didn't really see it that way.

"After you left for Seattle, I focused on my classes. It was lonely and I was heartbroken."

He started to speak but she held up a hand to stop him.

"I was young. I hadn't even turned twenty-two yet. You were my first love and, of course, I was devastated. I was a bit of a late bloomer, so I hadn't experienced that kind of intense relationship before." She swallowed, mustered the courage to say the rest. "It wasn't your fault that I had been so sheltered until then."

She waited to see if he had anything to say. When he didn't, she moved on.

"For the next two years, I hung on to the idea that you would be back." She laughed softly. "I was confident you loved me just as much as I loved you and that you'd come back and all would be well again."

His expression changed then. The defensive face melted into something softer, something aching.

"Then my father became ill, and I had to leave school to take care of him. I only had two semesters left, but there was no putting off going home. He was very, very sick."

She fell quiet for a moment, remembering those pain-filled days. Her father was the only family she'd had left. Saying goodbye to him had been so very difficult.

"Before he died, he made me promise that I would go back and finish school. So I did. I left everything at the farm just as it was and completed my final semesters. By that time I felt as if I could go back and pack things up. Do what I had to do. It took a couple of months, but I got it done. The farm sold practically before I could put it on the market. I decided I wanted to go someplace where I could disappear into the energy and excitement. Atlanta felt like the place."

"You went to work for Clayton and Ross, and the rest is history," he said, the defensive face and tone back in full swing.

"I had no idea the accounting firm had anything to do with the Armone family." She shrugged. "I had no idea who the Armone family was. The firm offered a very competitive salary plus a bonus. They would pay for my master's. It was a win-win situation. I found a small apartment and even bought a new car with part of the money from the farm." She shook her head. "I was so happy. It felt like a fresh beginning. I had been lonely and sad for so long."

Jax stood. "Then what? Let me guess. Armone came in and swept you off your feet. You had no idea who he was. Thought he was a knight in shining armor." He walked over to where she sat and crouched down to her eye level. "But you stayed married to him for five years. *Five years.* Nearly two thousand days and nights. You had to have figured out who he was way before that much time elapsed. But you stayed." He pushed to his feet. "You're doing the right thing now, and that's great. I'm here for you. But for far too long, you pretended you had no idea who the man you were crawling into bed with every night was."

Fury and regret made her lips tremble. "There are things you don't know."

He planted his hands on his hips. "Tell me."

She shook her head. She couldn't tell him those things. Ever. The idea of how he would look at her was too painful. She couldn't bear it. Let him think what he would. She had tried to make things right between them.

"I guess there's nothing else to say."

With that pointed announcement, he walked away.

That was the thing with Jax. He always walked away.

THE SUN HAD DISAPPEARED, and darkness had settled over the landscape. The thin layer of snow reflected the light from the moon. Jax had spent the evening checking the perimeter and ensuring all was locked up tight.

Ali's words about being sad and lonely kept echoing in his brain. He didn't want to feel the regret that had crowded into his chest. She had made her own decisions. Yes, he was the one to leave. But he'd been young, damn it. A fool. And yes, it took him a long time to see that fact, and by then it was too late.

Why did she feel compelled to keep trying to make him understand?

He didn't understand. He didn't want to understand. He wanted to keep an emotional distance between them, because he didn't want to feel what he was feeling.

Damn it.

She had said there were things he didn't know.

Probably just another excuse. She'd had everything she wanted. Money, power, prestige. Who knows what prompted her to decide to testify against the old man? Maybe she was afraid she would be next after he executed his own son.

Or maybe she and the old man had something going on.

He closed his eyes. Hated himself for even thinking such a thing. Anger, resentment, regret—all those emotions were driving him right now. He had to work through this. To keep his head clear.

Brannigan had mentioned the pain she had endured. Did that have something to do with the part she refused to share with him?

Before going back in the house, he put through a call to Holloway.

"Everything okay?" The worry in the other marshal's voice was palpable.

"Yeah. Everything's fine."

"You don't sound fine."

Holloway knew him well enough to hear the doubt in his voice.

"I need to see the entire file." A part of him wanted to argue with his own words. That part of his instincts that warned he would regret knowing nudged him. He ignored it. He had to know the whole story.

Holloway didn't respond for a bit. Finally, he said, "If she wants—"

"She's not going to tell me," Jax said, cutting him off. "Holloway, I wouldn't ask if it wasn't necessary. If Brannigan can be briefed on the part I don't know, I can, as well. I need to get my head screwed on right with this."

More of that lingering silence.

"You said this wouldn't be a problem. Tell me now if you were wrong. I don't want Ali at even more risk because you can't get beyond the past. As for what I shared with Brannigan, that was necessary. I needed his input."

"I can handle her security," Jax argued. "I just need to know the rest so I can get…" He exhaled a big breath. No use lying to the man. He would see through it. "I need to get my personal feelings sorted out, and I can't do that until I understand what she isn't telling me."

"This is her life, Stevens. She doesn't have to tell you anything."

"You know I'll hear it at trial," Jax reminded him. "Better for me to know now and be prepared."

Holloway was the one letting go of a sigh now. "You're right. Maybe I should have given you the whole story to begin with. But understand, this is intensely personal. You don't need to know in order to do your job."

He was aware that Holloway was only agreeing to indulge his personal needs.

"I don't want to go into this on the phone. I'll make sure you see the entire file tomorrow while you're in Nashville for the teleconference. There's a video you need to see. I think that will take care of whatever is nagging at you."

"All right." He could wait until tomorrow. "I appreciate it, Holloway."

"You may change your mind when you see the video."

His gut tightened. "Better to know the whole truth," he argued.

"Sometimes maybe not," Holloway countered. "Just keep her safe, Stevens. This might sound lame, but if anyone has ever needed a real-life hero, it's this woman."

The call ended, and Jax stared at the house. Ali had been standing at the window watching him, but she wasn't there now.

He'd said too much. Every time they talked about the past, his anger got the better of him. Not once in his adult life had he had this problem with anyone else. He'd always been easygoing, nonjudgmental.

But he couldn't maintain his objectivity in her presence.

This was the real problem. He still had feelings for her, and it drove him crazy.

He didn't want to feel any of this. He just wanted to do his job.

Inside the back door, he locked up and removed his jacket. Maybe he should make another pot of coffee and see if she would open up to him. Why hear the truth from a stranger when she was right here?

He emptied the carafe, rinsed away the old grounds from the brew basket and prepared a fresh pot. When it started to brew, he went in search of her. She'd already shut herself and Bob up in her room. He stood outside her closed door and tried to think of something to say.

Finally he shook his head. Tomorrow would just have to be soon enough to hear the rest of her story.

ALI STOOD AT the door, her hands pressed to the cool wooden surface. She closed her eyes and laid her cheek there. As much as she wanted his forgiveness, his understanding, she could not tell him the details of her marriage.

It was too painful. She couldn't bear to see the pity in his eyes.

When this was over, he would go on his way, and she would go hers. Vying for his understanding was a selfish luxury that was not necessary to her continued existence. She would get over the hurt. It wouldn't be the first time she'd had her heart fracture over Jaxson Stevens.

He moved away from the door. She felt his withdrawal more than heard it. She moved away, as well.

It was only eight o'clock. Going to bed this early was a little ridiculous, but it was safer than allowing that little voice in her head to goad her into telling him the whole story.

What he didn't know wouldn't hurt him or change what he was assigned to do. It would, however, devastate her.

In hindsight, there were parts she wished she hadn't shared in those initial interviews. But she had been desperate, vulnerable. The story of her marriage to Harrison Armone had poured out of her like a poison her body had needed to expel. Each time she fell silent, the interviewer was there, prodding her for more. No one would ever hear those parts, the agents had promised.

As time moved on, she had slowly but surely been informed that it might become necessary to use those details as proof of her motivation for coming forward. The fear, the humiliation and endless abuse she suffered could be an incredible asset for setting the tone for the jury.

Ali was a victim, and the jurors needed to see that victim. They needed to feel her pain.

She paced the room. Keeping Jax out of the courtroom was likely impossible. He would hear all the gory details, and there was nothing she could do to prevent it. But at least she wouldn't have to look at him. She would focus on the man questioning her.

As much as she dreaded that part of the questioning, she would do whatever necessary to see that the bastard went away. He could not be allowed to get away with all that he and his son had done.

It was time he paid.

She climbed onto the bed and closed her eyes. After all she had endured, it would be almost worth it to see the look on his face when the jury announced, "Guilty."

Chapter Eight

Two days until trial

Tuesday, February 4

Ali pulled on her jacket and finished off her second cup of coffee. She stared out the window over the sink. Thin patches of snow lingered here and there, but it would be gone by midday with the subtle rise in temperature. The interstate to Nashville wouldn't be a problem either way, but some of the back roads might still be icy this morning.

Jax had said back roads would be the word of the day. The only person who knew their exact route was Marshal Holloway, and even he didn't know the turn-by-turn details. Both she and Jax trusted him implicitly. They'd spoken this morning. She was so thankful he had been released from the hospital late yesterday. He was still on leave because of his injuries, but he was healing. Ali appreciated all that he had done for her this past six months. The first marshal assigned to her hadn't been so friendly. She had gotten the impression he had considered her a lesser life form. But he had done his job and gotten her out of danger when the time came.

"You ready?"

She turned to the man who had spoken. They hadn't said a word to each other since that unpleasant exchange late yesterday. Not even good morning.

He'd gone outside and checked his SUV. Not that he'd told her what he planned to do when he walked out the door. She'd watched from a window. He'd gone over the vehicle very carefully. Surely if anyone who had intended to do harm had found their location, they would have burst into the cabin and done so last night. Then again, she supposed it was better to be safe than sorry.

When he'd finished his inspection, she was back in the kitchen pulling on her jacket. She decided not to worry about her purse. All she needed was her driver's license and lip moisturizer. Those she carried in her left jacket pocket. The emergency cell phone Holloway had given her was in the other pocket.

"I am," she said in answer to his question. She rinsed her cup and placed it on the counter before turning to face him.

"We should get started just in case we run into any closed roads."

She crouched down and gave Bob a hug. "You take care of the place while we're gone."

His tail wagged, and she gave him a scratch on the head as she stood. She followed Jax out the front door and to his SUV. A minute later they were rolling down the treacherous road that led back down to the paved one below. Ali found herself holding her breath more than once.

Once they were on the paved road and moving along at a faster speed, she relaxed. She'd pinned her hair up and back in a makeshift twist this morning. She rarely wore it that way, but it was important not to look like her usual self.

No matter that she had prepared for the trial, trepidation was building inside her. She tried to tamp it down, but there was no holding it back. In forty-eight hours, she would have the opportunity to tell the world just how evil the Armone family was. Truly, viciously evil. She wanted to do this. Nothing outside of a bullet to her brain would stop her.

But that didn't mean she wasn't scared.

Of course, she said this to no one.

Jax rolled to a stop at the Highway 64 intersection. He reached across to the glove box, and she found herself holding her breath again. He popped it open and pulled out a pair of sunglasses.

"Put these on."

She accepted the eyewear and slid it into place. "Thank you."

The half hour that followed was thick with tension and silence. He drove around, bypassing Winchester proper. The road they were on now felt like a tunnel through a dense wood. Traffic was light. School buses were already off the roads. The other time she'd gone to Nashville, it had only taken ninety or so minutes but Marshal Holloway had taken the interstate. This would likely take a lot more time. But they had plenty.

She closed her eyes and allowed his scent to envelop her. After ten years how was it she could recall the scent of him so precisely? Whatever aftershave he wore, it was subtle. Earthy like amber, with the slightest hint of something sweet like honey. She'd loved the smell and taste of his skin. They had been so young—all they wanted to do was get lost in each other.

He was her first love, her first in every way.

Her eyes opened, and she forced away the memories. Not a good idea to get lost in those.

"Do you have any questions or concerns about today?"

She dared to turn her head to study his profile. Those lean, angular features tugged at her. The swell of his lips, the straightness of his nose. High cheekbones. His thick hair fell over his forehead. How many times had she seen that face in her dreams?

She blinked, faced forward. What was wrong with her this morning? "No."

He was doing his job, not trying to make conversation. He had made that very clear last night.

Could she blame him for not understanding how she came to be Mrs. Harrison Armone? Not really.

I guess you had to be there.

Last night she had decided not to pursue trying to make him understand. This was her burden to carry. The idea of him feeling the way he did about her forevermore was painful, but she had no power to control his feelings. She could only control her own, and she had spent far too much time as a prisoner to someone else's desires and demands. She would not be a prisoner any longer.

"We'll stop just before we arrive in Nashville for a break."

He didn't ask if she was good with that, simply made the statement. To her way of thinking, a response was not required.

She closed her eyes and rested her head against the seat.

It was time to think about the future. For months she had feared she wouldn't have a future. Finally she could see the tiniest flicker of light at the end of the tunnel. Why not make a plan just in case she did survive?

THE TELECONFERENCE WAS scheduled in the Estes Kefauver Federal Building on Ninth Avenue South, only steps from Broadway and countless legendary country music spots, like the Ryman Auditorium and the Country Music Hall of Fame.

Rather than park in the designated parking area, Jax drove over a street and parked in the lot of a huge church. From there he called an Uber that would take them right up to the door. Considering only half a dozen people—people he knew—were aware of this meeting, he hoped he didn't have to worry about a leak, but he wasn't taking the risk.

Ali had answered the few questions he had when they started out, but she hadn't said a word otherwise. He'd said too much last night. That he'd felt tremendously guilty only minutes later made no difference, since he'd opted not to apologize. In forty-eight hours, this assignment would be over. He could manage two more days without running his mouth off again.

He'd received the color and make of the vehicle as well as a picture of the driver when he made the reservation, so he spotted the tan-colored sedan when it turned into the parking lot. He allowed the driver to go past their position before getting out. Since he drove slowly, Jax was able to identify him.

"That's our ride. Don't get out until I'm at your door."

He climbed out and went around to the passenger side of the car. After surveying the area, he opened her door and she emerged. He hit the lock button for his SUV and waved down the Uber driver.

Once they were in the sedan, Jax leaned forward and said, "We've changed our mind about where we want to go."

In the rearview mirror, Jax watched the guy's eyebrows lift in question.

"Estes Kefauver Federal Building. Ninth Avenue entrance." He passed the man a fifty.

The driver shrugged. "Works for me."

The walk would have only been two blocks, but that wasn't the point. The point was to maintain some semblance of cover until they reached the entrance.

Jax scanned the street in both directions, the sidewalks. He watched to ensure no vehicles were braking near where they wanted to get out. All they had to do was get out of the car on the passenger side and hustle across fifteen or so feet of sidewalk.

When the car stopped the driver asked, "You need an updated receipt?"

"No, thanks." Jax opened the door and climbed out.

He scanned the street and sidewalk again and then motioned for Ali to get out, as well. Once she was out of the car, he shoved the door shut and rushed her across the span of sidewalk and through the doors.

Once they were beyond the security checkpoint, he relaxed. The third floor was their destination. Ali stopped him before they reached the elevators.

"I'd like to find the ladies' room."

He nodded. "This way."

A short corridor right off the lobby led to the restrooms. He stopped her before she pushed through the door.

"I need to check it out first."

She started to argue but then shook her head.

Keeping her close to his side, he pushed the door open and shouted, "Hello! Anyone in here?"

He waited three beats, and when no one responded, he walked inside with Ali.

"You shouldn't be in here," she said.

He held up his hand. "As soon as I know there's no one else in here, I'll get out of your way."

One by one he checked the stalls. Looked all the way around the room. Clear.

"I'll be right outside."

She nodded and watched until he was out the door. He stationed himself directly in front of it to ensure no one else went inside until Ali was finished.

After they'd gone through security, he noticed that she looked a little pale. She was more nervous than she wanted him to know. Understandable.

She wore jeans as she had every day since he arrived, but today she wore a pink sweater instead of the usual sweatshirt. The color made her look even more vulnerable. He doubted that had been her goal. Her wardrobe was limited, but he had seen a black skirt and jacket in a hanging bag. For court, he assumed.

He shifted his weight to the other foot and wondered what was taking so long. Just when he'd decided maybe he'd poke his head in and check on her, the door opened with a hydraulic *whoosh*.

They continued to the bank of elevators. He moved in front of her as an elevator opened. Two people emerged, and only when he ensured the car was empty did they walk through those doors. He selected the floor and hoped the elevator didn't stop on two.

When the elevator stopped on three, she looked at him. "Will you be in the room?"

"Only long enough to ensure you're settled, and then I have some things to take care of across the hall. But I won't be more than a few steps away."

She nodded, her expression clearly relieved.

AUSA Knowles and his assistant waited in the conference room, along with Tom Phillips, another of the marshals assigned to Nashville, and FBI special agents Willis and Kurtz. These were all people Jax knew well.

Introductions were made, and the teleconference began. Once Ali's attorney and the AUSA from Atlanta were online, Jax slipped out and went across the hall. Agent Kurtz followed. He had agreed to prepare the file and accompanying videotaped interview for Jax's perusal.

"Good to see you, Stevens." Kurtz said as he opened the laptop on the table. "How's Holloway?"

"He's doing better," Jax said, "but he'll be out of commission for a while yet."

Kurtz pointed to the screen. "This file contains all the case documents. This one has the video interview. I'll be across the hall if you need anything."

Jax thanked him and turned his attention to the laptop. The room was a small meeting area designed for separate discussion when the need arose during a larger meeting across the hall.

First, he skimmed the documents. A good deal of the file was compilations of the material gathered over decades regarding the suspected activities of the Armone family. He read page after page of how Ali had come to know Harrison Armone and when they had married. He hadn't known the more intimate details, like the fact that he'd run into her in the lobby at the firm where she worked and then he'd shown up at her office every day until she agreed to have dinner with him.

The words sickened him. He kept seeing that bastard touching her. He closed his eyes and shook his head. If he didn't know better, he would think he'd just gotten jealous reading about some other guy with Ali.

No way.

This was something else altogether. He just couldn't name what it was.

He plowed through the fairy-tale first year. Travel, expensive jewelry, lavish shopping sprees. The castle of a home.

He cleared his throat of the bile that threatened.

Then the day a covolunteer had asked the question that changed her life.

You're married to Harrison Armone?

On that day, she opened her eyes.

Her first mistake had been discussing the question with her husband.

The evidence and the terror started to build until there was no way for her to pretend. She had tried to keep up the pretense but Armone had felt the change…saw it in her eyes…felt it in her touch.

The fairy tale was over.

Then I became his prisoner.

The statement startled Jax. He read it three times before moving on.

The file then referenced the videotaped interview. It was standard procedure to record statements. For the purposes of a jury trial, it was always better to have a living, breathing witness, but in the event something went wrong, the video could make the necessary difference.

Jax closed the folder and moved on to the one containing the video. He double clicked the icon dated just over nine months ago and waited. The screen opened, and Ali came into focus. The interviewer instructed her to recite her name and other pertinent information. She did this. He was impressed with how calm and strong she looked as she spoke. She recited a lengthy monologue that basically recounted what he had read in the file.

He stretched his back and repositioned himself. His body felt as if he'd been sitting here for hours when it had only been forty or so minutes.

"How was Mr. Armone able to keep you prisoner?" the interviewer asked. "Did he lock you in a room? Shackle you in some way? The jury needs to understand why you continued to live with a man like Armone and why you didn't come forward sooner."

Jax would like to understand that, as well.

Ali's chest rose with a deep breath. She moistened her lips. "He told me what he would do if I ever left him."

"What did he tell you he would do?"

Another big breath. "He said he would kill me and bury parts of me all over the city."

Jax felt his shoulders tense.

"How could you be sure his threat was real? Had you seen him murder anyone?"

She shook her head.

"You'll need to voice your answers," the interviewer reminded.

"No. Not then. I had overheard phone calls about taking care of situations and cleaning up problems. But he was very careful what he said over the phone. It was the discussions between him and his father that warned me I shouldn't doubt what he was capable of. They would drink and smoke cigars once a week in my—in Harrison's study. I started taking every opportunity possible to listen in."

"Did you learn anything specific?"

One by one, she listed names and dates of "fixes" and "cleanups." Jax didn't need to refer to the file to know those were dates that major power shifts occurred. Bodies showed up. New people took over in the Armone operation.

The interviewer referenced a document that would

be listed into evidence. The document was a time-line that laid out the murders that occurred on the dates she recited.

"You were gathering this evidence for a reason?" he asked.

"Yes. I wanted to have enough for the FBI to arrest him and his father."

"Again, I ask, how did he keep you from leaving for so long?"

She blinked, looked away from the camera for a moment before answering. Jax watched her eyes, saw the fear mingling with the determination.

"In the beginning, when he wasn't home, I was forced to spend part of the day shackled in my room. Whenever I was allowed to leave the room, one of his men accompanied me. To the bathroom, when I showered. Anywhere I went—to the dentist, shopping, whatever, I was escorted. I was never out of his sight. Never."

"But you attempted to escape, did you not?"

She nodded. "The first man, Tate. I'm not sure whether that was his first name or his last." She stared at her hands a moment. "Harrison had a big dinner party coming up. I told him I needed to go to the spa for my hair and nails. He ordered Tate to take me there and shopping for something new to wear. At the spa, when I went back to change into a robe was the first time Tate had not followed me into a changing room. He got a call on his cell. I guess he was distracted."

"What did you do?"

"I went out the back and ran."

She stared at her hands again.

"But he found you."

"Tate caught up with me. He took me back home and called Harrison. He came home immediately. I was terrified."

"What did he do?"

She lifted her gaze and looked directly into the camera. "He shot Tate right in front of me. Told me his death was on me." She swallowed hard. "Then everything got worse."

"Worse? He'd just killed a man in front of you. What could be worse?"

Her eyes glittered with emotion. "There are worse things than dying."

She dropped her gaze for a moment.

"The jury will need to understand what that means, Ms. Armone."

Jax's gut tightened at hearing her called that. He rubbed at the back of his neck. Sweat had popped out on his skin.

"He punished me severely for forcing him to kill an old friend."

Jax drew slightly away from the screen.

"Punished you how?"

"He withheld food. Water. Kept me shackled naked in my room for days with the lights off and the blinds closed tight. Once he felt I had been suf-ficiently punished for trying to run away, he removed the shackle and told me he had decided on new rules."

The silence throbbed for too many seconds.

Every muscle in Jax's body had grown rigid with tension.

"He told me what to wear. Clothes, makeup. Everything. How to walk. When to speak. When to eat. If I made a mistake, he…"

She stared at her hands as she went on. "He tortured me."

Those three words stabbed deep into Jax. He wanted to push away from the table. To shut off the volume. But he had to keep listening. He had to know the rest.

"Sometimes he used a leather whip. The number of lashes I received was determined by the severity of my mistake. Did I say the wrong thing or wear the wrong perfume?

"Over the course of the next two years, I had a dislocated shoulder. A fractured arm. Two concussions and a series of burns." Her breath caught, yet somehow she managed to go on. "There were other, more intimate methods of inflicting pain he utilized, depending upon my infraction."

Jax stared at the face on the screen. It hurt to breathe. The crushing sensation against his chest was unbearable. Why hadn't she told him any of this?

Why the hell hadn't Holloway told him?

"Were you taken for medical attention?"

"His personal physician always came and attended

to my injuries." A single tear rolled past her lashes and slid down her cheek.

"This was a very painful time for you."

"Yes." She flinched. "But I never cried."

She shook her head. "I would have died before I let him see my pain. He'd already taken my pride, my hopes and dreams. I wouldn't allow him to have anything else."

"On May 2 of last year, you witnessed one last travesty. Describe that event for the jury."

"My father-in-law, Harrison Sr., came for his weekly visit. He and Harrison went to his study for the usual evening of cigars and scotch. I recognized an added layer of tension between the two."

"Was there anyone else in the house?"

"Always. But Harrison had sent them outside. He and his father preferred complete privacy."

"Did you overhear anything different this night?"

"I didn't have to try and overhear this time. Mr. Armone asked me to join them. He told me to stand by the window so he could look at me as he and Harrison spoke. I was very uncomfortable. Harrison only laughed. I suppose he had bragged to his father about how he was punishing me."

She paused to draw in a deep breath.

"Mr. Armone suddenly announced that he was aware of what Harrison was doing—attempting to take over the business. Harrison denied the allegation. He stood and paced the room, ranting about how someone was only trying to cause trouble between them. Mr. Armone ordered him to sit. He did as his father said. Then Mr. Armone circled him as if considering what to say next. He paused, drew a handgun from his jacket and fired a single shot into the back of his son's head. Harrison slumped forward in his chair."

"What did you do?"

"Nothing." She blinked. "I stood there the way I'd been told."

Outrage burst inside Jax, so powerful that he couldn't stay seated. He pushed to his feet, his hands searching for a place to land.

"What happened next?"

"Mr. Armone looked at me and told me that now I belonged to him."

Jax hit Pause, his gut pulsing with the need to vomit up the sick details he'd just heard. He stared at her face...at her pale skin, her weary blue eyes.

He had been wrong. Dead wrong.

The one thing he knew for an absolutely certainty was that the bastard would never get his hands on Ali again.

He'd have to go through Jax to get to her, and that was not going to happen.

Chapter Nine

"Everything go okay?"

Jax asked even though he was aware that it had. He'd caught the last fifteen minutes of the meeting. Ali had sounded strong and calm. The AUSAs had sounded satisfied that she was ready for trial.

The two of them had left the building the same way they arrived. He'd had the driver circle the lot where his SUV was parked three times before he stopped. During those slow circles, he had carefully surveyed their surroundings as well as his SUV. When the other car had driven away, he'd checked the SUV more closely before they loaded up.

For the first fifty or so miles, she hadn't spoken and he hadn't, either. On some level he had known if he said anything he would say too much. The things he'd read…the words she had said in that video had ripped him apart inside. A whole new guilt had settled on him then. It was his fault this had happened. If he hadn't left…if he had stayed, she would never have gone to Atlanta and met the SOB.

But he hadn't stayed. He'd left her alone. He hadn't even come back when he'd learned her father had passed away. It was days after his funeral when Jax discovered that he'd died. Why hadn't he come back then? There had been nothing left holding her in Georgia at that point.

Pride. Plain and simple. He had practically begged her to go with him ten years ago, and she'd said no. He wasn't going to ask again. This time she would have to make the decision on her own. What a fool he'd been. He should have realized she was devastated by the loss. Overwhelmed with settling her father's estate. He should have come back, been supportive. Then if she hadn't mentioned wanting to try again with him, he would know he had done all he could do. He would have done the right thing.

Too late now.

His pride had kept him away, and the longer he'd stayed away the easier it had become.

"Yes," she said in answer to his question. "It was basically the same as the last conference call. Nothing I wasn't expecting."

"Good."

He clenched his jaw before words he couldn't say burst out. If he said he was sorry, she would ask about what, and then he would have to tell her something. Anything he said would likely lead her to understand that he had seen the video. He was in hell. Trapped in this place where he now knew the truth but couldn't tell her. She would feel humiliated and betrayed. He didn't want to add to the pain she had already suffered.

What he wanted was to kill Harrison Armone Jr., except the bastard's father had already done that. His gut clenched at the idea that the old man had dared to kill his own son and then assume he could claim his widow for his own.

"You want to stop for food?" He hadn't intended to stop, but he was confident they were in the clear. He had taken a different route, still back roads, but not the same ones they had used on the drive up.

"I'd just like to get back to Bob." She turned, allowed her gaze to meet his but only briefly. "If you don't mind."

"No problem. We should reach Huntland in about thirty minutes."

The silence closed in on them again. He didn't attempt to restart a conversation. Maybe later.

He had to find a way to say the words burgeoning in his chest. He owed her an apology. He needed her to understand that he hadn't meant to...

What?

Leave her vulnerable? Be a coward?

That was the real problem. He'd blamed her for not choosing him over everything else in her life when the truth was he had known she wouldn't desert her father. He had been a coward. She had consumed his entire existence. He hadn't been able to think of anything but her. They had both been so young.

He'd needed time.

But he'd taken too long.

It was far too late to make that right now.

ALI WAS GRATEFUL when they started the precarious climb up that narrow mountain road. Not really a road, she decided. Just a really long, infinitely tight driveway. The snow was gone now. But the sun was slipping downward and the temperature was dropping. This gravel and dirt road would be truly treacherous with a layer of ice on it. The drop-off on the cliff side provided no leeway for mistakes.

At the top of the rise, the house came into view. No matter that it was still daylight, the gloom that hung from the darkening sky warned that more snow might just show up. The last few minutes of the trip, she hadn't been able to bear the silence any longer, so she'd turned on the radio. When the hour rolled around, the local news had included a weather forecast. The meteorologist mentioned the possibility of another dusting of snow. Probably not more than an inch.

Jax parked and got out, locking her in until he was certain the house was clear. Per the usual protocol, she waited while he had a look around. He checked the front door and started around the house. He would make a complete circle and then take her inside.

She glanced toward the woods. It would be dark soon. It had been a long day. She didn't like reviewing the horrors of the past five years, but it was necessary to ensure her testimony went smoothly. It wasn't like she would ever forget a single moment of the horror—not if she lived a thousand years.

Movement at her door made her jump.

Jax.

She pressed a hand to her throat, her heart threatening to burst out of her chest, then reached for the door.

"Get down," he ordered through the glass. "Stay down until I tell you otherwise."

Fear pulsing through her, she scrambled to the floorboard, hunkered down to make herself as small as possible.

She kept her eye on the window of her door and reminded herself to breathe. The idea that any second she might hear gunfire seared through her. Jax could be killed. She would be next.

What about Bob?

What felt like long minutes later but was likely only a few, Jax appeared at her door once more. This time he opened it and extended his hand to help her out.

"What happened?" She struggled to ease her hips between the seat and the dash.

"The back door was standing open."

That fear that had twisted deep inside her expanded now. "Where's Bob?"

"He's not inside."

Ali rushed to the house. She started to call his name the instant she was through the door. Jax had told her he wasn't in the house, but she needed to see for herself. She bounded up the stairs and checked the bedrooms.

No Bob.

Jax waited for her at the bottom of the stairs.

"We have to find him." She shook her head. "Why would someone break in and take him?"

His eyes told her the answer without him having to say a word.

"No." She shook her head.

"Let's not go there just yet," he said gently, more gently than he had spoken to her since he walked back into her life. "I checked the lock. It doesn't stay latched every time, so it may not have been an intruder. I locked and unlocked it several times. If the latch doesn't catch properly, it doesn't lock. Bob may have swiped past it and caused it to open. Maybe the house has settled and the door is no longer square in its frame." He pushed it to and showed her how the door drifted open on its own when the lock wasn't fully engaged.

Her heart slowed to a more normal rate. "So he's probably out there in the woods somewhere." Her gaze sought his. "Lost. It's going to be cold tonight. We have to find him."

"We'll look for him. Let me get the flashlight from my SUV just in case it gets dark on us before we find him."

"Thank you."

She didn't know why he had suddenly started to

be so nice to her, but she didn't care as long as he helped her find Bob.

They walked around the perimeter of the property and called the dog's name. The third or fourth time, they got a response. Bob started to bark.

Ali scanned the tree line. "Where is that coming from?"

They moved faster now, calling out to him to prod him to bark again.

"This way," Jax said as he turned and hurried toward the side of the property that overlooked the valley below.

Ali's heart dropped into her stomach. If he was on that side…

The barking was louder now.

Jax called out to him, and Bob barked as if he understood they needed to follow the sound.

Please let him be okay.

The cold had cut through her clothes and invaded her bones. Her fingers felt numb, but she didn't care. They had to find him.

At the edge of the cliff, Ali stood, her heart pounding as she stared into the gloom enveloping the trees and brush that covered the mountainside.

His bark was more enthusiastic now. He was close, and he recognized their nearness.

"Where are you, boy?"

"I can't see him," Jax muttered, roving his flashlight over the area below them.

"I need to climb down," she said, worry clawing

at her. It was the only way to find him. Obviously he was trapped somehow. Or possibly injured. Otherwise he would have run to them by now.

"You stay put," he ordered. "I'll go down."

He removed the weapon from his shoulder holster and handed it to her, butt first. "Don't hesitate to use it. Holloway says you're a good shot."

Ali nodded. She couldn't have spoken if her life depended upon it. She turned around a dozen times, checking behind her, while Jax disappeared below. Bob's bark had grown frantic.

Her body started to shake from the cold and maybe from the fear. Adrenaline or something.

Finally, she heard Jax coming back up.

Even in the darkness she spotted the big old black lab in his arms. She rushed to help him.

"We have to get him to a vet," Jax said. "I believe he has a broken leg."

ALI SAT IN the back seat holding Bob as Jax drove toward Winchester. He had called Holloway, and he'd made arrangements. Burt Johnston was more than happy to meet them at his veterinary clinic in Winchester.

"Did you get lost or spooked, boy?" Ali rubbed his head and wished she could do something for the pain. His nose was warm, and his respiration was quick and shallow. She felt so helpless.

"I'm thinking he got outside and chased some animal that wandered into the yard. He got too close to the edge and slipped over. Broke his leg in the fall."

Ali cringed. Couldn't bear to picture him falling.

"Considering the drop, I'm surprised he's not hurt worse."

"Are we almost there?" She had no idea where the clinic was. Wherever it was, getting there was taking far too long.

"According to my GPS, we're almost there."

Ali stroked the animal and hummed softly to him. It was the strangest thing, but he liked when she hummed to him—like a kid. She smiled. She wondered if Bob was the closest thing to a child she would ever have. How could she have gone her whole life and not known the love of a dog?

"Here we go," Jax said as he slowed for a turn.

Relief rushed through her. "It'll be okay soon, boy."

A man who looked to be around their age met them in the parking lot.

He opened the back door and reached in to stroke Bob. The dog tensed. "Easy now." He looked to Ali and then to Jax. "I'm Tommy Wright, one of Burt's vet techs. We should get this guy inside."

It took some maneuvering, but they finally got him out and into the man's arms. "What's his name?"

"Bob, and I'm Ali—Alice Stewart," she said. "He's four years old and, to my knowledge, in good health. I hope he's not hurt too badly. He fell quite a distance."

Holding the door, Jax said, "About eight feet."

When Tommy had gone through the door, Ali followed. Jax closed the door. She heard the click of the automatic lock.

"What do we have here?" A tall, older man asked as they entered what looked like an operating room.

Tommy repeated what Ali and Jax had told him.

"I'm Burt, by the way." The older man glanced at her and smiled. "The best vet in these parts, and the county coroner."

A smile spread across her lips despite the worry twisting inside her. Burt Johnston was seventy-five if he was a day. His demeanor was kind and even a bit charming. She was grateful.

"Why don't you two have a seat in the corridor beyond that door and we'll take care of Bob."

As much as it pained her to leave him, Ali did as Burt asked. Jax sat in the hard, plastic chair next to her. When they had sat in silence for a while, her gaze glued to the activities beyond the open door, she pulled her attention to the man beside her.

"Thank you for rescuing him."

"Holloway says he's in the best hands available with Burt. He's been taking care of animals his entire life."

Another smile tugged at her lips. "I wonder how he became the coroner."

Jax chuckled. "I don't know the answer, but I guarantee you it's quite a story."

She sighed. "I miss this."

He turned to her. She didn't have to look—she felt the heat of his stare.

"Sitting in a cold corridor with me?"

She smiled again in spite of herself. "No. I mean, the small-town way of life. Everyone knows everyone else. Neighbors help each other out. I didn't realize until now how much I missed that sense of family."

"I know what you mean," he said.

She turned to him, surprised. "I thought you were all about the city."

Wasn't his desire to go to Seattle in part about being part of a thriving city atmosphere?

"Seattle is a nice city. Going there was about being close to my family. As you recall, they live only an hour outside Seattle, in a small town very much like Winchester."

"Right." She wanted to throw in that she'd forgotten, but that would be a lie. She remembered everything about his family.

"Why did you move to Nashville?"

She shouldn't be asking personal questions since she certainly didn't want to answer any of his, but she had to know. He'd wanted to get back to Seattle so badly ten years ago. Why the sudden change of heart?

He shrugged. "It was a career move. I won't be here long. Maybe another year at the most. If all goes well, I'll end up back in the Seattle area with the experience I need for a supervisory position. If it works out, I'll be there for the rest of my career."

"Oh." It was the only thing she could think to say. He had a long-range plan.

"What about you?"

"I just want to get through Thursday, and then I'll go from there."

They both fell silent, staring straight ahead. The urge to ask him if there was someone in Nashville or back home—someone special—prodded her.

No. She wouldn't ask.

"You can start over. Put all this behind you." He looked at her but she couldn't meet his gaze. "You never have to look back, Ali."

Burt started toward the door, and she stood. Anything to move on from the moment.

"Is he going to be okay?"

Burt nodded. "He surely is. We'll need to keep him overnight. Make sure nothing else crops up considering he took quite the tumble. You can pick him up tomorrow afternoon."

Ali wasn't sure what to say to that. Tomorrow afternoon she would be in Atlanta, readying for trial.

"We'll actually be out of town for the next couple of days," Jax explained. "Can he stay until we're back?"

She darted a glance at Jax. He was awfully confident she would be coming back. Her stomach suddenly rolled, and she fought the urge to heave.

Nerves, she reminded herself. She would get through this.

"Certainly. We'll take very good care of him." The last part he directed to Ali. "Would you like to say goodbye? He's sedated now so he might be a little woozy."

"Thank you."

Bob didn't raise his head as she came nearer, but his eyes followed her movement. She stroked his head and whispered in his ear.

She would be back for him.

Somehow.

Chapter Ten

It felt strange to be completely alone with Jax.

Bob had been a sort of buffer, at least in Ali's mind.

She sat on the sofa now, staring at the fire. It was late. She should go to bed. Tomorrow was a big day. The day after would be an even bigger one.

But sleep would not be possible. Not just now.

The one question she had been asked today would be the hardest to answer on Thursday.

Why did you stay after you found out what he was?

Shock, disbelief...fear.

She had asked him about the reaction of her co-volunteers. From that moment he had known that the fantasy was over.

I knew the truth—at least a small fraction of that truth.

In today's world of fearless women and total independence, no woman on the jury would understand her simple truth.

When she was in college and then after when she started her career, she had heard friends say that no man would ever rule them. Ali remembered feeling exactly the same way, especially considering how Jax had broken her heart.

But Harrison had been different. He had not been a mere man. He had been a monster. Taught by the mother of all monsters…his father.

Ali had been lucky to escape with her life.

If the jury chose not to believe her story, she could do nothing to change their minds. All that mattered was that they believed her when she stated who had shot and murdered the man to whom she had been married.

Nothing else about the trial mattered. It was not about her redemption or somehow proving she was not a total fool. It was about taking that bastard all the way down.

Jax was suddenly standing over her. She hadn't heard him come into the room.

"You should eat."

How many times had he suggested she eat the past few days? She was not a child. She could decide for herself when to eat.

"If I wanted to eat, I would eat." Her tone was far sharper than she'd intended.

He lowered to the coffee table, settling there so that he sat directly across from her. Too close. She drew back into the sofa cushion.

"Thursday I'll be in that courtroom with you. If

there is anything you want to discuss with me now, it might make that day easier."

She stared at him then. Why did he care? "I'll be answering the questions in front of all sorts of strangers. Why would I feel any differently about you?"

Her words hit their mark. He flinched.

"Because I want to hear them from you before all those strangers."

She was tired. Tired of all the pomp and circumstance of preparing for this trial. Tired of being protected. Tired of being alone.

When this was over, no one who had been involved with this case would care what happened to her. She would be left to fend for herself. Anger ignited in her chest. She wasn't a person to those people who wanted so desperately to destroy the Armone family. She was evidence. Nothing more.

She looked directly into his dark eyes now. Eyes she had gazed into and gotten lost in all those years ago. "You want to hear all the dirty details of how he kept me in line? What prevented me from running away and going to the authorities sooner?"

He didn't answer, just sat there staring at her with such concern and regret. Yes, regret. She wanted to laugh out loud. *He* regretted what she had gone through. He most likely had no idea exactly what that was. But he understood it was bad.

"All right. I'll tell you why I stayed until the day I watched his father put a bullet in his head."

He swallowed hard, then visibly braced himself.

In that clarifying moment, she understood without doubt that he already knew something. Part of her ugly story, at least.

Maybe he would even enjoy hearing her say the words. Only one way to find out. "At first he assigned a full-time bodyguard to me. I wasn't allowed to go into a bathroom without him. I wasn't allowed to walk around the gated and guarded property without my personal guard at my side. At night one ankle was shackled to the bed."

She shrugged. "Maybe he worried that I would kill him in his sleep and try to run. This way, if I did shove a knife into his chest or use a hammer to bash in his head, I was stuck with his dead body."

She had considered both those methods for freeing herself. She closed her eyes for a moment. Not once in her life had she ever considering harming another human being until then. Thank God her parents were long gone. They would have been so ashamed of her.

"How long did this go on?"

His voice was too soft. She didn't want his pity. She looked away from him. "We had been married a year and a half when one of the other volunteers at the center asked me if I was his wife. One by one, over the next couple of weeks, they all started to shun me. Eventually I asked him if there was something he failed to tell me before we married. Things went downhill from there."

Jax shook his head. "How did you survive?"

She laughed. "I can tell you I wished for death many times, but it didn't come." Her mind went back to those darkest days. "Once I even asked my guard to kill me." She closed her eyes and thought of the look on Tate's face. He had laughed and told her she was trying to get him killed.

And she *had* gotten him killed.

The burden sat heavily on her shoulders…on her heart.

"Harrison could have killed me." Another shrug. "At first I didn't understand why he didn't. I slowly realized that he didn't want me dead. He wanted to punish me for taking away his fantasy. With me he could pretend he wasn't who he really was. He could be the wealthy businessman whose wife spent her time helping those less fortunate. The man whose wife looked at him with such adoration and respect. But I took that away from him. I suppose in part he wanted to keep up the facade. I helped him represent a different life than the one he actually lived."

"He would have had to admit that he'd made a mistake," Jax suggested.

She looked straight at him again. "Men don't like to admit when they've made a mistake. I have the scars to prove it."

He lowered his head, staring at the floor before she could get a glimpse of his reaction to that revelation.

Did he think she'd been held prisoner for more

than three years and escaped unscathed? How nice that would have been.

She didn't want to do this anymore. Her emotions were churning, and she just wanted to escape the memories...the feelings. When she would have stood and announced as much, his words stopped her.

"I made a mistake."

He lifted his gaze to hers, and for several beats she couldn't move. She could only stare at him, searching his eyes for the sincerity in his words.

Then the realization that it didn't matter slammed into her chest, forcing the air out of her lungs. She launched to her feet. "Well, this has been..." There was no way to describe how this felt. "Anyway, I'm calling it a night."

He stood, putting himself toe to toe with her. "I made a mistake."

She didn't want to look at him. Didn't want to see what he might show her. But her body had a mind of its own apparently. Her eyes met his. "You said that already."

"I'd barely settled in out in Seattle when I realized that. We were so young. I figured we had time. So I kept an eye on you."

His words took her aback. "What do you mean, you kept an eye on me?"

"I checked on you. I had friends in Glynco. I had them make sure you were doing okay. That's how I knew when your father got sick."

What was he saying? This made no sense. She shook her head. "Why didn't you simply call me?"

"Pride? Stupidity? Take your pick."

This was a pointless waste of time and emotion. "I really—"

"I almost came back. I knew how hard things were for you."

A realization barreled into her. "It was you."

Surprise flared in his eyes then he blinked it away. "I don't—"

"That private nurse who came to help with my dad because we couldn't afford to hire help…that was you."

The nurse had said a private donor paid her salary. She would never say who. Ali had assumed it was some of her father's friends who had gotten together and pooled their resources. God knew they had brought food every day. But she should have realized none of them could afford such a luxury any more than she could.

"My family pitched in, too," he confessed. "We wanted to help."

Ali held up her hands. This was too much. "I genuinely appreciate what you and your family did. I can't tell you how comforting it was to have a nurse to help."

Tears burned her eyes, but she couldn't let him see. Her chest felt so full she would hardly manage a breath.

"When you went back to college, I was really

happy for you. I knew how much that meant to you. I thought maybe when you finished I'd show up at your graduation and give you a hug to congratulate or something."

"I'm sorry, I really don't understand why you just didn't call." This made no sense.

"I thought there was time. I didn't want to interfere with you finishing college. I was working hard to establish my career. Move up the ranks."

If he was watching her, why on earth hadn't he stopped her from marrying the bastard?

Before she could demand an answer to that question, he said, "I was sent on an extended undercover assignment, and while I was off the grid, you moved to Atlanta and got married."

So he did know. "You knew I had married into that family and you didn't warn me?"

This time she damaged him. Her demand shook him. His face told the story.

"I couldn't see how you didn't know what he was. I thought you'd decided you wanted what he had to offer regardless of who and what he was."

How could he have thought such a thing? "Then you didn't really know me at all."

He stopped her when she would have moved away from him. His hands seemed to burn her skin through the sweater she wore. "I was wrong." He shook his head. "My ego was bruised. I thought that if you married someone else, you couldn't possibly have cared about me the same way I did about you.

I was jealous. Shocked. Torn up. I never checked on you again."

Whether he knew her as well as he should have, she did know him. He meant what he said. She had hurt him by marrying Harrison. But how could she have known Jax still cared or that Harrison was a monster?

"For that," he said, his fingers tightening around her arms as if he feared she would run away, "I am truly sorry. It's my fault this happened to you. Instead of turning my back, I should have come to you and told you the truth. We could have worked things out. But I couldn't see past my bruised ego."

She searched his eyes, felt the weight of his pain for her. "I wished a thousand times that you would show up and rescue me." She laughed, tears slipping down her cheeks no matter how hard she tried to hold them back. "I thought of you so often. I think those little fantasies of you showing up to carry me away from the nightmare are what kept me from giving up." Ali sucked in a sharp breath. "But you never came."

"I'm here now, and I will keep you safe. I can't change the mistakes of the past, but I can make sure they don't happen again. I will not let Armone touch you."

All those months that had run into years, she had longed to hear this man say those words. But now that was the part of all this that terrified her the most. She fully understood how ruthless Armone was. He wouldn't hesitate to have Jax murdered. If he had the slightest idea Ali had feelings for Jax, he would relish the act of taking his life.

She had realized when she arrived in Nashville this morning that she had only one opportunity to do what she had to do. She'd already tried with Holloway, and it hadn't worked out. But it was done now.

"I was thankful you weren't in the room for most of the meeting this morning."

Tension riffled through him, tightening his hold on her even more. "Why is that?"

"I spoke to AUSA Knowles. I told him I didn't want you in Atlanta. He agreed that having you there would be a mistake. So once the plane lands in Atlanta, you'll get on a flight back to Nashville. You won't be leaving the airport. Another marshal will take over from there."

Anger flashed in his eyes. "I see what you're doing. You think you need to protect me. You're wrong." He pulled her closer—too close. "I can take care of myself. I don't need you protecting me."

She stared at his lips as he spoke. No matter that she hated herself for doing it, she couldn't help herself.

"I will call Knowles and straighten this out. There is no way I will let you out of my sight. If they try and stop me, they'll have a fight on their hands."

Worry that she'd made yet another mistake twisted inside her. "You can't do that."

"Oh yes, I can. This time I'm making sure nothing

happens to you. I took my eyes off you once. That won't happen again."

More tears spilled down her cheeks, and she wanted to scream at herself for falling apart.

Then he kissed her. Slow and deep and sweet. The way he had kissed her hundreds of times before. She remembered his taste, every nuance of the way he kissed. And her heart ached with longing.

She could not do this. If she let herself fall this time and he left again, she wouldn't survive it. She wasn't strong enough.

She pressed her palms to his chest, for one single moment savored the feel of him, and then she pushed him away. "We can't do this."

"Yes—" he pressed his forehead to hers "—we can."

She pulled free of his hold, her knees bumping the sofa. "*I* can't."

Moving as quickly as she dared with tears clouding her vision, she hurried up the stairs. A long hot bath would help. Then she was going to go to bed and attempt to sleep.

Tomorrow was the beginning of the end.

ALI HAD NEVER been so grateful for a tub. Usually she preferred showers, but after this day she needed a long, hot soak. Strangely enough, she'd found some bubble bath under the sink, and all the necessities were available. Towels. Soap. Shampoo. She suspected the kind sheriff had ensured those items were on hand. He'd stocked the fridge and a few items in the pantry, too.

Winchester and the surrounding communities were growing on her. So many of the people she had met were so nice.

Once the tub was full enough and bubbles frothed up to the rim, she peeled off her clothes and slid into the welcoming heat. Her entire body sighed. She laid her head back, closed her eyes and did something not so smart by allowing that kiss to fill her senses. The way he'd tasted—pure Jax. In a hundred years, she wouldn't have forgotten his taste. His strong arms around her had made her feel completely safe and far too needy.

"Don't make another mistake," she murmured. Whether the words were an order or a plea for strength, she wasn't sure she could hold back if he came near her again.

She had dreamed of kissing him, making love with him a thousand times—perhaps more—over the past decade. Even when her monster of a husband had held her in his arms, she had found it necessary to push aside the memories of Jax. He had been such a part of her...so deeply entrenched in her soul.

She sighed. Let go of the last of the tension and sank more deeply into the sweet-smelling bubbles. Her muscles slowly grew completely pliable. She felt as if she could melt into the hot water and just slip away.

Except tomorrow was coming, and there was no way to change what she had to do.

If Jax stood between her and a bullet—

She squeezed her eyes shut and blocked the images.

If something happened to him because of her— she couldn't live with that. There had to be a way to prevent him from going to that courthouse with her. She slid beneath the water, allowed it to cover her completely. She lay there for a half a minute, listening to the heavy sounds of the beating of her heart. Then she sat up, pushed her hair back from her face, pulled her knees to her chest and pressed her cheek to them.

She closed her eyes again and allowed memories of their time together to fill her. Maybe it was selfish, but she needed so badly to feel alive again, even if only for this one moment. Her body shivered with an abrupt rush of need. She should have responded more deeply to his kiss. Lost herself in his touch.

Who knew what tomorrow would bring?

What did it matter who did what ten years ago? He had been looking after her those first few years. Maybe if she hadn't married that bastard, things would have been different. Jax would have come back for her.

Why hadn't she swallowed her pride and gone after him once her father passed away? She could have looked him up, said hello and…

But she had been too hurt by his leaving.

Lonely and alone.

A dangerous recipe, which led to utter disaster.

"Ali." He knocked softly at the door. "Can I come in?"

She hugged her arms around her knees more tightly. Did she dare? When he looked at her body, he wouldn't see the smooth flawless skin from ten years ago. There were scars. Small and not so deep, but so many of them.

Could she bear the pity on his face when he saw them?

"I don't want to talk anymore." She pressed her forehead to her knees. Squeezed her eyes shut.

If he came in and saw all of her, there would be more questions.

Could she bear to tell him all the things that bastard had done to her? How he had nearly broken her? Actually, he had broken her, and somehow after witnessing his life ending, she had pulled herself together enough to run.

She should have trusted Jax all those years ago. Should have followed him to Seattle. Coming home to take care of her father wouldn't have been a problem. Jax would have understood. Still, she wouldn't trade those last months with her father for anything. As certain as she was of that, she was also certain her father would not have wanted her to suffer the way she had the past few years.

Before his death he had asked her twice what happened to the nice young man who was training to be a marshal. She never told him that she had given him up to stay close to home.

All of that was behind her now. It was very possible that in another twenty-four hours she would be dead. Why deny herself this time with Jax? Whether she lived or died, he would move on to his next assignment and it wouldn't be her.

He would be gone.

"Come in." The words were out of her mouth before she could stop them. Her mind still resisted, but her heart and the rest of her no longer wanted to refrain.

The door creaked open, and he walked inside. She was thankful for the deep bubbles. Maybe he wouldn't see.

He knelt next to the tub, his forearms resting on the edge. "I'm sorry."

She frowned, searched his dark eyes. "Sorry for what?"

"I should have manned up and come after you when your father was sick. I could have brought both of you to Seattle. I was a fool, and you paid a terrible price."

"I appreciate you saying so, but it wasn't your fault. You did what was right for you. Far too often we don't do that, and it's usually a mistake. When you left, I wanted to go. Desperately. I should have. I should have gone to my father and told him we were moving. I shouldn't have used him as an excuse. I should have done what was right for me. His health was already deteriorating. Looking back, I believe there was a good possibility he would have agreed."

"Hindsight," he said, his lips smiling just a little, "is twenty-twenty. What you know now and what you knew then are two different things. You did the right thing." He shrugged. "Maybe we both did, but there were consequences, and I am truly sorry you suffered the brunt of them."

Tears slipped past her restraint. "Thank you."

He reached for the shampoo. "Let me help you out with this bath. You deserve a little pampering."

He washed her hair, slowly, using his fingers to massage her scalp until she felt ready to moan. She ducked under the water and rinsed the shampoo away. When she surfaced again he washed her back, touching each tiny scar. She shivered. Hated for him to see. Then he leaned forward and kissed her skin, over and over.

As he kissed his way up her neck, he shed his shirt. She reached out and unfastened his jeans. When he'd toed off his shoes and peeled off his jeans and socks, the boxers went next.

And then he was in the water with her.

The feel of his body against hers cleared all the hurt and worry from her mind. She could only feel his skin sliding against her own. His hard body pressing all the soft, needy places of hers.

The sense of belonging…of being home filled her. Whatever else happened, *this* was right in every way.

When his mouth covered hers, she stopped thinking at all.

Chapter Eleven

One day until trial

Wednesday, February 5

Ali stared at herself in the mirror over the bathroom sink. Today they would drive to Huntsville, Alabama. It was less than an hour away. There was an airport there. She would be on the noon flight to Atlanta. Yesterday it had been decided that a commercial flight would be safer than driving. A more controlled situation, AUSA Knowles had said.

Jax hadn't agreed, but he had been overruled. Last night he hadn't mentioned his concerns, and she hadn't asked.

She had needed to escape.

Her eyes closed as her mind immediately replayed their lovemaking. Even though she had loved Harrison in the beginning, her feelings for him had been different than her feelings for Jax. Their intimacy had been completely different. She had no other experience to which to compare, but being with Jax was in a whole other league. There was a depth to their connection that had been missing with Harrison. The absolute certainty that they were meant for each other had never been present in her marriage.

Whatever happened tomorrow, she would cherish last night. This time she understood things were different. They were both mature adults and had their own lives to get back to. Not that she had much of a life anymore. She would be busy—assuming she survived beyond the trial—building a new life. After last night, it was easy to picture that life with Jax wherever his career took him.

But she wasn't foolish enough to believe that one night of lovemaking and truckloads of guilt had resurrected what he had once felt for her.

They were different people now.

She studied her reflection again. The glimpse of fear in her blue eyes tied a knot in her belly. She was no longer that naive young woman. Of course she was a little afraid. But that fear would not stop her from going into that courtroom and telling the truth.

Nine months she had waited to tell the judge and jury the sort of monster Harrison Armone Sr. was. She had been fully apprised of her rights. Instructions on how to proceed with her testimony had been drilled into her head. She had been questioned and cross-examined in an attempt to confuse and frighten her, since this was what would happen in the courtroom.

She was ready.

A dark suit—skirt and jacket—as well as conservative flats had been provided for her to wear. She was to arrange her hair in a twist or bun so that she looked more reserved. No makeup or jewelry. She never wore makeup, anyway. Wore very little jewelry except when her husband had insisted.

Ali turned away from the mirror and left the bathroom. She couldn't hide any longer. She had still been asleep when Jax got up this morning. When she had awakened, she had smelled the delicious scent of coffee brewing. She'd showered and dressed, taking her time.

It wasn't as if they hadn't made love before, she reminded herself as she descended the stairs. But this was different. She hadn't seen him in a decade. He had seen her more recently. She'd been stunned at the idea that he had looked in on her and that he and his family were the ones to help with the private nurse. She needed to write a letter to his mother. Such a dear, sweet lady. How nice it would have been to have her for a mother-in-law. Ali imagined she was an amazing grandmother.

The yearning for children wrapped around her heart and tightened. Ali stopped at the bottom of the stairs and marveled at the sudden reawakening. It had been so long since she dared wish for anything normal. But, she realized, she wanted a family. A real husband and at least two children.

Had making love with Jax roused those long-forgotten hopes and dreams?

As if the idea had summoned him, he was suddenly at the kitchen doorway, smiling. "Good morning."

She had been certain this morning would be awkward. That she would be embarrassed. But she wasn't, at all. Instead, she melted instantly. He was the most beautiful man she had ever met. "Good morning. You were up early."

As she walked toward him, her heart started to pound and her pulse raced. She would love nothing better than to make love with him again, right now. When he'd left the bed this morning, his absence had pulled her from the most magnificent sleep she had experienced in years.

"I checked the perimeter. Made coffee and whipped up a little breakfast."

A smile pulled at her lips, and her stomach reacted to the delicious smells coming from the kitchen. Looking at him had blocked all other stimuli, but his words drew her senses beyond him.

"Smells wonderful."

"Pancakes," he said, stepping aside so that she could walk into the kitchen. "Tanner is a good shopper. He didn't forget the syrup."

As good as the pancakes smelled, Ali walked straight to the coffeemaker. She filled a mug and took a sip, relishing the taste and the heat.

Jax touched her arm and she turned to face him. "Come sit with me."

She allowed him to usher her to the table. They took their seats, and she smiled at the not quite round pancakes.

"They're a little misshapen, but they taste good." He added a couple more to his plate and drizzled syrup over them.

Ali did the same. "Thank you. This is very nice."

She drizzled the syrup and then took a bite. He was right, the pancakes were really good. "Yum," she said and watched his smile broaden to a grin.

"I've learned a few things living alone all these years."

She didn't say as much, but Ali wished she had been with him all these years. They would likely have children by now. A sigh whispered out of her, and she quickly poked another bite of pancakes into her mouth.

He sipped his coffee then set the mug aside. "I'm certain now that my mother was correct."

Ali cradled her mug of coffee, warming her hands. It was cold this morning. The fire was roaring but still, it was chilly. Or maybe it was just nerves.

"I told you about Seth, my little brother."

The memory tugged at her heart. "You did. Yes. It was a such a tragedy. I'm certain it devastated your entire family."

He nodded, stared at his now empty plate. "My

parents have told me hundreds of times that it wasn't my fault, but I couldn't change how I felt."

"Your parents were right. You were a child yourself. You did everything you could. More, actually."

Ali remembered the story vividly. The family had been at their lake house. Jax and Seth had gone fishing on the pier. He had told his little brother repeatedly to stay away from the edge, but he hadn't listened.

When he fell in, Jax tried to save him. The autopsy confirmed that Seth had hit his head on the way down, so he'd been unconscious when he hit the water. Rather than struggling to reach the surface, he had sunk like a rock to the very bottom of the murky depths. Jax almost drowned going down over and over trying to find him.

By the time he did, it was too late.

His hands were flat on the table on either side of his plate, his gaze focused there as if the answer he needed would come to him. "I should have watched him closer. Made him sit down."

"Even the coroner said that it would have been sheer luck to have found him in time. The water was too dark around the bottom." She hated to see him carry that burden. He'd only spoken of that day once in all the time they were together. Yet it was more than apparent that it was with him every day, particularly back then.

He nodded, finally lifted his gaze and met hers. "My mother swears this is why I'm not in a long-term relationship. She says I don't trust myself to take care of a family." He grunted. "She believes the reason I became a marshal was to prove to myself that I could save lives. But nothing I do is ever enough, according to her." He searched Ali's eyes for a moment before saying the rest. "She says it's the reason I let you get away."

Ali's breath stalled in her throat. She, too, had wondered if that long-ago loss had kept him from wanting to fully commit, but she had been too young to trust her own instincts. It was easier to believe that he just hadn't loved her as much as she loved him.

"Your mother was right, Jax. It wasn't your fault, and maybe you have been afraid to commit fully. If you recognize that now, you can choose differently moving forward." This conversation was too much. She couldn't do this. She stood, her chair scooting back. "Thank you for breakfast. It was very nice."

She took her plate and fork to the sink. Since he had cooked, she could certainly do the cleanup. That was the way it was done, wasn't it?

He moved to her side, placing his plate and fork in the sink on top of hers.

She grabbed a paper towel from the roll and readied to wash their dishes. She couldn't look at him. That awkwardness she had feared this morning was now thick between them—at least from her perspective. She couldn't get enough air into her lungs. Her skin was on fire just being near him.

"I was wrong, Ali. I shouldn't have left without

you. I've always believed a person made his own fate happen. Whether this moment was fate or not, we have an opportunity here. The potential for a do-over. And we can do it right this time."

Her hands stilled, suds dripping from her skin. How long had she dreamed of hearing those words? How often during those first years after he left had she heard the doorbell or the phone and rushed to answer, hoping it would be him?

But she had been disappointed every time. Then she had run headlong into that horrible mistake of a marriage. From that moment she had known there was never any hope that she would see Jax again. Having a life with him was never, ever going to happen. Her dream had shattered, and she had clung to a new one that turned out to be a living nightmare.

She turned to the man standing so close beside her. He was right. They did have an opportunity here, but she was terrified it wasn't what it seemed. "It's possible," she said, the words hardly able to squeeze out around the lump in her throat, "that what you're feeling right now is nothing more than guilt."

He started to argue with her, but she stopped him. "You felt guilty, which is why you helped when my father passed away." She didn't want to believe her own words—she wanted to believe that he had done it because he cared, but she couldn't take that risk. "When you learned I had married into the Armone family, you were angry. You despised me, I imagined."

"No." He shook his head. "I—"

She held up her hand, stop-sign fashion. "Don't lie to yourself now, Jax. It's time we both faced the truth about our lives. We made mistakes, yes. You made far better choices than me. I made terrible mistakes, and I paid—" she drew in a sharp breath "—for those mistakes."

The pain on his face told her she'd read him right. He was only human.

"Whatever you think," he said, "you're wrong. *This* isn't about guilt."

When she would have argued, he touched his fingers to her lips. "Whether you've ever fully trusted me or not," he said, "trust me now. I know what I feel. I know what I want."

She closed her eyes to block the hope in his. This was far too important to take the plunge without being absolutely certain. Deep breath. She opened her eyes and met his, that desperate hope in his squeezing her heart.

"I trust you completely, Jax." She hated herself as that hope evolved into happiness. "But I don't want a relationship with you based on anything other than the real thing. True love and nothing else."

His hands dived into her hair and clasped her face. "I love you, Ali. If I ever doubted that, I was wrong."

Her damp hands rested against his chest to slow things down. Her heart felt ready to burst. "I want that to be true. So very, very much. But we're in a high-pressure place right now. Fear and desperation make people do things they normally wouldn't do."

He stroked her cheek with his thumb. "I won't change my mind tomorrow or the day after or the day after that."

"Let's make a deal, then." It was so incredibly difficult to think clearly with him touching her, looking at her this way. But she had to be strong, had to think clearly. This was far too important. "When this is over, if you still feel the same way, we'll give us a new go."

He turned her face up so he could gaze deeply into her eyes. "Count on it."

Then he kissed her, and her fingers fisted in his shirt with longing.

Before the moment got completely out of control, she drew her lips from his. Pressed her forehead to his chin.

If she lived through this day and the next, she was going to spend the entire weekend making love with this man somewhere far away from here.

JAX WATCHED ALI come down the stairs with the garment carrier that held her trial clothes. Over her shoulder she'd slung the backpack that held the rest of her things.

"Let me help you with those."

When she reached the bottom step, he took the two bags. "I'll put these in the car with mine."

"Thanks."

Taking his eyes from her was not easy, but he managed. They'd made a deal, and for now he had to focus on keeping her safe. He couldn't allow anything to distract him.

As he exited the house, he scanned the perimeter. Once he'd tucked the bags into the cargo area, he locked the SUV and did a walk around. It was damn cold, but otherwise all was as it should be.

Back inside, he heard Ali talking in the kitchen. He locked the door and moved in that direction.

"I know," she said.

She was using the small cell phone Holloway had given her.

"It's a lot to ask," she sighed, "but I'd feel better if I knew Bob was going to be okay. If you can't take him, Marshal Holloway, I understand."

She was making arrangements for the dog in case she didn't make it. Jax closed his eyes and steadied himself. All these emotions were tricky. Keeping his head screwed on straight was the most important part of what he had to do right now.

"Thank you. I really appreciate it." Pause. "Yes, I checked with Dr. Johnston, and he said Bob is doing great." Another pause. "I will. Thank you for everything, Marshal. You made the past six months bearable."

She ended the call and tucked the phone into her hip pocket.

"You'll be taking care of Bob yourself," he said.

She turned, surprised that he was standing so close. She nodded. "Hope so."

He was the one drawing in an extra-deep breath now. "It's time to go."

"Okay."

They walked through the house, made sure everything was turned off. Jax flipped the breaker for the hot water heater to the off position, and then he locked the door behind them.

Ali squared her shoulders and walked to his SUV. He opened her door, waited for her to buckle up and then closed it. Their eyes met for a moment, and the fear in hers tore him apart inside.

He loaded up, turned the SUV around and headed down that narrow road.

Just as they crossed the stream, his cell vibrated on the console. He picked it up. *Holloway.*

"What's up?"

He supposed his friend just wanted to ensure they were ready and on the road.

"There's been a change of plans."

Holloway's voice sounded as surprised and frustrated as Jax suddenly felt. "What kind of change?"

He glanced at Ali. She stared back at him with mounting uncertainty.

"AUSA Knowles is concerned about the commercial flight now."

"Fine," Jax said before he could continue. "I prefer driving." He would be more in control of the situation that way.

"He still won't agree to highway transport. He wants her on a plane."

What the hell? "So where are we going?"

"There's a private plane waiting at the Winchester Municipal Airport. Special Agent Wesley McEntire is waiting with the pilot."

Last-minute changes always made Jax nervous. But it happened. There were people whose job it was to assess transport options all the way down to the wire.

"Okay. Give me the directions." He listened as Holloway listed off the streets and turns he would need to make to reach the small local airport. "Thanks. I'll confirm when we're in the air."

"Good luck, Stevens. Take good care of her."

"If it's the last thing I do," he assured him.

He dropped his cell back on the console.

"I take it we're not going to the airport in Huntsville."

The slight hitch in her breathing as she spoke twisted his gut. "They've decided we're taking a private plane from the airport here in Winchester."

"Okay."

She stared forward. He did the same.

"Is it normal to have last-minute changes on a day like today?"

She didn't glance his way, and her words sounded stilted. He hated that she was afraid. Wished he could assure her, but every instinct he possessed warned that this was wrong somehow. Risky.

He glanced in the rearview mirror. No one behind them. He slowed and pulled to the side of the road.

She stared at him, worry clouding her face. "What's wrong?"

He hesitated, but then he said what he felt. "We don't have to do this."

"I don't understand."

"We can drive away. Go someplace where that bastard will never find you."

He sounded as if he'd gone over the edge. He recognized this. But the urge to take her out of this scenario and someplace else was overwhelming.

"No." She shook her head. "Your career would be over, and that monster would walk away scot-free. I have to do this, Jax. There is no other choice."

She was right. He didn't know what he'd been thinking.

Before he could apologize, she leaned across the console and kissed him. "Thank you for caring so much."

He forced a smile. "Let's do this, then."

Every nerve ending in his body was humming with a warning.

His instincts had only failed him once, and that had been ten years ago—when he walked away from this woman.

Chapter Twelve

The airport was smaller than she had expected.

A man in a dark suit identified himself as FBI, producing his credentials. Ali watched from the passenger seat of Jax's SUV as he spoke with the agent. He had told her to stay in the vehicle until he checked things out.

Her nerves were vibrating, making her restless. She wanted to get on that plane, get to Atlanta and finish this. Most of all she wanted Jax to come through this unharmed, and for the first time since all this began, she desperately wanted to survive. For months she had hoped to survive, but if she didn't— so be it. She would do this no matter how the circumstances ended for her. But now there was something to look forward to.

Jax wanted to try again.

He still cared about her.

Her pulse started to pound with the thought. She pushed away the tiny doubts that attempted to sprout. He had no reason to mislead her. It wasn't like he was attempting to persuade her to testify. That was a given. He had absolutely nothing to gain by suggesting that they needed to pursue their feelings.

This was real.

Jax returned to the SUV and opened her door. "They're ready."

She was ready, too.

Ready to put the past behind her once and for all.

He stepped to the back of the SUV and grabbed their bags from the cargo area. Ali climbed out and walked across the tarmac with him. They climbed the stairs and stepped into the small jet. Inside there were six leather seats. Jax guided her to the middle row and gestured for her to have a seat.

The jet was small but well equipped. This one was not nearly as large but similar to the one the Armone family owned. Sleek and luxurious from the lighting to the carpet. The seats were heavenly.

The hydraulic sound of the door closing drew their attention forward. Beyond the small partition, the pilot was adjusting controls and speaking into his headset.

Jax moved toward him. "What about the agent?"

The pilot glanced back at him. "My orders are to transport only the two of you." His attention shifted forward once more. "You and the other passenger need to prepare for takeoff. We have a tight schedule. If we don't land on time, they'll call out the cavalry."

Ali's nerves were jumping now. Jax was right—this didn't feel right. The fear and paranoia could be the root of her sudden uneasiness, but she worried that it was more.

When Jax had settled into the seat next to her, he pulled out his cell.

The plane started to roll forward.

Ali focused on breathing. This would not be a good time for a panic attack. Flying had never bothered her before, but today was different.

Jax dropped his cell back into his jacket pocket. "There's no service."

His tension made her all the more anxious.

To hold herself together, she focused on the mundane. She fastened her safety belt. Jax did the same.

"How long does this flight take?" She hugged her arms around herself. Cold had seeped into every part of her.

"Forty minutes, maybe. Less than an hour for sure."

Less than an hour. Good. "A car will pick us up and take us to the hotel?"

"Holloway said that had all been arranged by a Marshal Steadman from the Atlanta office."

"I remember him," she said, thinking back to the first big teleconference she'd participated in after arriving in Kentucky. She didn't remember him commenting during the meeting, but he had been at the table.

"Try to relax," he suggested. "This may be your last opportunity for any semblance of calm. There will likely be meetings this afternoon and final prep for tomorrow."

"I'll try, but no guarantees."

He smiled, and she relaxed the tiniest bit, allowing her arms to settle onto the armrests rather than hugging so tightly around her. His hand settled over hers, fingers lacing. The sensation of being protected slipped over her.

She almost drifted off. She really did, but she couldn't totally relax. Her mind kept going over all that had happened yesterday and last night—Bob's injury, making love with Jax…talk of the future. Excitement shimmered just beneath the worries about tomorrow. She allowed her mind to wander. She would be facing Harrison's father in the courtroom tomorrow. He would be sitting at the defendant's table. She would be in the witness box describing all the heinous details of his life and work.

His evil eyes would stare at her, hoping to intimidate her. She was well aware of the depraved things he did to those who angered or betrayed him. But she had made up her mind that fear was not going to stop her. She would see him go down for all the terrible things he had done.

Her eyes drifted shut, and she almost dozed off. The sound of the pilot's voice stirred her from that place between awake and asleep.

"Marshal Stevens?"

Jax unfastened his safety belt and walked to the front of the aircraft.

Ali leaned forward to hear the exchange. Her heart had started that frantic pounding again.

"We're being diverted," the pilot said.

"On whose order?" Jax asked.

"Marshal Steadman. There's been a security breach with DeKalb-Peachtree. They're diverting us to an airstrip about thirty-nine miles south of Atlanta. We'll prepare for landing in another ten minutes."

"All right."

As he moved back toward his seat, the hard set of his jaw as well as the thin line of his lips told Ali that something beyond another change in the itinerary was wrong. He was not happy about this second change in plans. Her stomach twisted into knots. She wasn't opposed to change—what worried her was his reaction to the changes. Jax had done this for a decade. His instincts were likely well honed. If he was worried, she certainly should be.

"How worried should I be?"

She saw no reason to beat around the bush. The next twenty-four hours were going to determine whether she had a future at all. The possibility that any future she might have could potentially include Jax had her even more determined to survive beyond tomorrow.

"We should be on alert," he said. "Anytime there are security breaches and changes are necessary, the risk factor is elevated."

Ali stared straight ahead. "He doesn't want me to

make it to Atlanta. If I don't make it, he walks. I'm sure he would do anything to make that happen."

She gritted her teeth. He could not get away with all he'd done. The fact that he'd murdered his own son wasn't even the worst of his crimes. Particularly since his son had been equally guilty. Ali suppressed a shudder. She had spent most of the past nine months attempting to evict memories of their time together from her mind.

Years would be required to erase him and all that she had seen and experienced.

She turned to Jax. He attempted another call on his cell. No luck. Staying in her seat was becoming more and more difficult by the moment. What if the marshal wasn't waiting for them at the airfield? What if it was Armone? Or some of his goons? They would all be dead within minutes of landing.

His gaze locked with hers. "We'll get through this," he promised.

She had to trust him. To do anything else would make the next minutes and hours unbearable. With that in mind, she mustered up a smile. "We will."

"Descending now," the pilot announced. "We'll be landing soon."

Jax took her hand again and returned her smile. Somehow just seeing his smile boosted her confidence. The plane started to descend, and Ali's pulse thumped harder and harder. Marshal Steadman would be waiting for them. Dozens of people were working on their security. This was, after all, the trial of the century.

Ali stared out the window as they drew closer and closer to the ground. The airfield looked to be nothing more than an airstrip in the middle of nowhere. There were no hangars or other buildings. There was only one small block structure that could possibly be an office.

Jax leaned over her to peer out the window.

There was no car waiting. That grim expression claimed his face once more.

The plane touched down, bounced and then settled back onto the ground again. The wheels bumped along the strip of asphalt. The plane slowed, the inertia forcing them forward in their seats. Her stomach always flip-flopped during landings. She appreciated that the landing was over fairly quickly, if joltingly.

Before stopping completely, the pilot turned the plane around to face the entrance to the airstrip. "Your transportation hasn't arrived yet. Marshal Steadman said you should stay onboard until your car arrives."

For a long minute, they stayed in their seats, just as the pilot had said. Ali stared out the window. The airstrip was so far outside Atlanta that all she could see in any direction were trees. Maybe the isolation was an added layer of security. Armone couldn't possibly have eyes on every airfield and private airstrip in the tri-county area. This was probably a good move.

Jax suddenly stood. He held out his hand. "I think we should wait outside."

She didn't second-guess him or hesitate. She stood and put her hand in his. "I could use some fresh air."

When they started toward the door the pilot repeated, "Marshal Steadman said—"

Jax reached for the weapon in his shoulder holster. "Open the door and lower the stairs."

The pilot, whose name she still didn't know, turned back to the control center and took the necessary action to start the process Jax had requested. The hatch-style door slowly opened, and the staircase lowered to the ground.

Jax moved down the staircase, pulling Ali behind him. When their feet were on the ground and they were clear of the aircraft, Jax pulled her close.

"Something is wrong here." He surveyed the area.

The sound of traffic in the distance suggested they weren't far from an interstate. But here, there was nothing. They could have been back on that mountain outside Winchester. There were no houses in either direction. A two-lane, unlined road with faded asphalt sprawled out in both directions. The problem was she had no idea exactly where they were. Thirty miles south of Atlanta, he had said. Her mind attempted to piece together a map and pinpoint a spot.

"We may have to make a run for it," he said, his gaze steady on the one entrance to the airstrip.

"I can do that." She'd done a good deal of running the last year of her marriage as well as since she'd moved to Winchester. That path she and Bob had traveled every day had been done in a dead run as often as in a leisurely walk.

Ali never wanted to be weak or afraid ever again.

"Pay attention," he said, "and do exactly as I say when I say it."

She nodded, her heart starting to race. "How will we be sure who's coming when the car turns in?"

The windows could be tinted. No one had told them what kind of vehicle Steadman would be driving. Worry gnawed at her.

A black sedan appeared in the distance.

"Looks like our ride," Jax said.

The plane's engine abruptly roared to life. Before the sedan she'd spotted had reached the turn to the airstrip, the plane was rolling toward takeoff at the other end of the airstrip.

"That's our cue," Jax said.

He was right. The pilot wouldn't be taking off before he confirmed that they had been picked up unless he had reason to flee.

He was leaving them here to die.

Jax was suddenly tugging her along behind him.

The plane had lifted off, and the sedan had made its turn. They hit the tree line and plunged into the woods.

Ali had never been more thankful in her life for the cold weather. The chances of stumbling upon a snake were slim to none. Bears would likely still be hibernating. At least she hoped so.

The sound of car doors slamming in the distance warned they wouldn't be running through these woods alone for long.

Chapter Thirteen

Ali ran as fast as she could.

Thank God for the running shoes she wore. And the warm socks and heavy jacket. Though it was warmer here than it had been in Tennessee, it was still cold.

Jax held tight to her hand and plunged through the woods, darting around trees, plowing through underbrush. There was no time to try the quiet route. His goal, she suspected, was to put as much distance between them and the bad guys as possible.

Slow and quiet could come later when they found some sort of cover or had gotten far enough ahead of those giving chase.

Limbs brushed at her legs. Roots snagged at her feet.

Don't fall! Don't fall!

Hang on tight to his hand.

Run.

She clung to his hand with all her strength. His grasp was firm, unrelenting. Her fingers were growing numb, but she ignored it. She had to keep going. Ignore the burn in her lungs. Hang on. Hang on.

A piece of tree bark popped into the air, pinged against her hair.

Then the echoing sound of bullets being fired exploded in her head.

They were shooting at them.

Move faster.

Jax suddenly stopped. She slammed into his back. He pulled her down to a crouch, his finger at his lips in a gesture of quiet.

The thick brush swallowed them.

He pointed to the water that was only steps away. Seemed too wide to be a stream…more like a river. She hadn't even seen it until he pointed at it.

Fear surged through her veins.

They were trapped.

He dropped to his hands and knees and crawled toward the water. She followed. He went in first, crawling until his body floated in the deeper water.

Ice seemed to form around her as she did the same. The water was so cold.

How could they escape like this?

They would surely die of hypothermia first!

He suddenly disappeared.

Her breath caught. Where was he?

His hand tugged her downward.

She inhaled long and deep and slid beneath the surface. The water was murky, but not so dark that she couldn't see the rocky bottom. She wasn't sure how long she could hold her breath.

Suddenly they were in total darkness. She drew back. Needed to surface. He pulled her onward. She needed air. She couldn't stay under any longer.

Suddenly he was pulling her upward. When her face broke the surface of the water, she gasped for air. Her lungs seized with need. Her body quaked from the icy water. He pressed his finger to her lips. She could barely see him. Why was it so dark? Light filtered in, but only a tiny amount.

She forced her brain to think—to analyze their surroundings. The water was up around their waists, not quite to their chests. Sunlight filtered through… limbs and twigs and other natural debris. She understood now. A large tree had fallen into the water and served as a dam-like object, holding fallen limbs and twigs and…wait. She blinked to adjust her eyes. Maybe not all the debris was natural. An old beverage cooler, the disposable kind. What might be a black jacket and other trash.

Distant shouting in the woods snapped her mind back to the danger close by. So damned close.

Jax pulled on her hand. Ali watched as he lowered to his knees, his chin level with the water's surface. She did the same, stretching to keep her nose and eyes above the surface.

The ones chasing them were at the riverbank now. Their voices drifted through the cold, crisp air. She couldn't make out every word, but obviously they were attempting to determine which direction the two of them had taken.

Her body shivered. She struggled to contain the quakes. If she made a sound, she might draw their attention.

Don't move, don't move!

More frantic talking. Judging by their voices, they were extremely disgruntled that they had lost their prey.

She closed her eyes and tried to ignore the odor of the water…of the rotting vegetation and something oddly musky. Where had that odor come from?

Jax squeezed her hand, and her eyes opened. Movement in the water drew her gaze there.

Snake.

Her heart stuttered to a near halt. She held her breath as the urge to flee fired through her veins. That was the musky scent.

Fear clamped like a vise around her chest.

The long brown-and-black body glided along the water's surface.

Ali bit her bottom lip hard to prevent screaming. The sound burgeoned in her throat. Pressed against the back of her teeth.

Had they inadvertently awakened a hibernating snake?

Were there more? Was this their home?

Jax held her hand so tightly she thought her bones might be crushed.

Adrenaline buffeted her chest, roared in her veins.

She could barely breathe. Prayed the thing would keep moving.

And it did.

As it glided away, the tension in her body lowered to a more tolerable level. Jax's grasp on her hand loosened a fraction.

She managed a shaky breath without dragging water into her nostrils.

The voices had faded.

Jax waited another minute. Each second ticked off like tiny explosions in Ali's mind. Her body had started to quake. She couldn't stop the reaction to the cold now seeped fully into every muscle and bone in her body.

When they still heard no sound, Jax started to move in the direction away from where they had entered the water.

Keeping their heads down, they progressed through the chest-deep water. A few minutes later, he was pulling her up onto the bank. Her body was numb. She shook uncontrollably.

He burrowed into the underbrush and pulled her into his lap, wrapped his arms around her and held her tight to him.

She closed her eyes and let the shaking overtake her. She couldn't fight it any longer. The air around them was quiet. Not a sound beyond the water moving idly along the banks. Her fingers felt like icicles, her arms and legs like frozen slabs. She had never been so cold in her entire life.

For what felt like hours but was certainly only minutes, they sat there, hugging each other, struggling to absorb each other's body heat—what little there was. He stood, pulling her up with him. She couldn't fathom how he found the strength to do so. She felt weak and shaky.

He pressed his face to hers and whispered, "We're going to move slowly for a while. Staying quiet is our goal."

She nodded her understanding.

Again, he pulled her along, ushering her forward when her body wanted to collapse in on itself.

Their only saving grace after that freezing dip in the water was that it was indeed warmer here than it had been in Tennessee. Still, she was so cold.

But cold was far better than dead.

THEY WALKED FOR what felt like miles. Her shoes still squished with every step, but her clothes were drying in some places. The legs of her jeans were reasonably dry. But the sweatshirt beneath her jacket remained soggy, as did the waist of her jeans.

She was still cold, but not the kind of cold she had been before they began walking. It was doubtful that she would ever truly be completely warm again. Her body was working hard to move quickly across the wooded terrain, which forced her muscles to heat up.

What she would give for a hot cup of coffee.

Jax stopped and listened.

She did the same.

He'd stopped once already to try and use his cell phone, but the water had killed it. They needed dry clothes and a phone, he'd said.

Ali wanted out of these woods. She had no desire to pee behind a tree again.

Jax hadn't said anything else. She understood that keeping quiet was extremely important. If those guys—she had no idea how many there had been—were still after them, they couldn't risk the sound of their voices carrying.

He didn't have to say the words for her to know that he was focused on reaching a phone to call in for more reasons than one.

Someone on his team had sold them out. The marshal, Steadman? The pilot?

When the type of transportation and the place for takeoff had changed, he had sensed something was wrong. She had as well, to a lesser degree. His training had him on the highest level of alertness.

As strong as she considered herself to be, she was depending solely on him to survive this new development.

The stillness in the air, the absence of noise had them moving forward again.

With the sun high in the sky, it had to be nearly noon. She had never appreciated the sun more than this moment. The bare trees allowed the rays to filter down to them. Her hair was dry, thankfully. She imagined it looked a mess, but she could live with a bad hair day. Jax's leather jacket was likely ruined. Like hers, his sneakers still squished now and then.

For the first time since this day began, her stomach reminded her that she hadn't eaten in a long while. Probably all the physical exertion. She pushed on, keeping pace as best she could with his long strides. Not an easy task. Her legs stung from all the slaps of brush against her jeans, particularly while they were wet.

A faraway honking sound brushed her ears.

Jax stopped. "Did you hear that?"

"Yes."

"We may be getting close to a highway."

He started moving again, pulling her forward through the waist-deep brush and dead grass.

More noise filtered through the trees.

The faintest sound of barking…a dog.

Jax slowed his pace.

Then the reason punched Ali square in the face. *Dogs.*

What if they were being tracked by dogs?

Fear shot through her heart like a bullet.

The barking stopped.

She tightened her grip on his hand. He turned to her. "It wasn't that kind of dog."

Relief flooded her, making her knees weak. She nodded. "Good to know."

They started forward again, moving slower and as quietly as possible.

A wood fence came into view. It seemed to run

for acres just beyond the tree line. Beyond the fence were rooftops.

A neighborhood.

More relief gushed through her. After reaching the fence, Jax stretched up and had a look. Ali waited, hoping this was perhaps someplace they could find a phone.

"We'll follow the fence line until we find the end."

She nodded. The going was easier here. For about three feet on this side of the fence line, the underbrush had been cleared. Fatigue was catching up to her now. Her muscles ached, and she was fading fast.

It felt like another mile before they reached a turn in the fence line. A man-made pond stretched out before them. Beyond that was a fenced playground.

Jax reached for her hand, and they started to walk again. Ali felt another shiver; she hoped anyone who looked out their windows would see them as just a couple out for a midday stroll around the pond. Except they likely looked like hell. Bedraggled and grungy. Thankfully it was a school day as well as a workday. If they were lucky, there wouldn't be many people home to see the trespassers.

"Should we just knock on a door?"

Jax was surveying the neighborhood, smiling as if she'd said something funny. "Haven't decided yet."

They walked the block, then made a left onto the next one. The street ended in a cul-de-sac where an empty lot and a home under construction rounded out the street with only one finished house. The finished house looked quite new itself and was for sale. Jax walked to the house under construction and studied it.

"Nice place," Ali said as she too pretended to survey the two-story skeleton of a home.

"It is." He glanced at her. "We're going to walk around the house that's for sale over there and see how difficult it will be to get inside."

"Ready when you are."

They followed the sidewalk to the house with the Realtor's sign in the yard. Jax pulled a detail sheet from the flyer box. From that point, they alternately studied the flyer and explored. They walked up onto the porch and then back down the steps and around the side yard.

"Looks as if someone is living here," Ali noted.

"Sure does. But I'm guessing they aren't home."

"How can you tell?" They were in the backyard now with nothing but trees and a fence that cut between this backyard and the one behind it.

"There were four newspapers in the swing on the porch. All still rolled and in wrappers."

She had noticed the swing but not the newspapers. "But if someone lives here, they probably have a security system."

"Mmm-hmm. But they probably don't have it armed so Realtors don't have to know the code to show the house. Too much of a hassle."

"Are we breaking in?"

"We are."

He walked straight to the rear of the garage, where a walk-through door led from the garage into the backyard. Using a credit card from his sodden wallet, he worked some sort of sleight of hand and opened the door.

"Did you learn that in marshal school?"

He closed the door and locked it. "I learned that in high school, but I'll take the Fifth on the rest of the story." He walked to the door that led into the house. "We won't be so lucky on this one." He tapped the lock. "This one has a dead bolt."

He turned all the way around, checking the garage. There was a sedan parked on one side. A neat row of shelves on the wall beyond it. At the end, near the door they had entered, was a workbench with drawers.

"What we need is a key."

Ali checked under the doormat. Jax felt along the top of the door frame. No key.

He moved to the sedan and checked the wheel wells for one of those magnetic key holders.

"Voilà," he announced.

Ali watched patiently as he unlocked the sedan and searched through it. He climbed out with a key ring loaded with keys.

"Maybe we'll get lucky."

She followed him to the door and watched as he tried key after key. Finally, he grinned. "This is the one."

As he opened the door, she held her breath. If an alarm went off…

But the keypad was not blinking. Jax checked the status. "Unarmed," he said.

He locked the door behind them and tossed the keys on the kitchen counter. There was a phone with a built-in answering machine. Next to it was a list of numbers.

She pointed to one of the numbers. "This one is for a hotel in San Francisco."

Jax picked up the list and turned it over. The homeowner's agenda was written out on that side of the paper. He, she or they had left on Tuesday and wouldn't be back until Sunday.

They were safe for the moment.

"Let's have a walk through before we get comfortable," Jax suggested.

Ali followed him from room to room on the first level, then repeated the same on the second one. He looked for cameras or any other devices that might notify the owner of their presence or record their activities. The master bedroom was the only one that appeared to be in use. The other two bedrooms had very little furniture, and there were no clothes in the closets or drawers.

Back downstairs, they returned to the kitchen and Jax checked the fridge. He grabbed two bottles of water and handed one to her. "Upstairs there was a laundry room. Throw your clothes and shoes in the washer and have a shower. I'll stay down here and make sure no one comes in on us. Once your clothes are washed and dried, you play lookout and I'll do the same."

"Are you going to call Holloway?" He would be worried. "We can trust him." She was certain of that if nothing else.

"I'll call Holloway, and we'll figure out what we do next. You go shower."

He didn't have to twist her arm. She was still cold, and she was so tired she could scarcely remain standing. "Okay."

She forced her weary legs to climb the stairs once more. The master's en suite was gorgeous. Lots of marble and a huge soaker tub. But she needed a shower to rinse all that murky river water off her body. She shuddered as she recalled the snake that had slithered past. But then, they had invaded his habitat.

She walked back to the laundry room and opened the washing machine. She tossed her jacket, shoes and socks inside. Then peeled off her jeans, panties and sweatshirt. Bra, too. She threw the whole lot in the machine and added detergent and fabric softener. With the selection set to a quick wash cycle, she pressed Start and headed back to the shower. She turned on the faucet, set the temperature to hot and rounded up a towel.

For a long minute or two, she stood under the hot spray and allowed the water to rinse and warm her skin. She washed her hair and added some of the conditioner that smelled heavenly. Then she spent a good long while slathering her body with the lavender-and-vanilla body wash.

By the time she stepped out of the shower, she was warm and relaxed and felt relatively human again.

With the towel wrapped around her, she moved her clothes from the washer to the dryer and started the cycle. She padded back to the bathroom and combed her hair. Since she had to wait for the dryer, she might as well blow out her hair.

When she returned to the laundry room, she draped her towel over the hamper. Her panties, bra and socks were dry. With those items on, she walked back to the master bedroom and had a look in the closet. She found a Georgia Bulldogs T-shirt and pulled it on. The hem hit the tops of her thighs. Good enough.

Downstairs, Jax had prepared her a peanut butter sandwich.

"Your turn," she announced. "The rest of my clothes are still drying."

He looked her up and down. "I got no complaints."

She grinned. "Thanks for the sandwich. Did you reach Holloway?"

"I did. I'll tell you all about it after I get this river stench washed off me."

"You will feel like a new man," she promised.

"You keep your eyes and ears open," he called back from the stairs. "We're not in the clear yet."

Her smile faded. This she knew well. There were no guarantees how long they would be safe here.

There were no guarantees about any of this.

Chapter Fourteen

Jax had checked on Ali three times since his five-minute shower. Even five minutes was too long to allow her out of his sight, but one of them had to listen for any potential arrivals. Though the owners were out of town, a Realtor could stop by with a client at any time. For that reason, it was necessary to be vigilant.

He opened the dryer—finally his jeans were dry. He'd hung his jacket up in the garage. He wasn't sure how it would come out.

This was not an ideal situation. Breaking and entering and basically stealing water, electricity and food were not a part of his training. As much as he disliked the idea of doing this, it was necessary for Ali's safety.

Until they understood the full ramifications of what had happened with their transport, extreme measures had to be taken.

He had spent only fifteen seconds on the phone with Holloway. Though he trusted the man implicitly, that didn't mean someone else wasn't monitoring his calls. Holloway was aware they had escaped the ambush and were presently safe and unharmed.

While Ali had showered, he had poured a bag of rice into a bowl and stuffed his phone into the center of it. He'd removed the case hours ago, hoping the phone might dry out and still function. He'd also found some oil to take care of his weapon.

He would know soon enough if the phone was going to work again, he supposed.

Dressed now, he returned to the kitchen, where Ali's attention was glued to the television.

"You okay?" He asked the question because her face was pale, and her arms were hugged around her body.

"I've been watching the news for the past half hour, and there's nothing about what happened to us."

"I'm sure the situation is being kept quiet. The AUSA will not want anyone to know his one and only witness is out of pocket. Of course, Armone's people are aware of the situation, but they have no idea—hopefully—where we are at present."

She tipped her head in understanding. "So this—" she gestured to the television hanging on the wall "—is a good thing."

"A very good thing."

It was nearing four o'clock. He had to make a decision. "This might be a little too close to where things hit the fan. I'd feel more comfortable if we relocated to a hotel closer to Atlanta."

"Are we going to borrow the car in the garage?" She looked skeptical.

"We are. I'll leave a note for the homeowner in case they come home early. He'll be reimbursed. I'll make sure the car is returned when we're finished."

"Works for me." Beggars couldn't be choosers. She would be thankful for however they escaped the trouble on their heels.

"We should borrow a hat. Maybe a scarf for you."

"I'll go upstairs and find what we need."

"I'll make sure everything is squared away down here."

Jax walked through the first floor, ensuring all was as they'd found it. He'd already done this upstairs. He wrote a note to the homeowner and left it by the phone. Since he couldn't be sure who might come in the house between now and tomorrow, he didn't sign his name. No one needed to know they had been here until Ali had testified.

He grabbed a couple more bottles of water from the fridge, mentally adding it to his tab. He removed his cell from the bowl of rice and cleaned up the mess he'd made. He used a paper towel to go over the phone to ensure there was no more moisture clinging to it. So far so good. He pressed the button to boot it up and hoped for the best.

When the logo appeared and the screen flickered to life, he breathed a sigh of relief. He tucked it into his hip pocket. Since his jacket was still sodden, he'd opted to forgo the shoulder holster and carry his weapon in his waistband. To that end, he left his shirt untucked.

They would need to pick up clothes for tomorrow. A big supercenter-type store would be the best for the purposes of staying anonymous. He always carried a prepaid credit card with him for moments like this. He would use it at the hotel.

Ali descended the stairs. She'd used a scarf to pull her blond hair back. The way the fabric wrapped around her head, her hair was almost completely covered. She handed him a ball cap with the Bulldogs' logo.

"Thanks." He gave her a nod of approval. "Good job on disguising your hair."

"I'm hoping there are sunglasses in the car."

"We're ready then." He settled the hat into place.

Once they were in the garage, he locked the door leading to the house. Ali settled into the passenger seat and fastened her seat belt. He pulled on his own, as well. She checked the glove box and then the console.

"Aha. Sunglasses for everyone." She passed him a pair and slid her own into place.

He tucked the sleek-looking pair she'd given him onto his face. "Nothing like traveling incognito."

They stared at each other for a long moment. He didn't have to see her eyes behind the dark eyewear. She was afraid. She should be. But he would do all within his power to keep her safe.

"Let's do this."

He hit the garage opener and waited while the door slowly slid upward.

Then he backed from the garage, tapped the button again to close the door and then eased out onto the street.

Dusk had fallen, but it wasn't quite dark enough to give him any extra confidence. All they had to do was roll through the neighborhood without drawing any attention and without running into trouble.

ALI REMINDED HERSELF to breathe. Every person on the street seemed to be staring at her as they drove past. But she understood it was her imagination. Other cars glided slowly along the street. Residents coming home from work, probably. A suffocating mixture of worry and fear enveloped her as they met each vehicle.

Would this be the one carrying the bad guys?

How many were searching for them now?

Could they possibly hope to survive the night?

Another turn and they were on the main road, Highway 92, moving away from the neighborhood. The suffocating sensation seeped away. She relaxed against the seat and drew in a big breath. The first hurdle was behind them. Now all they had to do was find a decent motel or hotel close enough to the courthouse but still off the beaten path.

Someplace no one would expect to find them.

As they drove across town, traffic was murder. Their timing couldn't have been worse. Commuters were leaving work, heading home, and everyone wanted to get there first. Patience was less than zero, and aggression was over the top. Ali couldn't help scanning the faces in the cars jammed beside them, in front of them and behind them.

Her nerves were strumming, her ability to breathe constricted again. She recognized the symptoms. She was barreling toward a panic attack. She'd only ever had a few, but she remembered each one distinctly.

It was the most awful feeling. A sensation of being utterly out of control with an overwhelming sense of doom.

"Breathe slow and deep, Ali."

His voice was low and soft, comforting. She would love for him to take the next exit and pull over somewhere so she could get out of this stolen car and run around in circles. Anything to work off the excess adrenaline rushing through her veins.

She struggled to do as he said. Slow, deep, deep, deeper breath. Hold it, let it out slowly. She closed her eyes. Could not analyze another face. This was enough. Enough. It wasn't like they could escape if a car pulled up beside them and the driver or a passenger pointed a weapon at them. There was no place to go in this bumper-to-bumper traffic.

Another slow, deep breath.

Then another.

"We're almost there," he said, the deep resonance of his voice softening the sharp edges of her anxiety.

He took an exit.

Thank God.

She leaned forward and noted the street was North Avenue. He merged into traffic on North and headed east. Then another turn onto North Highland. Traffic wasn't so bad here.

Another slow, steady breath.

A final turn into the parking lot of an inn. He chose a slot far away from the street and shaded by a group of trees and shrubs.

"When we go inside," he said, "I want you to go into the ladies' room. There will be one somewhere close to the lobby. I'll follow you there and ensure there's no one inside. Go into a stall and lock yourself in. When I have a room key, I'll knock on the door and say 'home free.'"

"Okay."

He stared into her eyes, his showing more worry than she suspected he wanted to. "I don't want you standing in front of that counter for the amount of time it will take to get checked in. Plus, it's better if I check in alone. They'll be looking for a couple. Later, we'll go someplace and find clothes for tomorrow. We need to wait until it's quieter on the streets."

"I understand."

He leaned across the console and kissed her forehead. "You're doing great. This has been tough, and you've hung in there every step of the way."

She managed a smile. "Thanks."

Jax scanned the parking lot as they moved toward the side entrance to the lobby. No need to go through the main entrance since they had no luggage and didn't need the assistance of a bellman. Two guests were at the counter checking in, so the clerks paid no attention to them crossing the lobby.

The restrooms were only a few feet down the corridor beyond the registration desk. Directly across from the bank of elevators. He waited at the open door while she checked to ensure no one was in the ladies' room.

"It's clear."

"Lock yourself in a stall, and I'll be back as quickly as possible."

The door closed with a swoosh, and she inspected the four stalls, deciding on the one at the end. She slid the lock into its slot and closed the toilet lid. She sat down and pulled her knees to her chest. If someone came in, maybe they would think this stall was out of order.

The crack in the door was quite narrow, but if anyone really looked they would see her in here.

Hopefully that wouldn't happen. Jax wouldn't be gone that long.

She pressed her chin to her knees and struggled to relax. It was almost over. This time tomorrow she would be out of Atlanta. The AUSA had promised that as soon as she had testified and been cross-examined, she was free to go.

The hydraulic whoosh of the door opening had her head going up. There had been no knock. No code word.

A distinct click, drag and shuffle vibrated in the air.

Ali held her breath. Didn't dare breathe.

A stall door banged inward.

Click. Drag. Shuffle.

Then another door banged inward.

Why didn't the woman pick a stall already?

Unless it wasn't a woman looking for a stall.

The urge to lean down and look beneath the stall wall was overwhelming, but the act would be impossible without dropping her feet to the floor.

The third stall door banged inward. Then another *click*.

Ali's gaze glued to the floor and the metal legs of something beyond her stall door...and white leather shoes...

A sharp rap sounded on the door. "I see you in there."

Ali's heart thundered. She blinked. Her gaze slid around the stall. Stainless steel safety bar. The door had opened outward rather than inward.

Oh hell. She was in the handicap-accessible stall.

"Sorry. I... I'm finished."

Ali slid the lock back and cracked open the door. An elderly lady glared at her as she backed up a step with a click and a drag of her walker and a shuffle of her rubber-soled shoes.

"I'm sorry." Ali slid through the partially opened door. "I was upset and not paying attention."

Thin gray eyebrows arched high on her wrinkled forehead. "I hope you flushed the toilet."

A solid knock on the door followed by, "Home free," saved her from an explanation.

"I did. Sorry."

Ali rushed to the door, pushed it open enough to see Jax and practically fell into his arms.

"You okay?"

"I am now."

THEY ORDERED ROOM service and devoured the food. Somehow, despite the near panic attack she'd had, Ali dozed off on the ultra-soft king-size bed. She hadn't intended to fall asleep, but she'd crawled onto the down comforter and snuggled into the mound of pillows to wait for Jax to say they were ready, and just like that, she was out.

When she opened her eyes again, it was almost eight. She bolted upright.

"Why didn't you wake me?"

He grinned. "You were exhausted. I didn't want to disturb you. You have a big day tomorrow."

Like she could forget.

She scooted off the bed and hurried to the bathroom. She relieved herself and finger-combed her hair. She was a mess. She desperately needed a hairbrush and a toothbrush.

When she'd made herself as presentable as possible, she rejoined Jax, who waited at the door.

"Let's go pick up some clothes."

"I'm as ready as I'll ever be."

He checked the security viewfinder and then opened the door. "The stairs are on this end of the corridor. They'll take us down to that side door."

Obviously he had done some exploring or research of some sort. The car was parked near that entrance, which would making escaping without being seen far easier.

"Do you know where we're going?" She knew of several supercenters within a twenty-minute drive. She doubted one was any better than the other.

"The closest place and then back here to hole up for the night."

Every moment they were out in the open, the more danger they faced.

"Have you spoken to Holloway or anyone?"

"I called him on my cell." He glanced at her. "It works, but not very well. I managed to get across to him that we would be at the courthouse on time in the morning.

"He said something about an arrest, but I didn't catch all of it. Too much static. I'm assuming that means whoever leaked information about our whereabouts has been found."

"That's good news."

"Holloway is reporting directly to AUSA Knowles, who passes info along to Keller. But he doesn't have our location. No one does. Not even Holloway."

"We should be safe, then," she said, hopeful.

"We should be, yes."

Until tomorrow, when they had to walk into that courthouse.

At the supercenter, they moved quickly through the aisles. Toiletries and other essentials were first on Ali's agenda. Jax grabbed a razor and toiletries of his own. She kind of liked his shadowed jaw. He hadn't shaved since yesterday morning. It was sexy.

"Why are you smiling?" He nodded to the shampoo she held. "You imagining how luscious it will make your hair feel?"

She shook her head, glanced at his chin. "No. Just thinking how much I like this scruffy look."

He rubbed his hand over his jaw. "I'll keep that in mind."

His grin told her he was flattered. She liked his smile. Always had.

"Clothes," he said.

"Right."

The store was more known for its casual wear than for courtroom apparel, but she found a dress that would work. A sweater and shoes plus undergarments and she was good to go.

Jax selected a pair of trousers and a button-down shirt. Socks, shoes and underwear. On second thought he grabbed a belt, too.

Ali's nerves were jittery until they had paid for their merchandise and made their way back to the borrowed car. She liked to think it was *borrowed* rather than stolen.

She hoped none of this came back to haunt Jax. If his helping her jeopardized his career somehow, she would be devastated.

Driving back to the inn, he asked, "Are you feeling calmer now?"

"Yes. I am. I feel we've made our way over the biggest obstacles and we can see the light at the end of the tunnel."

"We'll get through this," he promised.

The same parking slot was available when they reached the inn. He backed into the space so the license plate wouldn't be visible to anyone cruising through the lot. They hurried inside and up the stairs. Once they were in the room and Jax had done a thorough search, Ali relaxed.

"You hungry? Room service ends in about an hour. Speak now or you're out of luck."

She grabbed the room service menu and perused the offerings. "Cheeseburger, fries and a soft drink."

He made the call and ordered the same as her. While they waited, they hung up tomorrow's wardrobe, content to let the silence settle between them. She thought of all they had been through this day, and she couldn't repress a shudder.

"Jax."

He turned to her, his expression expectant.

"I want you to know that no matter what happens tomorrow, I am very grateful for all you and Marshal Holloway have done." She took a big breath. "I'm not sure I can adequately articulate what it means to me to have had the past few days with you. I never imagined we'd find each other again." She smiled. "Whatever tomorrow brings, this time with you means the world to me."

He pulled her into a kiss. He said everything she wanted to know with his mouth and hands and then with his body.

Chapter Fifteen

Trial day

Thursday, February 6

"There are four FBI agents, four marshals besides me and a good number of Fulton County deputies watching everyone who enters the building."

Jax waited for her to catch up with all that he was saying.

Ali looked worried. Worried and scared and yet strong and brave somehow. However terrified she was, she was damned determined to get this done. He was so proud of her.

But he didn't want to lose her. If there had been any questions whatsoever, those doubts and uncertainties had vanished last night. He had held her against his body and he'd known that she was the part of his life that had been missing all these years. He hadn't wanted a long-term relationship with anyone else because his heart had always belonged to Ali.

"Do you have a route planned out?" she asked as she stared at the map of downtown Atlanta he had spread across the desk.

"We're not taking any direct routes." He pointed to the map. "We'll take North Highland all the way down to Irwin. Then we'll zigzag around and head up to Ivan Allen before dropping down to where we need to be."

"Where will we park?"

"We'll do the same thing we did in Nashville. Park at some church a few blocks away and call for a driver to take us to the front entrance. Sheriff's deputies will come out of the woodwork when I give the signal and form a line on either side of the entrance so no one can get to you from the street between exiting the car and gaining entrance."

"What about some shooter who might be in a neighboring building? Taking aim from some window?" She shook her head. "I've probably seen far too many movies, but when I think of how vicious and ruthless Armone is, I know he's capable of anything."

"We have that covered. Before we so much as step out of the vehicle, the deputies will cover and surround us, ushering us into the building. Making that shot will be virtually impossible. Inside, the marshals will take over and get us to the courtroom."

Ali moistened her lips. "Sounds like a good plan."

"We are prepared to react to anything that occurs."

"What about a bomb?" She tugged at the neck of

the new dress. It was a floral print, and she looked so young and innocent in it.

"Bomb squad is standing by. AUSA Keller isn't taking any chances."

She turned to him. He let her look her fill without saying anything. The cheap trousers, shirt and tie would do. The jacket would work to cover his weapon. The clothes were far from spectacular. Yet she stared at him as if he were some celebrity dressed in a thousand-dollar getup.

"You'll be in the courtroom?"

He smiled. "I will. Security is on high alert. No one is getting into that building with a weapon unless he's a marshal, FBI agent or sheriff's deputy."

It was going to be a long day. Her testimony would take hours, and then there was the cross-examination. As soon as the judge dismissed her, Jax was getting her out of there.

They had made their plan last night. He had already scheduled a few days to visit his parents, but he'd put that off for this assignment. He wanted to take her to Seattle this very evening. She had agreed.

No one was going to stop him.

She had been worried about clothes. He had laughed and said he would buy her a whole new wardrobe.

He held out his hand. "We should get going. You ready?"

"I'm ready."

He'd already done the in-room checkout, so there

was no reason to stop at the registration desk. They exited via the stairwell again. The parking lot was clear. They were in the car and exiting the lot in under three minutes.

The route he'd mapped out went off without a hitch. He found a church at which to park and made the call for an Uber pickup.

Ali grew more nervous with each passing moment. She couldn't keep her hands still. Her eyes roved the parking lot.

"I was thinking," he said, drawing her attention to him. "My apartment is kind of small, and they don't allow pets."

Her gaze widened at the idea that Bob wouldn't be allowed at his place.

"Once we've spent a couple of days with the family, we should probably look for a house. Something with a yard for Bob."

Her lips spread into a smile, and the sheer joy in her eyes affected the rhythm of his heart. "Are you sure that's what you want to do?"

"I am absolutely certain," he confirmed. "I want us to start our new life right away. No more waiting. No putting anything off. Life is too short and too precious."

She stretched across the console and kissed his lips. "I want you to promise me something."

Her face had gone completely serious now.

"Name it." Anything she wanted, if he had the power to make it happen, he intended to.

"Promise me that if you suddenly realize that you've made the wrong decision—" He opened his mouth to argue, but she stopped him with her fingers. "If you've made this decision out of some sense of guilt and you come to realize that going back to what we had before is not what you really want, swear to me that you'll tell me. I don't want you spending your life trying to make up for a decision you made at twenty-two."

"You have my word," he said instead of countering. "If I decide for some reason that I don't want to spend the rest of my life with you or that I don't want you to be my wife and have children with me, then I'll let you know."

She blinked, startled. "What did you say?"

"Which part?" He might be enjoying this a little too much.

"The part in the middle just before the mention of children."

"I want you to marry me, Ali. Tonight, tomorrow, next week, whenever is good for you."

She threw her arms around him, and they hugged. "I love you," he whispered against her hair. "I have for more than a decade."

Ali drew back and looked into his eyes. "I love you, too."

He swept a strand of hair from her cheek. Before he could say more, he spotted the car he was expecting. The driver matched the photo he'd been sent.

"Here's our ride."

He climbed out and walked around to her door. When she emerged, she took his hand and said, "Don't get shot, okay?"

He grinned. "You got it."

THE CAR PULLED to the curb in front of the entrance to the federal building. Ali's heart was pounding so heart she could scarcely breathe.

Immediately a line of uniforms formed on either side of the car door from which they would emerge.

"Ready?"

She nodded.

As the car door opened, something large and black like some sort of tarp was stretched out overhead. Jax climbed out of the car and reached for her hand. She joined him on the sidewalk. As planned, the uniforms closed in around them. She and Jax hunkered down and moved with the mass of uniforms through the doors.

Once they were inside, she managed a breath. The other marshals took over from there, surrounding them and ushering them toward the elevator.

They stepped into the car, and Ali struggled to hold back a looming panic attack. She would not let this happen. Not now. What she was about to do was one of the most important steps in her life. She would not fail.

She and Jax were sequestered in a private room until it was time for her to enter the courtroom. There hadn't been time to don bulletproof vests. At this point it was no longer necessary. They were inside, well guarded, and anyone who stepped into that courtroom would be, as well.

A few minutes later, she was escorted to the courtroom, Jax at her side. Silence fell over the room as she walked to the witness box. Jax sat behind the AUSA. She stood facing the courtroom, and her gaze immediately lit on Harrison Armone Sr. She stared at him, unflinching. He was surrounded by a team of attorneys, but they would not win. Not this time.

While her former father-in-law stared at her, she took the oath to tell the truth and nothing but the truth. She sat down, and as she did, she smiled at him. She wanted him to know how very much she intended to enjoy this day.

MORNING HAD GIVEN way to late afternoon by the time Ali was finished. They had taken a lunch break and she'd spent that time in the private room with Jax. She hadn't been able to eat. She wasn't sure she could again until she was far away from here.

When she was dismissed, she was escorted out of the courtroom just as she had been when she entered.

Another few minutes were required for her and Jax to be whisked away from the courthouse via a route where they wouldn't be trapped by reporters. Jax had turned over the keys to the borrowed car and given one of the other marshals a list of items owed to the owner.

To Ali's surprise, Marshal Holloway and his friend Chief Brannigan showed up to drive them to the airport.

"You're looking far better," she said to Holloway.

"I don't feel as much like death, that's for sure," he said with a laugh.

She hugged him gently and thanked him again for all he'd done to keep her safe for six long months. He promised to see that Bob arrived safely in Seattle in a couple of weeks. Jax hadn't told her until they were out of the courthouse that he'd already put in for a transfer back to Seattle. He would be on vacation until the transfer was approved.

Two and a half hours later, she and Jax were sitting in first-class seats headed to Seattle.

"I'm thinking," she said, "we should take a honeymoon." She was feeling bold after a lovely cocktail.

Jax chuckled. "Don't you think we should get married first?"

She leaned her head against his shoulder. "Maybe we'll just do it simultaneously. You know, go to some exotic place and get married there."

"We could," he agreed. "But then we'd have to face the wrath of my mother and my sister. They've been waiting for this wedding for a long time."

Ali laughed so hard she lost her breath. "Usually that would be the bride's line."

He pressed his forehead to hers. "We'll do whatever you want to do, Ali. As long as you say, 'I do.'"

"Well, I can do that right now, Marshal. I *so* do." She sealed that promise with a kiss.

* * * * *

DISRUPTIVE FORCE

ELLE JAMES

I dedicate this book to my three children, who are now grown and successful adults; to my husband, who supports my crazy habit of writing books; to my mother, who has encouraged me from the beginning; to my sister, who started this journey with me; and to my father, who taught me the value of hard work and perseverance. Family is everything and I love all of them dearly.

I miss you, Dad.

Chapter One

Are you still assigned to help me? CJ Grainger hesitated before she sent the text to Cole McCastlain. The former member of Marine Force Reconnaissance now worked for Declan's Defenders, the small but dedicated agency created to help fight for justice when the police, FBI and CIA couldn't get the job done.

A week ago, CJ had helped Declan's Defenders by providing them information she'd found on the dark web about a potential assault on the National Security Council meeting.

That attack had gone down as predicted. The VP and Anne Bellamy, a mid-level staffer for the National Security Advisor, had been taken hostage, amid another plot involving a deadly serum. Fortunately, Declan's team had been ready. They'd rescued the vice president and the staffer, killed two Trinity sleeper agents embedded within the White House staff as well as two other agents who'd worked with them to abduct the hostages.

Trinity.

Even the thought of the name and organization

made CJ break out in a sweat. She'd spent the past year hiding in plain sight. One of very few who'd escaped Trinity and lived.

I'm here, Cole texted.

Again, CJ hesitated. On her own for so long, she'd survived because of her independence and ability to disguise herself. She'd been very careful not to leave a trail a trained hacker, private investigator or Trinity-trained assassin could follow. And she didn't have anyone to be used as leverage. No Achilles' heel, no loved one Trinity could hold hostage to get her to come out into the open.

The part about no loved ones had been one of the reasons she'd been recruited into the Trinity training program in the first place. And by "recruited," she meant stolen out of a foster care home she'd been placed in by Virginia State Social Services.

The state of Virginia hadn't spent a lot of time and resources looking for a child nobody wanted.

Years ago, as a young adolescent, she'd been assimilated, brainwashed and forced to learn how to fight, how to defend herself and how to kill people Trinity ordered her to eliminate.

Until one year ago.

They'd ordered her to kill a pregnant woman. The wife of a senator. When CJ had sighted her rifle on the woman, who'd been probably eight and a half months along in her pregnancy, she hadn't been able to pull the trigger. She'd hesitated, wondering if the baby was a boy or girl and thinking that if she killed the child's mother, she'd be without a parent. And knowing that if Trinity decided the father was of no further use to them or was a risk who could expose someone within the organization, the father would be eliminated, as well. That would leave the child parentless.

Having been parentless, CJ had refused to let that happen to the unborn child.

Her hesitation hadn't helped the woman. Trinity had a second assassin waiting on a rooftop to do the job if CJ wouldn't.

The shot was fired, the bullet piercing the woman's belly, killing the baby instantly. It wasn't until much later that CJ learned the mother had died in transit to the hospital.

After she'd failed to take the kill shot, CJ had known what would happen next. Since most Trinity agents didn't get second chances if they failed an assignment, she knew the man who'd assassinated the pregnant woman and her baby would be turning his rifle on her.

CJ, anticipating the inevitable, had ducked low, out of the sight line of the rooftop from where the gunman leveled his sniper rifle and pulled the trigger.

The bullets flew well over her head. She'd tucked her rifle into the golf bag she'd carried up to the rooftop and then crawled to the door and descended to the first floor. There, she hid her golf bag under the last step of the staircase, planning to retrieve it after the furor died down.

In the meantime, she'd pulled a hooded jacket out of her satchel and slipped it on over her sweater. The added bulk made her appear heavier. She slipped on a pair of black-rimmed plastic glasses and tucked her hair under the hood of the jacket. Then she jammed her hands into the pockets of her jeans and hunched her shoulders like a teen trying to be invisible. Slipping out of the apartment building, she'd blended into the rush of people heading home from work.

Instead of going to her apartment, she'd kept walking. Nothing in that apartment meant anything to her. It had been a place to sleep and shower. She always carried everything she needed in the satchel she'd slung over her shoulder. A laptop, a couple changes of clothes, three wigs in varying colors, makeup and her Glock 9mm pistol. She'd also had a burner phone in her pocket, along with a wad of cash and a couple of credit cards that would have to be shredded since she'd become a target for the same organization she'd worked for.

For the past year, she'd been on the run, dodging shadows and living from day to day looking over her shoulder.

Are you in trouble? Cole's second message brought CJ back from her memories to the task at hand.

Are you still digging into Trinity conspirators? she texted.

CJ didn't want help, but she had to find the leader of Trinity before he found her. Two or three people searching the internet was better than one person using borrowed internet from public libraries.

Yes.

Look into Chris Carpenter, the Homeland Security Advisor for the National Security Council.

Cole's response was quick.

Got anything to go on? Any clues?

CJ hated to say she had a gut feeling about the man. A trained assassin relied on cold, hard facts, disregarding emotion and luck.

Prior to the attack in the NSC, the conference room coordinator received a text from Carpenter.

The guy who helped kidnap Anne Bellamy and the vice president?

Yes.

His assistant, Dr. Saunders, was the woman who was almost killed in a hit-and-run accident, wasn't she?

That's the one.

On it.

CJ had been doing her own digging on the dark web via the Arlington Public Library. She'd hacked in, making it past the firewall of the phone system used by Chris Carpenter to his billing information. She'd narrowed her search of his calls to the day of the attack. She'd gone through his phone records, searching for a connection to Terrence Tully, the conference room coordinator for the NSC meeting, and found one.

Terrence Tully had been one of Trinity's sleeper agents, embedded in the White House, waiting for his call to serve.

That day, he'd helped orchestrate the kidnapping of the VP and Anne Bellamy, the woman CJ had contacted to warn about the attack.

Can we meet? Cole asked.

CJ frowned. Any contact she had with others put them at risk. She'd already broken the first rule she'd made for herself upon her defection from Trinity: stay away from anyone or anything to do with the organization. Including people who were actively searching to destroy it.

She'd broken that rule by contacting Anne to warn her of the attack.

Then she'd involved herself in Declan's Defenders' rescue effort. If that wasn't bad enough, she'd gone to their base location at Charlotte Halverson's estate. The Defenders knew more about her than she'd wanted to divulge, including what she looked like. And they'd assigned one of Declan's men to be her protector and backup.

CJ snorted. Like she'd let that happen. If she allowed anyone to get that close to her, it would be one more way for Trinity to find her and the agent would be collateral damage when Trinity came to kill her.

Being a loner was better for all involved.

She typed, If I need you, I'll find you.

CJ backed out of Carpenter's phone records she'd been perusing and went back on the dark web, digging into anything she could find that might lead her to Trinity's leader, the best kept secret in the entire organization.

When she'd first left Trinity, her main focus had been on staying alive and out of their way. It didn't take her long to realize, however, that she'd never be truly safe until the organization was destroyed. And the best way to do that was to find its leader and destroy him. Because of the recent Trinity activity in the DC area and the fact that it was a world capital, she felt confident that Trinity's head was somewhere in the vicinity.

A little more than a week ago, she'd found a particular website with a forum where anyone could anonymously arrange to hire a hit man. It seemed assassins for hire didn't like that Trinity was an exclusive organization they couldn't crack. Some of the people on the site had it out for Trinity and had made it a personal challenge to identify its leadership and/or to sabotage the organization's hits. It was on that site through online chats and more that CJ had learned about the potential attack on the White House during the NSC meeting.

Going to the site, CJ went directly to the message board.

Still looking for the Director, she typed.

A few seconds later she received this response: They're still looking for you.

Weary of the chase, the worry and living below the radar, she wrote, Time to stop T.

The time will come. We will find the Director.

Today?

Probably not.

The next message made her pulse pound.

Someone knows where you are.

CJ frowned.

How do you know?

Message traffic on another site, listing IP address of Arlington library.

She glanced out the glass window of the computer room to the library beyond. Moms were helping their children carry stacks of books to the counter, and a college student with a backpack leaned over the desk to ask the librarian a question. No one looked like a Trinity assassin. But then, she had been one and had been trained to blend in.

Where are you seeing this? she typed.

No time.

He's here now?

Now. Run. Don't go home. Compromised.

CJ cleared the browser, cleared the screen and logged off the computer. She ducked low, pretending to get something from her backpack. Instead of putting something in, she took out the blond wig cut in a short bob, pulled it on and quickly stuffed her own auburn hair beneath it. Then she took off her black leather jacket and crammed it into the backpack, straightening her pale pink T-shirt with the cartoon kitty on the front. Setting a pair of round sunglasses on her nose to hide her green eyes and popping a piece of bubble gum into her mouth, she stood.

Disguise in place, CJ exited the room through the opposite door from where she'd entered and slipped through the stacks, weaving her way along the travel section into the how-to books.

A gray-haired man peered at a gardening book for beginners. A young woman perused a book on designing websites.

CJ moved past them. She'd have to go through the front entrance to get out without setting off any emergency exit alarms.

A group of two women and six children ranging in ages from five to fourteen loaded books into bags and headed toward the door.

The college student stood at the magazine display, leafing through the tabloids.

CJ crossed the open space in front of the checkout desk and trailed the group of women and children out of the building and into the parking lot. She looked around, keeping the door to the library in her peripheral vision.

CJ moved across the parking lot in the opposite direction of the children, not wanting them to be collateral damage should the situation get sticky. She kept walking, figuring the farther away from the library she got, the better. Once she knew she'd shaken whoever might be after her, she'd hop on a bus and head for…

Hell if she knew. If the apartment she'd rented had been compromised, she couldn't go back there.

Footsteps sounded on the pavement behind her.

CJ stepped around a large SUV and chanced a look back.

The college student had followed her out of the library. He had slipped his backpack off his shoulder and was reaching inside.

CJ made it to the sidewalk, quickly passing shops and other buildings until she found the right one. She ducked into the restaurant and walked to the back. The dim lighting forced her to remove the sunglasses. Following a waitress, she entered the kitchen.

"Sorry, miss, you can't be here," the waitress said.

CJ grimaced and glanced over her shoulder. "Is there a rear exit through here?"

"Yes, but for employees only."

"My ex-boyfriend is following me. He won't leave me alone. And he's abusive." CJ touched the waitress's arm. "Please. I need to get away from him."

The woman's eyes rounded and she looked through the glass window of the swinging door. "Dark hair and backpack?"

CJ nodded. "Yes."

The waitress grabbed her arm. "Come with me." She led CJ to the back door and out into the alley. "My husband is waiting for my shift to end. He can take you where you need to go, as long as it's not too far." She glanced down at her watch. "I get off in fifteen minutes." She took CJ's hand and led her to an older model sedan with a faded paint job.

The man in the driver's seat was asleep, his head tilted back against the headrest.

The woman tapped on the window.

Jerking awake, the man sat up and rolled down the window. "Hey, Bea, are you off already?"

"No," Bea said. "But I want you to help this woman get away from an abusive ex-boyfriend. Take her where she needs to go. I'll be ready to go when you get back."

She turned to CJ. "Ronnie will take care of you. He's a good guy, my man is." Bea opened the back door and held it for CJ. "Hurry, before he figures out which way you went."

CJ nodded, hating that she'd lied, but needing to get away. "Thank you." She climbed in and hunkered low on the backseat while Ronnie drove away from the restaurant and out onto the busy street in front.

CJ waited until they were half a block away before she looked up over the back of the seat in time to see the college student run out of the restaurant and look both directions.

When he turned and walked toward the library, CJ let out a sigh.

"Was that the guy?" Ronnie asked.

CJ nodded. "He just won't let go." Which was true. Trinity assassins were trained to keep after their target until the target had been eliminated. He'd find her again. And when he did, he wouldn't let her slip away a second time.

CJ had Ronnie drop her off at a metro station two miles from the library. She slipped onto the train headed for a neighborhood she'd been through several times. The one where Cole McCastlain lived. She wasn't ready to admit she needed help, but she'd found a furnished town house for rent near his. If it was still available, she'd crash there and regroup. She needed time to think about her next move. Maybe it was time to openly join forces with Declan's Defenders. They were all after the same thing. To bring an end to Trinity. To do so, they had to bring down the Director.

COLE SAT AT his desk in the town house he'd rented, his body tense, his gaze glued to the computer. He'd seen the messages come across the website he'd been following. He'd known Trinity was closing in on CJ. And he'd been unable to do anything but warn her. Frustration was too weak a description of what he was feeling. Cole needed action.

But CJ had refused to let him or anyone else from

Declan's Defenders overtly assist her in their mutual objective to bring down Trinity. She'd insisted she was better off alone.

He'd been lucky today. The messages had come in just in time for him to warn CJ to get out of the Arlington library. Hell, he'd been able to locate her based on the IP address of the computer she'd logged in on. She'd been perusing the internet on sites known for helping people find assassins for hire. What scared him was that if he was able to find her, others could easily do the same.

He'd invested in a burner phone. Next time she texted, he'd give her that number and insist she use it with a new burner number. Trinity had to know Declan's Defenders were out to destroy the organization that had most likely put out a hit on John Halverson. Declan's Defenders would not exist but for the trust and generosity of Halverson's widow, Charlotte—Charlie.

John Halverson had been on a mission to stop Trinity's illicit activities. He'd scratched the surface and had probably gotten too close to finding their leader, thus making them desperate enough to eliminate the threat.

As much as Charlie had done for Declan and his band of former Marine Force Reconnaissance men, they wanted to return the favor. Their mission was to find the leader of Trinity, the Director. The theory was to chop off the head of the snake and the rest of the organization would die.

According to Halverson's records, he'd been

searching for the same thing. It had taken him years to get as far as he had, and yet, he'd not found the Director or, at least, not been able to identify him before he was murdered.

Cole had been working with Jonah Spradlin, Charlie's computer guy. They'd been hacking into the computer system at the White House to deep dive existing background checks on people who worked there ever since CJ had given them the heads-up on a planned assault on the NSC meeting at the White House. The problem, of course, was that there were over four hundred people who worked in the White House. Narrowing them down to the few who might present a threat had been a challenge. Four had evaded their background check prior to the hostage taking at the NSC meeting. Four Trinity assassins had been embedded in the White House staff.

Those four were no longer a threat. But how many more were slipping past them? The background checks didn't tell them much. They had to dive deeper into their private records, bank accounts, emails and phone records. The task was monumental given the number of White House staff.

The cell phone beside him buzzed with a text message. He glanced down at the screen. *Unknown Caller.*

His pulse beat faster as he unlocked the screen and stared down at the message.

Thank you.

Are you okay?

Yes.

Need a place to stay?

No.

If you do, I have room. So does Charlie.

Thanks.

Let me help more.

You are. Dig into Carpenter.

Will do. Be careful out there. I'm here whenever you need me.

Good to know.

Got a burner phone. Need to stop using this number in case it's being monitored. Call me for the number.

Cole waited, hoping she'd call. For several minutes, he didn't hear anything, text or voice. Then his personal cell phone chirped.

Unknown Caller.

"It's me," he answered.

"Number?" a female voice said.

He gave her the number and waited for more.

The call ended.

Disappointment piled onto frustration made Cole clench his fist. How could he do the job of protecting CJ if she wouldn't let him get close?

His burner phone vibrated. His pulse leaped and he lifted it to his ear. "It's me."

"It's me," she echoed.

Cole smiled. CJ's husky voice flowed over him like warm chocolate, oozing into every one of his pores.

"Better," he said. "Now, tell me…did you find a place to stay?"

"For now."

"Did you have any trouble getting away from the Trinity guy after you?"

"No."

She wasn't very forthcoming with information. Cole sighed. "What are my chances of actually seeing you so that I can protect you?"

She laughed, the sound like music in his ears. She almost sounded like a different person. "Slim to none. I don't need protection."

"Would you have made it out of the library without my help?"

"Yes."

"Did my assistance help you make it out without an altercation?"

She hesitated. "Yes. Thank you for the heads-up."

"It can't be easy searching the web on public computers. Charlie has a room full of computers in a secure location."

"Thanks, but I'll manage."

He felt her pulling away. "CJ?"

She didn't answer, but the line didn't go dead.

Cole continued. "I really want to help you."

"Find the Director."

"We're working on it," he said, wanting to reach through the airwaves and grab her hand.

"I'll be in touch."

And the call ended.

Cole sighed. At least he'd heard from her and gotten her onto a more secure line. He wanted her to be more tangible, to see her, touch her and know she was close so that he could protect her. At the same time, the woman was still alive after living a year outside of Trinity. She knew what she was doing and having someone else hanging around might slow her down.

Patience was never something Cole had in abundant supply.

He lifted his personal cell phone, not the burner phone he'd used with CJ, and dialed Charlie Halverson's estate.

Declan O'Neill answered. "Hey, Cole. Got anything new?"

"Heard from CJ."

"Good to know," Declan said. "Was wondering when she'd make contact."

"Dig into the Homeland Security Advisor, Chris Carpenter, since he'd texted Terrence Tully prior to the NSC incident."

"I'll get Jonah on it." Declan paused. "Did she say anything else?"

"No." Cole explained what had gone down with

messages on the dark web and Trinity finding her at the library in Arlington.

"Does she need a place to stay? Charlie would happily put her up for as long as necessary."

Cole shook his head, though Declan couldn't see it. "She said she has a place for now. I gotta tell you, this assignment is killing me. How do I protect a woman I can't see?"

Declan chuckled. "It's like she's a ghost. Most likely she's gun-shy."

Cole snorted. "I know I would be if I had a target painted on my back. Trinity doesn't like to lose one of their own."

"To Trinity she's a loose end that needs to be tied up."

"With a bullet." Cole's jaw tightened.

"That's why you need to get closer to her and keep that from happening."

"Tell me about it." Declan was preaching to the choir. If only Cole could get close enough. Then he might be able to do his job.

In the meantime, all he could do was continue to sift through clues and data to find the Director.

Until CJ came out of the shadows, she was on her own.

Chapter Two

Contrary to what she'd told Cole, CJ didn't have a place to stay that first night after abandoning her apartment. She'd slept behind some bushes in a quiet neighborhood, leaving just before sunup to sneak into the twenty-four-hour gym she'd joined, paying for her annual membership in cash. After weight lifting and a run on the treadmill, she hit the shower and changed into clean clothes. She didn't think she'd be able to come back to the gym. Trinity had come too close the day before. If she was smart, she'd leave the DC area and start a new life in a different state. Hell, a different country wouldn't be far enough.

After a breakfast of a protein bar she had stashed in her backpack, she went in search of a new place to live. She'd done her own homework about the man assigned to protect her. Cole McCastlain lived in a town house in Arlington.

Last night, CJ learned that a town house a few doors down from the one Cole lived in was being sublet. The owners had just left on a world cruise and wouldn't be back for six months. She paid the deposit with money she'd earned designing web pages, gave her fake identification and quickly passed the background check. By noon, she had moved into the fully furnished home.

She didn't waste time settling in. While Cole and Declan's Defenders searched the web for information on Chris Carpenter, CJ would follow the man and learn what she could about his habits and who he talked to. She might be chasing shadows, but the text he'd sent to Tully prior to the NSC assault was all she had to go on. It could have meant nothing. The text could have been a legitimate effort to make sure all was in place, nothing more.

All other coordination for the meeting had been done via emails throughout the weeks prior to the get-together. A text would have been appropriate for a last-minute adjustment to the arrangements. Or it could have been information regarding the attack.

Though CJ had a laptop and could access the internet by tapping into Wi-Fi at internet cafés or libraries, she couldn't delve into the dark web anymore. Somehow, Trinity had found her and traced her IP address to the library. She could continue to hack into phone records and other sources of information, but they were getting too close.

Needing additional clothing and disguises, she shoved her hair up into a ball cap, dressed in a long gray sweater that hid her figure, and sunglasses. Disguised as best she could, CJ left the town house to visit a couple thrift shops. She found items that would help her to blend in and make her as invisible as possible. She even found a skirt suit that might come in handy if she wanted to get closer to some of the politicians on Capitol Hill. The total of her purchases barely made a dent in her cash. Afterward, she made a quick trip to the grocery store and stocked up on a few items she'd need to keep from having to eat fast foods. Once she'd unloaded the food and staples in the refrigerator and pantry, she put on a black wig, a different pair of glasses and a hooded sweatshirt and went out to scout the neighborhood thoroughly. Knowing where to go on short notice was always a good idea.

Stepping out on the sidewalk, she started toward Cole's place. On the bottom step of the next town house, a stooped old woman stood with one hand on a cane, the other on a leash. At the end of the leash was a white ball of fluff.

"Good afternoon," the woman called out with a smile. "You must be the one subletting the Anderson place."

Normally, CJ didn't stop to talk to anyone. But the woman and her dog didn't appear to pose a threat. "Yes, ma'am. I'm Rebecca." She didn't bother holding out her hand since the older woman's were both occupied.

The woman nodded. "Gladys Oliver."

CJ squatted beside the dog. "And who do we have here?" The little dog wiggled and jumped up on CJ, excited to meet someone new.

"Sweet Pea, named after one of my favorite flowers," Gladys said. "Down, girl." Her gentle tug on the dog's leash had little effect. "My granddaughter got me the dog, but she's still a puppy and needs a lot more exercise than these old bones can give her. I'm thinking I might have to give her back." The woman's brow furrowed. "She's such a sweet thing. I hate to give her up."

"I'm going for a walk now," CJ said. "I could take her with me, and she could burn off some energy, if you like."

The old woman's blue eyes brightened. "You would do that?"

"Certainly."

"I mean, it's not like you're really a stranger. I know where you live and all." Gladys handed over the leash. "She's really no trouble. Just needs to move a little faster than I do. If you're sure it's not a bother…"

"We'll do just fine together." CJ smiled at Gladys. "We'll be back in twenty or thirty minutes."

"I'll be inside. Just knock when you're back. I'll come to the door." Gladys leaned down to pat the little dog on the head. "You be a good girl for Rebecca," she said and scratched Sweet Pea behind the ears.

Her disguise complete with a dog in tow, CJ walked along the sidewalk, letting Sweet Pea take her time sniffing every tree, mailbox, bush and blade of grass along the way. The dog's interest in her surroundings gave CJ plenty of time to study the homes, the street and places Trinity agents could be hiding, or where she could hide if she needed to.

Soon, she passed the town house where Cole lived. It looked much like the rest of the homes on the street.

Two-story, narrow front, a four-foot-wide gap between it and the townhomes on either side, which
she walked through to learn more. A five-foot-tall
wooden fence surrounded a postage-stamp-size backyard. Nothing CJ couldn't scale, if she had to. Without
actually climbing the fence, she couldn't see what the
back of the house had to offer in the way of doors,
windows or trees. It was comforting to know he was
only a few doors down from where she was staying.

She moved on, back to the front, studying the other
houses and alleys all the way to the end of the long
street where it turned onto a busy road. CJ turned left
and kept walking, sticking to the sidewalk. A block
away, there was a small strip mall with a hamburger
place on one end and a pizza joint on the other. In
between was a liquor store, a nail salon and an insurance agent.

Across the busy thoroughfare was a tattoo parlor,
a pawnshop and a Chinese restaurant.

For the first few blocks, Sweet Pea led the way,
tugging at the leash, eager to keep going. When she
started to slow and hang back with CJ, it was time to
turn around and get her home to her owner.

CJ performed an about-face and started back.
When she turned the corner onto the street where
she lived, her gaze went to Cole's place. She wondered if he was home. How easy would it be to stop
in and say hello, like a regular person?

Still a few houses away, she heard the sound of
running footsteps coming from behind.

CJ spun to face a man jogging toward her, wearing

only shorts and running shoes. His body was poetry in motion, his muscles tight and well-defined. Every inch of exposed skin glistened with sweat.

Cole McCastlain. The man who wanted to be her protector.

She recognized him from the one time she'd been to Charlie Halverson's estate, immediately following the rescue of Anne Bellamy and the vice president of the United States. At that time, CJ hadn't been wearing a wig. She'd been without any disguise, her auburn hair hanging down around her shoulders.

Using the back of his arm, he wiped the sweat from his eyes and kept running toward her.

A tug on the leash reminded CJ of Sweet Pea. The dog had crossed the sidewalk to the opposite side, her leash creating a line in front of Cole. CJ crossed to the same side of the sidewalk to keep Cole from tripping over the leash.

He ran past her, the muscles in his legs flexing and tightening with each long stride.

A rush of relief washed over her, at the same time as a flush of heat.

The man had tone and definition in each muscle of his body, from his shoulders, down his chest, to his abs, thighs and calves. She bet she could bounce a quarter off his backside.

As he passed, he shot a sideways glance her way. For a brief moment, his eyes narrowed. He didn't slow, or stop, but kept moving. When he reached his town house, he ran up the steps and disappeared inside.

CJ inhaled a deep breath, amazed at how much

she needed it. Had she forgotten how to breathe in the presence of the former marine? She told herself she wasn't ready to do anything that would connect Cole to her. If Trinity was watching Declan's Defenders, and CJ was hanging out with them, they'd find her and eliminate her before she had a chance to expose the Director. She couldn't let that happen. There were a lot of lost children, teens and young adults being held captive and indoctrinated into the Trinity family of assassins. They didn't deserve the life of violence for which they were being groomed. The Director ruled the organization with an iron fist. If they found and destroyed the Director, Trinity would fold.

At least, that was the theory.

As she passed Cole's townhome, CJ kept her face averted, focusing on the sidewalk in front of her as if she were only out to walk her dog. In her peripheral vision, she watched the windows for movement. Was that him, standing in the corner of the front picture window?

Her heart pounding, CJ kept moving, walking past Gladys's house and her own for another block before she returned.

The old woman met her at the door. "I thought I saw you go by with Sweet Pea. I guess she needed a little more of a walk." The woman leaned over, her back hunched as she reached down to pet her tired dog. "Thank you for taking Miss Sweet Pea for a walk. I bet she sleeps all afternoon, now." Gladys looked up. "Can I pay you for your trouble?"

CJ could always use the money, but she couldn't

take it from the kind old woman. "No, ma'am. It was my pleasure. Sweet Pea must give you a great deal of comfort and companionship."

"She does. Since my children all grew up and moved away, and my husband passed, I've been lonely. Sweet Pea is my surrogate baby. I love her so much." The woman's eyes welled with unshed tears. "I'm sure you don't want to hear me blubbering about loneliness. But if you ever need a companion to walk with, Sweet Pea and I would be happy if you take her."

"Thank you, Ms. Gladys." On impulse, CJ leaned down and kissed the woman's cheeks. She reminded her of a grandmother she might once have known, who'd died before her parents' auto accident. Her heart swelled with emotions she hadn't felt in a very long time.

"Thank you again," she said and turned toward her town house.

"If you ever want to share a cup of tea or coffee, stop by anytime," Gladys called out. "I'd be happy to make some."

"I'll keep that in mind," CJ responded, knowing she couldn't do that. If Trinity was watching now, her short interaction with the old woman and her dog would place them in danger. Trinity wasn't above using others to lure their defectors out into the open. And they weren't above killing innocent people to get what they wanted.

And they wanted CJ dead.

WHEN COLE ENTERED his town house, he stopped long enough to catch his breath and then turned to the window. He could swear he knew the woman he'd jogged past, but he couldn't put his finger on who it was or where he'd known her.

The black hair wasn't ringing any bells. And the dog? He was certain he'd seen it with someone else. Didn't it belong to the old woman who lived several doors down from his place?

Maybe that was it. The woman was a daughter, granddaughter, niece or something to the old woman. Perhaps that was where he'd seen her before.

He waited at the window for her to pass with the dog. When they did, he looked hard, still unsure of where he'd seen her before. But he knew he had. The way she walked, the sway of her sexy hips, the tilt of her nose and the long, thick eyelashes should have been dead giveaways.

His phone rang in the armband he used when running. Cole tapped the earbud in his ear. "Yeah."

"You coming in to do some heavy-duty computing?" Declan O'Neill's voice sounded in his ear.

"I am. Just showering. I can be there in thirty to forty-five minutes."

"See ya then," Declan said.

When Cole glanced back out the window, the woman had disappeared, dog and all.

Cole showered, changed into jeans and a T-shirt and headed out to the Halverson estate, driving the Hummer he'd purchased prior to exiting the Marine

Corps. Thankfully, Charlie Halverson had hired him before he'd had to sell it for money to live on until he'd gotten a decent-paying job.

Once he passed through the gates, he drove up the winding drive to the sprawling mansion.

Roger Arnold, Charlie's butler, met him at the door and let him in. "They're waiting for you in the war room," he said.

Cole went straight for the study and the trapdoor that led into the basement of the mansion. All of Declan's Defenders were there.

Declan stood at a large whiteboard with photographs taped to the surface. Jonah Spradlin sat at a desk against the wall, an array of computer monitors displayed in front of him.

Mack Balkman sat in a chair near Declan. He ran a hand through his black hair, his blue eyes studying the whiteboard. Beside him sat the former Russian operative, Riley Lansing. Gus Walsh stood on the opposite side of the table, the woman he'd helped rescue standing at his side.

Jasmine Newman, aka Jane Doe, was as much a key to their operation as CJ Grainger. Jasmine had been a Trinity agent before John Halverson recruited her to help him fight the organization. Combat trained and fluent in Arabic and Russian, she was a formidable opponent and a worthy ally. They'd "killed" her off and given her a new name and identity to keep her off Trinity's hit list. So far, she'd managed to remain out of sight, but she would always be looking over her shoulder as long as Trinity remained a threat.

Jack Snow, the team slack man, sat beside Anne Bellamy, the mid-level staffer who'd been recruited by John Halverson to spy on politicians and staffers in the West Wing. She still had the bruises from her kidnapping ordeal by the Trinity sleeper agents a week before.

Frank "Mustang" Ford stood with his girl, Emily Chastain, the college professor. He turned as Cole entered the room. The brown-haired, brown-eyed former point man was as used to action as Cole. He paced the room like a caged cat. "Nice of you to join us."

Cole shook his head. "I'd have been here sooner, if I'd known you wanted me here." They were all tense. After the attack on the National Security Council meeting, they knew they had to bear down and come up with some real leads. Trinity had far too much power and had infiltrated too many places. Picking the agents off, one by one, would take too long and never be effective as the organization continued to "recruit" new agents. They had to find the lead man and take him down.

"Based on your woman's intel," Declan said, "Jonah's made some headway that might be useful." He turned to Charlie's computer guru.

Cole wanted to correct Declan. CJ wasn't his woman. He barely knew her and had seen her only once in the very room where he stood now. An image of a black-haired woman walking a little white dog rose in his mind.

Jonah pointed to one of the monitors. "Chris Carpenter is in debt up to his eyeballs. He's maxed out every credit card he owns—and he has quite a few—and he's struggling to make the minimum payments on all those. He's in a house that far exceeds his pay scale and he's gone through everything his father left him in a trust fund."

"The man is barely able to keep his head above water," Declan concluded. "It's a wonder he got a security clearance."

Cole shrugged. "CJ thought he might have a connection to Trinity since his was one of the last texts Tully received on his cell phone prior to the attack on the NSC conference room. How does his financial woes make him a likely suspect?"

"A man that deep in debt can usually be bought," a female voice said from behind Cole.

He turned to face Charlie descending the stairs, carrying a tray loaded with glasses and a pitcher of lemonade.

The butler followed with another tray of sandwiches Cole suspected were prepared by Charlie's chef, Carl.

Cole took the tray from her and set it on the conference table.

Charlie took over hostess duties, pouring lemonade into clear, crystal glasses. "It's not whiskey, but then I thought you might want to have clear heads for this discussion."

She handed out glasses to everyone who wanted one and then nodded toward the picture of Carpenter that had been taped to the whiteboard. "If Carpenter is in debt that deep, an offer to bail him out might convince him to do favors for anyone who is willing to pay for them."

"I've worked with Chris Carpenter for the past two years." Anne Bellamy shook her head. "It's hard to believe he would work for Trinity."

"Desperation changes a man," Charlie said. "If he's in over his head and drowning, he'll take any life raft thrown his way to get out."

"Just because he's in debt, doesn't make him a traitor," Cole said. "We need solid proof. Got anything else?"

Jonah's lips twisted and his gaze narrowed. "He's made several payments to a marriage counseling center."

Cole sighed. "Again, a marriage on the rocks isn't much to go on."

"We need more," Declan agreed. "Do you have access to CJ?"

"We're communicating by burner phones," Cole said, and held up the phone he'd purchased for just that purpose.

"Get her on the line," Declan commanded.

"I can't guarantee she'll answer," Cole said. "She's very skittish."

"That's the only way she can stay alive if Trinity is actively pursuing her," Jasmine said. "It's a miracle she's still alive after escaping over a year ago. And to be in an area known to be prime Trinity territory..." The former assassin shook her head.

Cole hit the redial button on his phone.

After the fourth ring, CJ answered. "What did you find?" she asked without preamble.

"I'm with the team. Can I put you on speaker?"

"Yes."

Cole hit the speaker button. "We learned more about Carpenter, but not enough to accuse him of conspiring with Trinity." He filled her in on the Homeland Security Advisor's financial troubles and the fact that he was seeing a marriage counselor.

"I doubt he's meeting with any Trinity contacts inside the West Wing. I'll follow him," CJ said.

"That puts you at too much risk of being discovered," Cole insisted. "I'll follow him and let you know what I find."

"I've seen him go into a bar close to the metro station after work," Anne Bellamy interjected. She gave them the name of the bar and the street where it was located.

"Anne and I will keep an eye on him in the West Wing during the day," Jack offered. He was still posing as Anne's office assistant.

Anne nodded. "We can follow him at lunch and see if he talks with anyone."

"Good," Cole said. "But he knows you two and wouldn't want you to know who he's meeting with. I'll go to the bar tomorrow night ahead of him. He doesn't know me and won't think anything of me sitting there sipping on a beer."

"I can let you know what time he leaves," Jack added. "And follow him in case he doesn't head for the bar."

"Deal," Cole said. "CJ, we'll keep you informed."

"Understood," she concurred and ended the call.

"Not a woman of many words," Gus noted.

Cole snorted. "No, she's not."

"You've heard the phrase 'loose lips sink ships'?" Jasmine asked.

"Yeah, but she's like a ghost. If she hadn't shown up after the NSC attack, here in this room, in front of all of us, I'd still wonder if she exists."

"She wants to bring down Trinity," Anne Bellamy said.

Cole silently agreed. They all wanted to bring down Trinity. He understood CJ's reluctance to trust anyone but herself with her life, but she didn't know the benefits of working with a good team, one that had her back and was pushing toward the same goal.

"And she can't do it if she's dead," Charlie reminded them, her mouth set in a grim line. "As we all know. John wanted to bring down Trinity, but look where that got him."

John Halverson had been murdered. The person who'd done it had never been caught.

Cole had no intention of being Trinity's next target. And something in him stilled at the thought of CJ meeting John Halverson's fate.

Not on his watch.

Chapter Three

CJ spent the next day logged on to her laptop at a coffee shop with free Wi-Fi. It was an unsecured network, but sometimes she found being one needle in a haystack of browser users helped mask her more than logging on to unique systems with huge firewalls. Trinity had a way around firewalls. She'd searched for the first half of the day, tapping into computers, trying to find the IP address for Chris Carpenter's home computer and digging into the man's bank and phone records.

She didn't find any large sums of money deposited to Carpenter's account. If he was involved with Trinity, he might have a secret account set up in a foreign location like the Cayman Islands. She'd need access to whatever computer he used to find whatever information he might have stored regarding secret accounts and passwords. In the meantime, she wanted to follow Carpenter to find out for herself if he was meeting with anyone who had any connection to Trinity.

After a lunch of a peanut butter and jelly sandwich, she donned the black wig, knocked on Gladys's door and took Sweet Pea for a walk, going the opposite direction from Cole's town house. Somehow, she managed to stroll around several blocks, making a complete circle that landed her in front of Cole's place, though. He didn't jog by this time, and she didn't see him peering through his window, looking for her.

A stab of disappointment struck her. She couldn't understand why. She'd bet her life on remaining alone. Why would seeing a stranger occasionally mean anything to her?

Because, after a year of being alone, she knew there were people out there who had her best interests at heart. She wasn't truly alone anymore. And it felt good.

That thought warmed her cold soul. For too long, she'd had to squelch all emotions. Her training with Trinity had emphasized that point. Any recruit who cried was punished severely. After one or two beatings, she'd learned to hold back her emotions, to swallow the tears and get tough. By doing so, she lessened or erased the pain.

When she'd been tasked with killing the pregnant woman, it had been the first crack in the wall she'd built around her heart. Having the backing of Declan's Defenders was chinking away at more of the mortar that held her emotions at bay. Talking via voice or text with Cole reminded her of the vulnerability of emotions. It scared her to open up to anyone, to leave herself exposed to the kindness of others.

Hell, even the happiness Sweet Pea displayed when

she'd come to take her for a walk had pinched CJ's heart. She needed to be alone, to remain aloof, to fight her own battles.

But Trinity was bigger than one person could deal with. She'd had to get help. She'd had to trust others to get the job done.

After she left Sweet Pea with Gladys, she went back to her sublet town house, showered and changed into a little black dress she'd picked up at the second-hand store, black heels and the long blond wig. Taking a circuitous route to the nearest station, she rode the metro into DC and got off near the pub Carpenter frequented.

She arrived well before five o'clock, found a stool at the far end of the bar and ordered vodka and cranberry juice, figuring it was girlie enough for a blonde woman wearing a sexy black dress. CJ preferred whiskey or beer, but the drink was cool and refreshing. Now all she had to do was wait for Carpenter to arrive.

If he arrived.

The first thirty minutes passed with a couple tourists wandering in and ordering beer. They left after they'd finished their beers to find someplace to eat.

The bartender asked a couple of times if he could get her another drink, which CJ politely declined.

A glance at the time on her cell phone indicated it was well past five thirty and creeping up on six. CJ had begun to think Carpenter wouldn't make his usual stop and her time there would have been a waste.

Then the door opened and a man in a dark gray suit entered and found a table in a shadowy corner.

From the pictures CJ had found online, the man was Chris Carpenter.

She studied him out of the corner of her eye, taking in the nice suit and tie, the highly polished shoes and the fact that he was staring at the entrance as if he was worried or expecting someone.

CJ kept her head down, watched and waited.

A couple minutes later, another man walked through the door and took a seat at the bar. He wore an Atlanta Braves baseball cap, jeans and a Led Zeppelin revival T-shirt. After ordering a drink, he removed the cap and ran his fingers through his hair, making it stand on end. He ordered the whiskey CJ wished she was drinking.

When he turned his profile toward her, she sucked in a sharp breath.

Cole.

She couldn't forget the close-cropped, dark brown hair, square jaw and his nose that wasn't quite straight but had a bump in it like it had been broken at some point in his life.

Another man walked through the door and sat on one of the stools in between CJ and Cole. He ordered a draft beer. When the tall mug came, he lifted it, turned in his seat and looked around the bar.

Was this a man who'd come to talk to a traitor?

CJ stared at the mirror behind the bar, watching the man's every move. He turned to her, got off his stool and moved to the one next to her.

He hitched his leg up on the stool and set his mug on the bar. Then he leaned toward her. "Hey, beautiful, you come here often?"

She shook her head, not wanting to start a conversation with him.

"Can I buy you a drink?"

Again, she shook her head and lifted the half-empty glass of the drink she'd been nursing for the past hour and a half. The ice had melted and the liquid had grown lukewarm. CJ didn't care. She didn't want another drink as much as she wanted to find the leader of Trinity and put an end to the terror.

"Not much of a talker, are you?" the man said and leaned closer. "That's okay, talk is overrated. What say you and I go get some supper, then find a place with some music?"

The idiot couldn't take ignoring him as an answer. Apparently, he had to have things spelled out for him.

CJ drew in a deep breath and spoke softly but with a steely edge. "I'm not interested."

"If you want to wait until you finish your drink, I'm flexible," the man said.

She didn't look at the man, just set her drink on the bar and started talking.

"Sir, I'm not interested in drinking, eating or sleeping with you, now or in the future. You might as well move on."

The man's lips pressed into a thin line. "I'm being really nice. Asking all polite, and everything."

CJ slipped to the edge of her bar stool, ready to take the man down if he so much as touched her.

Meanwhile, a brunette, wearing a slim-line black skirt with a white button-down blouse, entered the bar, pushed a long strand of her chocolate-brown hair out of her face and looked around, as if trying to get her eyes to adjust to dim lighting. After a few minutes, she scanned the interior. She must have found who she was looking for because she didn't stand around long. Hiking her cross-body purse up onto her shoulder, she walked past Cole, CJ and the man bugging the fire out of her and slipped into the booth beside Chris Carpenter's. She sat with her back to Chris.

"You sure look hungry," the guy beside CJ was saying. "What would it hurt for you to come share a meal with me?" Obnoxious Man couldn't get the hint that his attention was unwanted.

"Darla, honey." The familiar male voice cut into Obnoxious Man's continued pressuring. "I'm sorry I was late." Cole slipped an arm over her shoulder and bent to brush a kiss across her lips.

CJ was so surprised, she forgot to breathe. When Cole set her at arm's length, he turned to the man beside her. "Do I have you to thank for keeping my fiancée company while she waited for me to get off work?"

The man's brow furrowed. "Don't know what you're talking about. Didn't know the lady was spoken for." And obviously hadn't seen Cole sitting at the bar a few stools away.

"No worries," Cole said. "My baby knows how to take care of herself." He winked and looked down at CJ. "Ready to go? We have a few stops on the way home."

She smiled, though she wanted to frown. What was his game? Then she shot a glance at the booth where Chris Carpenter had been sitting. He was gone. And so was the female who'd sat in the booth beside his.

CJ hopped up from her stool, slipped her arm through Cole's and started for the door, muttering beneath her breath, "How did you know it was me?"

"Wasn't positive at first, but once the light shone on your green eyes, I knew." He grinned as he held the door for her to leave the bar and step out onto the sidewalk.

"We've met only once before. How did you remember I had green eyes?"

He shook his head. "They reminded me of the color of the live oak leaves on the trees back home in Texas, but that would be a lie. They are actually the color of the paint job on my Hummer, a kind of gray-olive color."

CJ glanced left then right, not seeing their quarry immediately. "I'm not quite sure if that's an insult or a compliment, and I really don't care. Do you see him?"

Cole had been looking. "There. Looks like he's headed for the metro."

"Let's catch him before he gets away."

Cole had replaced his ball cap on his head. Taking her hand, he walked at a quick pace.

Though several inches shorter than Cole, CJ kept up with him and they made it to the station at the same time Chris Carpenter climbed aboard the train with the same woman who'd been sitting in the booth beside his.

COLE SPOTTED CHRIS and a woman stepping onto the train. He hurried CJ along and entered a different car before the doors shut and the train slid out of the station.

"Any idea who the woman is?" CJ asked beside him. Like him, she was staring through the windows separating their car from the next one.

Carpenter and the woman sat side by side, facing them. Cole didn't recognize her, but based on her business suit, she probably worked somewhere on Capitol Hill or in one of the business offices nearby.

What her relationship with Carpenter was, Cole could only guess. They didn't hold hands, touch or even talk to each other. But they sat together.

Cole glanced at the train map on the inside of the car. They were headed toward Arlington, Virginia. He noted that the train had several stops to make as it moved through the city toward the countryside.

Carpenter and his lady friend weren't on for long. At the second stop, they got off.

Cole and CJ stood at the exit to their car until Carpenter passed. Once they were well past them, Cole and CJ left the train and followed Carpenter and the woman to a hotel.

"I guess that explains why he's seeing a marriage counselor," CJ said.

"I'd bet my last dollar that woman he was with wasn't his wife," Cole said.

"Is it worth hanging out to find out for sure?"

"You can if you want," Cole said. "But I'm thinking it might be a good idea to plot our next move. With Carpenter being a creature of habit and going to the bar every day after work and getting a little frisky afterward, we might use that time to get into his home computer."

"You think, like I do, that he'd keep any information of value on his computer at home?"

Cole shrugged. "It would be safer at home than in the West Wing. We just need to ascertain Mrs. Carpenter's schedule and work around it."

"Tomorrow night, maybe?" CJ confirmed. "That would give us time to figure out the best plan."

"Tomorrow, as long as Mrs. C is also out of the house."

CJ held out her hand to Cole. "We're on for tomorrow night."

"Partners?" Cole took her hand in his, an electric awareness zipping up his arm and spreading throughout his body.

Her eyes narrowed. "I like to work alone. But I guess it would be better to have someone looking out for me."

"Then it's a date." Cole grinned.

"If breaking and entering someone's home is what you consider a date," CJ said, "then I guess it is."

Cole grinned all the way back to the metro. When they got on the same train heading farther into Arlington, he leaned close to her and asked. "So that was you yesterday with the black hair, walking the white dog, wasn't it?"

CJ's chin lifted. "I don't know what you're talking about."

Cole's grin broadened. "Right." He'd bet his favorite semiautomatic rifle that he was right.

Working with CJ would be a challenge. The first part of which would be getting her to trust him enough to stick around.

For a late-evening ride, the train was still crowded with people trying to get home from the city.

Aware of the fact Trinity wanted CJ dead, Cole kept a vigilant watch on the passengers, considering each and every one of them a potential Trinity agent.

A couple passengers, in particular, captured his attention. Every time he looked over at them, they were staring at CJ. Granted, in the little black dress and the blond wig, she was a knockout. But there was something else. A furtiveness about them. When they thought someone was watching them, they looked away quickly.

One was a young man wearing jeans and a brown leather jacket, his hands in the pockets.

Cole moved to place his body between the young man and CJ in case one of those pockets contained a handgun.

The other potential Trinity operative was a woman with long black hair and dark eyes. Tall, slim and athletic, she looked like she could take down a linebacker with a few well-placed side kicks to the knees.

"Is it getting warm in here to you?" CJ murmured in a low tone.

He understood what she was talking about. "Could be."

The train rolled into a station three stops from the one closest to his town house. A few people got off, but not the two Cole had his eye on.

A second before the train doors were due to close, CJ slipped out.

Cole didn't have time to react before the doors closed and the train jerked into motion.

The two people he'd been watching turned toward the platform as the train left the station.

Already, CJ had disappeared from sight.

Cole worried for her safety. Trinity agents didn't give up easily. But then CJ had survived for a year on her own. She knew how to escape and evade.

Having been a part of a combat team, Cole knew a little about stealth and camouflage. CJ brought it to an entirely different level. He hoped that by teaming with her, he didn't put her at more of a risk than she already was. If Trinity thought he could be an asset they could hold over her to force her out into the open, they wouldn't hesitate to use him. With that in mind, he pulled the same stunt as CJ at the next stop. He waited until the last moment.

As the doors started to slide closed, he stepped out onto the platform. The doors closed with the two people he'd been watching staring at him through narrowed eyes.

Cole didn't wait around for anyone else to catch up

with him. He took off on foot and jogged the rest of the way to his town house, taking a twisting, turning route, checking behind him as he went to make certain no one was following. Not that it would make a big difference. If someone wanted to find him, they could. His whereabouts weren't a secret like CJ's.

When he arrived at his place, he entered, locked the door and checked all the other locks to ensure they were secure.

Once he was certain he was alone and fairly safe, he texted CJ. Make it back?

No response.

Cole waited for the next hour, giving her time to return. When she still didn't respond, he called Declan and reported on the night. Declan promised to swing into action if needed but urged him to hang tight a while longer in case CJ came home.

He stayed awake for a long time, wondering if she was still alive and what he could have done differently to keep her from getting away without him.

He knew he couldn't have acted any faster. She had the advantage. CJ knew what she was going to do next. No one else did. Hopefully, that paid off for her and kept her alive until they could bring Trinity down.

Chapter Four

When CJ got off the train three stops short of the one leading to her sublet, she knew she had a tail. She'd hoped that by getting off at the last minute, she'd shaken any follower. Unfortunately, he'd been watching closely and hadn't been in the same car with her, so she'd not seen him until it was too late.

As soon as she stepped off the train, he dived out of the other car.

CJ quickly left the station, moving among other passengers in a hurry to the parking lot where commuters left their vehicles to catch the train into DC. When she made it to a line of cars, she ducked low, rolled under an SUV and rummaged in the satchel she'd carried in place of her usual backpack. Quickly taking off the wig, she stuffed it into the bag, pulled out a baseball cap and wound her hair up into it.

The dress was a little more difficult. Lying beneath a vehicle, she couldn't get out of it. Instead, she removed her heels, pulled out a pair of sweats, slipped them up her legs and over the short dress. CJ struggled into a hooded sweat jacket and zipped it. She slipped on her running shoes, shoved her heels into the bag and tucked the bag under her jacket.

When she was ready, she remained where she was, timing her move for when the next train was due to arrive. She looked beneath the chassis of the vehicles, searching for the feet of her pursuer. When the time came, and she didn't see any movement, she rolled out from under the SUV and straightened slowly.

Figuring her tail would be looking for her to move away from the train station, she hunkered over like a fat man in a tracksuit and lumbered toward the metro stop, arriving at the same time as a train pulled in.

Men and women in business clothing got off the train, their faces tired, their clothing creased from hours of sitting behind desks. As soon as the car emptied of the passengers for that stop, CJ boarded and found a seat near the door, dropped into it and pulled her ball cap low over her face. The man she'd seen get off the train when she had was nowhere in sight. She'd checked as she'd gotten on, looking in the other cars on either side of the one she'd stepped into.

Only a few people remained on the train headed out of DC into the neighboring municipalities, all looking like they'd had a long day and were ready to be home.

CJ stayed on a stop past the one closest to her rented town house. She didn't trust that she was still alone, though she'd lost her last follower. Always vigilant, she would walk the extra blocks to save herself from being caught.

By the time she arrived at her sublet, she was exhausted and took only a few minutes to unpack her satchel and repack her backpack with clothing she might need for quick changes the next day.

She dug out the burner phone from the satchel and glanced down at a text from Cole: Make it back?

Her heart warmed. He wanted to make sure she'd returned to her place safely. Whether it was because she was his assignment didn't matter. Someone cared enough to ask. Her fingers hovered over the letters that could spell out a response, but she held back. The more she relied on him, the more vulnerable she became, the more at risk he became. Shoving the phone into a pocket on the side of the backpack, she finished packing it for the next day.

CJ took the pack with her into the bathroom, brushed out the three wigs she kept on hand and packed them into one of the large pockets. When she was done, she stripped out of the jacket, sweats and dress, and climbed into the shower.

For the next twenty minutes, she let the water wash over her, the spray pounding into her shoulders, easing the tension. When her skin started to shrivel, she shut off the water, grabbed a towel and dried her body. As she stepped out of the shower, she heard something that sounded a lot like breaking glass.

Immediately alert, she slipped into a T-shirt and the sweatpants she'd removed minutes before and jammed her feet into the running shoes. Quietly opening the door to the bathroom, she eased out with her backpack, hurried to the bedroom door, closed and locked it quietly.

Downstairs, she could hear the crunch of some-one walking over the broken glass in heavy shoes or boots. CJ opened the French doors off the mas-ter bedroom and stepped out onto the balcony over-looking the minuscule backyard, carefully closing the door behind her.

Knowing she had only moments to spare, she slipped the backpack over her shoulders, grabbed the balcony railing and eased her legs over the edge. She lowered her body, holding on to the railing until she was as close to the ground as she could get, and let go.

When her feet hit the ground, she bent her knees and rolled onto her side to absorb the impact. A crash above indicated her intruder had smashed through the master bedroom door.

Her heart thudding against her ribs, CJ sprang to her feet and ran as fast as she could, diving into the shadows of the town house next door. She kept mov-ing, clinging to the shadows until she came to the town house Cole lived in.

For a moment, she considered running past and disappearing into the night. Leaving Cole out of her life was the right thing to do. He could easily be-come collateral damage in Trinity's quest to bring her down.

But CJ was tired.

Tired of running. Tired of fighting this battle. Tired of being alone. Knowing she would regret it later, she stopped and peered through a gap in the blinds. Cole sat in a chair, a beer in one hand, his burner phone in the other. Was he waiting for her response to his earlier question?

Before she could change her mind, she tapped on the window softly. If he didn't hear it, she would move on. She couldn't make a lot of noise and she didn't have time to stand around. Her intruder would soon figure out that she'd jumped off the balcony and would be hot on her trail.

CJ glanced around, her pulse thundering, her muscles tense, ready to move out swiftly if she needed to run.

When she looked back through the gap in the blinds, she didn't see Cole sitting in the same spot. In fact, she didn't see him at all.

Then the back door to the town house opened and the barrel of a gun poked out, followed by Cole's head.

"Don't shoot," CJ whispered. "It's me, CJ."

"What the hell?" he said in a hushed tone.

CJ hurried toward him.

When she came within reach, he grabbed her arm and yanked her through the door, closing it softly behind him.

The first thing CJ did was move out of the site of the door frame and deeper into the house, turning off lights as she went.

Cole followed her, his gun still gripped in his hand. "What's going on?"

"What? I thought you wanted to be a little closer so that you could protect me," she said as she closed even the slightest gaps in the blinds. The only light illuminating the rooms came from the streetlamp in front of the town house shining around the edges of the curtains.

Cole's hand on her arm brought her to a stop. "Seriously, what happened? Why did you ditch me on the train?"

She shrugged. "We had a tail, so I got off." CJ glanced away, her lips thinning. "My tail got off at the same time."

"Damn it, CJ." Cole's fingers gripped her shoulders, forcing her to face him. "How can I help you, if you don't let me?"

Her chin rose and she stared straight into his eyes. "What could you do that I didn't?"

"What did you do?"

"I hid, changed disguises and waited for the next train. When I got on, he didn't." She breathed in a deep breath and let it out. "But he found where I lived and broke in."

Cole swore again. "That's it. You're staying with me." He held up a hand. "I don't want to hear any argument. You and I are going to be like Siamese twins, joined at the hips."

Her lips twitched, a smile forming. His words struck her as funny. If she wasn't in such a hurry to get away from whoever was following her, she might have laughed at the image his words invoked. "We can't stay here. If he found me once, he'll find me again."

"Give me a second to put on shoes." He moved

her to the shadows of the hallway and pointed at her chest. "Stay."

"I'm not a dog."

His eyes narrowed. "On second thought…" Cole took her hand and led her into his bedroom. "I'm keeping an eye on you. You have a habit of slipping away."

"I won't this time," she promised.

"Yeah. And I'm supposed to believe that?" He shook his head and stripped out of his sweatpants.

CJ's eyes widened at the boxer briefs he wore beneath them. They fit his tight backside like a second skin. When Cole turned to face her as he shook out a pair of jeans, CJ's breath caught in her throat.

The thick bulge in front was evidence the man was built and that he was a little turned on at the moment.

He jammed his legs into the jeans and pulled them up and over the hard ridge.

CJ was almost sad he'd zipped himself into the tight denims.

He didn't bother to tuck in his T-shirt; instead, he pushed his arms into a leather jacket and shrugged it on over his shoulders. "Ready?"

She snorted. "Always. You're the one that needed to get dressed." CJ glanced around. "Got a ride?"

"In the garage."

"If we go out, he'll see us leaving."

"Then we go out with you tucked down low."

"If they know where to find me, they might also know you're involved with me in some way. That makes you as much of a target as I am." She shook her head. "I shouldn't have come."

"Too late. You did. I'm stuck with you, and we're getting out of here together." He winked. "Trust me. I'm smarter than you think."

CJ knew he'd been a competent marine, or he wouldn't have made it into the elite Marine Force Reconnaissance. But how would they get the vehicle out of the garage without attracting the attention of the man who'd broken into her town house?

The answer was…they wouldn't.

COLE INSTRUCTED CJ TO get down on the floorboard as he jumped into the driver's seat. His Hummer was facing out. He almost always backed into his garage so he could be ready to roll whenever duty called. As he jabbed the automatic door opener button on his visor, he started the engine.

Like a thief who'd just robbed a bank, Cole stomped on the accelerator and roared out of the garage onto the street, turning away from the town house CJ said she had occupied.

Just when he thought he'd made it out without encountering resistance, the back window of his Hummer exploded, spitting glass through the interior. Since the bullet hadn't gone all the way through the front windshield, Cole assumed it had lodged into the back of one of the seats.

He didn't wait around for a repeat performance. His foot pressed all the way to the floor, he raced down the street, putting as much distance as he could between them and the active shooter. Three blocks farther, he turned onto another road. If the shooter had a vehicle or a driver waiting nearby, they could catch up to them. The Hummer wasn't known for being a great getaway vehicle. Thus, distance before the shooter could mount up was key.

"CJ?"

"Yeah," she replied.

"You all right?" he asked.

She unfolded, sliding up into the passenger seat. "I'm okay." Looking over her shoulder at the shattered back window, she grimaced. "Which is more than I can say for your vehicle. I'm sorry. I shouldn't have come to you."

"Don't say that. The window can be replaced. If you had been hit…" Cole shook his head. "Well… dead is dead. There's no replacing someone."

CJ snorted. "There would be no need to replace me. I don't have a family who depends on me. Really, no one would care whether I lived or died."

Cole reached out and took her hand in his. "I'd care."

She gave him a weak smile. "Don't feel like you have to humor me."

"Don't worry. I won't feel obligated." His lips twisted. "Now, quit feeling sorry for yourself and keep your eyes peeled for anyone following us."

"Gotcha." CJ turned in her seat and peered through the shattered glass.

Racing through the residential streets of Arlington, he avoided the main arteries and aimed for one of the side roads that led to the Halverson estate. Whoever had guessed he and CJ had a connection would also know the connection Cole had to Charlie Halverson. After the kidnapping and subsequent rescue of the vice president of the United States, more people would know of the existence of Declan's Defenders. If not by the team's moniker, then by their personal names. If anyone was following Cole and CJ, they'd soon discover the meeting location at the Halverson estate.

In which case, he should get there as quickly as possible to avoid any Trinity agents who might try to beat him by using a more direct route.

He thought of calling ahead to let the team know he'd be coming in, possibly with a tail, but he put all his focus on the drive instead, mapping out the best route in his head. He'd phone when they were closer and knew more.

Finally on the country road leading to Charlie's estate, Cole increased his speed, determined to get inside the safety of the Halverson gates and wall.

At every curve, he slowed, expecting to find a vehicle blocking the road on the other side of the bend. Coming out of the last turn, he could almost taste the home stretch to the gate. That's when he saw something lying across the road. It appeared flat, like maybe a strip of construction material that had fallen off the back of a truck. It was hard to make it out in the dark. He didn't have enough time to slow down before he reached it.

He was going fifty miles per hour when, at the

last minute, he saw what it was and slammed on the brakes. Too late. His tires hit the spike strip and exploded.

"Get down!" Cole cried out.

The steering wheel jerked in his hands. He held on as best he could but had little effect as each tire hit the spikes. His Hummer careened out of control and skidded on flat tires and bare metal rims on the pavement. When they ran out of pavement, the metal wheels dug into the shoulder and the vehicle flipped, rolling down into the ditch, landing, by some miracle, upright, airbags deploying and pushing them both back in their seats.

"Get out!" CJ yelled. "Get out and run!" She struggled with the airbag and her door. When she couldn't get it open, she used the gun in her hand and hit it with the grip, breaking through the window. With the barrel, she cleaned away the jagged pieces, grabbed her backpack, pulled herself through and dropped to the ground.

It took Cole several attempts before he finally managed to shove open his door. He reached into the glove box, grabbed his handgun and dropped out.

"Run!" CJ shouted, already halfway up the other side of the ditch, heading into the darker shadows of the woods.

Cole stumbled, then found his footing and raced after her.

He'd barely reached the tree line when he heard a blast. Less than a second later, he was thrown to the ground by the force of an explosion. Metal, glass and fragments of what had once been his Hummer filled the air around him.

His ears rang as he pushed to his knees and searched the gloom for CJ.

Over his shoulder, flames rose from the burning fuel that had spilled onto the road.

Movement captured his attention out of the corner of his vision.

Slinging her backpack over her shoulders, CJ staggered to her feet, her body visible in the light from the fire and silhouetted against the darkness of the trees.

Though his head spun, and his ears rang, he realized that if he could see CJ, others could, too. Could see both of them. Hunkering low, he ran toward CJ.

"Get down," he said as he got close. "Get down!" When she didn't drop fast enough, he hit her from behind, tackling her like a linebacker.

She crashed to the ground as the sound of gunfire echoed through the trees and splinters of bark rained down on them.

The rapid report of multiple rounds being popped off indicated the shooter had a semiautomatic rifle.

"Move, but stay low," Cole urged. On his hands and knees, he clung to the shadows, following CJ as she crawled through the underbrush, moving deeper into the woods.

Crouched as they were, they wouldn't stay ahead of their attackers for long. Though his eyes had adjusted to the darkness, it was difficult to know which way they were going. As long as they kept moving away from the light of the fire, they were headed in the right direction.

The gunfire ceased and silence stretched like a bad dream. Any movement made noise when they crossed over dried leaves and twigs. But it couldn't be helped. They didn't have armored vests and helmets to protect them from gunfire. And Cole didn't have his M4A1 rifle to fire back. He'd have to get close enough to use a pistol to kill his opponents. That was too risky.

When he thought they were out of range of the rifle, Cole pushed to his feet.

CJ rose, as well.

Grabbing her hand, he took off running, zigzagging through the trees.

Not ten seconds later, gunfire announced that their pursuers weren't far behind.

Finding a wall of brush, Cole pulled CJ in behind it. Together, they lay low to the ground and waited. Perhaps someone would notify the police of the fire by the road. Hopefully, they could hold out long enough for help to arrive.

If not, Cole would wait until their opponents passed in front of them. At that point, he'd have a chance of hitting his targets with the handgun he'd jammed into his waistband.

Footsteps crashed through the underbrush, heading toward them.

With the barrel of his Glock, Cole pushed aside the brush and peered through the opening.

Two men ran through the woods, carrying what

appeared to be AR-15 rifles. The lead man aimed ahead and fired several rounds.

Cole and CJ ducked as low to the ground as they could get.

A siren wailed in the distance.

At first, the men running toward them didn't hear the emergency vehicle's alarm. They were almost to where Cole and CJ lay hidden when they stopped running and listened.

One swore. "Gotta get back to the vehicle."

"What about our target?" the other asked.

"Can't stay, or they'll find our van. Empty your clip. Maybe we'll get lucky." The lead guy turned and fired into the trees. His partner did the same.

Cole moved, covering CJ's body with his as the barrage continued for the next thirty seconds.

He lay still and waited, even after the gunfire ceased. Afraid to make a sound, he didn't dare move.

The shuffle of feet indicated the men were moving again, heading back the way they'd come.

As their footsteps faded, Cole moved off CJ's back and looked through the bushes.

Their pursuers were gone.

Cole remained hidden behind the greenery for another full minute before he spoke. "Clear."

CJ rose up to a kneeling position. "The fire's dying down."

The siren grew louder. Through the trees, they could see the flashing lights of a fire engine and the blue lights of a law-enforcement vehicle.

Cole stood and held out his hand.

CJ took it and let him draw her to her feet.

They walked back through the woods, hand in hand.

As they neared the scene of the explosion, CJ stopped in the shadows. "I'd rather not make my presence known."

Cole nodded. "Follow this road for a quarter of a mile to get past this circus. I'll call to have one of the guys come get us. But right now, I need to let the fire department and law-enforcement personnel know the driver of that burning vehicle is not dead." When CJ turned, Cole held on to her hand, forcing her to stop. "Promise me you'll be there when I shake loose of this mess."

She hesitated for a moment.

Cole squeezed her hand gently. "You've trusted me so far, why stop now?"

Her fingers tightened around his. "I'll be there."

Not sure he trusted her to keep her word, Cole pulled his gun out of his waistband and laid it in her hand that he'd been holding. "Take this. I don't want to have to declare it to the law."

She slipped it into one of her jacket pockets.

"CJ?" He cupped her cheek in his palm. "We're going to figure this out. I promise."

She looked up, the lights from the fire engine flashing in her eyes. "That's the plan."

He bent and brushed his lips across hers. "Not just a plan." He kissed her again. "A promise." He pulled her close, crushing her in his arms, his mouth coming down over hers.

Her body stiffened in his arms. But as he continued to kiss her, she relaxed, melting against him, her lips opening to him. Her hands crept up around his neck and she leaned into him.

For a long moment, the world faded away around them and Cole caressed the back of CJ's neck and slid his tongue along hers in a kiss he didn't want to end.

When he raised his head, he let go and stood back.

CJ touched a hand to her lips. "Why did you do that?"

"I don't know." He reached out and brushed his knuckles across her cheek. "But if you don't go now, I'll do it again."

She caught his hand in hers and pressed her lips into his palm. Then she turned and ran. CJ moved like a cat, slipping through the darkness, her supple body all grace in motion.

Once he was certain she was far enough out of range, Cole pulled his phone out of his pocket and called Declan.

"Cole. Tell me you aren't on the highway headed to Charlie's?"

"Sorry, but I was."

"We heard an explosion and came out to see what was going on. Was that you?" Declan asked.

"Afraid so. I was on my way to Charlie's when all hell broke loose." Cole explained what happened from CJ showing up at his door to the men blowing up his Hummer. "We're going to need a ride to Charlie's after I check in with the first responders. I'm supposed to meet CJ a quarter mile from the scene. She might have passed you in the darkness. She probably won't come out until I show up."

"Got it. We'll turn around and wait for you to come out. I'll let Charlie know. She might have some connections to get you out of there sooner rather than later."

"Thanks." Cole ended the call and emerged onto the highway amid the emergency vehicles.

At the center of the crew working the fire, Cole found the sheriff and firefighter in charge. While he gave them a rundown on what had happened, he was careful not to mention anything that had occurred prior to his being on the road where the incident had occurred. He pretended he didn't have any idea why someone would want to attack him.

Once the sheriff and the fire chief finished with him, he gave them his phone number and promised to be available to answer any further questions that arose.

"Need a ride?" the sheriff's deputy asked.

"No, thank you," Cole responded. "Already called a friend." He left the emergency crews doing what they did best and jogged down the road. He found Declan's truck less than a tenth of a mile away. Mack had moved to the backseat of the king cab. Cole jumped in and leaned forward as they drove slowly along the road to the approximate location where he'd asked CJ to wait.

All the while, he prayed that his kiss hadn't scared her off, that she would be there. Based on her reaction to his kiss, she hadn't seemed angry. Just the opposite. She'd kissed him back. What worried him was why. Had she responded the way she had because she'd liked it? Or had she given him what he wanted with the intention of ditching him and moving on by herself without raising his suspicion right away?

His breath lodged in his throat, Cole scanned the roadside, searching for the woman who'd captured his attention, his admiration and might just conquer his heart.

Chapter Five

CJ hunkered low in the shadows, watching the road, waiting for Cole, as she'd promised.

The CJ who'd been living on her own for the past year, remaining aloof and independent of anyone, itched to run and keep running. And she might have.

If not for that kiss.

Her lips still tingled and an ache she had never felt before built deep inside her.

Why had Cole kissed her? Did he think that would change anything?

She pressed her hand to her chest. It was so tight she could barely breathe. Was that a reaction to the kiss or the brush with death?

Vehicles lined up, close to the accident, their drivers waiting for the road to clear.

One by one, they moved through, the line shortening as law enforcement and firefighters cleared one lane of traffic.

A truck approached from the other direction, moving slowly. When it came within a hundred yards of her position, it stopped. The passenger door opened and a man got out. The light from the cab flashed on and then off as the door opened and closed.

CJ couldn't see who had climbed out or who was driving. She waited, sinking lower in the shadows.

"CJ?" Cole's voice called out.

Her heart skipped several beats and then slammed against her ribs, racing like a marathon runner's at the end of a course. She rose from her position and almost sprinted out into the road. Survival instincts kicked in and she stopped, looked around, searching the shadows for anyone hiding, waiting for her to come out. The men who'd come after her might only have moved down the road from the burning vehicle. They could be close, watching for her to relax and appear where they could easily pick her off.

"CJ?" Cole called again.

"I'm here," she responded, loud enough for him to hear.

"Keep talking." He headed in her direction. "Tell me when I'm getting warmer."

"You're getting warmer," she said, a smile pulling at her lips. She hadn't played hide-and-seek since she had been a little girl when her parents were still alive. The memory warmed her.

"Don't come out," Cole said, lowering his voice. "Let Declan bring the truck to us."

"I've no intention of presenting myself as a target," she said. "Keep coming."

When Cole was within range, she reached out and grabbed his arm, pulling him into the shadows with her.

"Thank God," he said and wrapped his arms around her.

She chuckled. "Did you think I'd run?"

He tipped her chin up and cupped her face with his hand. "Yes, I did."

She clucked her tongue, her pulse racing, her body on fire where it touched his. "So little faith in me," she said with forced lightness.

"So much understanding of your situation," he said softly. "You're alive because you relied on yourself and your instincts." He bent to touch his lips to hers and then raised his head. "I thought I'd scared you away."

"Me? Scared?" She gave a shaky laugh. She had been scared. Afraid of how she felt. Afraid of falling for someone and making him a bargaining chip Trinity could use to get to her.

Cole kissed her again. Hard this time. Then he stepped back. "Ready to make a run for it?"

No. She was ready for another real kiss. "I'm ready."

Cole pulled her against him, shielding her body with his. "Let's go."

Declan had moved the truck as close to the edge of the trees as he could.

Cole and CJ took off in an awkward jog toward the vehicle, Cole using his body as the first line of defense against any bullets that might be lobbed their way.

When they reached the truck, he yanked open the door and shoved her into the front passenger seat. "Stay on the floorboard," he said and jumped in behind her, slamming the door shut behind him.

CJ crouched, her arms on Cole's knees, her chin on his lap.

Declan shifted into gear and took off, spitting up gravel from the shoulder as he lurched onto the pavement.

They hadn't gone far when something pierced the back windshield and traveled through the cab and out the front windshield.

Declan cursed and slammed his foot down on the accelerator, launching the truck forward. He zigzagged across the road to make it harder for the shooter to get a bead on them. "Mack, Cole, get down!" Declan hunched over the steering wheel, keeping his head as low as possible.

Cole leaned over, covering CJ's head and shoulders with his broad frame.

Another bullet smacked the rear window.

Declan jerked the steering wheel, sending the truck careening to the left.

CJ held on to Cole's legs to keep from falling over.

Declan grunted and straightened the truck. "I think we're pulling away from them."

"I don't see a vehicle behind us," Mack said from the backseat.

"Then they were on the ground," Cole said. "They were using what appeared to be AR-15s. I doubt they could have hit us if they'd been in a vehicle."

"It won't take them long to catch up."

"Then we'll just have to stay ahead of them," Declan said, an edge to his voice. He maintained a breakneck speed, barreling down the highway.

Cole sat up and looked around. "Only about a mile

to go to get to the gate." He pulled out his phone and hit some buttons.

CJ shifted to ease a cramp forming in her calf.

"Someone open the gate and be ready to close it immediately," Cole said into the phone. "We're coming in hot and might have a tail."

When he ended the call, he looked down at her. "Are you okay?"

CJ gave him a grimace. "I'm fine." She tilted her head toward Declan. Blood dripped from his side onto the seat. "But your friend isn't."

Declan's face was pale and his knuckles were white on the steering wheel. "I'm fine," he said through gritted teeth. "We're almost there."

Cole ripped off his jacket and pulled his T-shirt over his head.

"Where were you hit?" he demanded.

"Doesn't matter. We can take care of it when we get to Charlie's."

"Where?" Cole snapped.

Declan's lips pressed into a tight line. "Right side, just below my ribs."

Cole leaned over and pressed his T-shirt against Declan's side.

Declan took his hand off the wheel for a second, to direct Cole's hand to the spot, and winced.

"You keep your hands on the wheel. I've got this," Cole said.

CJ knelt on the floor and leaned over the console. "Let me," she said.

She slipped her hand beneath Cole's and held the shirt in place, applying pressure to the wound.

Declan slowed the truck.

Cole put his hand around CJ's hip and held on as they turned and passed through an impressive iron gate.

As soon as they were through, the gate shut. Men holding AR-15s waved them past and turned to face the gate and any threat that might present itself.

Declan picked up speed, taking them along the winding road into the estate, coming to a stop in front of the Halverson mansion. Declan shifted into Park and leaned his head against the headrest. "I can take it from here," he said, reaching around to the wad of T-shirt soaked in his blood.

"The heck you can. I've got this until they get you out and someone else can take over." CJ maintained pressure on Declan's wound.

Charlie Halverson, her assistant Grace and her butler Roger Arnold hurried down the steps to the truck.

"We're going to need an ambulance. Declan caught a bullet," Cole said as he dismounted and came around the other side.

"Calling 9-1-1." Mack hit the numbers on his phone while climbing out of the back.

"Help me get him out," Cole said.

Arnold joined Cole as he opened the driver's door.

Grace stood behind them, her eyes wide, her face pale.

"I'll get blankets, towels and sheets." Charlie ran back inside.

Cole reached in, hooked Declan beneath his shoulders and dragged him across the seat and out of the cab.

"I can get myself out," Declan said through gritted teeth.

"Right," Cole grunted as he took the bulk of Declan's weight, looping his arm over his neck as the injured man stumbled down out of the vehicle.

Arnold slipped under Declan's other arm.

CJ scrambled across the seat and out to walk behind them, pressing the shirt against the wound in Declan's back.

Grace hurried up the stairs and opened the other side of the double doors, her face tight, her expression worried.

Guilt stabbed CJ in the heart. Declan was injured because the shooters were gunning for her. If the man died, it would be CJ's fault.

Collateral damage.

She shouldn't have gotten them involved. This was her battle. She should have fought it alone.

An overwhelming desire to turn around and run from here swamped her. But if she did that, she'd be abandoning them. They were in it with her, whether she wanted them now or not. She had to stay. To help. Just as they'd helped her.

Charlie met them in the front foyer. "Bring him into the sitting room. I spread sheets out over the sofa."

They carried Declan in and laid him on the sofa.

"You're making a big deal out of a little flesh

wound," Declan said. He grunted as they rolled him onto his stomach to better see the wound.

CJ shrugged out of her backpack, dropped it on the floor and pulled her knife out of the scabbard strapped to her leg.

Cole gripped the hem of Declan's shirt and held it tight.

CJ dug her knife into the fabric to cut an opening, then sheathed her knife and ripped the fabric up his back, exposing the bullet hole.

Grace gasped. "Oh, Declan."

"Grace, I'm all right," Declan said, his voice muffled against the sofa's cushion. He held out his hand.

Staying out of the way, Grace sank to her knees and held his hand. "Sure, babe. Just a flesh wound." A tear slipped from the corner of her eye. She glanced away. "Any news on that ambulance?"

"On its way," Mack confirmed. "ETA five minutes."

Arnold approached, folding a hand towel into a square. He placed it on the wound and applied pressure.

"Who's on the gate?" Cole asked.

"Mustang, Gus and Jack," Mack said.

"They know to check before they open the gate?" Cole asked.

"Roger," Mack said. "Just got off the phone with them."

CJ stood back, watching as the team rallied around their injured comrade. She wanted to help, but they had everything under control.

Her gaze met Cole's.

He stepped away from the sofa and captured her arm in his, drawing her with him out of the sitting room. "Are you all right?" he asked.

She nodded. "I'm fine. It's your friend who's injured. He wouldn't have been if I hadn't gotten into the truck."

Cole shook his head. "Did you shoot him?"

CJ's brow dipped. "No. But—"

"Then it's not your fault. Those men shot him."

"But—"

He pressed a finger to her lips, shaking his head slowly. "You don't have to do this alone anymore. We are going to help you."

"You don't understand," CJ said. "Trinity won't stop until I'm dead."

"Then we have to stop Trinity. That was our goal. Whether we'd met you or not." He smiled down at her. "You've already helped us once. You might as well stick with us."

"Are you speaking for everyone on your team?" CJ shook her head. "They might not agree."

"Your situation is exactly why we established Declan's Defenders," a voice said from behind Cole.

Cole turned to face Charlie Halverson and smiled. "Right. It's what we do."

Charlie smiled at CJ. "And until we stop Trinity, you can stay here."

"I can't impose on you," CJ said.

"Yes, you can. What's the use of having a big house if I can't share it?" She nodded to Cole. "And since you're assigned to help CJ, you'll stay, as well. If you want, I can show you to your rooms."

"If it's all the same to you," CJ said, "I want to wait until I know Declan will be okay."

As if on cue, Mack exited the room. "Fire truck, ambulance and two sheriffs' vehicles just passed through the gate."

Charlie spun and headed for the sitting room. "How's our patient?"

Mack followed. "Cranky."

"He has a right to be." Charlie's voice faded.

CJ started to follow.

Cole gripped her arm, his eyes narrowed. "So, you'll stay?"

Her lips tightening, CJ hesitated. She might be making a big mistake, but she nodded. "I'm staying."

Cole relaxed. "Good. It will be easier for me to help you, if I know where you are." They stood outside the door of the sitting room, staring in at Declan who was lying on the sofa, holding Grace's hand. "I'm not sure how you've managed to lie low, but I'm willing to bet it wasn't by talking to the police or sheriff's deputies."

She glanced out the window at the vehicles pulling up to the front of the estate. "True."

"You might want to disappear while they're here," Mack called out. "We'll avoid mentioning you as a passenger in the truck."

"Or the Hummer," Cole added.

Once again, they were putting their lives and integrity on the line for her.

Cole touched her arm. "Just go with it and get scarce."

CJ nodded. "Thank you."

Charlie led her to another room in the house that would allow her to watch without being spotted and questioned.

These people had gone above and beyond for her. No one had done that for her since…

She couldn't remember.

Her eyes stung and filled. She blinked hard, appalled at the sudden emotional response. Hadn't she learned anything from Trinity? Crying showed weakness. Never cry.

COLE HOVERED IN the massive entryway as the EMTs worked to stabilize Declan and load him into the ambulance. He kept a close watch on the door Charlie had led CJ through. He didn't trust her not to run. The woman was skittish and rightly so.

The same first responders who had been at the scene of the Hummer fire were the ones who'd arrived in front of Charlie's home.

While Declan was being cared for, the law-enforcement professionals spent a lot of time examining the truck and asking questions of Cole and Mack.

The ambulance left for the hospital with Grace riding in the back, still holding Declan's hand.

What seemed like hours later, the sheriff's deputies departed.

CJ emerged into the foyer, joining Charlie, Mack, Roger Arnold and Cole.

"After two attacks, I think it would be best to maintain perimeter security for the night," Cole said.

"Arnold and I will help Charlie's security guards. Mustang, Walsh and Snow will cover the night perimeter," Mack said.

"I can pull night duty to relieve someone," Cole offered.

"That goes for me, as well," CJ said.

Mack shook his head. "We can only cover so much. If anyone gets by, Cole will be your only defense."

CJ stiffened. "I can defend myself."

"Which is a huge advantage," Cole said. "It means while I'm watching your six, you can be watching mine. We're a team, now. As a team, we look out for each other."

"That's right," Mack agreed.

"And we will also be Charlie's last line of defense," Cole added.

"With everyone but you and Cole on the gate and walls, I'll feel a lot better knowing I have two trained professionals watching out for me," Charlie said.

CJ slung her backpack over her shoulder.

Charlie took her hand. "Now, if you two will come with me, I'll show you where you can sleep."

Cole followed CJ and Charlie up the sweeping staircase to the second level.

"You can have the blue room, CJ, and Cole will be in the room beside you, should you need assistance." She opened the door and stepped inside. "There's a bathroom across the hall. I'll bring you something to sleep in, and I'll have your clothing cleaned and ready for you by morning."

"I don't want to be a bother," CJ said. "I have some things of my own. Although, nothing in the way of sleepwear."

Charlie laughed. "Just so you know, you're not the first one of our rescues to stay here. Grace and I have amassed a stash of clothing in different sizes. Seems we're getting people who come to us in similar circumstances. You know, on the run, with nothing but the clothes on their backs." Charlie's brow furrowed. "It's nothing to be ashamed of. And we love to help. I would hope that if I find myself in a similar situation, someone will help me."

"Thank you," CJ said. For the second time in one day, that stinging feeling swept through her eyes and she blinked hard. She dropped her backpack on a chair.

"I'll be right back with those clothes." Charlie left CJ in the room with Cole.

"Are you all right?" Cole asked.

CJ blinked, squared her shoulders and faced him. "I'm perfectly fine."

He touched a hand to her cheek. "Then why are you crying?"

CJ batted his hand away from her cheek and wiped her hand across a damp spot, appalled that a tear had slipped out of her eye and made a trail down her face. "I don't cry," she said through gritted teeth. "I never cry."

"There's no dishonor in crying." Cole's fingers curled around her arms.

"There is if it's me."

Cole's jaw hardened. "Is that what you learned from Trinity?"

"I learned it even before Trinity, when they placed me in a foster home. No one cares about orphans. They're expendable. Like their parents."

"No, CJ. They aren't. Every child deserves to be loved and looked after."

She snorted and turned away. "You grew up in a different world than the one I grew up in."

"That doesn't make mine the only way to grow up," Cole said.

"Or mine wrong," CJ whispered. "Just different. And we learn to adapt to our environments."

Cole dipped his head. "Granted." He cupped her cheek again. "But you don't live in that world anymore."

"Don't I?" She stared up at him, her heart pinching hard in her chest. "Until Trinity is wiped off the face of this planet, I will never have another life. I will always be on the run, looking over my shoulder, expecting someone to shoot me in the back."

"You have me, now. I've got your back." He leaned close and kissed her cheek where the tear had been. "I promise to do my very best to keep you safe from harm." He kissed the other cheek.

"You don't understand Trinity," CJ murmured, her heart fluttering. "They're relentless."

With his thumb, he tipped her chin up. "I can be relentless, as well."

CJ shifted her gaze from his eyes to his lips. How she wanted him to press his mouth to hers. She could almost taste his lips. "It could take years to end their terror."

"I'm in this for the long haul." He lowered his head, his lips capturing hers.

For a long moment, he held her until footsteps echoed in the hallway.

Cole released her and stepped back as Charlie entered the room with an armload of clothing. "I forgot to ask you what size you wore, so I grabbed a few things in a couple different sizes."

Heat rose in CJ's cheeks. She held out her hands to take the pile. "Thank you. I'm sure I can find something that will work."

"If you'll leave the things you're wearing now outside the door, I'll have Roger collect them. We can have them cleaned and back to you by morning."

"Please, I can do my own laundry, if you point me to the washing machine," CJ said.

Charlie shook her head. "Roger won't let anyone touch the washer or dryer. He just replaced them with a fancy new set and insists on doing all the laundry. He lets others help fold, but he won't let anyone near the new machines." Charlie chuckled. "You'd never guess the man is former British Army."

CJ's eyes widened. "How did you get such a man to be your butler?"

Charlie shrugged. "My husband hired him. I think

he was looking for a less dangerous position after he was injured and retired from the SAS, the Special Air Service, the Brits' special forces."

Cole snorted. "How's that working out for him?"

Charlie grinned. "Let's just say his skills as a butler are impeccable. But his skills from his SAS days have saved our butts on more than one occasion." She looked around the room. "If you need anything else, just ask me, Grace or Roger. Although, Grace will be at the hospital until Declan is released. Which, by the way, should be soon. I received word the bullet missed all the vital organs."

CJ drew in a deep breath and let it out in a long sigh. "I'm glad to hear that." A weight lifted off her chest and she breathed freely for the first time in a few hours.

"The doctor said he'll be fine as long as he doesn't get an infection. He's got Declan on antibiotics and pain medications." Charlie's lips thinned. "We have to find the people who are doing this and put a stop to their brand of terrorism."

CJ and Cole nodded.

Charlie's face lightened. "On that note, I'll leave you two to rest. Good night." The widow left them and walked to the far end of the hallway to her suite of rooms.

Once the door closed, Cole turned to CJ. "You need rest. If you need anything else, all you have to do is yell. I'll hear you."

"I'll be fine," CJ said. "I'm glad your teammate will be okay."

Cole shook his head. "It would take a lot more than a mere bullet to bring that man down." He smiled. "And that's not the first bullet he's caught." He crossed to the door. "You can have the shower first. I want to go check on a few things with Jonah."

Still holding the collection of clothing, CJ nodded. "Thank you for being there for me. I know it's your job, but I still appreciate it."

Cole's brow furrowed. "It's not just a job, CJ." He closed the distance between them, took the clothes from her hands and laid them on the bed. Then he cupped her cheeks in his hands. "It's more than the job. I kinda like you." Then he kissed her hard, his mouth descending on hers, taking and coaxing her to give back.

She gasped, her lips opening to him, allowing him to sweep in and kiss her like their tomorrows were uncertain.

When he finally raised his head, he stepped back, his hands falling to his sides. "You have every right to slap my face. And I encourage you to do so, if you don't want me to do that again."

She pressed a hand to her throbbing lips, her tongue tied and her voice lodged in her throat.

"Now, I have to go before I do something we might both regret." He spun on his heels and left the room, closing the door behind him.

CJ should have been relieved, but she couldn't help wondering what he might regret doing. Her only regret at the moment was that he didn't do whatever it was.

Chapter Six

Cole fought the desire to stay with CJ, pick her up and toss her on the bed. Then he'd make sweet love to her through the night.

He adjusted his jeans, without hope of loosening the tight constraints. Time would accomplish that. Or a cold shower.

He needed to meet with Jonah to see if the young computer geek had any information for them to go on. They had been operating in the dark for far too long.

Any one of them could have taken that bullet. Mack, who'd been seated in the backseat, had been lucky it hadn't hit him.

Cole descended the staircase, the taste of CJ's mouth lingering in his. She was so tempting. And he'd been wrong to take advantage of her when she'd been through so much over the past year. Hell, over her entire life. She didn't need a man coming on to her. She'd had enough men in her life telling her what to do and when to do it. She deserved to make her own decisions, not have him forcing one on her.

But then, she hadn't fought him. In fact, she'd

kissed him back. But was that because she'd wanted to? Or had she gone along with him because that was what was expected?

Cole could have kicked himself for succumbing so easily to his desires without taking CJ's wants and needs into consideration.

Bottom line, he had to keep his hands and lips to himself.

Jonah was in the war room beneath John Halverson's old study, tapping away on his computer keyboard.

Cole sat at the computer beside his and clicked the mouse to bring the computer to life. "Anything new?" he asked, hoping and praying for a fresh lead. Anything that could steer them in the right direction. They'd had so little to go on so far.

"I got word that the FBI and Secret Service investigators followed up with Chris Carpenter about the text message he sent to Tully before the attack. Carpenter swears he didn't even have his cell on him that morning. He'd left it at home."

"Interesting," Cole muttered. "If he didn't send the text, who sent it for him?"

"It might be worth tapping into his computer at home to see if we can find anything, but he doesn't leave it on or tied into the internet when he's not at home," Jonah said. "I've tried for the past few hours and, apparently, he doesn't log on very often. There's a limit to what we can get from here. We need to send someone in to do a download of everything on his hard drive."

"What about his desktop at work?"

"It might be worth getting into, but he has it secured with a password and government common access card. It would take me a lot more time to hack into it than it would to send someone in to swipe his card and access it while he's away from his desk."

"Can you get me and CJ inside the West Wing like you did for Snow when he went to work for Anne as her assistant?"

Jonah grinned. "Already have you and CJ in their system. You as yourself and CJ as Charlotte Jones. All I need are pictures to go on the cards and you're golden." He tilted his head toward the camera behind him. "If you'll stand in front of the camera, I'll get yours ready right now."

"I can have CJ come down after she showers so that you can take her picture."

Jonah nodded.

"I can do it now," a voice said from behind them.

Cole turned to find CJ standing at the bottom of the staircase leading into the basement war room.

"I thought you would be in the shower."

She shrugged. "I needed a drink of water. When I came downstairs, I heard your voice and came to see if you'd learned anything else."

"Well, good. We can take care of this now." Jonah stood and stepped behind the camera.

"Aren't you concerned someone might recognize you?" Cole said. "We got some of the Trinity sleepers who'd been working at the White House. There could be more."

CJ raised a single finger. "Hold that thought." She turned and ran up the stairs.

Cole could hear her footsteps ascending the staircase, moving quickly. Then they were coming down again and CJ entered the war room, her backpack in her hands. She placed it on the conference table in the middle of the room and rummaged inside.

A moment later, she pulled out a black wig and a blond wig and held them up. "Which would be more appropriate for the office?"

"Blond," Jonah said at the same time Cole said, "Black."

CJ's brow furrowed. "Seriously?"

Cole frowned at Jonah and then faced CJ. "You'll be a little more invisible with the black wig."

"Then black it is." She pulled her auburn hair up and secured it in a ponytail that she then wrapped around the base several times, securing it in place using pins. Tipping her head down, she pulled the wig over her scalp and tucked in any stray strands of dark red hair.

Straightening, she slipped a pair of black-framed glasses onto her nose. The transformation was uncanny.

Jonah chuckled. "Perfect."

Her costume didn't make CJ any less desirable in Cole's books. In fact, it made him want her even more. Though CJ was a knockout with black hair and those thick, black-framed glasses, Cole wanted to tear them off her and reveal the beautiful woman she was beneath. She shouldn't have to disguise who she really was.

"If you'll step in front of the camera, I'll get this ID card made for you. I've set you up as Chris Carpenter's temporary assistant. You'll be filling in for Dr. Millicent Saunders until she's back from medical leave."

"The woman who was run down over a week ago by Trinity," Cole confirmed.

Jonah nodded. "I understand she'll be out on convalescent leave for a couple more weeks. Cole is coming in as tech support to manage a work order Carpenter put to have his office rearranged, moving his desk, phone and computer to a different wall."

"A worker out to move his stuff?" CJ asked.

"He put in the request over a month ago. I imagine it's been low on their priority list," Jonah said.

"You sure we'll get in with these cards?" CJ stood in front of the camera and waited for Jonah to snap the picture.

"I got Jack Snow in, I can get you in," Jonah said.

"Remind me not to make you mad at me," Cole murmured.

"I can get you in, but you'll have to figure out how to get a backup of Carpenter's hard drive without him catching on to you."

"We'll get Anne and Jack to show us the ropes," Cole said.

"I'll have the kinks worked out by the time you leave for work in the morning." Jonah clicked on the computer and waited while the information and image imprinted on the card. When it was done, he handed the card to CJ. "Run it through the scanner." He tipped his head toward the card reader set up in the corner of the room. "It should work the same at the West Wing. I'll also create a Virginia driver's license matching your assumed name—in case the Secret Service question you. Anne said they've tightened security since she and the VP were involved in that foiled kidnapping."

"Great." Cole shook his head. "What are the chances we'll have our cover blown before we even get inside?"

"One in ten?" Jonah quipped.

"Odds aren't all that great," Cole said, digging into a drawer and pulling out two tiny, flat, round disks. He held them up. "These look like watch batteries. We need to drop one into Carpenter's pocket. That way, we can track where he goes. He might lead us to whomever is pulling his strings, if in fact he's one of Trinity's agents. Even if he isn't part of Trinity, they might be using him to get what they want."

Cole glanced over at CJ.

She didn't look convinced about their ability to get inside the West Wing.

"I can get Anne Bellamy to help me get into Chris's office. You don't need to go."

"What excuse will Anne have to be in his office?" CJ shook her head. "No, I need to go. As a temporary replacement for Dr. Saunders, I would have more reason to be in Carpenter's office than Anne would. No use in her getting caught snooping. If I lose my job there, it's no big deal. I'm only a temporary employee."

"Like I said," Jonah interjected. "I'll have all this squared away by morning, and I'll have Cole with administrative authority to get onto Carpenter's computer." He waved them away. "Go on. Get some sleep."

"What about you?" Cole asked.

"I can sleep tomorrow. You two need this by morning. I'll have it ready." Already, Jonah was back at his computer, his fingers flying over the keyboard.

CJ removed the wig and stuffed it into her backpack along with the black-framed glasses. "Thankfully, Charlie had a skirt, a white blouse and some black pumps in the stack of clothing. Hopefully, it'll be sufficient business attire for the job."

"I'm sure it will be." Cole took CJ's elbow. "We'd better leave the man to his work." He led her up the stairs and turned toward the kitchen instead of the staircase. "I could use a drink and something to eat."

CJ's stomach rumbled. "I hadn't realized that I haven't eaten since breakfast."

Cole shook his head. "Come to think of it, neither have I. Let's see what Charlie's chef left in the refrigerator. Carl's one of the best cooks the Navy let get away."

He opened one side of the double-door refrigerator. "I think we hit the jackpot." He pulled out a glass platter filled with slices of ham. "Care for a ham and cheese sandwich?"

"I'd love one." CJ pressed a hand to her belly. "Know where I can find plates?"

Together they unearthed condiments, plates and a knife. Minutes later, they had two thick ham sandwiches lying on plates and two glasses of milk.

"And I thought I was the only one who liked milk with my sandwich." He grinned.

"I'm all for strong bones. A big glass of milk with my sandwich is one of the few memories I have from my childhood before I went to train at Trinity." She took a bite and closed her eyes, a moan rising up her throat.

Cole's groin tightened. "You need to stop that right now," he said through gritted teeth.

Her eyes opened and widened. "Stop what?"

"Never mind." Cole focused on his sandwich and milk, refusing to look up at CJ. The woman was making him nuts. He finished his sandwich and milk and was surprised to see that CJ had finished hers as quickly. They rinsed their plates and glasses and placed them in the dishwasher.

Back at the top of the stairs, Cole walked CJ to her door and waited while she entered before he headed for his own room.

"Cole," CJ called out.

Cole turned, his pulse picking up. He wanted so badly to take CJ into his arms and hold her. He couldn't understand how he'd come to this point so quickly with a woman he'd known only a short time.

She stared at him for a long moment. "Why did you kiss me?"

He closed his eyes, drew in a deep, calming breath and let out it before opening his eyes again. "To tell the truth... I don't know. I can't seem to stop myself."

CJ's eyes flared and her tongue swept across her lips. "Are you sorry you did it?"

His gaze captured hers. "Are you?" He held his breath, wanting to know the truth but afraid of her response.

UNSURE OF THIS mating game people played, CJ finally shook her head. "No, I'm not sorry you did it." In a lower voice, she continued. "I'm only sorry you won't do it again."

Cole crossed the floor, pulled her into his arms and kissed her before the last consonant rolled off her tongue. He crushed her mouth with his in a soul-capturing kiss that rocked her to her very core.

When he finally allowed her to breathe again, he pressed his forehead to hers. "I can't keep doing this."

"Why not?" she asked.

"Because, the more I do it, the more I want."

Her heart fluttered, an unusual feeling to the hardened warrior inside her. "That's funny," she said with a little laugh.

"Why is it funny?" he asked, pulling back to look into her eyes.

She met his gaze unflinchingly. "Because that's exactly how I feel." CJ reached around him and gave the door a gentle push, letting it swing shut behind Cole. Her breath hitched as she made a decision. "Don't go. Please."

"Are you sure this is what you want?" Cole shoved a hand through his hair. "I can leave now. But if I stay, I'll want much more than just a kiss. Tell me to leave now."

CJ grabbed his hand and brought it to her lips. "I need a shower after rolling around in the woods." Her lips curled upward on the corners.

"So do I."

"Care to join me?" she asked, her voice thick and gravelly, strange to her own ears.

Cole pulled her close to him, again in a long, passionate kiss.

When he tore his mouth away, he scooped her up in his arms. "A shower for my lady," he said and kissed the tip of her nose.

With his hands full, he couldn't maneuver the door handle.

CJ reached out, twisted it and pulled it open.

Cole carried her through and across the hallway to the bathroom where he set her on her feet.

Grabbing the hem of her shirt, CJ pulled it up over her head and let it fall to the floor. Then she gripped his T-shirt and tugged it up his torso, stopping halfway up.

Apparently impatient to get naked, Cole tore his shirt the rest of the way off and tossed it into a corner.

CJ reached behind her back for the clasp to her bra.

Cole brushed her hands away and fumbled with the hooks, releasing them and sliding the straps slowly over her shoulders and down her arms. As he did so, her breasts fell free of the garment.

With her breath arrested in her lungs, she fought to draw more in. As her chest rose, so, too, did her breasts, into Cole's cupped palms.

How warm and rough they were against her nipples. Sweet abrasion that made the heat rise low in her belly and her center ache for more.

He trailed kisses from the corner of her mouth down the long line of her neck and over her collarbone.

"I'm not very good at this," she admitted, her voice breathy, her hands spanning his hard chest, touching the smooth planes, reveling in the strength of his muscles beneath her fingertips. She had to see more, feel more, and press her body to his in all the right places.

CJ undid the drawstring of her sweatpants, kicked off her shoes and pushed her sweats down her legs, stepping free.

Cole reached into the shower stall and turned on the water. When it had warmed, he finished undressing, toeing off his boots and shucking off his jeans. When he stood naked in front of CJ, she had trouble breathing.

The man was beautiful from the shock of dark hair to the tips of his toes. His broad shoulders seemed to fill the bathroom.

He took her hand and stepped into the shower, ducking beneath the spray, letting the water run over his head and shoulders and across his chest. When he was good and wet, he turned and let her stand beneath the spray.

A shower had always been a means of cleansing her body, nothing more.

Cole showed CJ how much more a shower could be. That it could be a gentle ministration, something tender and sexy at the same time. He lathered a bar of soap in his hands and rubbed the suds over her shoulders and along the long, smooth line of her arms. Then he captured her hips in his soapy hands and followed the curve of her waist up to cup her breasts in his palms.

CJ sucked in a sharp breath, the movement pressing her breasts more firmly into his hands.

He thumbed her nipples and circled them, again and again, the suds washing free of her skin as the spray sluiced over her body. Then he bent to take one of them in his mouth, sucking gently on the little rosy-brown bud. Flicking it with his tongue, he had her so worked up she could barely breathe.

Cole cupped the backs of her thighs and lifted her, pressing her against the cool tile. "You're driving me crazy."

"That's my line," she said, kissing the droplets off his forehead. She wrapped her legs around his waist and sank down until the tip of his shaft nudged her entrance.

He closed his eyes, as if he was in pain, and then opened them again. "Not yet."

He set her on her feet, poured shampoo into his hands and lathered her hair.

CJ had never had a man wash her hair. His hands were gentle, and he kissed her often before he turned her back to the water, tipped her head beneath the spray and rinsed the suds from her strands.

Then he lathered his hands again and smoothed them over her entire body from the back of her neck to the tips of her toes, slowing to dip his fingers inside her, making her legs shake and her entrance slick with more than soap.

When Cole was done, CJ took over, lathering his body, exploring every square inch of skin. When she came to his jutting erection, she circled it with both hands and slid her fingers up and down, loving the contrast of the velvety softness of the skin encasing his hardness. She knelt in the shower's spray and took him into her mouth, tonguing the tip and then tracing a circle around the circumference.

Cole's body tensed and his fingers dug into her hair, holding her close. When she took all of him into her mouth, he sucked in a breath and held it.

She leaned back, letting him out almost all of the way before taking him in again.

Settling into a rhythm, she sucked him in and out until his fingers dug into her scalp and he pushed her away.

"Too close," he said through gritted teeth.

She shook her head, a smile curling her lips. "Never." When she tried to take him again, he pulled her to her feet and set her outside the shower on the bath mat. "We're done here."

She blinked the water from her eyes, a frown pulling her brow downward. "Done?" No way. She wanted so much more.

"Done. Here." He nodded toward the shower as he stepped out beside her on the bath mat. With quick, efficient movements, he toweled her dry.

Using a big, fluffy towel, CJ returned the favor, lingering over that prominent protrusion, her body on fire, begging to consummate their time together. She might never have this kind of opportunity again. Being from completely different backgrounds, what were the chances that what they were feeling and doing would last more than a night, maybe two? She'd take whatever she could get and save the memories for when she was alone once again.

Once they were dry, Cole wrapped a towel around his waist and one around CJ's body. Then he scooped CJ up into his arms and strode toward the door.

She reached down to twist the knob, open the door and peer out. "Coast is clear."

Cole strode across the hallway, nudged open the door to her bedroom and carried her over the threshold. He didn't slow until he reached the bed. He set her on her feet and backed her up until her knees bumped into the mattress and she sat.

"Don't move." Cole stepped away from her and rummaged in the nightstand. When he didn't find what he was looking for, he left the room and returned to the bathroom.

CJ leaned over, her gaze following him through the door until he disappeared. She held the towel up over her breasts, her body on fire, barely cooling, even after he left her alone.

Cole was back in moments, carrying his jeans,

pulling his wallet from the back pocket. He dug into the folds and pulled out a small foil package with a triumphant grin.

"I'm glad someone is thinking." CJ stood and took the packet from his fingers. At the same time, she let the towel slide down her body to pool at her feet. "Now, where were we?"

Cole jerked the towel free from his hips and sent it sailing across the room. "I think we were about to rock the world."

She tore open the packet and slid the protection over his engorged shaft. Backing up to the bed, she sat and scooted backward across the mattress.

Following, Cole climbed up onto the bed, settled between her legs and leaned over her. His staff nudged her opening.

CJ let her knees fall to the side, ready to take him into her.

Cole hesitated, bending to claim her lips. "Not yet," he repeated.

"Seriously?" she said, her voice a breathy whisper. "I want you. Now."

"I promise. I'll get there. But first…" He trailed kisses along her jaw and down the length of her neck. When he reached her breasts, he cupped one while he tongued, nipped and licked the tip of the other. When the nipple tightened into a hard bead, he moved to the other breast and gave it the same treatment.

CJ's blood hummed through her veins, molten hot. Heat coiled at her core, her body willing him to take her. But he wasn't ready.

Cole worked his way down her torso to the triangle of hair covering her sex. He paused, parted her folds and blew a warm stream of air over that special place. Without giving her time to breathe, he thumbed that nubbin of flesh and replaced his thumb with his tongue, tapping, flicking and laving her until she writhed beneath him.

When she thought she couldn't take any more, he flicked her again, sending her shooting over the edge. She arched her back, digging her heels into the mattress. Her channel throbbed with the intensity of the sensations splintering through her.

What seemed like seconds later, she fell back to earth, her need still strong, her desire to have Cole washing over her. All of Cole. Inside her. Now.

She laced her fingers into his hair and dragged him up her body.

"Hey, the hair is attached," he said, chuckling as he leaned over her, his gaze capturing hers. "Ready?"

"What do you think?" she quipped as she gripped his buttocks and guided him home.

He sank into her, moving slowly, letting her adjust to his girth. When he'd gone as far as he could, he pulled back out and started all over again.

The pace was far too slow for CJ. She wanted all of him, hard, fast and completely. Her hands still on his buttocks, she set the rhythm, showing him how she wanted it.

He complied, taking over to the point she let her hands fall to her sides where she curled them into the comforter and raised her hips to meet him thrust for thrust.

Cole moved in and out of her, pumping hard, his face tight, his body tense. After one last thrust, he buried himself to the hilt and held steady, his shaft throbbing against the walls of her channel.

A few moments later, he collapsed on top of her and rolled her onto her side, maintaining their intimate connection.

Cole draped a hand over her bare hip and sighed. "I didn't intend to make love to you," he said.

"And now that you have?" she asked, holding her breath for his answer, sure he'd say he wished he hadn't.

"Now that I have, I don't know how I'll keep from doing it again." He leaned close to her and pressed a kiss to her lips. "You are amazing."

CJ let out the breath she'd been holding and laughed. "You're not so bad yourself."

"What are we going to do now?" he asked.

"What do you mean?" CJ asked. "Just because we had sex, doesn't change anything."

A frown dented Cole's brow. "The hell it doesn't. It changes everything."

"How so?"

"I'm thinking, since I'm too involved in you, I might lose my situational awareness." He cupped her cheek. "I might not be the right person to protect you."

CJ stiffened in his arms. "Are you trying to quit on me?"

"I don't want to, but how can I provide your protection when all I want to do is make love to you again?"

"I never said I needed protection," she reminded him.

"But you know, as well as I, that you do need someone to have your six."

"Let me put it this way. I don't want anyone providing my protection—which I don't need—unless it's you." She frowned across at him. "Unless you're trying to break it off with me. If that's the case, you don't have to come up with any excuses. You can just leave."

She held up her hand to cut off his next words. That stinging sensation burned her eyes. CJ held tightly to her emotions. "And don't worry, you won't break my heart. I never had one to begin with."

It was a lie. If she didn't have a heart, why the hell did it feel like it was cracking…right down the middle?

Chapter Seven

Cole lay for a long time after CJ went to sleep, going over her words in his mind. The woman was delusional. *Never had a heart to begin with?* That was horse hockey. The woman had more heart than even she knew. When they'd first encountered her and learned of her defection from Trinity, she'd told them the triggering event had been her assignment to kill a pregnant woman. The fact that she couldn't pull the trigger on the woman and her unborn baby said it all. And she'd risked her own safety, coming out of hiding to alert Anne Bellamy to an attack on the White House.

The woman cared more than she would admit. And he'd be a real bastard to think he could make love to her and walk away.

CJ had been left behind as a child, sucked into a killer organization at a young age and given little to no love. That she cared enough to help others was amazing in itself. One didn't learn that in the environment where she'd been raised. That kind of compassion was as much a part of her as the color of her glorious auburn hair.

Cole stared at her in the little bit of starlight making its way through the windows into the bedroom. He'd been right, telling her that he was the wrong man for the job of protecting her. With her around, he'd have a hard time concentrating on the little clues that might pop up. His attention would be on her and his mind on what he could be doing with her behind closed doors.

If he wanted to remain her protector, he had to be careful and retain his focus. No matter what, he couldn't let anyone slide through his defenses and get to her. All it took was one well-aimed bullet to end her life.

Though Cole hadn't known her for long, he realized he wanted to know her even more. One night of making love to the strong, determined woman could not be the end. He wouldn't let it be. But until they captured the head of Trinity, they would all have to be looking out for each other and their special guest.

The thought of letting someone else take over her protection was enough to kill him. If he couldn't be with her every moment of every day, he'd be worried and on edge. No. He'd force himself to keep his eyes open and stay alert. He had to be the one to cover her six. He wouldn't hesitate to take a bullet for her.

He must have fallen asleep because the next thing he remembered was the blaring of the alarm clock on the nightstand beside CJ's bed.

CJ slapped the alarm, killing the irritating sound.

She leaned up on one arm and stared down at him, the sheet falling away from a bare breast.

Cole blinked open his eyes and smiled. "You look like a Valkyrie lording it over your conquest."

"I feel like one." She sat up and stretched her long arms over her head. When she brought her arms down, she turned and snuggled back into his embrace, resting a hand across his chest. "Do we have to sneak into the West Wing today?"

"I'd much rather stay here with you." Cole brushed a strand of her hair from her cheek. "Can we put it off for another day?"

"Though I love the feeling of your hands on my skin, I know we can't wait another day to take down Trinity." Her fingernails curled into Cole's flesh. "I wish Trinity didn't exist. Then things could have been different between us. I could spend all day with you, just like this."

"If Trinity didn't exist, we might never have met," he pointed out. "For that reason alone, I'm glad they exist. Not that I'm glad you were recruited, but...you know what I mean."

She nodded. "Still, I'd rather stay here with you."

"If it's any consolation to you and me, I'll be with you all day." He gave her a lopsided grin. "Albeit, fully clothed and hands-off."

CJ snorted. "Not the same," she said, twirling a finger around one of his little brown nipples, tickling him. "I guess we don't have time to...you know."

Cole turned on his side and ran a hand over her

shoulder, cupped a breast and tweaked her nipple between his thumb and forefinger.

She gasped, her body arching toward him.

"We can't go all the way there without protection, but that doesn't mean we can't have a little fun." He traced a line down her torso to the juncture of her thighs.

CJ shifted, parting her legs, letting him in to strum that little nubbin of tightly packed nerves.

She closed her eyes and let his fingers do all the talking, flicking, tapping and dipping into her channel for the warm juices that made his digits slide across that sensitive spot.

Before long, he had her poised on the edge, her body tense, her hips rocking to his tender ministrations. One more flick and she stiffened, her body rising up to meet his hand. He continued touching her there until she sank back to the mattress, her body limp, glistening with a fine sheen of perspiration.

Cole leaned over and kissed her, drawing her into his arms, pressing his engorged staff against her belly. He wanted more, but he didn't have anything left in his wallet. No protection. No making love.

CJ wrapped her fingers around him and moved up and down the shaft.

His breath caught and held. He could let her do what she was doing, but he'd want to take it to the next level. Instead, he captured her hand in his and held it still, shaking his head. "We have to get ready for work."

"But I want you to feel what I felt," she whispered.

"I did," he said. "Through you." He smacked her bottom and sat up. "Come on, we have some undercover work to do. The sooner we catch Trinity's leader, the sooner we can laze around in bed doing what we like doing better."

Cole rose, wrapped a towel around his waist and leaned down to capture her mouth in one last kiss. Then he was out the door, leaving her to dress and prepare for a day at the West Wing, gathering information about Chris Carpenter's role in the attack. That is, if in fact he had a part in the kidnapping of the vice president.

Grabbing his toiletries, he headed to the bathroom to shave. He returned to his bedroom, dressed in his only suit and tie. When he was ready, he fully expected to have to wait for CJ. Opening his bedroom door, he was surprised to see CJ standing there wearing a simple black skirt, a white blouse and black pumps on her feet. She'd tucked her gorgeous auburn hair up into the black wig and had on her black-framed glasses with the clear lenses. Even in the supposedly frumpy disguise, she was sexy as hell.

Cole pulled her into his arms and kissed her hard.

She opened to him and he slid his tongue along hers in a caress he didn't want to end.

When it did, he stood back and ran his gaze over her from top to toe. "You look amazing."

"I didn't think you could look better than when you wore your jeans and a T-shirt. But this look?" She nodded. "Sexy as hell."

He held out his elbow. "Ready to conquer the world?"

"I am." She slipped her hand through the bend of his elbow and walked with him down the staircase to the ground floor.

Cole led her toward the voices he heard coming from the kitchen.

Mustang, Charlie, Anne, Jack, Jonah and Carl the chef were busy setting the table, toasting bread and pouring coffee and orange juice into mugs and glasses.

They all settled at the table and discussed the day ahead.

Anne gave them a brief description of the layout of the offices in the West Wing and where they could find Chris Carpenter's.

"I put together a small tool kit for you to use when you move Carpenter's desk around," Jonah said. "Nothing in the kit should raise any alarms with the guards at the entrance. I even packed several types of batteries so that the two GPS disks will look like any other small, flat batteries. I also gave you the printout of the work order."

"Thank you." Cole scooped fluffy scrambled eggs onto his plate and a couple of slices of crispy bacon.

"It would be better if you and CJ don't show up at the West Wing at the same time." Mustang held up a hand. "Don't worry. Anne and Jack can walk her in to make certain she isn't targeted."

Cole frowned. "I don't like being that far away from her. She's my assignment."

CJ stiffened beside him, making him realize how callous his words sounded.

"I mean, I want to be the one to protect her." He turned to CJ. "I've been with you the longest."

"I can manage getting into the West Wing without a bodyguard," CJ said. "For that matter, it might be better if I don't get too close to any of you. Trinity is likely to know by now that you're all working together to bring them down."

"She has a point," Charlie said.

"In which case," Mustang said, "since I'm not one of the people going to work in the White House, I could wear a disguise and go with CJ as far as the entrance to the West Wing."

Cole didn't like the idea of being separated from CJ for even a minute, but they were right. Trinity had to be watching Charlie's estate by now and anyone coming and going. He nodded. "We'll have to take separate vehicles to the train station."

"I'll drive CJ all the way in and let her off near the Capitol," Arnold said as he joined them at the table.

"I can catch the train, change shirts in a bathroom and put on a ball cap before I get off at Farragut station," Mustang said. "I can position myself at a crosswalk, where you can drop off CJ, and walk near her the rest of the way to the West Wing."

The more complicated the plan got, the less Cole liked it. "I'll be there as soon as I can get there by metro," he said. "Wait for me to do any snooping around."

CJ dipped her head. "I'll get in and check Carpenter's schedule and let you know via the burner phone what times he'll be out of office. You can schedule your work order around him leaving for a meeting." She frowned. "You can give me one of the GPS devices. I can slip it into his jacket, since I'll be with him all day."

Cole nodded. "I'll do that after I get the tool bag through security."

With plans in place, they finished breakfast and loaded up into separate vehicles. Mack and Gus arrived by the time they were ready to leave and tightened up the convoy of vehicles heading for the metro and DC.

CJ rode with Cole as far as the metro station.

"I'll see you soon," Cole said. "I'd rather be with you, but Mustang will take good care of you."

CJ opened her mouth, but Cole pressed a finger to her lips with a smile. "I know. You can take care of yourself. But it's nice to have backup." He squeezed her hand before he got out and boarded the train.

Anne, Jack Snow and Mustang arrived in separate vehicles. They got onto different train cars without acknowledging each other's presence. As far as curious onlookers could tell, they didn't know each other. And by watching the rearview mirror and looking behind their little caravan, Cole had determined that no one seemed to have followed them from Charlie's estate. But they couldn't take any chances. Trinity had an entire network of individuals swarming all over DC and surrounding areas.

Cole found a seat and studied the people on board, wondering if one or more of them worked for Trinity. How could he tell? The Trinity sleepers who'd been inside the West Wing looked like everyone else who worked there. It was impossible to tell the difference.

He prayed CJ's disguise was sufficient to get her in and keep her safe until he arrived.

Chapter Eight

CJ sat in the back of the SUV, relying on Roger Arnold to get her through the heavy morning DC traffic. Thankfully, they'd left far earlier than most and missed a significant portion of rush hour until they neared the heart of the political scene. By the time they'd arrived at the agreed upon drop-off point, the traffic had slowed to a crawl. In some places, it was more stop-and-go than a crawl.

Mustang stood at a bus stop not far from where CJ got out of the car. He wore an Atlanta Braves baseball cap and a light gray sweatshirt. CJ walked past him headed toward the White House. In her peripheral vision, she saw Mustang fall in behind her. Moving with purpose, she didn't take long to reach the West Wing of the White House.

As predicted, the security was still tight following the attack and subsequent kidnapping of the vice president and one of the mid-level staffers. CJ still felt responsible for getting Anne Bellamy involved in that mess. But when she'd learned that John Halverson had asked Anne to spy on people in the White House, looking for anyone who might have connections to Trinity, CJ had reached out to her. She had seen mentions of a potential attack on the White House and had felt obligated to warn someone on the inside to be aware and safe.

What she hadn't expected was for Anne to be kidnapped along with the VP and used as leverage to lure CJ out of her hiding as a trade for the lives of Anne and the vice president.

She'd offered to make that trade to free two innocent people. But Declan's Defenders had had other plans. With her help, they'd brought down the Trinity sleeper agents, freed Anne and the VP and saved the day without bringing CJ out in the open.

She owed them a lot for their sacrifices and the risks they'd taken to rescue the hostages. They had been right in assuming a trade would accomplish little. Trinity wasn't known to leave anyone alive to identify their agents in a lineup. Had they made the trade, CJ, Anne and the VP would have died.

Using the information Anne had provided about entry and location of offices, CJ stepped through the doors, scanned her card and proceeded through the metal detectors. The card worked, the metal detectors didn't find anything amiss, and she was on her way into the West Wing.

One hurdle crossed, on to the next. She found the office of the Homeland Security Advisor, Chris Carpenter, pasted a smile on her face and entered.

Having seen several pictures of the man, CJ recognized Carpenter at once. He stood in the middle of the front office, waving a stack of papers at some poor woman.

"How am I supposed to get anything done without help?" he asked.

"I'm only on loan until they bring in a temp to replace Dr. Saunders," the woman said. "I have work to do in my other office, as well. I can't do everything."

CJ cleared her throat to gain their attention. "Are you Mr. Carpenter?" she asked, knowing the answer before he gave it.

"Yeah. Who are you?"

"HR sent me as a temporary replacement for Dr. Saunders."

"Oh, thank goodness," the other woman said and rushed for the door.

CJ held out her hand to the man standing in the middle of the room. "Charlotte Jones. You must be Chris Carpenter, my new boss for the time being."

He gripped her hand absently and gave it a brief shake. "Can you type? Ever done any fact checking?"

CJ nodded. "Both."

"Are you even set up on the computer network?" Carpenter shook his head. "I don't know why they send me replacements when we have to spend the next two weeks getting them up and running on the server. By that time, Dr. Saunders will be back from sick leave."

"Let me see what I can do before we get tech services involved," CJ said. "Where will I be sitting?"

"You'll have to sit at Dr. Saunders's desk. And, speaking of tech services, they'll be in today to rearrange the connections in my office. And about damned time. I'll be out most of the morning and early afternoon to meetings. You'll have to familiarize yourself with the office on your own." He stared down at the papers in his hands. "These will have to suffice until I can make the changes." With one last glance, he headed for the door. "I'll be back before the end of the day."

After Carpenter left the office, CJ sat at the desk he'd indicated and tapped the mouse. The screen came to life. She stuck her access card into the reader on the computer base unit and entered the password Jonah had set up for her. Like magic, the computer came to life and let her into the server used by the staff of the West Wing. Once there, she sifted through various files searching for ones created by Chris Carpenter.

None of the files on Dr. Saunders's computer provided any information, clues on the attack, a connection to Tully or the Trinity sleeper agent, posing as a Secret Service agent who'd set off the explosion. But then, CJ hadn't expected to find anything obvious. She needed to get onto Carpenter's computer to see if there were any files or emails stored there that could lead them to the man in charge of Trinity.

Until Cole arrived, she didn't dare walk into Carpenter's office or log on to his desktop computer. Having a representative from technical services gave her a good excuse to be in the Homeland Security Advisor's office. Or better yet, she would be the first line of defense should people want to go into Carpenter's office. She could waylay them with the news Chris was in meetings all day. At the same time, she could warn Cole someone was outside the door.

He only had to have enough private time to download the contents of the computer onto a portable hard drive. Then he'd make the adjustments to the office as requested, to the best of his ability, and get the heck out before anyone discovered he wasn't really part of the tech services team.

CJ spent the first half hour using the bug sweep device Jonah had given her to check the entire outer office for any signs of hidden cameras or microphones. When she was certain there weren't any, she carried a document into Carpenter's office, leaving the door open in case someone walked in. She had the excuse of leaving the document on his desk as the reason for being caught in his office.

The bug scanner came up empty. With both offices clear, she felt more confident Cole would be able to do what he had to do without being observed.

With nothing else to do to pass time, CJ studied the data pertaining to the Department of Homeland Security. She received emails from Carpenter giving her a list of tasks to accomplish by the time he returned to the office that afternoon.

CJ wasn't sure what she was supposed to do with some of the items on the list, but she gave it her best shot. Thankfully, Trinity had insisted all of the children placed in their hands be educated in math, the sciences, English and foreign languages. What she didn't know, she searched on the internet for information.

By the time Cole appeared, she was ready to get

on with the work they'd come to do. And seeing him again brought back memories of their night together. Her body warmed.

"I've checked the offices for bugs," she said in a low voice. Though she'd checked, she still didn't fully trust that the device she'd used was fail proof. In a louder voice, she asked, "Are you the technical services representative here to move Mr. Carpenter's office around?"

"I am." Cole waved the work order in his hand. "Point me in the right direction and I'll get to it."

She led him to Carpenter's office, opened the door and let him in. "I take it you know what has to be done?"

He nodded. "I've got a work order with detailed instructions."

"Let me know if you need anything from me," CJ said. "I'll be out here, manning my desk." She left the door open only a crack. Enough that Cole could hear her, but not enough that anyone could see him sitting at Carpenter's desk, downloading data onto a portable hard drive.

CJ sat at her desk, facing the door to the hallway, her nerves on edge, fully expecting guards to come storming in looking for her with her fake clearance and identifying her as the person tapping into a computer hard drive. They'd haul her and Cole off and send them somewhere to be interrogated. Maybe even Guantanamo Bay to perform a little waterboarding on them to get what little information they could out of them.

Though she didn't care much what happened to her, she didn't want to see Cole thrown in jail for trying to help her find the Director of Trinity and put a stop to its form of terrorism.

A few minutes crawled by. CJ tapped her fingernails on the desktop, wondering how long it would take to make a complete backup of a desktop computer's hard drive.

She had just risen to go check on Cole's progress when a dark-haired young woman with a smooth, white complexion and coal-colored eyes entered the doorway to the hall and smiled. "I heard we had a replacement for Millicent." She entered, holding out her hand. "I'm Katie Wang, I work with the director for Europe and Russia."

CJ shook the woman's hand, trying to think of some way to get her out of there as soon as possible. "I'm Charlotte Jones. I'm just temporary staffing, filling in for Dr. Saunders. Is there something I could help you with?"

"I just wanted to let you know that I was working with Millicent on a project involving some connections in Russia. Mr. Carpenter knows about it. If he asks you to pick up the ball and run with it, you can call me. I can fill you in."

"Thank you. I'll be sure to do that. You're in the directory?" CJ asked.

"I am. Anything you might need, feel free to call." Katie headed for the door. "We were all sorry to hear about what happened to Millicent. I visited her in the hospital. She's home now recovering."

"I'm glad to know that. I'm sure she will be missed while she's out."

"At least HR got it right on sending a replacement." Katie wiggled her fingers. "See ya around. And good luck."

As soon as Katie Wang left the office, CJ pushed through the door into Carpenter's office. "How's it going? Need help moving furniture?"

"Not yet. I need another five minutes to complete this download." Cole nodded at the computer and the flash drive sticking out of the front.

"Carpenter is supposed to be out of his office all morning," CJ said. "I don't expect him back anytime soon."

"Convenient. Maybe you can help me. The work order shows he wants the credenza moved to the west wall."

"Let me check out front and then I'll be back." CJ dashed out into the front office. Since it was empty, she turned back to the Homeland Security Advisor's office. She was just about to push through the door again when she heard voices in the hallway. One in particular was very familiar and had her heart racing.

She ducked her head into the inner office. "Got a problem. I hear Carpenter heading this direction."

"I can't stop the download now, or I'll have to start all over again." Cole glanced at the monitor and shook his head. "I need another three minutes."

"I'll do the best I can," CJ said and ran to her desk in time to take her seat.

Chris Carpenter entered the area with another man

CJ didn't recognize at his side. "I have that file on my desk. I'll only be a second."

CJ stood and blocked Carpenter's path. "Oh, good. I'm glad you came back. I'm stuck and need a little guidance on one of the items on your list."

The Advisor tried to step around her. "I don't have time to help. Ask someone in one of the other offices to assist. I need to grab a file and go."

"Sir, the technical services guy just got here." CJ went to Carpenter's office door and stopped, her fingers curling around the handle. "Did you want to give him any directions on how you want your office arranged? He's ready to begin but had some questions."

"It's about time tech services got here. I put that work order in over a month ago. Yes, I'll speak with him." He turned to the man waiting in the doorway to the hall and held up a finger. "Give me two minutes."

The man nodded.

CJ prayed Cole had managed to cover the flash drive as she pushed the door open. "Mr. Carpenter is here. You can ask him what you wanted to know now."

Cole stood by the blank wall, away from the computer and monitor. "Is this the wall you wanted the credenza on?"

Carpenter nodded. "It is."

"Did you want it centered or offset to the right or left?"

CJ walked around the desk and stared at the wall with her head tilted to one side. "Centered would look good," she said. She shot a glance at the computer monitor. Cole had turned it off. Though the computer hummed as the files and data downloaded to the flash drive, having the monitor off made it appear as if the computer was powered down or in hibernation mode.

"Yes, centered," Carpenter was saying. "And I want my desk positioned in front of it with a gap between them similar to the one I have now. I need room to get in and out of my chair."

"Got it," Cole said.

The computer humming stopped and the light on the flash drive blinked off. The download had completed, CJ noted, just as Carpenter turned toward the desk.

"One other thing, Mr. Carpenter," Cole said, directing the man's attention back to him. "Did you want me to wire your computer for two monitors while I'm at it?"

"I don't need two monitors. One is more than enough."

While Carpenter's back was turned, CJ reached out, snatched the small device from the USB port and slipped it into her pocket.

Carpenter crossed to his desk, grabbed a file folder sitting on the corner and turned toward the exit. "Just move the desk and credenza. Everything else needs to stay the same. I'll be back later this afternoon."

Carpenter left the room and joined the other man waiting in the outer office, holding up the file. "Got it."

CJ followed them to the door. "If you need anything, Mr. Carpenter, all you have to do is call," she said.

He ignored her and disappeared down the hallway.

Once the Homeland Security Advisor was out of sight, CJ returned to the inner office. "Need help moving that furniture?"

He nodded. "Let's do it."

It took longer than expected to empty out drawers and shelves before they could move the furniture and reconnect the computer to an electrical outlet and ethernet port across the room. When they were done, it was noon.

"I'm going to get some lunch," CJ said. "Care to join me?"

"Don't mind if I do." Cole gathered his tools into the bag Jonah had equipped him with and they left Carpenter's office and exited the West Wing.

As they walked toward the food trucks lining the street for the lunch hour, Cole asked, "Think they'll miss you when you don't return from lunch?"

"I left a note on Carpenter's email telling him that I had been called to fill a permanent position and appreciated his understanding of the change." CJ grinned. "Hopefully, he won't be looking for me, or asking HR about me."

Cole dug his phone out of his pocket and placed a call. "Jonah, Cole here. We're out of the West Wing." He paused, listening. "Good. Then we'll head to Carpenter's home next. Thanks for taking care of it." He ended the call and nodded at CJ. "Jonah's on it. He shows Charlotte Jones as having been terminated from the HR database as of today, with the reason that you found other employment."

"Good. So, we're off to visit Carpenter's home next?"

"We are. Roger has what we'll need staged in a van off F Street, three blocks down. Everything is in that van."

"Address?" she asked.

"In Foxhall Village. Not far from here."

"Then let's do this." She picked up the pace, eager to get to Carpenter's place with the hope they'd find something, anything, that would lead them to the head of Trinity.

"What if Carpenter isn't our connection?" CJ said.

"Then we would mark him off the list and keep looking. I have to believe that text to Tully has to lead somewhere."

"He said he didn't have his phone that day."

"He could have lied," Cole pointed out.

They paused at a crosswalk and waited for the walking-man signal to blink on.

CJ was careful to check both directions. After Dr. Millicent Saunders had been run down crossing just such a street, they couldn't be too careful.

They made it across the street and hurried down F Street. At the third block, a white van was pulling out of a parking garage. The lettering on the side read *Bug-B-Gone*. Roger Arnold was at the wheel, wearing a white coverall with a patch with the same Bug-B-Gone logo embroidered over the right breast.

The side door slid open and Mustang waved them in.

CJ stepped in first, followed by Cole.

As soon as they were inside and the door was closed, Arnold headed for Foxhall Village. Next stop was Carpenter's home. CJ hoped they struck information gold. They needed a break. John Halverson had spent years searching for the answers. It was time to lay Trinity to rest. Preferably in a graveyard.

Chapter Nine

Cole sat on the floor inside the van, shaking his head. "You're kidding, right?"

"It's the perfect cover, isn't it?" Mustang grinned across at him.

"Did you get it?" Jonah sat on a bench in front of a laptop and an array of three monitors, holding out his hand.

CJ handed Cole the flash drive.

Cole placed it into Jonah's open palm. "When did we get a communications van?"

Mustang's grin broadened. "Charlie and Jonah had it in the works. This is its maiden voyage. Check it out." He pulled a panel across, hiding Jonah and his computers from sight. On the panel were face masks, gloves and plastic jugs of bug spray like those used by exterminators. "There's another panel near the rear door just like this. Anyone who just happens to look inside would never suspect there was a man and a bank of computer equipment inside."

Mustang reopened the panel, exposing Jonah at

work, plugging the flash drive into a USB port on his laptop.

"I'll be looking through the data you collected from Carpenter's work computer while you collect the same information from his home computer." Jonah didn't look up as his fingers flew across the keyboard and mouse pad. The monitors flashed data on the screens.

"In the meantime, we need to dress for the part." Mustang handed them each a white coverall with the exterminator logo patch. "This is how we're getting into Carpenter's house. They're due an annual termite inspection. We're just going to do it earlier than they expected."

CJ's brow furrowed. "What about Mrs. Carpenter or the help?"

"Mrs. Carpenter is scheduled to meet with her hairdresser this afternoon. She should be gone during the time we're conducting our termite inspection," Mustang said.

"What if she gets done early?" Cole asked.

"That's why we have our communications van," Jonah said. "You, CJ and Mustang will have two-way communications. If we see anyone coming home early, we'll notify you. Hopefully, in time to get out."

Cole frowned. "Hopefully?"

"The house should have at least a front and a back door and possibly one in the kitchen," Arnold said. "You should be able to get out of one of them if I notify you as soon as someone shows up."

"We should," Cole said. "At the very least, if Mrs.

Carpenter returns early and catches us at it, we can say Mr. Carpenter authorized us to conduct the termite inspection."

"If it comes to that, I can jam her cell phone signal," Jonah said, "long enough for you two to get out."

Mustang slid his legs into a white jumpsuit and pulled it up over his body. "I'll be on the outside, keeping watch, as well as to make sure we don't miss anyone sneaking in from other directions."

"Where are Gus and Jack?"

"Jack's still in the West Wing with Anne," Mustang said. "We can't be certain Trinity has been eradicated from the White House. Gus is following up on a tip from the dark web. A dog trainer in the Virginia countryside thinks there's a terrorist training camp in the hills near him. We sent Gus out with a drone to check it out."

CJ's eyes widened. "I remember being in the hills when I was in training with Trinity."

"Think you could find it again?" Cole asked.

She shook her head. "Operatives are taken out of the camp blindfolded. Only the trainers know how to get in and get out."

"What about flying over?" Mustang zipped up his coverall.

CJ's eyes narrowed. "Maybe. I remember being in the woods, though. Even the buildings were surrounded by trees and hidden beneath the canopy."

"I look forward to Gus's report when he gets back," Cole said.

"Me, too." CJ glanced at the coverall in her hands.

"I'll need to lose the skirt if I want to get into this," she said.

"I brought your backpack from the car," Arnold said from the driver's seat. "It's in the corner storage bin."

"Perfect." CJ found her backpack, tucked away the glasses and heels, and dug out a pair of gray leggings. Without hesitation, she slipped them up under her skirt. Once she had them on, she unzipped and stepped out of the skirt, folding it neatly before stuffing it into her backpack.

The coveralls went on over her leggings and shirt. She pulled them up over her hips and torso and slid her arms into the sleeves. The coveralls were two sizes too big, but she zipped them anyway and rolled up the sleeves. She shed the wig and rearranged her ponytail before fitting one of the green Bug-B-Gone hats over her head. Once more, she dug in her backpack and unearthed a pair of running shoes.

Cole marveled at how the woman could change her appearance so quickly and completely. No one would think she was the same person who'd stepped into the van wearing the black skirt and white blouse. She looked like a guy. A smallish guy with feminine facial features. "Do you carry everything in your backpack?" he asked.

"Everything I think I might need for a quick change in disguise." She lifted her chin. "It's kept me alive for the past year."

Cole held up his hands. "I'm not judging. I'm impressed."

"We'll be there in two minutes," Arnold called out.

Cole hurriedly dragged his coveralls on over his suit trousers. Removing his jacket and tie, he tugged the coverall sleeves on and zipped the white fabric over his shirt. He pulled on a cap and tugged paper booties over his dress shoes.

Jonah turned to Cole. "The Carpenters have an alarm system on their house. I've hacked into the company that services it and disarmed it for now."

"Good to know. Did you hack into their locks?" Cole gave Jonah a crooked grin. "Lock picking wasn't one of the skills we learned as Marine Force Recon."

"I've got that," CJ said.

Mustang shook his head, his lips twisting. "Trinity life lesson?"

CJ nodded. "From a young age."

"Need any tools?" Jonah asked.

One more time, CJ dug in the backpack and pulled out a thin file. "No. I've got it covered."

"Good," Arnold said. "Because we're here." He pulled to a stop on the side of the road between two large homes. He nodded at one. "Carpenters live in the gray brick house."

"Guess that's our cue," Cole said.

Jonah handed each of them an earbud. "These are your radio headsets. Turn them on and leave them on so you can hear me if I need to warn you of someone coming."

Mustang, Cole and CJ tested their communications devices one by one. When they were satisfied they could hear and be heard, Mustang closed the panel, hiding Jonah.

Cole opened the van's side panel and stepped out.

CJ followed and Mustang brought up the rear, carrying a jug of bug spray.

"I'll go around to the left, you two take the right," Mustang said. He left them and started around the front of the house, squirting bug spray as he went.

CJ led the way around the other side of the house. The house had a detached garage with a covered walkway between it and the kitchen entrance. CJ stuck her file into the lock on the handle, jiggled it once and had the kitchen door open within seconds.

Cole let out a low whistle. "I'm impressed."

She shrugged. "Like I said, they taught us the skill at an early age."

Cole followed her into the house, closing the door behind them, locking it in case someone did enter while they were there and were alerted to the fact the door wasn't locked.

They made quick work of the ground level. It consisted of a formal dining room, chef's kitchen, and a formal living room sporting a baby grand piano. In the back of the house was a den with a couple of comfortable sofas and lounge chairs.

CJ met Cole in the hallway near the staircase.

"His office must be upstairs," Cole said.

"All clear out back," Mustang said into Cole's headset.

"All clear in front," Arnold echoed.

Cole led the way up the stairs where they found three spacious bedrooms, a bathroom in the hall and the master suite at the end. Off the side of the master suite was another room with a desk, file cabinet, computer and a wall full of bookshelves.

"I'll download," Cole said.

"I'll look through his files." CJ crossed to the file cabinet. It was locked, but she opened it with no problem.

Cole clicked the mouse only to find the computer was password protected. "Any idea what password he might use?"

"Try his birth month and year." Jonah gave him the numbers.

Cole keyed them in. It didn't work. "Next?"

"His wife's birth month and year." Again, Jonah fed him the numbers.

Cole entered them and he made it past the first hurdle. "Bingo." He stuck the flash drive into the USB port and started the download. While the computer was copying the files to the portable drive, he searched through Carpenter's emails, social media and internet cookies.

Many of the links were to news, travel and government sites typically visited by officials. One of the travel sites contained information about Russia. Another link took him to the site for the Russian embassy. In particular, to one of the embassy staff members, Sergei Orlov.

Cole pulled out his cell phone and snapped a photo of the name to remember later. He took another photo of the internet browser history.

With four more minutes to kill while waiting for the download to complete, Cole clicked on one IP address after another. Halfway down the list, he hit on one that brought up an image of the Trinity knot. The same symbol found on a ring John Halverson had in his collection. The same symbol that kept popping up in connection with the Trinity organization.

A gasp sounded from behind him. "That's the Trinity website."

He turned to find CJ standing behind him, a file in her hand, her face pale.

"They have a website? I would have thought they'd want to be a lot lower key."

"They use it to recruit young people to their organization."

Cole clicked on the link. It took him to a video of teenage boys and girls, wearing camouflage, learning combat techniques and how to fire military-grade weapons, including AR-15s and grenade launchers. "I thought they took children from foster care?"

"They do, but they also recruit teens who rebel against authority or are looking for a place to fit in."

The video went on to show the young people sitting around a campfire in the woods, laughing and smiling.

CJ snorted. "They had to have used stock videos for that shot. We never sat around a campfire laughing and smiling. If we weren't training for combat, we were studying languages and other subjects to help us fit in to just about any situation or country."

"We've got company," Arnold said into their earbuds. "Silver Mercedes just blew into the driveway. Female getting out. I assume it's Mrs. Carpenter, by her appearance. She was going so fast I didn't realize she was going to stop until she turned in."

"Can you two get out?" Mustang asked from his position outside the house.

"We're upstairs," Cole whispered. "We'll hide and wait until she leaves." He exited the Trinity video and checked the status of the download. They needed two more minutes. He left it running in the background and prayed Mrs. Carpenter didn't notice the flash drive in the USB port.

"If she doesn't leave soon, we'll come up with a diversion to lure her out," Arnold advised them.

The sound of a door opening downstairs echoed up to the office off the master bedroom.

CJ tipped her head toward a closet at one end of the little office.

Cole followed CJ through the door, closing it behind them almost all of the way, leaving a little gap to let in light and sound. The closet was barely big enough for one person to fit inside, much less two. It contained a stack of file boxes, shoe boxes and one umbrella. CJ had moved to the side as far as she could to allow Cole to get his entire body inside the confined space.

He reached for her hand and held it, squeezing gently. He liked how soft yet strong her fingers were against his.

Footsteps sounded on the staircase and then in the upper hallway, heading in their direction.

Cole peered through the sliver of a gap in the doorway at the woman who entered the bedroom in a hurry, a cell phone to her ear.

"He's not home," she was saying. "I know… I had to come back. I forgot to clear the browser history before I left earlier. I know… I know…it was stupid and careless. But I'm here now and deleting it as we speak. He's been at the office all day. He'll never see it." She sat at the desk and clicked on the keyboard, hitting the delete button several times until she was satisfied. "There. All the browsing history has been wiped clean. I'll be there in twenty minutes." She smiled. "I'll be there soon, my love."

She ended the call, stood and looked down at the computer.

Cole tensed.

Had she noticed the flash drive? Or had she brought up the screen showing how many minutes were left on the download?

Mrs. Carpenter ran her fingers through her hair, closed her eyes and tipped her head back. Then she left the little office and hurried through the bedroom to the bathroom on the other side.

"What's happening?" CJ whispered against his ear.

"She's in the bathroom," Cole answered so softly only CJ could hear.

The sound of the toilet flushing and water running in the sink was followed by Mrs. Carpenter leaving the bathroom and heading into the walk-in closet.

"Mustang?" Cole whispered softly into the head-set.

"I read you," Mustang responded.

"Put a GPS tracker on her car," Cole said. "Now."

"Roger," Mustang responded.

Mrs. Carpenter emerged from the closet wearing a soft gray dress and red high heels. She slipped her arms into a black trench coat and left the bedroom, descending the stairs much slower than she'd climbed them.

A moment later, Cole heard the sound of the kitchen door clicking shut.

"The missus has left the building," Mustang said into Cole's headset.

"Did you get the GPS tracker on her car?" Cole asked.

"Roger."

"Good. We'll be down as soon as her car leaves the street," Cole told him, pushing the closet door open. "Be ready to track her." After checking that he couldn't see the driveway through the window, he strode to the desk and checked the status of the download. It was complete. He removed the flash drive and slipped it into his pocket. Then Cole pulled CJ into his embrace and dropped a kiss onto her lips. "I've wanted to do that all day. And I'd kiss you longer—"

"—but we have to follow that duplicitous Mrs. Carpenter." CJ took his hand and led him down the stairs and out through the kitchen door.

Mustang was already in the van when CJ and Cole climbed in.

"Follow her," Cole told Arnold as he handed Jonah the flash drive. He also texted him the two images he'd taken of the IP address to the Trinity recruiting site and of the Carpenters' browser history. "It's apparent that one of the Carpenters has a connection to Trinity. Seems it could be Chris Carpenter, Mrs. Carpenter or the man she'd called *my love* on her cell phone. Or it could be all three."

"Hopefully, one of them will take us to their leader," Jonah commented, his back to the others, busily tapping the keys on his laptop.

Cole prayed they would. He was ready to take down Trinity and put an end to their reign of terror. Then he could get back to making love to CJ without worrying someone was waiting in the sidelines to put a bullet through her head.

CJ UNZIPPED THE coveralls and stripped out of them. She sat cross-legged on the floor of the van, staring at the tracking device Mustang held in his hand in the passenger seat, directing Arnold through traffic.

"They aren't going to get anywhere really fast in this snarl," Mustang commented, looking at the bumper-to-bumper stream of cars.

"Neither are we," Cole pointed out, leaning over the back of Mustang's seat. "Where does she appear to be headed?"

"She's headed east on Reservoir Road," Mustang said. "No, wait. She's turning north on Thirty-Seventh Street."

Arnold drove the van out of Foxhall Village onto Reservoir Road.

A few moments later, Mustang reported, "Now she's on Tunlaw Road."

CJ leaned forward, her brow furrowed. "Isn't that close to Embassy Row?"

"I found a lot of travel sites in their travel history," Cole mentioned. "Wanna make a guess as to where?"

"Russia," Jonah said from behind them. "Someone was searching for flights to Moscow."

"Do you think Mrs. Carpenter is cheating on her husband with a Russian?" CJ asked.

"She's stopped in front of the Russian consulate," Mustang said. "Even if she's not cheating on her husband, she's meeting someone close to the consulate."

"There's no crime in that," Cole noted.

"No," CJ said. "But there is crime in attacking the White House and kidnapping the vice president and a mid-level staffer."

"True, but just because Mrs. Carpenter is stopping close to the Russian consulate doesn't mean she's meeting someone from the consulate, or that she was involved in the attack on the White House," Cole said.

"But she could be," CJ insisted, peering out the front window of the van as if she could see as far ahead as the consulate.

"She's moving again," Mustang said. "Heading for New Mexico Avenue."

"We're not far behind now," Arnold commented.

When the Carpenter woman stopped in front of the consulate, they'd gained ground and were now less than a couple of blocks behind her.

Her pulse pounding, CJ watched through the window, searching for a silver Mercedes. Ahead, traffic came to a stop at a light. The car in front of them turned onto a side street, leaving two cars between them and the silver Mercedes.

"There she is," Cole said.

"And she has someone in the car with her," Mustang noted.

The light turned green and they made a left onto Nebraska Avenue and a left on Arizona.

"I think they're headed for Chain Bridge," CJ said.

The light changed to red before they reached Arizona Avenue. The vehicle in front of them stopped. Had they been first to the light, CJ was certain Arnold would have blown through it. Instead the gap between them and Mrs. Carpenter lengthened.

By the time the light changed and they were moving again, the silver Mercedes had crossed Chain Bridge and merged onto George Washington Memorial Parkway heading north.

"Can we move any faster?" CJ asked, leaning over Arnold's shoulder.

"Only as fast as the people in front of us. We can gain some ground when we hit the parkway," Roger said.

Once on the major highway, they picked up speed. Roger adeptly zigzagged through the traffic, gaining on the woman in the Mercedes. Once again, they had closed the distance between them. Soon, they could see the silver sedan moving in and out of the fast lane.

Roger kept two cars between theirs and Mrs. Carpenter's, following her close enough to keep up, but far enough not to alert her to their presence.

A black sedan whipped past, swerving dangerously close to the vehicles in front of them. When it moved up alongside the silver Mercedes, it turned sharply into the side of the smaller vehicle. The Mercedes swerved violently, crossed the lane of traffic to its right and ran off the road, hitting a ditch and rolling several times before coming to a stop upside down.

Traffic slowed and Roger was able to get to the side of the road.

As soon as the van stopped, Cole ripped open the sliding door and they jumped out.

Cole was first to reach the crashed vehicle. CJ was next.

Mustang, Jonah and Roger brought up the rear, his cell pressed to his ear, reporting the accident to the 9-1-1 dispatcher.

Cole dropped to one knee and peered into the vehicle. Lying upside down, the top of the car had caved in several inches. "Doesn't look good." He tried to open the door, but the damage kept the door from budging.

CJ squatted beside Cole and looked in through the window.

Mrs. Carpenter lay crumpled against the ceiling. The man who'd been in the passenger seat lay across her, blood soaking his forehead. No airbags had deployed, making their injuries worse.

Neither moved.

"Let me in there," Arnold said.

Cole and CJ moved aside. Roger placed a tool against the window and the window glass exploded, creating a hole the size of his fist. Using the other end of the tool, he scraped the glass away from the frame.

Cole leaned in and touched two fingers to the base of the neck of the man lying over Mrs. Carpenter. He shook his head. "Not getting a pulse." He tried to get to Mrs. Carpenter's throat but couldn't with the man on top of her. "I can't get to the woman," he said.

Cole grabbed the man's arm and pulled. The dead weight and the angle didn't make it easy. "Help me get him out."

An acrid scent stung CJ's nose. "I smell gasoline." Smoke rose from the engine. "Need to get them out now!" She reached in, grabbed the man's other arm, braced her feet on the side of the vehicle and pulled with all her might.

With Cole pulling as well, they inched the man's body past the steering wheel and toward the window.

When Mustang could get close enough, he gripped the man's arm and added his weight to the tug-of-war.

The man broke free of whatever was holding him in and slid all the way out. "Check for identification," Cole called out and turned back to the upside-down vehicle.

CJ reached in, searching for Mrs. Carpenter's arm. A bloody hand grabbed her wrist.

She stared into the woman's open eyes through the blood staining her face. She tipped her head back to look into CJ's gaze. "Help me," she whispered, her words gurgling.

CJ held on to the woman's hand and pulled.

Cole reached in and hooked his hands beneath her shoulders and slid her the rest of the way out.

The woman kept a death grip on CJ's hand as Cole lifted her and carried her away from the vehicle.

Smoke turned to flame as the leaking gasoline caught and burned.

Cole, Mustang, Roger, Jonah and CJ ran up the embankment, putting as much distance as they could between them and the burning Mercedes.

No sooner had they reached the top of the embankment, the fire reached the gasoline in the tank and erupted in a blast that sent them to their knees.

Cole laid Mrs. Carpenter on the ground, covering her body with his as the ash rained down on them.

Sirens wailed in the distance, moving closer. Traffic had slowed and backed up with rubberneckers eager to see what was happening.

The hand on CJ's wrist slackened and the fingers released her.

CJ stared down into Mrs. Carpenter's eyes. "What do you know about Trinity?" she asked.

The woman gave a slight shake of her head. "They…did…this."

"We don't doubt that. We need to know who their leader is," CJ said, leaning closer. "Tell us."

Mrs. Carpenter shook her head. "Never."

"You'd let him kill you, rather than tell us who it is?" Cole leaned over the woman. "Trinity has to be stopped."

"Not until it's done."

"Until what's done?" CJ asked, tempted to shake the woman until she got answers.

"Soooonnn." Lydia Carpenter inhaled a shallow breath. Then all the air left her lungs, as if on a sigh, and she breathed no more.

Cole cursed.

CJ checked the woman for injuries. Other than a gash on her forehead, she appeared to be fine. She hadn't been wearing her seat belt. Nor had the man who'd been with her. Internal injuries could have taken their toll. CJ couldn't let it go. She pressed the heel of her palm against the woman's chest and pumped several times.

Cole felt for a pulse and shook his head.

"She knows something," CJ said through gritted teeth as she knelt beside the woman and performed CPR, continuing until the EMTs arrived and took over.

They worked on Mrs. Carpenter even as they loaded her into the ambulance and drove away.

CJ wiped the blood from her hands down the sides of her leggings, her heart pinching hard in her chest. "She knew something," she repeated.

Cole slipped an arm around her middle and pulled her against him. "We'll follow that lead. Everyone she's been in contact with. We'll look at her phone records and check into her passenger's identity. Surely he had connections to Trinity, as well."

CJ nodded. She'd seen her share of dead bodies, but this person had been the closest to being able to give her the answers they so desperately needed. So damned close.

"Come on. We need to get back to Charlie's estate and fire up the main computers." Cole turned her toward the exterminator van. "We have work to do."

Chapter Ten

It took Arnold over an hour to get them back to Charlie's. As always in the DC area, roads resembled a
parking lot.

While Jonah worked on picking through the data
on the flash drives as they sat in traffic, Cole could
do nothing without a computer of his own. They'd
tracked down the leads they'd had. Now they had to
dig deeper into these new ones.

"Do you think Chris Carpenter is involved?" CJ
asked.

Cole shook his head. Based on what they knew
so far, he doubted it. "He could have been telling the
truth when he said he'd left his phone at home the day
of the attack. Likely his wife sent the text to Tully."

"Someone should question him about his wife's
connection with the Russian."

"Sergei Orlov," Jonah called out from his position
at the laptop inside the van. "I got a look at his wallet prior to the EMTs arriving to collect the bodies."

"What have you got on him?" Mustang asked.

"He works at the Russian consulate as some kind

of staffer," Jonah reported. "He's been in the States for over a year and has no criminal record."

Cole pulled out his cell phone and dialed the estate.

"Halverson Estate, Grace speaking."

"Grace. How's Declan?"

"He's here, refusing to take pain meds and grouchy as a grizzly bear with a sore paw. But he's alive. Want to talk to him?"

"Yes, please," Cole said. "Put him on."

"Cole. You gotta get me outta here. These women are going to smother me to death. I'm fine. I can go back to work."

"The doctor said two weeks without lifting anything heavier than your hand," Grace said in the background. "That means lifting a gun is out of the question."

"My gun is not that heavy," Declan grumbled. "Forget about me, Cole. What's happening?"

Cole brought him up to date on the visit to Carpenter's office and home. When he got to the part about the phone conversation between Lydia Carpenter and her lover, Declan interrupted.

"She was having an affair with a Russian?" Declan whistled. "Affairs in Washington are practically public knowledge. No one in DC ever gets away with anything juicy like that for long."

"Apparently, Mrs. Carpenter was."

"And you caught her," Declan said.

Cole went on to explain about the accident and the Russian's death and Mrs. Carpenter's words.

"By the way," Jonah said. "I hacked into the hospital records. They called it. Lydia Carpenter is officially deceased."

"Chris Carpenter should be on his way to the hospital, if he's not there already."

"I'll have Snow intercept Carpenter to see what he can find out about the missus and her lover," Declan said.

"We're headed back to the estate," Cole said. "Unless you can think of anywhere else we should go at this point."

"No," Declan said. "We need to put our heads together and think about our next steps before we take them."

"You don't need to do anything but take your pain meds and sleep," Grace said in the background.

"I'm beginning to regret the relationship portion of this gig. I liked it better when I made my own decisions about what my body could or couldn't take," Declan grumbled.

"You can't let your wound get infected," Cole said. "Let yourself heal before you jump back into the thick of things."

"Great," Declan muttered. "All I need is one more person telling me how to recuperate."

"Like I said," Grace murmured in the distance, "grizzly bear cranky."

"You would be, too, if you were stuck with a bullet wound when your team is out risking their lives." Declan cursed. "See you guys when you get here. If I haven't died of boredom by then."

Forty-five minutes later, the van pulled through

the gate of the Halverson estate and rolled to a stop in front of the mansion.

Declan, Jack and Grace met them at the top of the steps.

Declan held a hand over his middle, his forehead creased.

"You didn't have to come out to greet us," Mustang said.

"I needed some air," Declan said and turned, wincing. "Hurts like the dickens."

"It wouldn't hurt as bad if you'd take the pain medication the doctor prescribed," Grace reminded him, slipping her arm around his back.

Declan draped his arm over her shoulder and leaned into her. "I can't take those drugs. They make my brain fuzzy. I get the feeling we're on the cusp of something big. I need a clear mind to think through what's going on."

"Fine. But at least find a place to stretch out," Grace said softly. "I don't like it when you're in pain."

He kissed her cheek. "I'll be okay. You're not getting rid of me anytime soon."

"I hope not. I haven't had nearly enough time with you. I want more."

Declan laughed. "Even when I'm surly?"

She smiled up at him. "Even when you're surly." Then she rose up on her toes and pressed her lips to his in a light kiss. "If you'll follow us, I had the guys set up a lounge chair in the war room for Declan before Gus left."

Declan tipped his head toward Jack. "Snow

checked with the hospital to track down Chris Carpenter. He never showed up. Mack's in the war room, going through the video images that Gus is transmitting via the drone."

Carrying his laptop and the two flash drives, Jonah ducked past the people standing at the entrance and hurried inside.

Declan watched as he disappeared into the study. "Has Jonah found anything useful from Carpenter's computers?"

"The URLs and IP addresses were the most interesting items we found on the Carpenters' home computer. Jonah's digging into Sergei Orlov's background. All we know so far is that he works at the Russian consulate."

They entered John Halverson's study and descended the stairs into the basement war room.

Jonah was already hard at work, searching the internet for clues and answers.

Mack sat at the other computer with a screen showing the tops of trees, roofs on houses and barns and an occasional pond.

"Anything?" Declan asked.

"Nothing yet," Mack responded. He glanced up briefly. "Heard you guys had an interesting day."

Cole snorted. "To say the least."

Mack grinned. "Didn't expect to uncover a politician's wife cheating with a Russian, did you?"

"No, we didn't," CJ said.

"At least it was interesting. I've been staring at this screen for over an hour and haven't found anything nearly as cool as what you guys did." He returned his attention to the monitor.

CJ crossed the room to look over Mack's shoulder. "The compound where I was trained was pretty much buried in foliage. It won't be that easy to spot from the ground or air. Want help?"

"Sure." Mack pulled another chair close to where he was sitting. "Between you, me and Gus, three sets of eyes ought to be able to find something." He pointed to the monitor. "The dog trainer who gave us the info has a training facility here." He pointed to a spot on the screen where trees had been cleared and all that remained was a green grassy area. "He said the facility is off a road a couple of miles from his place to the northwest."

"What made him go that way?" CJ asked.

"He lost a dog he'd been boarding and went looking with a tracking dog. He found the animal, but also heard a lot of gunfire. When he got up close, he noticed the facility was surrounded by chain-link fence topped with razor-sharp concertina wire."

"Gunfire could be from a couple of guys out target practicing with pop cans, getting ready for deer season," Cole said, coming to stand behind CJ.

"Yeah, but they weren't firing single rounds, they were firing semiautomatic and automatic weapons, from what the dog trainer said." Mack pointed to the northwest of the dog facility. "The trees are dense here, and there are more hills to hide in."

CJ leaned closer to the monitor, looking for anything that didn't fit in, like the straight edge of a roofline or vehicle. The more she looked, the more the green leaves of the trees blended together. Until she came to a dark, rusty line in the middle of a canopy of trees. "There," she said, pointing to the line. "Is that a corrugated tin roof?"

Mack zoomed in on the image, blowing it up to twice the size on the screen. "Looks like it."

Following the line of the roof, CJ found another shape that wasn't natural for a forest, a gray, curved bowl. "Satellite dish?" she said, her brow dipping.

Mack nodded and pointed to another straight line. "That appears to be another building tucked beneath the trees."

Soon, they'd identified several potential buildings.

Mack picked up a satellite phone and called Gus. "Any way you can get closer to these coordinates?" He gave Gus the numbers and waited.

When Gus finally spoke again, Mack's brow furrowed. "Got it. So, it's like the dog trainer said. Did you hear any sounds of gunfire?"

CJ could hear Gus talking, but couldn't make out the words.

Mack's gaze met Cole's. "No sounds. Maybe they've moved from that site." He paused while Gus spoke. "You did? I'd say it's time to go in and investigate, boots on the ground."

"We're in." Cole glanced across at CJ.

She nodded, her pulse pounding hard against her eardrums. Heading back to where it all began seemed insane, but necessary. They might find the leader of Trinity there, supervising the training of even more

Trinity agents. A bunch of babies being led into a life of violence.

If she had any way of getting them out, she would. "Let's go."

"We'll get back with you when we have a plan and timeline," Mack assured Gus. "Stay low and don't get caught." Mack ended the call and turned to Cole. "We need communications equipment, bulletproof vests, weapons and some smoke grenades."

"Are we going in prepared to shoot kids?" Cole asked.

"No, but we're going in prepared to defend our lives," Mack said.

"Who's going where?" Charlie's voice sounded from the top of the stairs.

All gazes turned to the woman who funded their little band of brothers.

Charlie Halverson looked like a million bucks. Dressed in a long, silver-beaded, satin-and-lace gown, she looked like royalty as she descended the stairs one step at time.

She glanced around the room. "I thought everyone was headed in for the night." Her gaze settled on Declan. "And that Declan was going to get some rest."

"We think we may have found one of Trinity's training camps," Mack said.

Charlie moved forward, her eyes widening. "Do I need to stay home tonight and help monitor activities?" she asked.

Declan frowned. "You're going out?"

"I had an invitation to a special event where the president is scheduled to speak," Charlie said.

"Charlie, you have to go to the event," Grace said. "That's more important."

"If anything, we could wait to move in on the training camp until another day," Declan said. "If they're still using the camp, I doubt they'd get out of there sooner."

"No." Charlie held up a hand. "You do what you have to do."

"But we can't leave you unprotected. Someone needs to go with you to the event," Declan insisted. He tried to rise to his feet, but he couldn't bend over enough to lean forward. Instead he sat back in the lounge chair and winced. "I'll go with Charlie to the event. As soon as someone helps me out of this chair."

"You're not going anywhere," Grace said. "I'll go with Charlie."

Declan frowned. "You aren't trained in hand-to-hand combat and they won't let you in if you carry a gun." He glanced around the room, his gaze landing on Roger Arnold, who was just descending the stairs carrying a tray filled with a pitcher and glasses. "Arnold and I will go to the event with Charlie. The rest of the team will check out the compound. If you determine the place is a Trinity training camp, you are not to engage. You will fall back and call in the FBI, national guard and whoever else we need to round up all of the operatives."

"And don't forget the children," CJ said. "They'll

need special handling. They'll be well on their way to being brainwashed."

"If you're going with Charlie, I am, too," Grace said.

"I can't get everyone in. I can only bring a plus one," Charlie said. "Roger will be my plus one." She turned to him with a frown. "We'll need to have you fitted immediately with a tuxedo."

"I have one, ma'am," Arnold said.

Her eyes widened. "You do?" Then her brow dipped. "Why did I not know this about you, Roger?"

He straightened to his full height, shoulders back and chest puffed out like the military man he'd once been. "Because you never asked."

Charlie smiled. "Roger, you take such good care of me."

"Yes, ma'am," he said.

"You'll have to stop calling me 'ma'am' if you're coming with me tonight."

"Yes, Charlotte," he said, his voice softer.

CJ hid a smile. She might not be an expert in the ways of the heart, but she could swear there was something there in Roger's eyes. A flash of desire or longing? Or was CJ projecting her own feelings for Cole into those around her?

CJ sighed. Until they resolved the Trinity issue, she couldn't have any kind of long-term relationship with anyone without putting them at risk. As much as she loved being around Cole, she'd have to cut the ties forming and leave. A heaviness settled on her chest. She hadn't felt that kind of weight since she'd lost her parents.

Mack had risen and gone to the cabinets against the wall. One by one, he pulled out weapons, grenades, bulletproof vests and communications devices.

Jonah helped him organize and store them in a couple of large duffel bags.

"I'll bring the SUV around to the front of the house," Roger Arnold offered and left the room, climbing the stairs, his limp barely noticeable.

Charlie's gaze followed him up the stairs, the corners of her mouth curling upward. "Arnold—Roger," she corrected, "never ceases to surprise me. And we've known each other since I met my husband. He was in the SAS when the three of us met in a bar in London." She smiled. "At first I was more attracted to Roger than John." She pressed her hands to her chest. "There's something about a man in uniform that makes a girl's heart flutter." She drew in a deep breath and let it out. "Alas, Roger deployed to some godforsaken place in Africa and John swept me off my feet." She turned to CJ, her eyes misty with unshed tears. "I loved John with all my heart."

CJ nodded, not knowing what to say to the woman. She had no experience with love. Her gaze went to Cole as he loaded rounds into magazines to be used in the weapons they would take. What would it be like to be loved by a man the way John had loved Charlie?

Dragging her gaze away, CJ squared her shoulders, grabbed a box of bullets and fit them into still more magazines. Though they weren't going in with the intention of starting a fight, they might be forced

to defend themselves and the children who'd been recruited by Trinity.

"The most important thing we have to be aware
of is Trinity's leader," Cole said. "If he's at the compound, we can't let him escape."

"True," Declan agreed. "If it comes to a choice
between losing him or engaging with the enemy…
engage the enemy to save the children."

CJ loaded more magazines. If they had to engage
the enemy, they might be shooting teenagers and children. She prayed it didn't come to that.

For the first time in a year, she had a chance at
finding and neutralizing the leader of an organization
that had ruined the lives of many children, including
her life. They had to make this opportunity count. She
didn't know if she had the strength to continue a life
of looking over her shoulder.

CJ wanted more. She wanted love and maybe a
family of her own.

She'd never even considered children as part of her
future, never saw them fitting in, so she'd not given
the possibility any thought. Now, though, she realized there were many things she wanted that she'd
simply refused to allow herself to contemplate as a
member of Trinity and then as an escapee from their
evil grasp.

But, yes, she wanted children, damn it. After all
she'd been through, all she'd been trained to be, she
hadn't considered herself fit to be a mother. Hell, she'd
thought she wasn't fit to be the wife of a good man.

But now—now she had dreams.

Chapter Eleven

Cole rode in the middle row of seats of the SUV. Mack drove, Jack claimed shotgun and CJ sat beside Cole. Mustang sat in the backseat as they drove through late-evening DC traffic to the Leesburg airport outside of the city. Charlie's connections had arranged for a helicopter to ferry them to a location close enough to the compound that they could set down in a field and hike in from there. Gus, who would meet them on the fenced perimeter, would wait to move in until they were all there.

The helicopter was a model used for sightseeing. The pilot was a former army helicopter aviator. He didn't ask questions about the gear they brought on board in two large duffel bags. All he needed was the weights to balance the load and they were off, heading west farther into Virginia.

Where it had taken forty minutes for them to get from Charlie's estate to Leesburg Executive Airport, it took less than thirty minutes for them to fly the distance from the airport to the landing site in the Virginia countryside.

Cole stared down at the traffic on the highway at a standstill in the evening rush hour and said a prayer of thanks for Charlie and her connections. It had taken Gus over an hour and a half to drive the same distance during the middle of the day, not at rush hour.

The pilot put down in the dog handler's field after Jonah had called ahead to get permission. The helicopter and pilot would remain in the field until one of the team released him to leave. If someone ended up getting hurt, they might have to airlift him out to get medical attention—quicker than waiting for an ambulance.

Cole hoped that didn't happen, but it was nice to know they had the helicopter as backup if they needed a quick getaway.

By the time they landed, the sun had just dropped below the horizon, casting the land into the gray shadow of dusk. They could see, but night would consume them quickly. The sooner they moved out, the better. Their night vision would adjust as the light faded.

Cole grabbed one of the bags and Mack took the other. They divided what was in them among the five members of the team, carrying an extra rifle for Gus who'd gone out with the drone and a handgun. Each person plugged the radio communications earbuds in their ears and buckled into bulletproof vests.

"How do we find Gus?" CJ asked.

"He's got the drone and it's wired with a GPS tracker." Mack held up a tracking device. "I have him, as long as he's still with the drone."

As they took off through the woods, Cole dropped back behind Mack and Jack. Mustang brought up the rear.

Cole reached for CJ's hand and held it as long as he could without tripping over branches and underbrush. Eventually, he was forced to let go. The darkness made it difficult to see what they were stepping on and into.

He wanted to ask her if she was all right, but the others would hear anything he had to say since they were all connected with the earbuds. He had to be satisfied that she was near him. Cole wasn't sure it was a good idea for her to go back into the compound if it was the one where she'd trained. Being back was sure to ignite a firestorm of memories that could end up derailing her concentration.

By the time they reached Gus, darkness had settled in and the stars had come out. A few clouds scudded across the sky, blocking out some of the light, but they could see well enough by moonlight to move through the forest without use of flashlights.

They found Gus seated beneath a tree, the drone on the ground beside him. When he saw them coming, he rose to his feet. "I did what I could to recon the area, but without wire cutters, I couldn't get past the fence without digging under."

"What did you find?" Cole asked.

"First, I checked, and this facility is not owned or operated by any federal or local authorities. It's private. The front gate has two sentries, each armed with AR-15 rifles. There's a guard at the rear of the compound inside the fence and one on each side. All are armed. I couldn't tell if the fence is designed to keep people out or in."

"Both," CJ answered.

Cole dug into his pocket, pulled out a pair of wire cutters and held them up. "Point us in the right direction and we'll get this party started."

Gus led them down a ravine and up the other side, over a ridge and back down to a fence that rose up out of the forest floor, eight feet high. It was topped with two more feet of concertina wire.

"The guard is a couple hundred yards to the south," Gus whispered.

"Cutting the wire is likely to make noise," Cole warned.

"We'll have to be ready in case he comes to check it out," Gus said.

Mack turned south. "Gus and I will keep an eye out for movement."

"Mustang and I will take the opposite direction," Jack said, "in case our man on the back side of the compound comes snooping."

CJ stood guard on Cole while he snipped through the chain-link fence one link at a time. He was glad she had his back. Standing at the fence, he would be easy to spot should anyone come anywhere close on the other side.

When he had cut enough of the links that a person his size could fit through, he stopped. Slipping the wire cutters into his pocket, he held the flap of fence to the side for CJ to go through first.

"We're in," he said into his headset.

Mack and Gus returned to his location and ducked through.

"We took care of our guard. He won't be warning the others of our arrival."

Mustang and Jack showed up at that moment. "We took out our guy. He won't be a problem. And we circled around to the far side and knocked out the one over there."

"Which leaves the two on the gate," Gus said.

After everyone else made it through, Mack held the fence for Cole. When they were all on the other side, they moved out slowly, staying low and clinging to the shadows.

Gus and Mack led the way based on the information they'd gleaned from the images the drone had collected. Treading quietly, they eventually could see several long buildings with corrugated tin roofs and clapboard walls.

"Dormitories," CJ whispered. "This is where they brought us. The one on the right is for the younger kids. The one on the left is for the teenagers. It's all coming back to me. In the center is a two-story house. It's the headquarters building. It's where the instructors live and dole out punishment."

"Get down," Mack said into the headset. "Someone's coming."

Several men carrying five-gallon jugs rounded the corners of the dormitories, shaking the contents of the jugs up against the sides of the buildings.

The scent of gasoline filled the air.

"That's gasoline. They're soaking the walls," CJ said. "They're going to burn the dormitories." She leaped to her feet and started toward the long buildings.

Cole dived after CJ, tackled her to the ground and covered her body with his, praying the men with the gasoline jugs hadn't seen her.

"They'll kill them," she wheezed, barely able to breathe beneath the weight of the former marine on her back.

"We don't know if there are any people in those dorms," Cole whispered in her ear. "And we don't know if those men are armed."

Mack and Jack slipped through the trees, darting from shadow to shadow until they were close enough to the men slinging gasoline all over the buildings.

"They're armed," Mack said softly.

"I'll get the one on the right," Jack said.

"Better make it fast—someone just threw a match," Cole said.

"Let me up." CJ bucked beneath him. "We have to help them."

"I will as soon as you promise not to go off half-cocked."

"I promise," she said too quickly.

"They're armed, CJ. You can't help those kids if you're dead."

"I can handle them. Let me go."

Cole rolled off her. "Stick to the shadows and be careful." He didn't want to let her go, but he had to. She was a trained killer, and she'd find a way out of his grasp no matter what he did. Better to let her go and help her than to have her work without his knowledge. CJ could take care of herself.

As she took off toward the dormitories, he prayed that was the case.

HER HEART SLAMMED against her ribs as CJ ran toward the first building, the one that housed the youngest of the children.

When the man dropped the match, flames spread and rose up the walls like a dancing, heaving blanket, consuming the gasoline and eating into the wooden walls.

Mack, Gus, Mustang and Jack sneaked up on the two men swinging around the rear of the dormitory with their jugs of gasoline. The Defenders took the two men out without making a sound.

As smoke and flame rose, sounds came from inside the dorms. Sounds of children coughing and crying for help. The building had no windows. CJ remembered there being a back door and a front door. Since the guys with the gas hadn't made it all the way around the building, the back door was still clear of the fire. CJ ran to the back door.

Hands banged on the door from the inside and voices shouted and screamed there.

CJ's heart squeezed hard in her chest. She tried the doorknob, then realized there was a padlock on the outside, locked tight. The men had locked the children inside and planned on burning the building down and the kids with it. This would cause a stir and attention, something Trinity liked to avoid, but CJ guessed in this case they might want to send a warning to people like her who got out. Trinity was ruthless enough to kill dozens of kids just to let a traitor know they'd stop at nothing.

CJ used the handle of her pistol and slammed it against the padlock again and again. No matter how hard she hit it, it wouldn't break. Then she remembered the file she'd placed in her pocket. She pulled it out, her hands shaking, and almost dropped it on the ground. After two attempts, she had the lock opened and removed from the hasp. Then she tackled the lock on the doorknob, releasing it on the first attempt. Finally, she flung open the door. Children rushed out, wearing the T-shirts and underwear they'd gone to bed in. Smoke billowed out with the children.

Mustang, Cole and CJ ran into the smoky room, checking beds and beneath the bunks. When the building was clear, they ran out, coughing.

CJ's lungs burned and her eyes stung, but there was another dormitory full of people and the flames were burning hotter and brighter from that building.

Mack, Gus and Jack had moved on to take out three other men wielding jugs of gasoline. These three had come looking for their cohorts and found Declan's Defenders. They were in the midst of hand-to-hand combat when Mustang, CJ and Cole arrived on the scene from behind.

Cole took out the one closest to him and CJ side kicked the other, sending him flying into Jack's fist. CJ didn't wait around to watch the outcome. She ran to the second dorm. Like the first, it had been locked from the outside with a padlock. Using her file, she unlocked the padlock on her first attempt and then the doorknob lock. Teenagers spilled out as soon as the door opened.

The ones closest to the doors stumbled out of the smoke-filled room, coughing and hacking. Some helped others escape. Still others lay on the floor, having succumbed to the smoke.

While Gus, Mustang and Jack went after the men on the gate, Cole and Mack helped CJ get everyone out of the second dorm, some leaning on them for support, others having to be lugged out in a fireman's carry over broad shoulders.

When Cole went back into the dormitory for the last teen, CJ turned toward the main house where the trainers lived and held court. They'd been the judges, juries and hangmen of the compound, keeping order through threats of harsh sentences. If the leader of Trinity was anywhere around, he'd be inside the main house, packing his stuff to get out before the fire department arrived and found all the dead children.

Would he be here at all? Part of her thought a leader this cruel would enjoy seeing his sickening plans in action, might even take pleasure in seeing her suffer as she witnessed the tragedy unfolding.

Anger burned inside CJ hotter than the actual fire as she ran toward the house. An SUV stood outside, the engine running and the headlights shining. Several men were inside the vehicle. The driver's door hung open and no one sat in the driver's seat.

A smaller SUV stood in front of the larger one, also running but unoccupied.

A man came out of the house, got into the larger vehicle and started to drive around the one in front of it.

CJ couldn't let them get away. While running toward the vehicle, she pulled out her handgun, aimed for the tires and fired off one round after another. She hit the right front and rear tires. Windows lowered and guns poked out of them.

CJ dived to the ground and rolled behind the rusted-out hull of the abandoned 1957 Ford Fairlane that had been in the courtyard of the compound for as long as she could remember.

Bullets slammed into the metal and kicked up dust around her. She edged toward the opposite end of the massive pile of junk metal and fired several more rounds into the windows of the SUV. The driver swerved and hit the vehicle that had been parked in front of it, sending it sliding up against the front porch railing of the house.

A couple of the men dived out the doors onto the ground, rolled to their feet and started running.

CJ shot them in the legs. They fell to the ground, screaming and clutching at their wounds.

The flames from the burning dormitories lit the yard, making it nearly impossible for her to run across to the big house without being seen.

Taking a deep breath, she left the comparative safety of the Fairlane and sprinted across the yard, heading for the house. She zigzagged, making it harder for potential shooters to get a bead on her.

Shots rang out, kicking up dust beside her.

She didn't slow until she reached the porch. Taking the steps two at a time, she dived through the door into the front foyer, rolled to the side and came up on her feet, her Glock in her hand.

"Stop right there," a voice said. A man stood before her with a handful of documents, fire burning one corner of them, and a pistol in his other hand, aimed at her chest.

With her heart pounding against her ribs, CJ stared down the barrel of the pistol and then looked up into the face of a man she recognized. Not from her time spent in training, but from her short time in the West Wing of the White House. "Chris Carpenter," she said aloud.

He gave a slight nod and tossed the papers onto the floor among a larger pile of documents and folders. The flames spread, gobbling up more paper, sending a bright flame climbing into the air.

"It's about time you came back to the fold, CJ." Carpenter shook his head. He brought his free hand up to stabilize the one holding the pistol. "I didn't recognize you when you took Dr. Saunders's position, I wasn't here when you went through training and I only had grainy photos to go by, so it didn't come to me right away. But once I learned you'd been in my house, I compared videos of the woman in my office with the one in the exterminator's outfit and realized my mistake. We taught you well."

"I'm not here for compliments, nor am I here to rejoin Trinity," CJ said. "I came to put a stop to Trinity and keep them from stealing children and killing innocent people."

"Like you kept them from killing my wife and Orlov, her lover?" Carpenter snorted. "I put out that kill order as well as the one that put a stop to John Halverson's snooping."

"You were responsible for John Halverson's death?" Her teeth ground together, her finger itching to pull the trigger.

"I had to. He knew too much."

"Bastard," she ground out.

"Maybe so. We had a job to do, and he was in the way. But no more. The wheels are turning, the plan is in place." He gave her a smile that looked more like a sneer. "And you're too late to stop it."

"Too late?" She frowned. "What do you mean?"

His lip curled. "The remaining recruits are being eliminated as we speak and, after tonight, our primary purpose will have been accomplished."

CJ lifted her chin, her eyes narrowing. "And that is?"

"Assassination of the most prominent figure in US government. In doing so, we'll put our own man in position to effect change." Carpenter snorted. "It's finally happening. What we've been working toward for so long."

"The president? Trinity is going to assassinate POTUS?" CJ's heart slid to the pit of her belly and back up to pound against her ribs. "When? How?"

Carpenter's lips twisted. "Sooner than you think. And we'll finally be rid of the other half of the Halverson annoyance."

CJ shook her head. "Charlie Halverson?"

"We thought we'd done away with the trouble when the Director had me eliminate John, never expecting his widow to pick up the baton and run with it." His jaw tightened. "But that will all be behind us soon." He took his gaze off her for a brief glance at his watch. "Yes, soon. Now, I need to get out of here before the gasoline tanks explode. You're going to be my ticket past your bodyguards."

"What makes you think I won't shoot you first?" CJ held the gun steady, her finger resting on the trigger. She'd always been taught never to put her finger on the trigger unless she intended to shoot.

She intended to shoot.

"You don't have it in you to shoot. You proved that when you wouldn't shoot your target a year ago."

"I don't shoot defenseless pregnant women," she said. "You're neither a woman, defenseless nor pregnant."

His eyes narrowed. "I could pull the trigger first, but if you die, you won't have time to warn your friends of the impending explosion. If you come with me without a fight, I won't shoot you. You can tell your friends about the tank before it goes up, and be my ticket out. I'll take you back to the people you belong with. You'll be an asset to us, with all you've learned on your little…vacation away from Trinity.

But you only have a few seconds to make up your mind. What's it going to be?"

CJ didn't hesitate. She pulled the trigger, then dived to the side.

The sound of gunfire echoed in her ears and a sharp pain ripped through her shoulder as she hit the wooden floor hard, rolled and came up, her Glock pointed at the man still standing. He dropped the gun from his grip and stared across at her, his face pale. "Won't do you any good. This place will blow any minute... The president and Halverson—" he dropped to his knees, clutching at his chest, blood seeping through his fingers "—will be dead...and the Director—" Carpenter slid to his side and stared up at her "—will...be...in...charge." The corners of his lips curled upward. "You're too...late."

CJ turned, pain shooting through her at her sudden move. Warm liquid dripped down her left arm. She glanced at her jacket, surprised to see blood. It didn't matter. She didn't have time to deal with it—she had to warn the others.

As she stepped through the door, gunfire rang out. A bullet hit the door frame beside her. Splinters rained down on her.

CJ darted to the side and dropped to a prone position, flattening her body against the wooden slats of the porch. She searched the darkness for the shooter. A man stood beside the crippled SUV, aiming for her.

Before she could bring her weapon up to shoot the man, another shot rang out. Fully expecting to take the hit, CJ was surprised when she didn't feel the pain. The man by the SUV crumpled to the ground and lay still.

"CJ?" Cole's voice called out. "Are you all right?"

Her gaze swept the yard, landing on the man who'd captured her heart. He stood with his gun pointed at the SUV.

CJ's heart swelled. "I am," she said and rose to her feet. With no time to spare, CJ leaped off the porch and ran toward Cole. "We have to get everyone out of here. Now."

Mack, Mustang, Jack and Gus appeared, silhouetted against the blaze.

"The recruits are hiding in the woods," Gus said.

CJ shook her head, dread crushing her chest like an anvil. "We have to get them out of here. Now," she repeated. "They have explosives on the fuel storage barrels. It'll blow any minute."

"We'll round up the children and send them down the road," Mack said.

"Go!" CJ said.

The four men ran toward the woods behind the dormitory infernos.

"I'm afraid they'll be too late," CJ said to Cole. "I have to find the explosives." She started toward where she knew they kept the barrels of gasoline.

Cole's hand shot out and captured her arm. "You can't."

She shook loose. "I have to." Then she was running, her feet carrying her the fastest she could go toward the possibility of death. If she didn't get to the explosives before they went off, she'd be blown away and die a fiery death. But so, too, would Declan's Defenders and the children who'd been involuntarily recruited to become assassins.

She couldn't fail. Those kids deserved to be children. Cole, Jack, Gus, Mustang and Mack deserved to live long, full lives.

If she died, no one would care, but they deserved to live.

Footsteps pounded on the ground behind her. Cole caught up with her and kept pace as she dodged between storage buildings to the back of the compound where the fuel was stored. Eight fifty-five-gallon barrels stood in a line. She didn't know which were empty and which were full. It didn't matter. What mattered was finding the explosives and disarming them before their world erupted into a fiery crescendo.

Cole started on one end, CJ on the other, as they examined the barrels, searching for the explosives. They met in the middle, both locating the wad of C-4 smashed up against a full barrel with a timing detonator pressed into the middle. The red digital numbers indicated thirty seconds until detonation.

CJ tried to pry the detonator loose from the C-4 plastic, but she couldn't get it to release.

Twenty-five seconds remained.

"Let me," Cole said. He dug his fingers into the C-4 and pulled as hard as he could, but he couldn't get the device out.

Ten seconds ticked by and still, they couldn't free

the claylike plastic from the barrel or the detonator from the plastic.

Pulling her file out of her pocket, CJ rammed it beneath the C-4.

Nine seconds…eight…seven…

Cole found a stick and used it as well, prying the explosive free of the barrel with five seconds to spare.

He ran for the woods, cocked his arm and threw the device into the darkness. "Get down!" he yelled and dropped to the ground.

CJ dropped to her belly, closed her eyes and covered her ears.

An explosion rocked the ground beneath her. A loud cracking sound followed.

CJ looked up in time to see the dark shadow of a massive tree falling toward them.

"Cole! Run!" she cried. Instead of running away from the falling tree, she ran toward Cole.

He staggered to his feet and took off.

She caught up with him and they ran as fast as they could to get away from the massive tree falling toward the buildings of the compound and the barrels of gasoline.

As it fell, other trees slowed its descent, buying CJ and Cole enough time to get out of the way of the largest of the branches.

When it hit the ground, a branch full of leaves slammed into CJ's back, slapping her to the ground like a fly beneath a swatter.

Cole, a few steps away from her, staggered but regained his balance.

He parted the leaves and helped CJ to her feet.

They turned to survey the damage the giant tree had created. The acrid scent of fuel filled the air again.

"I smell gasoline," CJ said.

"The tree fell on the barrels. We have to go." Cole's quiet voice sent shivers down her spine.

CJ launched herself away from the tree, the barrels and the burning buildings that would soon catch the tree and the spilled gasoline on fire. They had only moments to spare.

As she ran, her ankle screamed with pain, until she was limping as fast as she could.

Cole slipped an arm around her waist and let her lean on him as they hurried away from impending disaster.

They were passing the main house when Cole veered toward the smaller SUV Chris Carpenter would have used as his getaway vehicle. It was still running with the driver's door still open.

Cole opened the passenger door. CJ dived in.

He rounded to the other side and slipped in behind the wheel. He'd just shifted into Drive when the barrels ignited, sending up balls of flames into the sky.

CJ could see the fiery reflection in the side mirror. "Go," she said. "We can't stop now. We have even bigger problems."

"What do you mean?" Cole asked.

Her fists clenched in her lap, a dull ache throbbing in her injured shoulder. "Trinity is planning a coup. They're targeting the president."

"When?"

"I assume tonight. Carpenter kept saying we were too late." She touched Cole's arm. "And they're taking Charlie out at the same time. They want the Director to take over as president."

"The only person who can do that is the VP. And if he's killed, then the speaker of the house."

"Where did Charlie say she was going tonight?" CJ asked.

Cole's fingers tightened on the steering wheel until his knuckles turned white. "She's at an event where the president is speaking."

"We have to get there." She leaned forward as they caught up with the children and teenagers walking down the middle of the road, heading for the highway.

They wore T-shirts and shorts, most barefoot, their eyes wide and scared. They looked like ghosts.

CJ's chest tightened. They would need years of counseling. What they'd gone through would have serious effects on them, much like PTSD for battle-weary soldiers.

She didn't have time to worry about them now. She had to gather the other men of Declan's Defenders and get back to the city before Carpenter's prediction came true and they were too late.

Chapter Twelve

Cole pulled up beside Mack, Mustang, Gus and Jack, each carrying a barefoot child piggyback. Sirens blared as fire trucks, law-enforcement vehicles and first responders pulled onto the dirt road leading to the compound, lights flashing like a parade with fast, colorful floats.

"We have to go," CJ said as the road became congested with people and vehicles. A smaller fire truck with paramedics on board was the first to reach them. The four Defenders handed over the children on their backs. Gus, Mustang and Jack got into the back of the SUV.

Mack gave the paramedic a brief explanation of what had happened and then backed away, slipping silently into the SUV.

Cole edged through the crowd of young people and headed for the highway, his pulse pounding, his hands holding the steering wheel so tightly he thought it would break. They couldn't get out of there fast enough.

Charlie had done so much for them. They couldn't let her down.

Jack was on his cell phone, desperately trying to contact Charlie, Roger or Declan. None of them was answering their cell phones. They would have made it to the downtown event center. Roger would be inside with Charlie. Declan would be with them, if Charlie arranged to have more than one escort. If not, he'd be nearby in case anything happened.

As soon as they reached the highway, Cole pressed the accelerator to the floor, sending the vehicle blasting toward the dog trainer's property and the waiting helicopter. Mack had called ahead to warn the pilot that they'd need to take off immediately.

The chopper was ready, the blades turning, when they pulled into the field.

Everyone bailed out of the SUV as soon as Cole pulled to a stop.

CJ and Cole hunkered low and ran toward the helicopter, climbing in.

Cole buckled his safety harness. When CJ fumbled with hers, he leaned over and pulled her harness over her shoulders. His hand brushed against warm, sticky liquid on her left shoulder. He leaned closer, staring hard at her in the limited lighting. "You're hurt."

She shrugged. "It's just a flesh wound." As if to prove it, she lifted her arm up and down. "See? I can still use it."

"We need to get you to a doctor."

"After we make sure Charlie and the president are okay, we'll have plenty of time to stick a bandage on this scratch," she said, her chin lifting in challenge. "Not any sooner."

Cole didn't like it. CJ was bleeding. She could have lost a lot of blood already.

As if reading his mind, she touched his arm. "If I'd lost a lot of blood, I wouldn't have been able to run to the helicopter. I was more worried about my ankle than my shoulder and it's fine. Both are fine. I'll survive. It would take a lot more to bring me down than a bullet or a 150-year-old tree." She cupped his cheek and smiled into his eyes. "I'm okay."

As soon as everyone was on board, Mack yelled into his flight headset, "Go! Go! Go!"

The chopper left the ground and rose into the air, turning in a tight circle toward the bright lights of the downtown area.

Because of the air restrictions around DC, the closest the pilot could land was at the Leesburg Leesburg Executive Airport. When the helicopter touched down, they dived out and ran for Charlie's SUV.

Mack drove, weaving in and out of traffic toward DC and the hotel hosting the event.

"We'll never get there in time," CJ said.

Traffic into the downtown area had thinned, allowing them to make good time, but they couldn't be certain they'd arrive before whatever Trinity had planned started.

Cole pulled out his cell. They couldn't wait another minute. "I'm calling in a bomb threat."

"We'll never get in after that," Mustang pointed out.

"No, but maybe they'll get out before Trinity attacks," Cole said.

They were five blocks away when police, fire trucks and ambulances raced past them toward the hotel. Traffic came to a halt.

"We have to get through before they barricade the streets," Cole said.

"Time to bail." Mack parked along the side of the street. The team got out and ran the remaining five blocks to the hotel.

By the time they got near, the police were setting up barricades across the road. Fire trucks and law-enforcement vehicles made it impossible for any other vehicles to access the hotel.

Guests streamed out of the hotel dressed in their finest. Men in black suits, wired with radio headsets, scurried around the entrances. Secret Service.

Cole stopped a man and woman walking away from the hotel. "What's going on?" he asked, knowing for the most part why they'd been evacuated.

"Someone called in a bomb threat. They've evacuated the entire building."

The woman shivered in the cool night air. "They wouldn't even let us get our coats."

"Did they get the president out?" Cole asked.

The man frowned. "The Secret Service gathered him and the vice president and took them out of the ballroom through the rear exit. I'm sure the president is back at the White House by now, sitting in front of a fireplace keeping warm. Unlike the rest of us." He draped his arm around the woman's shoulders and pulled her close. "Come on, we'll find a cab a couple blocks away from this nightmare."

"I can't walk too far in these shoes," she complained as they continued away from the hotel. "I wasn't expecting to hike in this outfit."

"What if they didn't get the president out of the hotel?" CJ said.

"We don't know how they plan to kill the president. It could be with explosives or they might plan on a sniper taking him out as he leaves."

"Carpenter said they would eliminate Charlie as well as the president," Mack said. "How would they do that and spare the others?"

Cole swore. "I might have made it that much easier for them by calling in the bomb threat."

"How are we going to get in?" Mack asked.

"Come on," Cole said. "I have an idea." Weaving through the crowd leaving the hotel, they found an ambulance parked near the entrance, a stretcher unfolded and ready for anyone who might need assistance. An EMT had just climbed up into the back of the ambulance for supplies, leaving the stretcher unattended.

Cole grabbed the stretcher and rolled it past a police car. "Mack, get the other end," he said. CJ swiped the EMT's tool kit and hurried after them.

With Cole walking backward and Mack pushing the other end, they walked right past the police but were stopped by the Secret Service men guarding the front of the building.

"We were told Charlotte Halverson is in need of medical support. Please, step aside," Cole said.

"We can't let you inside," the man in the black suit said.

"Mrs. Halverson funds half the hospitals in the DC area," Cole said. "Do you want to be responsible for her death and the cessation of funding to those hospitals?"

The man stood tall, his chest puffed out, a rifle in his arms. "Can't let you in."

"Very well," Cole said. "Let it be on your shoulders when she dies."

"Oh, dear Lord," CJ jerked and clutched her shoulder. "I've been hit!" She dropped to the ground and moaned. "They're shooting at us. I've been hit."

The agent crouched and looked up at the buildings surrounding them. "Get down!" he called out. Everyone within earshot ducked. Women dressed in evening gowns screamed and dropped to their knees.

In the confusion, the five Defenders slipped past the guards, entered the hotel, sidestepped the metal detectors and kept moving, following the signs leading to the ballroom. The first chance they got, they ditched the gurney.

Cole didn't like leaving CJ outside the hotel, but knew they had to get to Charlie and the president.

"CJ? Are you okay?"

For a moment, he thought their headsets had quit working. But then he heard the soft sound of her voice,

"I'm okay. I'll see you inside."

"Don't try. We'll take care of this."

A bad feeling hit Cole in the pit of his belly. What were the chances that CJ would stay put outside the hotel?

Slim to none.

If Trinity had its people inside and they ran into CJ, they'd take her out, as well.

Damn.

Cole fought the urge to turn around and run back out to the front of the hotel. They had a job to do. The fate of the nation and Declan's Defenders rode on the outcome.

Secret Service agents combed the ballroom. Several had bomb-sniffing dogs, checking every square inch of the room.

Cole stopped one of the agents. "Did they get the president out?"

The agent frowned. "Of course. Who the hell are you and how did you get in?"

"We're from the bomb squad," Cole lied. "We're here to defuse the bomb when you find it."

"Good. I'd like to keep all my parts in place." The agent nodded toward the rear of the ballroom. "They took POTUS and the VP out that way, along with that billionaire philanthropist, Halverson, and some guy." He shrugged. "Not sure why they took her. Maybe the president wants her to fund his next election campaign."

"Why that way and not out the front?" Cole asked.

"They have several escape plans for each event the president attends. Going out the front, going out the back and going up. If they go up, they have to hold until Marine One can get here. If the helo can't land on the roof, they'll call for a Navy SEAL team to extract them."

"We'll be around if you find anything," Cole said. "All you have to do is yell."

"Don't go far. If a clock is ticking, we might be on borrowed time," the agent said. He went back to work searching under chairs and tables draped in fancy white linens, set with gold charger plates and crystal glasses and candelabras.

A man in a black suit was on a ladder in the middle of the room, checking out the huge crystal chandelier.

Cole, Mack, Mustang, Jack and Gus moved through the room to the rear exit. Mack pulled out his cell phone.

"Calling Declan?" Cole asked as they pushed through the double doors into a hallway.

Mack nodded. "I don't know why they're not answering. If they were evacuated, they'd have been outside by now."

"Try Arnold," Cole said. "He was Charlie's date."

Mack dialed the butler's number.

A moment later, he looked up. "Nothing."

Then his phone pinged. Mack stared down at the screen. "It's a text from Declan."

The men gathered around Mack.

Head for the top. Trinity has POTUS, VP, Roger and Charlie. Take stairs.

"They're headed for the roof," Cole said. "Find the stairs."

AFTER CJ FAKED being shot and had everyone ducking to avoid being hit, she rolled away from the guard
at the door and ducked into the building following
another Secret Service agent. She dodged the metal
detectors to avoid setting off an alarm with the gun
she had stashed beneath the jacket she wore that was
splattered in her own blood.

She'd listened to the one-sided conversation she
could hear as Cole spoke with someone about them
being part of the bomb squad. She chuckled as she
headed down a hallway. When she heard them talk
about the text from Declan and needing to get to the
roof, she found a stairwell and started up. She ran,
though her ankle hurt and her shoulder throbbed.
They were the least of her worries. Charlie was in
trouble. And Trinity was planning to kill the president and possibly the vice president.

If they both died, the speaker of the house was
next in line for the presidency. Had the speaker of the
house been the leader of Trinity all along? CJ thought
about who that was and shook her head. The speaker
of the house was a man who had been married to
the same woman for thirty years, had two beautiful
daughters and five grandchildren. He went to church
on Sundays and volunteered at children's hospitals
in his home state and in the DC area. He couldn't be
the Trinity leader.

And the vice president had been kidnapped by
Trinity along with Anne Bellamy just a little while
ago, a plot foiled by the Declan crew. Trinity wouldn't
kidnap their own leader, would they?

Unless they wanted to throw others off. Who would believe they would kidnap their own leader? No one. But they hadn't killed him when they could have. They'd used the VP and Anne Bellamy to lure CJ out of hiding.

They'd succeeded in that effort. CJ wasn't hiding anymore. But they hadn't been quick enough to kill her. She'd stayed one step ahead. With the help of Declan's Defenders, she'd gotten that much closer to learning who was in charge of Trinity.

She'd hoped that when she'd discovered Chris Carpenter in the main house on the compound, that he would prove to be their leader. But he'd been pretty confident that Trinity would have someone in the highest office in the US soon. Since he wasn't with the president at the time, nor in position to take over the presidency, he clearly wasn't the guy.

Which brought it down to one of two people. The vice president and the speaker of the house.

CJ's money was on the vice president. The sooner she got to them, the sooner she'd find out.

Taking the stairs two at a time, she ignored the pain in her ankle and in her shoulder and powered through, climbing the eight stories to the top, her breath fast and heavy. When she reached the eighth floor, she found a smaller stairwell with a locked gate in front of it. A sign read Authorized Personnel Only.

CJ vaulted over the gate, landing on the first stair leading upward. Since she hadn't heard anyone in the stairwell or seen the others of her group, she assumed they were climbing a different set of steps to the roof.

She hoped they arrived around the same time as she did. They'd all need backup.

If it was true the Secret Service had evacuated the POTUS, VP and Charlie, they were probably Trinity sleeper agents who'd managed to get past the background checks to become Secret Service staff members. They'd be highly trained as assassins as well as having gone through specialized training for the Secret Service. They'd be formidable foes in hand-to-hand or weapon fights.

When CJ reached the top of the stairs, the door led out onto the rooftop of the hotel. A rectangular window allowed her to peer through before she made her move to step out onto the roof.

As far as she could see, there were air-conditioning units jutting out of the roof near her end of the long, rectangular building. A structure graced the other end of the building. It appeared to be a rooftop bar with large windows on the side she could see. Outside the windows, there was a patio area with tables, chairs and potted plants in large concrete containers. Based on the direction the bar faced, it had a view of the city customers would pay top dollar to admire.

"Declan just texted." Cole's voice sounded in her earbud headset and made her feel warm all over. "They're in the rooftop bar. He can see them through the window. The men dressed as Secret Service are holding the president, Charlie and Roger hostage."

"What about the vice president?" one of the guys asked.

CJ waited, her heart pounding, hanging on the edge, eager to hear Cole again.

Cole swore. "He's calling the shots."

CJ nodded. As she suspected. Vice President Gordon Helms would be next in command should the president die. He'd be the leader of the US until the next election.

"That's our guy. The bastard we've been searching for," Gus said in his gruff voice. "How many guns?"

Another pause before Cole answered. "Six men in black. And the VP is carrying."

Six. The trick would be to get inside the bar without being detected.

If they made too daring a move, Trinity would push the process forward and kill the president, Charlie and Roger before they had a chance to rescue them.

"How do we want to handle this?"

"None of us was able to bring in the rifles. All we have are small arms. We can't pick them off without several sniper rifles going at the same time." It was Mack's voice. "We have to get inside or get close enough to shoot through the glass."

"There are planters, tables with umbrellas, and chairs on a patio close to me," CJ interjected. "I can low-crawl to within a few feet of the windows."

"It's too dangerous," Cole said.

"I can do it," CJ insisted. "Going now. I'll let you know when I'm in position."

"CJ," Cole said.

She ignored him and slipped out of the door onto the roof. Keeping low, she moved in the shadows of the AC units until she reached the edge of the patio, partitioned off by a wrought-iron railing. CJ crept alongside the building where there were no windows and rolled over the top of the railing, landing on the patio. She lay still, listening for movement from inside. When she thought all was quiet, she low crawled on her belly, moving from the cover of a giant pot to the shadow of a table to another giant pot until she was close enough she could see through the windows to the people gathered around.

Her heart caught in her throat when she located Charlie. The older woman sat on the floor beside a body of a man in a tuxedo. His head lay across her lap and she held his hand.

Roger Arnold, the butler.

Charlie raised his hand to her cheek and held it there.

Was he dead?

The butler brushed his knuckles across her cheek and his lips moved.

CJ let go of the breath she'd been holding. "I can see the six men dressed as Secret Service agents, the vice president, Charlie, Arnold and the president. I have ten rounds in my gun. I can take them out, but not all at once."

"Wait until we get in position on the other side," Cole said.

From where she was, CJ could see that the patio extended around the front of the bar to the other side with a similar setup of tables with umbrellas, chairs and potted plants.

"Gus and Mack met up with Declan. They're going in through the back door once the war begins," Cole said. "Jack, Mustang and I can take out the four men close to the vice president."

"I can take the other two who are closer to my side of the bar," CJ said.

"What if they're not Trinity?" Jack asked. "What if they're really there to protect the VP and president?"

The vice president lifted his weapon and fired at one of the men in black. The man dropped where he stood. The others didn't flinch.

"I'd say that answers our question," CJ said.

"On three," Cole said. "One."

CJ positioned herself, holding her Glock steady with one hand braced beneath the handle.

"Two."

The vice president waved his gun at one of the men in black.

That man raised his weapon and aimed it at Charlie.

"He's going to shoot Charlie," CJ said, and fired on the guy.

Chapter Thirteen

CJ's bullet pierced the window with a clean, round hole and hit her target in the side of his head. He fell to the ground.

The president sank to the floor beside Charlie and Arnold, out of range of the bullets flying over their heads.

Cole and Jack dropped their men and CJ hit the second guy on her side in a clean kill, taking him down with a bullet through the chest.

That left the vice president as the only man holding a gun still alive.

Gus, Declan and Mack burst through the back door into the bar, their weapons leveled on Helms, but a second too late.

Helms had grabbed the president from behind and pressed his gun against the man's temple. Through the holes in the windows, CJ heard the VP say, "Drop your weapons or I'll shoot him."

CJ leaped to her feet and raced for the back door, coming to a skidding halt beside Mack and Gus. "If you drop your weapons," CJ said, "he'll shoot the president anyway, then he'll shoot you. That's what Trinity does. Isn't that right, Director?"

"I don't know what you're talking about," Helms said. "You worked for Trinity. You should know."

"He shot Roger," Charlie said, her lips pulled back in a sneer. "He told one of the men to shoot me."

"Shut up, woman," Helms yelled. "Or I'll shoot you myself." He jerked his head toward Mack. "Now, are you going to put your weapons down, or am I going to put a bullet in the head of your commander in chief?"

"You might as well give up now," CJ said. "Carpenter is dead. His wife and the Russian are dead. The compound is burned to the ground and your thugs are dead. You'll be sad to know your plan to burn the kids in the dorms didn't work. We got all of them out before we lost even one."

Movement from the floor caught CJ's attention.

Roger Arnold, Charlie's butler and former SAS soldier, lunged for Helms, knocking the gun away from the president's temple and up toward the ceiling.

Helms pulled the trigger. The bullet went wide, lodging somewhere in the ceiling.

Roger fell to the floor, spent.

Helms raised his weapon and aimed it at CJ.

Before he could fire, three bullets hit him, one each from Gus, Mack and CJ's guns, sending him staggering backward with each impact.

Still, he raised his weapon and aimed again at CJ.

A shot was fired from beside CJ, hitting Helms in the head. The man dropped and lay completely still.

CJ turned to find Cole standing beside her.

"Took you long enough to get here," she quipped and fell into his arms.

"I thought you had it all under control," he said, holding her close, his strong arms surrounding her.

She didn't care if she looked weak or like she couldn't handle one more Trinity agent. CJ was in Cole's arms and she liked it there.

COLE WAS GLAD to hold her. He'd gone through all kinds of hell worrying about her when she'd been out of his sight. And then to walk into the bar and see the vice president aiming his gun at her... He'd done the only thing he could do and shot the man in the head.

Declan reached a hand down to help Charlie to her feet.

She waved his hand away and scooted across the floor in her long gown to brush a hand across Roger Arnold's forehead. "My hero," she murmured.

"Mine, too," said the president. He rose to his feet, straightened his suit jacket and stood tall. "I don't know who you men are, but I owe you my life."

Declan straightened and, wincing, pressed a hand to his midsection. "These are my team of Declan's Defenders. I'm Declan O'Neill. This is Mack Balkman, my second in command."

Mack raised a hand.

Declan pointed to Mustang. "He's Frank 'Mustang' Ford."

Mustang nodded.

Declan waved a hand toward Gus. "Gus Walsh."

"Sir," Gus said, coming to attention.

Pointing to Cole, Declan said, "Cole McCastlain."

"Pleasure to meet you, Mr. President," Cole said without loosening his hold on CJ.

Declan pointed to Jack. "Our slack man is Jack Snow. The youngest man on the team."

Jack popped a salute. "It's an honor, sir!"

The president's eyes narrowed. "Prior military?"

"Yes, sir," Declan responded. "Marine Force Recon."

"The best of the best," the president murmured. "I take it you're not in the marines anymore?"

Declan's lips thinned. "No, sir."

The president's brow furrowed. "I'd like to know why."

"Sir, it's a long story," Cole said. "And some of these folks need medical attention." He looked down at CJ. "No argument."

"And this young lady is?" The president held out his hand to CJ.

"Nobody you need to concern yourself with," CJ answered, afraid she'd be arrested if anyone were to recall that Helms had just revealed she'd once been a part of the same organization that had just attempted to assassinate the president.

"You saved my life," the president said. "I'd say that you are well worth getting to know."

CJ couldn't ignore the man's hand and shook it.

"Thank you for coming to my rescue," the president said, his tone deep and sincere.

"You're welcome, sir," CJ responded, her face suffusing with color.

"Are you blushing?" Cole whispered close to her ear. She elbowed him in the side. "No."

He chuckled softly. "Liar."

"Mrs. Halverson." The president turned to Charlie.

"Please, sir, call me Charlie," she said with a smile.

"Your date had a major role in saving my life, as well. I'd like to get to know him better."

"Sir," Arnold said in his mild English accent, from his position lying on the floor. "Roger Arnold, the Queen's SAS, at your service. Pardon me if I don't rise. I seem to have caught a bullet."

Mack removed a headset from one of the dead Trinity gunmen who'd been undercover as a Secret Service agent and tapped into the radio frequency for the president's men. "We need medical assistance in the rooftop bar. And send more men up to guard the president."

"I think I'm better off with you gentlemen as my bodyguards," the president said. "Where does one hire such men?"

Declan turned to Charlie. "Sir, you'll have to go through our boss. Charlie's the one who had the idea to pull this team together. She deserves the credit."

"Far from it," Charlie said. "I only tapped on some talent the Marine Corps let slip through its fingers. When you get a moment when your life is no longer in danger, Mr. President, I'd like to have a meeting with you on that very subject."

"I'll be sure to have my people put you on my schedule. Would you like to meet at my place or yours?"

Charlie laughed. "Yours, of course. You travel with

far too much baggage." She winked and took Arnold's hand in hers. "I'll have my people get with your people to make it happen."

"Yes, ma'am," the president said with a smile.

The Secret Service men swarmed in on the bar and surrounded the president, hustling him out of the bar and hotel, and into a waiting limousine.

Charlie, CJ and the team waited for emergency medical technicians to arrive and lift Arnold onto the stretcher that was probably the one they'd appropriated to help them get past the guards what felt like hours before.

When Arnold had been loaded into the ambulance, Charlie insisted on going with him. Declan joined them, adamant that someone needed to provide for Charlie's protection. Based on the blood seeping through his shirt, he needed the trip to the hospital for a recheck on his gunshot wound.

Cole insisted CJ also go to the hospital. She refused.

"Charlie has a doctor who will make house calls," Mack said. "Let's get her back to Charlie's place."

Mack and Mustang hurried out to where the team had left the SUV parked several blocks away and drove back to collect the other Defenders and CJ.

By the time they'd returned, the blockades had been cleared and they were able to drive up to the front of the hotel.

Tired and dirty, Cole wanted nothing more than to climb into a shower with CJ and then lie in bed with her in his arms, making love until they both fell asleep from sheer exhaustion.

CJ sat silently beside him, all the way to Charlie's estate.

Cole couldn't believe it was over and CJ was alive. They'd helped rid the world of the Director in charge of Trinity, the man who'd tried to ruin her life and that of so many others. Along with the burning of the training compound, Trinity would surely crumble.

When they reached the estate, Grace met them on the steps of the mansion.

"Charlie called to say CJ was hurt," Grace said. She hurried down to her. "The doctor is in the sitting room. He'll take care of you. If it's serious enough for surgery, we'll get you to a hospital ASAP."

"It's only a flesh wound," CJ insisted as they entered the foyer.

Cole's jaw tightened. "That's what Declan said. He's just lucky the bullet didn't hit any of his internal organs." He held up a hand when Grace shot a worried look in his direction. "Declan rode with the ambulance to provide protection for Charlie and Arnold. He'll have the ER doctor do a double check on his own injuries. And, no, he didn't sustain any more injuries tonight."

"If you think you can handle things here," Grace said, "I'd like to go to the hospital and be with Charlie, Roger and Declan."

"Go," CJ said. "I'll be fine."

Grace squeezed her hand and ran out the front door.

"I'd rather just get a shower and something to eat," CJ said, dragging her feet across the foyer.

Cole shook his head. "You're seeing the doctor. He'll determine how badly you're injured."

"Does anyone know what happened to all the kids from the compound?" CJ asked as Cole led her into the sitting room.

Jonah appeared in the hallway, coming out of the study. "They've been taken to a church's gymnasium for now until they can all be identified and cross-referenced against the missing or exploited children's database. Charlie had offered to set up a commission to handle the children."

"I'd like to be part of helping them through the re-patriation process," CJ said.

"Later," Cole insisted. "You're having your shoulder examined right now."

"I know, but—" CJ started.

"But nothing," Cole grabbed the elbow of her good arm and marched her into the sitting room.

The doctor asked her to take a seat on a small ottoman.

Cole helped her remove her bloodstained jacket and shirt. The fabric stuck to her skin with the dried blood.

"I'll get a damp cloth," Cole said as he hurried out of the room.

Mack met him in the hallway with a towel, a bucket of warm water and a washcloth. "Thought she might need these."

Cole threw the towel over his shoulder. "Thanks."

Mack lifted his chin toward the sitting room. "Is she going to be all right?"

"Haven't got to the wound yet." Cole took the bucket and the washcloth. "I'll let you know."

"She was pretty amazing tonight," Mack said as he released the handle of the bucket.

Cole's chest tightened. CJ was everything. Skilled at warfare, a great shooter, tough, tender and had a heart buried deep in all that Trinity training. "Tell me about it."

"I don't know what's going on between you two, but she's a keeper. She could probably do better, but you can't." Mack grinned and clapped a hand on Cole's shoulder. "Be nice and she might stick around."

Cole walked back into the sitting room, mulling over what Mack had said.

The doctor draped the towel around CJ and used the washcloth and warm water to wet the fabric stuck in dried blood. Before long, the water did the trick and he was able to ease the fabric away from the wound and remove the shirt altogether. She sat in a white lace bra, completely at ease with her body and the fact that she was in the presence of two men in only her underwear.

Cole smiled. Tough and confident. That was CJ.

Once he had the wound cleaned, the doctor could better see how bad it was. "You're lucky. It doesn't appear to have damaged any muscle tissue," he said. After applying a local anesthetic around the gash, he removed the bullet and sutured the skin together with three small stitches. "You'll be fine, as long as you keep it clean and watch for infection. I'll be back to take the stitches out at the end of next week."

CJ nodded. "Thanks." Then she draped the damp towel over her shoulders. "Any problem with showering? I'd like to wash the rest of the dirt and soot from my body."

"No problem at all. Once you're done, apply this antibiotic cream to the wound and cover it in gauze and tape." He pulled out the supplies she'd need and gave her instructions on the care and cleaning of the wound for the next week. "If you suspect it's getting infected, don't wait, call me. I'll be back out."

Cole and CJ walked the doctor to the door.

"Not many doctors perform house calls anymore," Cole remarked. "Thank you for making the effort."

The doctor shook his head. "I would do anything for Charlie. She's done so much for me." He shook hands with Cole and CJ and then left.

"Seems Charlie has a fan club," CJ remarked as she headed for the stairs.

Cole followed. "The woman has saved so many lives through her generosity."

CJ glanced up at him as they climbed the staircase side by side. "Like yours and all of Declan's Defenders'?"

He nodded. "When we were dishonorably discharged, no one would hire us. And what skills did we bring to the table? Who wanted combat-trained men in their factories or businesses?"

CJ nodded. "I face the same situation, only worse. My résumé would read 'trained assassin.' The only people who are going to hire me are men wanting to off their wives to collect insurance money or to keep them from having to pay alimony or half their fortunes to an ex." She snorted. "I'm done with killing. I'd rather spend my time helping the children Trinity recruited to reclaim their childhoods before they become like me."

They were at the top of the stairs when Cole turned CJ to face him. "They'd be lucky to become like you. You're amazingly strong, both physically and here—" he touched a finger to her chest "—where it counts most. Even though Trinity tried to brainwash you into becoming a killing machine, you knew, deep down, right from wrong and fought for what you believed. That took more chutzpah than toeing the Trinity line and completing their list of hits."

He tipped her chin up and brushed at the line of soot smeared across her cheek. "You're beautiful inside and out." He bent to touch his lips to hers. "I wouldn't want you any other way."

She pushed up on her toes to meet his mouth, returning the pressure in a kiss as gentle as it was passionate.

When they broke apart, CJ laughed. "Look at us, all filthy when there's a shower not ten feet away." She took his hand and led him down the hall to the bathroom.

Once inside, she shut the door and pushed the jacket from his shoulders. It dropped to the ground, sending up a waft of soot to sting their noses.

Cole removed the towel from her shoulders and let

it slide to the floor to join his jacket. Then he helped her out of her leggings and shoes until she stood there in her panties and bra.

"Before we go any further, I have one question for you."

Her brow furrowed. "And what's that?" she said, reaching for the button on his jeans.

"What does CJ stand for?"

She laughed. "We've made love and you don't know?"

He shrugged. "Always seemed to get pushed to the back of my mind when I had other things to concentrate on. But now, I don't want to go any further until I know just who I'm making love to." He covered her hands with his before she could lower his zipper.

She looked up at him with a twisted grin. "It's not nearly as intimidating as the initials."

"I'm not looking to be intimidated." His fingers squeezed hers. "Tell me."

"I haven't been called by my given name since I was turned over to child protective services and placed in foster care. Right before Trinity stole me away from the home in which I'd been assigned."

He kissed her forehead. "You're stalling." Trailing kisses from her temple, across her cheek to her mouth, he paused. "Tell me."

"We need showers," she whispered. "How can you kiss me when I'm so dirty?"

"I like you dirty," he said and brushed her lips with his.

When she rose up again on her toes, he lifted his head. "Uh-uh. Not until you tell me."

CJ dropped back on her heels. "It's no big deal."

He let go of her and crossed his arms over his chest. "I'm waiting."

"Fine." CJ looked away. "My given name is Cara Jo Grainger. I go by CJ because Cara Jo sounds too soft and girlie."

"Cara Jo." Cole grinned.

CJ swung at him. "See? It's not me."

Cole pulled her into his arms and tipped her chin upward with a finger. "It's most definitely you. Because, you see, you might be the hard-as-nails CJ to everyone else, but I know beneath that outer shell is the soft Cara Jo, fighting to get out."

"I'm not soft," CJ said. "And I'm going for that shower, even if you aren't." She stepped out of his embrace, her panties and bra, and into the shower stall. The water switched on and she leaned out, a frown denting her pretty brow. "Are you coming?"

Cole didn't need a second invitation. He stripped off his shirt, jeans and shoes and stepped into the shower with her.

Half an hour later, the water had chilled, but their passion had not.

Cole gently dried Cara and wrapped her in a big, fluffy towel. He dried himself and looped a towel around his waist. Following the doctor's instructions, he applied the ointment to her wound and dressed it in the gauze and medical tape. Then he scooped her up into his arms and carried her across the hall into his bedroom and made love to her into the night, careful not to jar her, or cause her any pain. When they'd spent themselves, he lay beside her and slept the sleep of the sexually satisfied and thoroughly exhausted, knowing that when he woke, Cara would be beside him.

CJ SLEPT HARD for the first time in years, waking early before Cole stirred. For a long time, she lay on her side, staring at the man who'd been beside her, relentlessly looking out for her well-being and safety.

With the Director dead and the training camp burned to the ground, Trinity had lost its strength. But there were agents out there now who didn't have leadership or anyone to guide them. What would they do now that they were basically out of a job?

She'd struggled over the past year to find herself without Trinity. Job applications were difficult when she couldn't list a single skill that applied to being a clerk in a doctor's office or pass the background check for many positions in the DC area.

Had she used her real name, a background check could have done one of two things. First, it could have alerted authorities that she was a cold case of a missing child. Second, a Trinity sleeper agent embedded in whatever government office processing the background check could have found her. They would have eliminated her before she'd had the chance to save Anne Bellamy and the man she'd thought was a trustworthy vice president.

Now that Trinity was defunct, Cole wouldn't need to protect her. She could move out of Charlie's house and start all over somewhere safe. A place that would allow her to be anything she wanted. As long as she had a new identity. From what she'd seen Jonah was capable of, he could set her up with that new identity.

CJ rolled out of the bed, wrapped the towel around herself and crept into her room, where she dug into her backpack for her clothes and dressed quickly.

Once dressed, she headed down to the war room where she found Jonah at his computer.

"Do you ever sleep?" she asked.

"Good morning, Ms. Grainger." Jonah glanced up briefly with a smile. "I'll have you know that I slept like a baby last night." He went back to tapping on the keyboard. "Knowing the Director was taken care of and the man who'd killed Mr. Halverson was dead cleared my mind for the first time since John Halverson's death." Jonah's hands paused on the keyboard. "He was a good man."

"I wish I'd known him. Seems he had a way with bringing people together," CJ said.

"He had a way of giving people a second chance. I was a snot-nosed kid hacking into bank accounts when he found me about to be caught by the Feds. He pulled me into his home and gave me a place to live. Hell, he made me part of his family. I loved him like the father I never knew. And Charlie…she's been there for me. I'd do anything for them."

CJ held up her hands. "I believe you. Charlie's amazing, and the team she hired has been nothing but professional and competent."

Jonah nodded and turned to CJ. "What brings you

to the war room so early this morning? I know it's not to hear about me or how I came to be living on the Halverson estate."

"No, but I'm glad you told me. I'm glad to know I'm not the only stray Charlie has taken in. She's got a good heart." She paused briefly before adding, "I need a new identity. A chance to start my life over."

Jonah nodded. "I can help you with that. Like I helped Jane Doe—I mean Jasmine Newman." He cracked his knuckles and turned back to his computer. "Who do you want to be? A teacher? A physicist? A police officer?"

"I want to be someone who helps children like those who were recruited into Trinity. I don't want what happened to me to happen to them."

"I can make you a social worker with a degree and everything."

CJ shook her head. "No, Jonah. I want you to give my life back to me. I want to be Cara Jo Grainger. But I don't want to be on anyone's database as having been a missing child or having been a part of Trinity. I want to go to college, get a degree and learn how to go about helping others. I just want to be me. Cara Jo Grainger."

Jonah turned to her and nodded. "I can help you with the database part, but you're going to have to find your way back to that person on your own. Trust me. I know. I've been there and I'm glad I don't have to do that again. And you can't go back and reclaim what you lost. You have to move forward and become the person you want to be." He stood and held out his hand. "We can start right now. Hi, I'm Jonah Sprad-lin. Pleased to meet you."

She smiled and took the younger man's hand. "I'm Cara Jo Grainger. The pleasure's mine." Then she pulled Jonah into a hug and let the tears slide down her cheeks. "Thank you, Jonah."

"Hey, what's going on here?" Cole's voice sounded behind them.

Jonah stood back and waved a hand at CJ. "Cole McCastlain, I'd like to introduce you to Cara Jo Grainger. She's new in town. I hear she's good with kids and she has a heart of gold."

Cole's brow furrowed and his eyes narrowed, but he went along with the introduction. "Miss Grainger, I'm pleased to meet you." He held out his hand.

CJ placed her hand in his. When his warm fingers curled around hers, she felt the electric current running between them. "Please. Call me Cara Jo."

"Cara Jo," Cole said. Then he pulled her into his arms and hugged her close.

"I'm ready," she said into his chest.

"Ready for what?" he asked.

"Ready to start over." She looked up into his eyes. "It's not too late, is it?"

"No, babe, it's not too late." He kissed the tip of her nose. "Just do me one favor."

"Name it," she said.

"Don't change who you are," he whispered.

CJ frowned. "But I can't be the CJ of the past."

He shook his head. "You'll always be the CJ of your past. It's what made you the kind, caring, incredibly strong woman you are today." He brushed his lips across hers. "It makes you the woman I'm falling in love with. The woman I don't want to let go of...for the rest of my life."

Her heart skipped several beats and then raced, pushing blood through her veins so fast she thought they might burst. "How could you fall in love with me? I'm a trained assassin." She had to admit to herself that his words of love were like a dream come true, but how could they be real? She didn't deserve his love. She'd killed people.

"Your past doesn't dictate your future. But it helps to shape you into the woman you want to become." He brushed a thumb across her damp cheek. "From where I'm standing, you're pretty awesome already. I want to be with you as you rebuild your life and you improve on the woman you already are."

"Mr. McCastlain, I don't think you know what you're getting yourself into."

"Oh, sweetheart, I know, and I can't wait to see what new adventures we'll come up with next."

She rested her hands on his chest where his heart beat strong and his muscles flexed when he moved. With a twisted smile, she stared up into his eyes. "Then hold on to your hat, cowboy. It's going to be a helluva ride."

Chapter Fourteen

Cole grabbed two longnecks out of the ice chest on the covered patio overlooking the pool at Charlie Halverson's mansion. After opening them, he handed one to Declan and the other to Mack.

"Aren't you having one for yourself?" Mack asked.

Cole shook his head. "No, thank you. I'm swearing off alcohol for the time being," he said and patted his midsection. "The older you get, the more weight you gain. I don't plan on developing a beer belly."

Mack drank half the bottle before he set it on the table in front of him. "Can I get you another rum and Coke?" he asked Riley Lansing, who sat in the seat beside him. He'd been holding her hand for the past hour as they sat staring out at the rippling water of the backyard pool and Charlie's rose garden, chatting with the rest of the team and their ladies.

"I can't believe it's been six months since I first met Declan, and he saved me from Trinity when they tried to kidnap me on Capitol Hill." Charlie leaned against Roger Arnold, an arm around his waist. "John would have been so proud of what you all have accomplished."

"What *you've* accomplished," Declan said, raising his bottle of beer to Charlie. "Had you not offered my team a job, none of it would have happened. Trinity would still be around and they could have had their leader as president."

Cole shook his head. "Our world could have been a very different place at this point in time. But, because you had faith in us, our presidency is safe, we have a new vice president who happens to be female, and the children of Trinity are learning how to be kids again."

"How's that going, Charlie?" Anne Bellamy asked from where she sat in the same lounge chair with Jack.

Charlie smiled. "Ask Cara Jo, she's been working as a volunteer since we set up the John Halverson Children's Foundation."

As all gazes turned to CJ, she smiled. "It's going to be a long road, but they're coming along better than expected. The discipline they learned from Trinity is coming in handy. Some of them have been rehomed in foster care. Others have chosen to remain in the foundation boarding school. We've set up a sports program to keep them busy and out of temptation. Many of them are showing a lot of promise in academics."

"How's the course work coming, Cara Jo?" Declan asked.

CJ's chest puffed out. "I made the dean's list this semester."

Everyone congratulated her.

Cole slipped an arm around CJ and pulled her close. "I was so proud of her, I knew if I didn't do something soon, I might lose her forever."

"What are you talking about, man?" Mustang asked. "Cara Jo's not going anywhere. She's one of us."

CJ's joy bubbled over at the compliment. Being a part of the team meant the world to her. Almost as much as being a part of Cole's life. She held up her left hand. "You guys are stuck with me. Cole asked. I said yes. We're engaged!"

Riley, Anne, Emily Chastain, Jasmine and Grace rushed forward to admire the ring and hug the happy couple.

"Have you picked a date?" Grace asked.

Cole's cheeks turned a charming shade of red. "Actually, we're getting married really soon. I need you all to clear your calendars for the weekend after next."

A collective gasp was followed by the women shaking their heads, and mentions of *impossible* and *that's crazy* were murmured.

Gus was the one to break through with the question everyone must have been wondering and one CJ was excited to answer. "Why so quick?"

Cole looked to CJ. "You want to tell them?"

She smiled and pressed a hand to her flat belly. "I'm pregnant. The baby is due in six months."

"So that's why you're not drinking alcohol?" Declan laughed. "I should have known something was up. You never pass on a good beer."

"As long as Cara Jo can't drink alcohol, I'm

swearing off." Cole kissed CJ's temple. "We're in this together."

Mustang chuckled. "Sounds like you're going into battle."

Cole ran a hand through his hair. "Sometimes I think I'm going into battle without a weapon. What do I know about raising a kid?"

CJ hugged him around the middle. "As much as I do. Don't tell me you're scared, because that would make two of us."

Grace hugged CJ and then Cole. "You two will be just fine. And that baby will have the love of a dozen honorary aunts and uncles."

"You bet. And a cousin to play with," Declan said.

Grace glared at him. "Shh. This is CJ and Cole's moment."

Cole's eyes narrowed. "Wait. What is this about a cousin to play with?"

Mustang leaned forward as Cole's gaze pinned Declan. The stares of the rest of the team and the women fixed on him, as well.

Declan winced and held up his hands in surrender. "Sorry, Grace. I just couldn't help myself." A grin spread across his face and he pulled Grace into his lap. "We're pregnant, too. But I didn't give up beer." Grace elbowed him in the gut. "But I guess I will now that the cat's out of the bag."

Roger Arnold stepped forward and cleared his throat. "While we're all confessing to big changes, Charlotte and I would like to make a couple of announcements." He turned to Charlie. "My love, you have the floor."

Charlie stepped forward with a paper in her hand. "I have with me a letter from the president of the United States."

Everyone grew silent.

"As you all know, I've been to visit the president on a number of occasions over the past few months since Declan's Defenders saved his life. Out of those meetings, we came up with the foundation to help the children of Trinity."

CJ's heart warmed, remembering how Charlie had gone into high gear to find a building with a dormitory and classrooms to house the children who would otherwise have inundated the state of Virginia's social services with too many children to place into foster homes. And with the need to teach them to think like regular kids, they were not good candidates to go straight into homes.

Charlie had spent millions of dollars to bring the facilities up to standard and make it more of a home than an institution for the children. CJ and the rest of the team—especially the women—had had a hand in helping paint, decorate and shop for everything they needed from clothing to toys and toothbrushes.

"I also made a special request to our commander in chief. I asked him to fix what was broken." She held up the paper and smiled. "Today, he came through. This letter confirms that each of my Declan's Defenders has had their military records expunged of the dishonorable discharge. You are all eligible to return to active duty and Marine Force Reconnaissance, if you so desire. The president says he would be honored if you would consider coming back to work for him and our country."

Declan stood, his eyes suspiciously shiny. "Seriously?" He paced the tiled patio, shoving his hand through his hair. "We're no longer listed as dishonorably discharged?"

Cole stood beside CJ, his hand tightening around her middle.

She knew how much being a member of the elite Marine Force Reconnaissance team had meant to him and the others.

She looked up at him, her heart thudding against her ribs. Her world on the cusp of yet another change. "If you want to go back to the Marine Corps, go. I'll support your decision."

"But would you come with me?" he asked. "It would mean moving away from the foundation, your college, Charlie and Roger."

She laid a hand on his chest. "I'll go wherever you go. Our baby will know her father."

"His," Cole corrected absently. "I could go back into the corps." He looked at Declan and his other teammates.

They all appeared to be in a state of shock.

Charlie frowned and chuckled. "This is not exactly the response I expected."

Mustang stood. "Charlie, don't get us wrong, we're thankful. It was a huge blow to us to be ejected from the corps we loved and swore our loyalty to."

"And worse, having the stigma of a dishonorable discharge on our records," Declan continued. "Having that expunged is a blessing."

Jack stepped forward, holding Anne's hand in his. "As much as we loved being a part of the military, of serving our country—" he looked around at the others "—we've loved being a part of Declan's Defenders." He frowned. "But maybe I'm speaking for myself, not the others."

"Snow's right," Cole said. "I didn't know how I would fit back into society after leaving the military. Who would ever need a man who knew how to fire a military rifle or a grenade launcher, or could drop a man at four hundred yards?" Cole shook his head. "I don't know about the others, but I was lost."

Mustang, Declan, Jack, Gus and Mack all nodded.

"If it weren't for Charlie, we might not still be together."

"Or we might have been statistics, like so many other guys who get off active duty and can't find their way home."

Silence settled over the men and women gathered at the Halverson estate.

CJ knew the statistics. Every day, twenty-two veterans took their lives. She couldn't imagine any of Declan's Defenders sinking to that level of desperation. They all seemed so confident and…happy. She pressed one hand to her belly, slid the other around Cole's waist and asked the question she wasn't sure she wanted to know the answer to. "So, what's it to be? Are you going to gather your team and report back to active duty?"

Declan pulled Grace up against his side. "What do you want me to do?"

Grace smiled up at him. "I want you to do what makes you happy."

"You'd follow me around the world?"

She nodded. "The baby and I will follow you wherever you go. We're part of your team now."

Declan kissed her and looked across the patio at his boss. "Charlie, if you still feel you need me, I'd be proud to serve on Declan's Defenders."

Charlie nodded. "Declan's Defenders has proved to be a viable and necessary organization. I'd be honored to have any and all of you continue to provide the service you've done so far."

Declan turned to his team. "If you feel the call to return to the corps, you need to do what is best for you. I'm staying."

Gus stepped forward. "So am I."

Mustang joined Gus. "Me, too."

Jack stepped up beside Declan. "I'm staying."

Mack slipped an arm around Riley. "I'm invested in the people here and the life we've begun. I'm staying."

Everyone turned to the last Defender. Cole.

"You're my brothers," Cole said. "Where you go, I go." He lifted his chin toward their benefactor. "And Charlie, Arnold and Jonah are family. I feel we found our way home when we came to work for you."

"Exactly," Declan agreed.

"But don't worry," Cole said. "We won't be moving back in with you anytime soon. Seems you need to keep rooms open for the strays you manage to attract." He glanced down at CJ.

Her heart swelled with the love she'd found in this man. She knew she could live without him—she'd done it before—but he completed her like no one had done in her past.

"I love you, Cole McCastlain. And I love the life we're creating." She leaned up on her toes and pressed her lips to his.

Roger Arnold cleared his throat again. "Charlotte has another announcement to make, if you would be so good as to give her your attention once more." He smiled and nodded to Charlie.

Charlie's cheeks flushed with color. The woman looked young again and excited. "I have a job opening for a new butler."

CJ frowned. "Roger, you're not leaving us, are you?"

He shook his head but pressed his lips together and waited for Charlie to continue.

"No, Roger is not leaving us." She reached out a hand to him.

He took it and stepped up beside her, his shoulders thrown back, his head held high. "What Charlotte is saying is that she's agreed to become my wife."

Charlie's smile spread across her face. "I know it's only been ten months since my dear, sweet husband passed. Deep in my heart, I know he would approve of my decision. You see, Roger and John had been friends for a very long time. I think if I had met Roger first, I might have married him. But then, I loved John with all of my heart and I wouldn't have traded any day with him for the world.

"Roger came to me when I needed him most. After John was murdered. I don't know what I would have done without his support. But it's more than that." She turned to Roger, her eyes gleaming. "I love him as much, if not more than I loved John. Life has proven to be short. I'm not wasting another minute of it alone when I can be with the man I love." She turned to face them and held up her left hand. "Looks like we're going to have a few weddings in our near future."

CJ was the first to hug Charlie and Roger, her eyes filling with tears as she wished them all the happiness their hearts desired. Then she stepped back into Cole's arms and felt as if her world had come full circle.

She'd lost her family at a young age and wandered through life trying to fit in. Now she had a man who loved her, a group of friends who would give their lives to save hers and a baby on the way.

After all the years of loneliness, her world was full of love. Trinity had stolen her childhood, but she'd found her way home to Cole and his team.

Cole stood behind her, his arms around her, a hand spanning her belly. They had a life ahead of them and a child to love.

CJ leaned back against Cole and looked at him over her shoulder. "I love you, Cole."

"I love you, too, Cara Jo. You're everything I could

have ever wanted and more." He kissed her temple. "And you're giving me the best gift of all."

"The baby?"

"Well, that, too. But I meant your love. I will treasure it, you and our children forever."

* * * * *

COMING SOON!

We really hope you enjoyed reading this book. If you're looking for more romance, be sure to head to the shops when new books are available on

Thursday 6th March

To see which titles are coming soon, please visit
millsandboon.co.uk/nextmonth

MILLS & BOON

LET'S TALK

Romance

For exclusive extracts, competitions
and special offers, find us online:

f facebook.com/millsandboon

🐦 @MillsandBoon

📷 @MillsandBoonUK

Get in touch on 01413 063232

For all the latest titles coming soon, visit
millsandboon.co.uk/nextmonth

MILLS & BOON

THE HEART OF ROMANCE

A ROMANCE FOR EVERY KIND OF READER

MODERN

Prepare to be swept off your feet by sophisticated, sexy and seductive heroes, in some of the world's most glamourous and romantic locations, where power and passion collide.
8 stories per month.

HISTORICAL

Escape with historical heroes from time gone by. Whether your passion is for wicked Regency Rakes, muscled Vikings or rugged Highlanders, awaken the romance of the past.
6 stories per month.

MEDICAL

Set your pulse racing with dedicated, delectable doctors in the high-pressure world of medicine, where emotions run high and passion, comfort and love are the best medicine.
6 stories per month.

True Love

Celebrate true love with tender stories of heartfelt romance, from the rush of falling in love to the joy a new baby can bring, and a focus on the emotional heart of a relationship.
8 stories per month.

Desire

Indulge in secrets and scandal, intense drama and plenty of sizzling hot action with powerful and passionate heroes who have it all: wealth, status, good looks…everything but the right woman.
6 stories per month.

HEROES

Experience all the excitement of a gripping thriller, with an intense romance at its heart. Resourceful, true-to-life women and strong, fearless men face danger and desire - a killer combination!
8 stories per month.

DARE

Sensual love stories featuring smart, sassy heroines you'd want as a best friend, and compelling intense heroes who are worthy of them.
4 stories per month.

To see which titles are coming soon, please visit

millsandboon.co.uk/nextmonth

MILLS & BOON
MEDICAL
Pulse-Racing Passion

Set your pulse racing with dedicated, delectable doctors in the high-pressure world of medicine, where emotions run high and passion, comfort and love are the best medicine.